THE YOUNG ALEXANDRIANS

A.C. METAXAS

THE YOUNG ALEXANDRIANS

BGSP

Published in 2021
by Maida Vale, an imprint of the Black Spring Press Group
Grantully, Maida Vale,
London w9, England, UK
United Kingdom

Cover design and typeset by Edwin Smet

ISBN 978-1-913606-45-9

Any typos or other errors spotted can be emailed to us at
info@eyewearpublishing.com for the second printing corrections.

BLACKSPRINGPRESSGROUP.COM

To my wife Margaret
and daughters
Nemone and Michele

Ricky (A.C.) Metaxas was born in Cairo and attended secondary school in Alexandria's Averofeio Gymnasium. He is an engineering graduate of London University, completing his doctorate at Imperial College, and holds a Life Fellowship at St John's College, Cambridge. A lifetime in research and academe has resulted in two named awards, a lifetime achievement award, membership of Bologna's Scientific Academy, two technical books on energy utilisation, the foundation of a European association and numerous peer-reviewed publications in his field of study. The author became aware of the plight of the Palestinians as an adolescent in Alexandria during the years following the Suez War. It is a subject that has preoccupied him for over half a century culminating in this novel.

Order of appearance of principal characters with ages as of 2018

Nestor Phundas	son of Nina and Tasos, 46
Nina Phuntas (née Schinia)	Averofeio school, 75
Tasos Phundas	Averofeio School, 77
Alexis Mani	Averofeio school, 76
Mary Mani	mother of Alexis, deceased
Mr Mani	husband of Mary, deceased
Pavlos Mani	brother of Alexis, 80
Yanis Lotas	Averofeio school, 76
Yeorgis Paphitis	fellow Scout at British Boys School, 77
Hermioni Mani	daughter of Alexis, 45
Joshua Schumann	Jewish friend of Mrs Mani, 99
Hannah Schumann	Jewish friend of Mrs Mani, deceased
Avi Schumann	son of Joshua and Hannah, 75
Rivka Schumann	daughter of Joshua and Hannah, 73
Abu-Ahmet	janitor at the Boy Scout grounds, deceased
Mr and Mrs Notiyan	owners of apartment block, deceased
Petros Kalos	Averofeio school, 76
Christos Papas	Averofeio school, 76
Carabet	Armenian shoe shop owner, deceased
Michalis and Mirto Saris	brother and sister at Averofeio school, 77, 73
Ismail el Kefr	Palestinian refugee, 79
Panos Yeoryadis	friend at British Boys School, 77
Thanos Metis	friend at Victoria School, 78
Ali Al Hakimi	leader of Hamas, 45
Abdul	adjutant to Ali, 36

Qasim Al-Jazari.	young recruit to Hamas, 44
Asim Al Balawi	second in command of Hamas, 43
Mustafa el Kefr	son of Ismail, 46
Marika	girlfriend of Christos & dancing partner of Alexis, 75
Rea Loizithou	cousin of Tasos, 75
Irini Samara	Averofeio school, 75
Mr Pateras	classics teacher at Averofeio, deceased
Erica	wife of Alexis, deceased
Kate	wife of Yanis, 72
Ingrid	wife Christos, 72
Vassiliki	wife of Petros, 73
Stuart	partner of Hermioni, 43
Myrna Papa	daughter of Christos, 44
Michael	married to Myrna, 44
Marinos Kalos	son of Petros, 46
Kaliopi	wife of Marinos, 44
Amalia	wife of Nestor, 43
Ahlam	owner of haberdashery shop, 74
Khalil	owner of coffee house, 77
Muhammad El Mazhiri	cousin of Ismail, 77
Ibrahim	second cousin of Ismail, 75
Leila	wife of Ibrahim, 70
Karima	daughter in law of Muhammad and Mother of Ramzi, 46
Ramzi El Mazhiri	Grandson of Muhammed and grand-nephew of Ismail, 19
Golda Schumann	wife of Avi, 75
Shimon Schumann	son of Avi, 45

Adina Schumann	wife of Shimon, 43
Aaron Schumann	son of Shimon, 20
Yuval Arvartz	billionaire Businessman, 55
Moshe	son of Yuval, 30
Muhammad El Mazhiri	cousin of Ismail, 77
Iqbal	head of the Al Mezan centre in Gaza, 50
Mahmood Sistani	Gazan industrialist, 57
Yousef Al-Fayeem and Ali	billionaire industrialist and his nephew 54,31

FROM ALEXANDRIA TO BEIRUT

GAZA STRIP

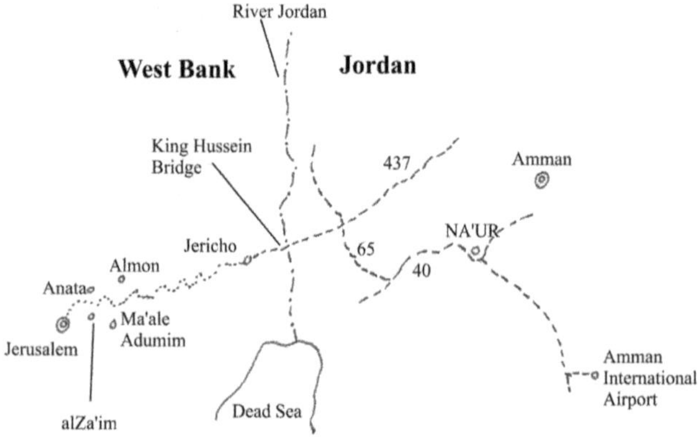

FROM AMMAN INTERNATIONAL AIRPORT TO JERUSALEM

1

Washington, December 6th 2017

The announcement by the President of the United States of his intention to move the Embassy from Tel Aviv to Jerusalem and house it in a new building stunned the world. To those in the know, his statement was not unexpected. This is because on March 2016, when he was a candidate for the Presidency he promised, in a speech to the American Israel Public Affairs Committee (AIPAC), America's foremost Pro-Israeli lobby, that he would do so. He chose to establish a temporary Embassy by May 14 the following year at the present US Consulate buildings in West Jerusalem to coincide with the 70th anniversary of the Declaration of Independence of the State of Israel. This could not be more provocative to the Palestinian Arabs who commemorate annually, on May 15, their eviction that preceded the formation of Israel. To the Palestinians, May 15 is Nakba Day or the Day of Catastrophe.

Nestor Phundas, an advisor to the President on foreign affairs, expressed dismay at the announcement which he objected to and warned his boss of wide condemnation by political leaders the world over. The President, who was shunned by fellow Republicans, and elected a year earlier against all odds by the slim margin of some key States against a formidable opponent and wife of a Democratic past-President, brushed aside any criticism stating that in his opinion this move was long overdue. Nestor cast his thoughts to the President's speech of March 2016 where he denounced the influence that Iran exerted in the Middle East and promised to the attentive audience that the US would always support Israel. He stated that Israel's security was to be paramount should he be elected President, that Palestinian Arabs are the terrorists who do not accept the existence of the State of Israel, and that Palestinian leaders from Arafat to his successors had rejected the many offers for a solution to the Israel-Palestine problem. As a deal-maker, he would be in a prime position to bring the two parties to the negotiating table and secure peace. The AIPAC audience were delighted with the content of his speech and interrupted him with frequent applause and standing ovations only to be followed by the Presidential candidate's murmurings, of "thank you, thank you."

A week after the announcement Nestor, a 47-year-old law graduate, drove home through the leafy suburbs of Washington and immediately rang his mother, Nina Phundas, née Schinia, in Athens. After only one year at Athens University he gained a scholarship to complete his study at Yale. After graduation he married a fellow Greek of the Levantine Diaspora who had studied music. The family settled in the USA but kept in touch frequently with his mother back in Athens. He proceeded to the garden to make sure that any bugging devices from the FBI or CIA did not interfere with his connection to Athens. When he was recruited his vetting unearthed that his parents were both born in Africa, his father in Johannesburg and his mother in Alexandria, so a confidential note was inserted in his file stating that he may have sympathy with Arab causes around the world. Nestor thought that his parents' background may have influenced the decision to recruit him to the staff at the White House in order to counter his other colleagues most of whom would naturally take a pro-Israeli stance.

"Grave news," he said to his mum and proceeded to explain that he had warned the President against making such an announcement, but alas he was overruled by other advisers, and by the President's own feelings about the present situation in Palestine.

"I did stress to the President that such a decision, however desirable or just in the eyes of many Jewish organisations and the Jewish lobby here in the USA, should surely be made by a consensus of people who know intimately the Israel-Palestine problem. In fact, this was the view expressed by the Rabbi who founded, and is the Director of, the Am Kolel Jewish Renewal Community of Greater Washington. It is such a sensitive issue that one wonders if the President made this announcement in order to divert attention from the other pressing issues he is currently facing."

"It is widely accepted that Jerusalem is a holy city not only to the Jews but Arabs and Christians alike," said Nina.

"Quite so," responded her son, "but try convincing the President to follow a more conciliatory approach."

Nestor's concern reflected many views of prominent Jewish people in the USA. A former Congressman of Florida and Chairman of the Jewish Democratic Council of America prophesied that the President's foreign policy was largely naïve and haphazard. Was it made on a whim, without thinking or reflecting on many issues that ought to be aired by both Palestinians and Jews taking part in any negotiations? Many commentators remarked that such a statement could pose grave consequences for the national security of both factions. Several ex-ambassadors to Israel warned the President not to go ahead with such a pronouncement, commenting further that past administrations had shied away from suggesting such a sensitive move because it could irrevocably damage any future Israeli-Palestinian peace initiative or at least considerably undermine it. The US should be doing its utmost to bring the various adversaries to the negotiating table rather than jettisoning any prospect of peace by such a provocative announcement. The international community was appalled by such a statement which was sure to trigger dire consequences on any peace talks and what is more would prevent the US acting as an honest broker in any future talks.

"I read in the newspapers only yesterday," said Nina, "that Patriarch Theophilous III, who as you know is the most senior theologian in Jerusalem, together with many other church leaders has sent a letter to the President condemning this decision and stating that it may result in hatred, conflict, violence and suffering in Jerusalem and the Holy Land."

"Of course, there are many Christian sites in the Holy Land and the concern of church leaders is the destruction of these as a consequence of his statement," replied Nestor, "the damage may be irreparable but I will do my best to reason with the President despite some in the administration welcoming such a decision."

"I bet there are many in Israel who are rejoicing as we speak, particularly those who lived illegally in East Jerusalem after the 1967 war when large areas were captured and later annexed by Israel," said Nina.

"I believe their number is some 200,000 living, as you say, illegally in East Jerusalem and they will be celebrating particularly as hard-liners in Israel have stated that Jerusalem should remain the eternal and undivided capital of Israel. I do hope the Palestinians will not take the view that there is no hope in any future negotiations and resort once again to yet another Intifada," said Nestor.

"Wouldn't the Israeli Government be thrilled if the rest of the world, including the EU, recognizes Jerusalem as the capital?" concluded Nina.

They continued to discuss the implications of such an announcement with Nestor promising that he would continue to discuss the matter with other advisors, to exert some pressure on the President to reconsider and hence avoid a rebellion by the Palestinian Arabs in both

Gaza and the West Bank. The protesters almost certainly would march near the border and throw stones or bricks and using rubber slingshots discharge small projectiles at the Israeli Defence Force (IDF) stationed at towers alongside the Separation Wall. The soldiers almost certainly would react with brutal force as they had many times in the past.

Such actions by Israel were long-standing and can be traced back to the incident in 1953 when Palestinians killed a mother and her two children and the policy instigated by the then PM of Israel David Ben-Gurion and his Cabinet, when brutal disproportionate retaliation had been established. Following these murders Israel chose the village of Qibya to retaliate and over 60 civilians died which stunned the world.

Nestor was well aware that the US support and aid for Israel was not always forthcoming. President Truman had started such aid but President Eisenhower in the fall of 1953 briefly suspended it following Israel's violation of the UN-negotiated agreement with Syria when the IDF entered the demilitarised zone in an attempt to divert the waters of the River Jordan and thus starve the Palestinian population of its precious resource. But gradually AIPAC grew in influence and although initially only liberal Democrats in the North supported American Jews and their associations, ardent opposition groups, such as the Republicans in the South, eventually came to support the Jewish lobby.

A CIA substation in London picked up key words

such as Israel, Palestinians, and Intifada through Nina's non-encrypted telephone line, and alerted the CIA permanent liaison officer in London.

"Nina Phundas and her son in Washington are once again discussing the Israel-Palestine problem. Let us keep an eye on their movements," was the encrypted message that was relayed straight to their counterparts at the CIA headquarters at Langley in Virginia. Ever since the killings of two CIA officers by Mir Qazi, claiming that he did it as revenge for the US Government policies in the Middle East and the killings of Palestinians by Israel, the security had been considerably tightened up to avoid a repeat of such an act of terrorism.

Langley immediately alerted Mossad about the conversation Nina had had with her son. They were not unduly alarmed as mum and son often discussed the situation in the Gaza Strip and the West Bank but Mossad's operatives in the Strip were alerted.

After the phone call Nina made a strong coffee and proceeded to her favourite spot by the window of her spacious apartment at Vrilissia overlooking the mount of Attica. She sat in her reclining chair slowly sipping her coffee, closed her eyes and reflected on happier times in Alexandria when she was a teenager. She would call her partner later that evening.

2

Alexandria, Easter 1956

A diffused beam of sunlight passed through the French shutters of the back room at the top apartment of a four-storey building in Rue Canope, Camp de César in Alexandria. It was Easter Monday in 1956. The stillness in the room was disturbed by the random buzzing sound of two houseflies beating their wings as they criss-crossed the beam of sunlight. Eventually one of the flies perched on Alexis' nose, and after a period of rumination, continued its exploratory journey along the adolescent's sleeping face eventually interrupting his slumber. Instinctively on waking up he stretched his arm to rid himself of the persistent fly still hovering.

Today was Sham el-Nessim, signalling the emergence of spring: an old Egyptian tradition going back to the time of the Pharaohs, celebrated on the first Monday after the Coptic Orthodox Easter by both Muslim and Christian Copts. Many other groups in Alexandria, and indeed throughout Egypt, such as the Greek, Armenian, Italian and Jewish communities, celebrated Sham el-Nessim simply out of custom. Alexis' mother, Mrs Mani, had arranged for them to spend the day in the countryside with friends at the resort of Palma, a few kilometres south of Alexandria. They would meet at Voras' apartment nearby and set off for Palma at around nine o'clock. It would be a jolly day with a leisurely lunch for all after which the youngsters would amuse themselves with games and exploring the surroundings.

"Wake up Alexis, it has gone eight o'clock," shouted Mrs Mani on her way to the kitchen.

Breakfast was soon over and shortly afterwards they were heading towards Voras' flat. Alexis' father, Mr Mani, had resigned from his long-standing tiresome administrative job and had formed a jazz band which was currently contracted to play in Sudan's capital, Khartoum. Alexis' older brother, Pavlos, was spending the day with friends at Sidi Bishr, a fashionable beach resort along the Eastern section of Alexandria's long coastal road, the Corniche.

On arrival at Mr Voras' apartment block they entered the main entrance on the ground floor and climbed the steps leading to the apartments above. As they approached the second floor landing a titter, characteristic of young girls, became more and more audible. Reaching the third floor they first came across Mona, Mr Voras' young daughter, who was playing with another girl whom neither Alexis nor his mum had seen before. After exchanging greetings, they entered the flat where they met other members of the party. Everybody was busy preparing for the trip while Alexis meandered aimlessly in the flat.

"Go and join Mona and her friend," urged his mother, but Alexis readily dismissed the idea, shrugging his shoulders. It was not that he did not wish to join them, but his innate shyness was too strong a barrier to cross and he stepped back. His mother smiled, as she realised how he felt, having experienced similar feelings herself as a teenager.

They were soon heading for Palma in Mr Voras' spacious Ford. Mrs Mani, Mrs Voras, Alexis and Mona's younger brother squeezed into the back while Mona and Nina Schinia sat next to Mr Voras. They crossed the suburbs of Alexandria, passed by the zoo at Nouzha and were winding along a snaking road between cotton fields in the Nile Delta. The scenery was often enriched by the presence of a fellaha attired in her long cotton galabieh wading through thickets while balancing a water-filled amphora on her head with native grace. As Alexis sat diagonally behind Nina he was in a perfect position to examine her youthful features. She was slim, with long brown hair, worn in two long pigtails with a fringe which made her look even younger than her early teenage years. Her profile shone brilliantly when the sunrays fell directly on her freckled cheeks. She was quiet and did not contribute much to the titbits that were going around, particularly from Mona, who seemed able to allude to the intricacies of the latest gossip and cause maximum embarrassment.

Mona talked to Nina incessantly. Alexis gathered that Nina had enrolled at the Greek School at Chatby, having previously attended the French School attached to the Sacré-Cœur Church near her home at Glymenopoulo, the fashionable quarter where better off expatriates lived in large elegant villas or spacious apartments. His school, the Averofeio Gymnasium was also at Chatby, next to the girls' school but he had not so far noticed her, perhaps not surprisingly as there were several hundred pupils and what was more the boys and girls attended lessons in different buildings. Co-education may have been practiced in Europe and some foreign schools, but the system of the Greek schools at Chatby adhered to a strict single sex education. Even the numerous courtyards of the adjacent schools were separated by high fences to ensure complete isolation of the genders while they attended school. Mona attended the Lycée Français, a school run by the Mission Laïque Française situated halfway between Chatby and Camp de César. It was natural therefore for Mona and Nina to revert to fluent French which filled Alexis with admiration as he could only grasp a fraction of what was said. Of the adults it was only Alexis' mother who spoke fluent French and impressed giggling Mona and Nina not only with her knowledge of the language but by her assertive interruptions.

Alexis' thoughts were interrupted by the jubilant outburst of Mona's brother as soon as he sighted the serene country resort next to Mahmoudieh Canal a tributary of the Nile. It was built near the eponymous port to supply water to Alexandria and other nearby neighbourhoods. A double-decked houseboat was anchored nearby, elegantly adorned with bouquets of flowers, and became the centre of exploration for the now enlarged group of youngsters from other families. Games were immediately organised with Mona giving orders with the proficiency of a British Sergeant Major. Alexis, rather reluctantly, joined in the games and felt very happy when Nina and himself were drawn in the same team to complete certain ludicrous tasks. He was intrigued by her mild aloofness and wished to know more about her. Often, they exchanged furtive glances only to be interrupted by Mona's outlandish instructions.

At around 6.30 in the evening Mr Voras suggested that he drive the youngsters back to their various homes while the adults stayed a while longer to enjoy some relative peace with some other friends who had joined them at the resort. It transpired that Alexis, being the eldest, could stay and return with the adults. Although under most circumstances that would have pleased him no end, he felt very disappointed not being near Nina on their return home. He was standing near Mr Voras' car feeling rather miserable when his mum and another adult approached him.

"Alexis," said his mother drawing him near the departing car, "would you mind leaving with the other youngsters so that there are no hard feelings? I will be back in a few hours."

Would he mind? Alexis found great difficulty supressing his sudden excitement, but managing to hide his brief elation, he regained his composure and replied, "Of course not, see you at home." He opened one of the rear doors and caused a certain discomfort when snuggling in as there were four youngsters already seated at the back. As the car drew away the adult turned to Mrs Mani and said, "It is a great tribute to the upbringing of your son Mary. Such empathy is rarely seen these days amongst teenagers."

The car was hurrying back to Alexandria through the April twilight as Mona's brother sat between Nina and Alexis. The silence in the car was occasionally broken by a youngster remarking how wonderful the day had been. Mona's brother suggested that Nina was his favourite girl. Alexis glanced at Nina who was oblivious of what had just been said and turned, fixing his eyes out of the window at the prevailing emptiness. His thoughts oscillated between scenes of joy, laughter and happiness of the preceding few hours to sadness that such a memorable day was coming to an end. The car reached Stanley Bay, passed through its residential areas and stopped outside an elegant two-storey building at Glymenopoulo. Nina said her goodbyes, thanked Mr Voras for inviting her to spend the day at the resort, ran to the entrance and swiftly disappeared. A little later Alexis was dropped off at Rue Canope and a few hours later his mother joined him.

"Did you enjoy the excursion?" asked his mother.

"Very much so."

"What did you think of Nina?" pressed his mother smilingly.

"She is very nice," replied Alexis hurriedly and went

on, "Why was she alone?"

His mother went on to explain that her father, a wealthy financier and her mother had urgent family business to attend to in downtown Alexandria and could not join them. Mr Voras suggested to Nina's mother that her daughter join the family outing.

Alexis could not sleep easily that evening. His thoughts swung to and fro between Palma and Glymenopoulo. He tried to remember his first reaction when he first saw Nina. He was left with a vivid recollection of her radiant face with the fringe, her suede jacket and her ankle-hugging boots. Eventually the conscious gave way to the unconscious and dreams replaced reality.

3

Cambridge, December 7th 2017

Alexis Mani had spent a week in Florence attending a conference on energy utilisation and boarded a flight from Pisa airport back to Stansted. After a bumpy landing he was driving back to his base at St John's College in the centre of Cambridge where he held a Life Fellowship. He was reflecting on two key questions posed by attendees on his keynote lecture when some dialogue on BBC Radio 4's News bulletin regarding the US embassy's move to Jerusalem prompted him to listen closer. He raised the volume and listened more attentively as the BBC's political editor in the USA was giving the latest reaction from the White House regarding the President's pronouncement a few days earlier of his intention to move the US Embassy from Tel Aviv to Jerusalem. He drove straight to St John's, parked at the Chapel car park, opposite the Round Church, and proceeded to his office. Images of his adolescent years in Alexandria and the troubled region in Palestine, the Gaza Strip, West Bank and Israel played rapidly in his mind. He picked up his mobile and rang his ex-Alexandrian school pal Yanis Lotas who had also settled and raised his family in England.

"I missed the President's announcement as I was in

Florence at a conference. Grim news?"

"Kate and I feel devastated," replied Yanis. "I don't think the President realises the feelings that his statement will arouse in Palestinians living in the Gaza Strip and the West Bank."

"I think he does realise," replied Alexis, "but perhaps he really believes that stirring matters up will prove decisive in the brokering of a settlement between Israel and the Palestinians. I fear this may prove to be a deal too far."

"Have you spoken to Hermioni? What is her reaction to the news?" asked Yanis.

"I can't reach her as she is in a meeting in Whitehall. Let me track her down to find out what the reaction has been of the British Government regarding the President's statement."

Hermioni was Alexis' 45-year-old daughter, a psychology graduate and a Liberal Member of Parliament for Hammersmith who was chairing a think tank on the UK's International Aid programme. There were many dissenting voices advocating that such aid should be curtailed or at least monitored very carefully because in a number of cases recently large parts of the fund intended for worthy causes seemed to have ended up in the pockets of the local representatives or channelled to fund subversive activities.

Alexis could not get in touch with his daughter, so he proceeded to the Combination Room at his College to have a spot of lunch. This stunning room, one of the most impressive in the whole of the Collegiate University, afforded excellent views of the second court where one of its oriel windows depicted an image of Queen Henrietta of France. Her engagement in 1624 to King Charles I was announced in this very room. Alexis was always pleased to show this room to guests while relating historical facts such as that General Eisenhower, the then Supreme Commander of the Allied Forces in WWII, had mock-ups of the Normandy beaches laid out on its floor while he briefed his generals days before launching Operation Overlord, the largest amphibious invasion in history. Alexis walked to the far end of the long rectangular oak table, sat down and glanced at the menu for the day offering a meat or a vegetarian choice, but opted for the cold alternative of smoked salmon salad. While lunching he chatted to fellow colleagues sitting adjacent to him about this and that but refrained from mentioning the President's latest pronouncement. Silver candelabras placed at intervals adorned the length of the imposing table, with candles unlit. He glanced at his watch, showing one o'clock which meant the time in Adelaide would be well into the evening. He returned to his office and rang his fellow Alexandrian Boy Scout pal, Yeorgis Paphitis, who in 1961 had emigrated Down Under. The two friends had kept in touch throughout the intervening years by e-mails or phone calls and met on Yeorgis' occasional visits to Europe or when Alexis visited Australia to present an invited talk.

"Dreadful news," was Yeorgis' reaction. "Cannot

believe that the President is serious but judging by his recent pronouncements on many other issues I fear he will go ahead despite the consequences."

"I am afraid he is serious and knows only too well the furore that his action may provoke," replied Alexis, and they went on to spend a good half an hour talking about each other's news but also reminiscing about the good old days in Alexandria during the late 1950s when they were both Patrol Leaders at the Scouts in Camp de César.

Mid-afternoon, Alexis rang his daughter again to learn that Westminster was aghast at the President's pronouncement. However, the PM had spent the last few days in Europe discussing the post-Brexit backstop relating to the border between Northern Ireland and the Republic and had not had time to digest or comment on the implications of the President's statement. Hermioni promised to get back to her dad as soon as she had more news.

Days later, Hermioni was on the buzzer once more. She had discussed the President's statement with key government advisors and surreptitiously tried to find out how well briefed the PM was vis-à-vis the Arab-Israeli conflict, the Palestinian Conundrum as he coined it, particularly its origins way back from the time of the British Mandate to the present day. The PM, Hermioni was told, was not likely to react to the President's latest announcement as she was totally preoccupied with Brexit but a file containing a summary of key developments in the Middle East was being prepared in view of the President's projected visit to the UK the following year. Hermioni, having chatted on numerous occasions in the past to her father about Palestine, was well-versed on the subject and took it upon herself to frequently engage with the PM's advisors.

"I will continue to feed the PM's advisors with more material about Palestine so that the dossier is representative of the whole picture and not just the Middle East before she meets the President. I will keep you abreast of developments."

"Good idea," replied Alexis, "but don't make a nuisance of yourself and switch them off." Alexis, knowing his daughter too well, was sounding a cautionary note.

"Don't worry, I will be diplomatic. By the way, have you rung Athens?" asked Hermioni.

"I cannot get through, so I will try later," replied her dad.

Alexis returned to his office and glanced at the stack of books on his side table regarding the Palestinian Conundrum. Over the years he had amassed a formidable array of material, the latest of which included *Israel and Palestine: Reappraisals, Revisions and Refutations* by Avi Shlaim, Emeritus Professor of International Relations at Oxford University, *One State, Two States: Resolving the Israeli/Palestine Conflict* by Benny Morris, Professor of History in Middle Eastern Studies at Ben Gurion University of the Negev, *The Ethnic Cleansing of Palestine* by Ilan Pappé, Professor of International Studies at the University of Exeter and *Palestine* by Ilan Pappé and co-authored with Noam Chomsky. He started leafing through *Palestine* and reflected on Chomsky's gravitas as earlier this year he was, along with two others, the recipient of the Seán MacBride Peace Prize, of the International Peace Bureau, the citation noting "his tireless commitment to peace, his strong critiques of US foreign policy, and his anti-imperialism."

4

Alexandria, May-July 1956

The boys at the school at Shatby had from the outset the choice to follow a commerce course and enrol at the Salvayios School or opt for the combined classics and science course and enrol at the Averofeio Gymnasium. Alexis after an entrance exam was admitted to the latter. After completing the second year another decision had to be made which this time meant whether a pupil would stay in the same stream and specialise in the classics or switch towards a more scientific course of which mathematics, physics and chemistry formed the core subjects. Although the final decision rested on the whim of the pedantic Headmaster, based on the pupil's first two years' performance, parents were encouraged to participate in the process. It was in such a meeting that Mary Mani came across the internal machinations of that school and the idiosyncratic Headmaster. The Gymnasium was housed in an imposing three-storey building with high-ceiling classrooms, surrounded by a large courtyard which came into life during the short free intervals between lessons. Such intervals were announced from the Headmaster's office by strains of classical music, such as the 'Largo di Händel', which emanated from two loudspeakers at carefully located vantage points in the courtyard.

Mrs Mani arrived at his office in mid-May and after some preliminary talk the Headmaster explained in a low tone that as Alexis had not shown remarkable progress in either disciplines it would be best for him to follow the easier of the two options, that of classics. Alexis, however, had on numerous occasions confessed to his mother that Homer's *Iliad* and its sequel *The Odyssey*, left him utterly cold; he could not see the point of spending a considerable time on mythology, although he appreciated the connection with his Greek heritage, when he did not derive any enjoyment from its readings. So, Alexis' mother, knowing the feelings of her son, had to counter the Headmaster's half-baked decision. She looked straight at the Headmaster and replied without hesitation.

"With due respect, Headmaster, Alexis has so far not shown what he can achieve. I have followed closely his progress and I am confident that a course in the sciences would suit him best. As Alexis hasn't yet seriously applied himself to his studies, when the time comes to do so he will have ample energy in reserve and that will hold him in good stead."

The scholarly Headmaster sensed that he was confronted by a strong-willed and determined mother who was close to her son and knew full well her son's range of ability. She deftly dismissed the Headmaster's reasoning and effortlessly tackled any awkward questions he threw at her. Her erudition came to the fore as she confidently formulated her counter-arguments about

Alexis' future direction. The Headmaster finally relented, which secured her son's admission to the sciences group. Although this outcome thrilled Alexis he was nevertheless surprised at his mother's confidence in his ability to tackle the tougher of the two streams, but he was delighted to be moving away from the classics.

At the end of June, the Averofeio Gymnasium School held its annual end-of-year examinations and a forlorn atmosphere prevailed amongst the boys and girls. Although Nina was still very much in Alexis' mind, they only saw each other fleetingly when they occasionally boarded the same tram on their way home from school. It was a brief encounter as Alexis lived only three stations away from Chatby to Camp de César while Nina continued for another half a dozen stops passing first the magnificent green fields of the race course adjacent to the Sporting Club before she arrived at her station at Glymenopoulo. During this short journey and amongst the rush of pupils getting on and off the tram they acknowledged each other with brief smiles. With the examinations over, Alexis looked forward to a leisurely summer. As usual it was scorching hot. By the end of July Alexis' natural tan added a healthy note to his youthful countenance.

On the morning of 26th July Alexis' mother informed him that she had arranged to go to the city to hear Colonel Gamal Abdel Nasser, Egypt's youthful President and ex-member of the Free Officers of the military, addressing his people. Joshua Schumann, a Jewish friend of the family, and his wife Hannah, a teacher at the Lycée Français, were to meet her there. Two years earlier Nasser, in a bloodless coup, ousted the anglophile General Naguib, who was behind the 1952 coup d'état when Egypt's King Farouk I was forced to abdicate. He was the last King of the Mahammad Ali dynasty, who not only inherited a fortune from his father, purportedly over $100 million, but was also left a seventh of all the arable land around the Nile that his father had confiscated during his reign. Just before his abdication, the playboy King had surrounded himself with a fleet of fast cars, priceless jewels, and other expensive ornaments. The people rejoiced following his eagerly awaited demise. The Anglophile King Farouk was such a thorn in the flesh of the young officers that after forcing his abdication the way was now clear to fulfil their aspirations for the future of their country.

Joshua had known Alexis' family from their days in Cairo. He was the son of a Jewish businessman who had recently passed away and left Joshua a considerable inheritance. Joshua too was born in Egypt and after he studied architecture in Paris moved his family to Alexandria and started his own practice. He was soon very successful and at present, while only in his late thirties, he had built a formidable reputation with his daring approach to aesthetics in modern buildings. He had built a luxurious villa in the fashionable quarter of Rushdi and had furnished it with a priceless collection of antique furniture, paintings and ornaments from the Far

East, especially China and Japan. Hannah, also Jewish, had studied philosophy at the Sorbonne. With their adolescent children, son Avi and daughter Rivka, the family was very much part of the Jewish community of Alexandria known as *Juifs d'Alexandrie*, but which cherished old acquaintances and friendships with the rest of the expatriate communities. Joshua looked forward to meeting a fellow erudite, Mary Mani, thoroughly enjoying their stimulating discussions.

Rumours abounded as to the content of President Nasser's speech and Avi, an apprentice at Alexandria's *Jewish Chronicle*, was asked to accompany the Newspaper's Chief correspondent. Mary Mani persuaded her son to come along and he agreed adding that they should stop by the local Boy Scout grounds where Yeorgis, a fellow scouter, had agreed to meet him, so he too could join them if he so wished.

Ever since Alexis' family had moved to Alexandria, he had joined the local Greek Scout movement in Rue Canope a few kilometres from the Mani apartment. Starting as a cub in group number three he progressed through the ranks and was now one of the leading Boy Scouts and a Patrol Leader in his Group, showing a remarkable commitment to the Baden Powell movement. Amongst the elder expatriates there was a consensus that scouting was a thoroughly worthwhile activity for getting through adolescence, where physical and psychological changes played havoc from puberty to adulthood. Yeorgis, a fellow Patrol Leader in the same Group, was tall, handsome, and dark-haired with strong muscular arms due to weightlifting and wrestling activities. He attended the British Boys School in Rue d'Aboukir opposite the Greek hospital Kotsikion. Unlike Alexis he had quite strong religious beliefs, often discussing his feelings with his atheist pal. They both shared an insatiable thirst for knowledge which culminated in endless discussions on multifarious subjects.

On this occasion Yeorgis agreed to join them and around mid-afternoon Mary Mani with the two boys boarded the tram at Camp de César and promptly arrived in the city. They met Joshua and Hannah who had driven direct from their home in Rushdi at the Yachting Club. They walked to the nearby Midan el Tahrir, the tree-lined square overlooking the law courts, where flocks of Arabs had already assembled. Alexis looked around him and spotted several marksmen located on the rooftops of the surrounding buildings. The place was awash with plainclothes policemen, some standing by the elevated platform and others mingled amongst the crowd. They did not have to wait long. Nasser appeared amidst his entourage and bodyguards, stepped up on to the podium, and greeting the audience warmly he started in his lucid, unmistakable voice. Although Alexis and his pal had not mastered Arabic, they got the gist of what he was saying. Basically, the President exclaimed, the Western powers had let Egypt down by refusing to finance the building of a High Dam across the river Nile at Aswan. Instead, he announced, Egypt would raise the necessary funds for the project by nationalising the Suez Canal and offering compensation to the owners. He mentioned the name Ferdinand de Lesseps three times which, unbeknownst to all present, was the coded instruction for the Egyptian army to move in immediately and occupy the Canal Zone between the towns of Port Said and Suez.

Although there had been a Low Dam at Aswan since 1902, the building of the High Dam would ensure better control of the flood waters by storing water and releasing it when most needed as well as generating hydroelectricity. This scheme, first conceived by the Greek-Egyptian agricultural engineer Adrian Daninos, was essential for the well-being of the regions adjacent to the Nile; however, over the years and after successive administrations including that of King Farouk, it was not implemented. It became the focus of the young officers who in 1952 overthrew the monarchy and were now at the centre of Egypt's governmental policy. Although the Western powers originally agreed to fund this project, they insisted on certain caveats, not least regarding the relationship between Egypt and Israel, which were totally unacceptable to Nasser, culminating in his decision to side with the Soviet Union who eventually assisted in funding and building the High Dam. During the speech he vehemently denounced the British in their role as Protectors in Egypt after the Ottoman Empire joined forces with Germany and Austria-Hungary during the First World War.

To the few non-Muslims mingling amongst the huge

crowd the President's message spelt grave foreboding, whereas to the jubilant majority his sentences aroused unprecedented nationalistic feelings – especially after he invoked his central theme in an emotional peroration. Alexis looked around and saw tearful faces gleaming with hope. He too was engulfed with excitement at what he was hearing and experiencing although hardly able to grasp the dire consequences that lay ahead.

After the speech Mary Mani, Joshua and Hannah went to the fashionable Café Trianon, no doubt to discuss the implications that lay behind Nasser's speech while Avi and his colleague made their way to the newspaper headquarters. Alexis and Yeorgis headed back to the Scout grounds almost certain to meet other pals. As time went by the Scout grounds at Rue Canope had attained a wider significance for Alexis and his mates than being merely a centre for scouting activities. As some of his close friends lived quite near it gradually became a convenient place to meet. The Arab caretaker, Abu-Ahmet, was in his late fifties with rugged features, large hands and a raucous voice. He wore a headdress in the shape of a white *keffiyeh* kept in place with a doubly wound *agal*. With his wife and their four young children, they occupied a ramshackle wooden house in one corner of the Scout grounds, with a front porch and tiny yard, thus affording rare but sought-after privacy. For a few piastres the youngsters could buy small bottles of Spathis, a local brand of sparkling lemonade, or bottles of Coca-Cola from a large wooden container kept near the entrance under the watchful eye of Abu-Ahmet. Large blocks of ice were delivered daily to the site, smashed into smaller pieces and dropped into the container.

A special bond developed between Alexis and Abu-Ahmet, with the young adolescent often going out of his way to render Abu-Ahmet's forlorn existence a bit more comfortable. After a carefully orchestrated campaign by Alexis and Yeorgis, consumption of the refreshments hugely increased thus somewhat augmenting the caretakers' meagre pay. Abu-Ahmet deeply appreciated such a gesture and allowed the two young Patrol Leaders special privileges such as using the grounds after hours or supplying them with soft drinks on credit.

In the weeks ahead Alexis and Yeorgis would soon realise why the elders felt so anxious after Nasser's audacious speech. However, with many more weeks of summer vacation before the start of the new term their thoughts turned quickly to sandy beaches and scouting expeditions. Nina was not far from Alexis' thoughts.

"I met a girl called Nina," he confided to Yeorgis as they turned into Rue Canope on their way to the scouting grounds.

"Oh really, what is she like?"

Alexis thought back to Easter and the Palma resort and replied, "She is slim, brown eyes, with long hair in two pigtails and a fringe …." Alexis hesitated.

"Well?" pressed Yeorgis.

"She is quiet and reassured. Although she attends the Averofeio School for girls at Chatby I have only seen her on the odd occasion when we usually board the same tram, so I hope to bump into her more often in the autumn," concluded a smiling Alexis.

After spending a couple of carefree hours with other friends at the Scouts, shooting a large ball into a makeshift basket or engaged on their long-term project of building a treehouse, Alexis and Yeorgis walked up Rue Canope and parted at the corner grocery shop Koukoulas, Yeorgis heading towards his apartment block opposite the Camp de César tram station while Alexis continued straight up Rue Canope. Echoes of Nasser's speech reverberated in his young mind as he approached Palestra, the Italian recreational club opposite the block of apartments where he lived. He hastily crossed the entrance hall, climbed three by three the tetragonal winding marble steps and reached the family's apartment on the fourth floor. His mum hadn't returned so he went to the spacious balcony and glanced down at the grounds of Palestra, where the professional was giving a tennis lesson. Basketball was his great love, a sport in which he had excelled since he was very young. He continued to watch the instruction without paying much attention to what was being taught.

When his mother arrived, she carried out a few chores, made herself a coffee, sat on her favourite rocking chair in the lounge and immersed herself in Jean Paul Sartre's *L'existentialisme est un humanisme*. Alexis stepped into the flat and caught his mum mid-soliloquy regarding Sartre's radical view about existence preceding the essence of a person, the key defining concept in existentialism. She lit a Craven A.

"Only a few pages to finish this chapter," said Mary Mani without looking at him. He sat silently close by watching his mother's eyes scanning the last few pages and then moving her head to and fro at an accelerating pace to complete the chapter. She placed the book on the metal-top coffee table, drew on her cigarette and looked at Alexis who had remained silent.

"You seem thoughtful?" she asked inquisitively.

Alexis explained that he was overwhelmed with excitement when he heard President Nasser's intention to nationalise the Suez Canal in order to finance the building of the High Dam at Aswan but on reflection he felt a tinge of sadness and now he swung between the two feelings without knowing why.

Hadn't Socrates expounded on the philosophical relationship between the two? He could not understand why such an occasion had so perplexed him. She listened to Alexis with her usual assiduousness, absorbed his semi-garbled arguments as though she wished to follow the myriad of migrating neurons of his evolutionary mind in search of plausible answers. When Alexis finished his narrative Mrs Mani started.

"Let us examine your feelings. Your happiness is quite understandable as you were surrounded by an elated group of people listening to their President's great emotional speech. Should he carry this out it would be a moral victory despite the dire consequences. Therefore, you felt happy for Egypt, the country of your birth. All our family were born in Egypt therefore we have a strong affinity with it. Your subsequent sorrow is a little bit more difficult to explain but has its roots in the natural sensibility that is embedded in all of us. With the rise of the nationalistic feeling amongst the mesmerised crowd, you have subconsciously sensed the beginning of the break of the bond between the expatriate communities and our Arab neighbours. Although it was only the major Western powers that were denounced in the President's speech it is difficult to dissociate ourselves from our Western heritage – our culture and ethics have remained too European. So, you see the position that such a situation puts us in – you consider Alexandria as your home and consequently any rift between its peoples is bound to cause some grief."

Alexis listened attentively to his mum. He was by now standing next to the window gazing at the dark starlit sky and was enveloped by the warmth of the July evening wafting through the wide-open French shutters.

"Is it wrong to nationalise the Canal?"

"Legally," continued his mum, "President Nasser will be breaking the law because there remain 12 years before ownership of the Suez Canal is passed to Egypt. However, morally he holds a much stronger position. You see, in 1875 Britain acquired, through Disraeli, control of the Canal Company, so the remaining 12 years must be compared with..." Mary paused, shut her eyes, moved her lips and carried out a quick mental arithmetic of the number of years the Canal was run by the Western powers. "... 85 years of Anglo-French rule. President Nasser's scheme of financing the building of the Aswan High Dam through the proceeds of the Canal traffic seems very courageous especially when he is bound to cause international irritation. But if it is true that he was let down by the West, well, this adds some justification to today's momentous proclamation. The building of the Dam is vital for Egypt's prosperity and agricultural programme and it would seem that the President was left with no alternative: either abide by the laws of the Canal company and perpetuate Egypt's impoverishment for over a decade or put the country and its people's welfare to the forefront and defy the laws, which incidentally, were agreed upon when colonialism didn't much care for the prosperity of the indigenous population."

Her trend of thought was interrupted by a slam of the flat's door. Pavlos came to the lounge stating that he was peckish.

"Well, let me prepare dinner," responded his mother, and stood up. "Your grandfather always insisted that he could not hold a serious conversation on an empty stomach. Calves' liver, French fries and salad is coming up," concluded Mary Mani to the approval of the brothers.

Pavlos withdrew to his room while Alexis stepped back onto the balcony, came to the edge and stared down at the grounds of the Italian Club Palestra. Its stately two-storey ambassadorial building stood at the centre of the grounds where on one side was the hardcourt used for tennis, basketball, and other sports, while on the other lay a long narrow clay surface used by the older members for *bocce*, that is, playing bowls. The whole area was surrounded by high walls and mature trees giving the club much sought-after privacy but not from the top flats of the adjacent apartment blocks. Alexis' balcony offered a superb vantage point from which to observe all the functions taking place in this graceful hideout of the Italian community.

The Italians were not the only community to establish their own little Italy where one felt at home as soon as one crossed its imposing iron gates. The Greek community found solace in two Clubs, Enosis near the Averofeio School at Chatby, and Ibrahimieh in the neighbourhood of Alexis' apartment. The Jewish community congregated at the Union Juive not far from the Scout grounds, while the Armenians had established Homenetmen-GAMK near the tram station of Sidi Gaber. The word GAMK, meaning will in the Armenian language, was significant in that it signified the will to achieve something. There was also the club at St Mark formed by pupils of the magnificent Coptic school bearing the same name and nearby was the only Arab club which interacted with the expatriate clubs, Tram, situated between the schools of Lycée Français and Institution Sainte Jeanne-Antide, built by the Sisters of Charity from Besançon. Although sport formed only part of the multifarious activities between these clubs it was mainly through sporting activities, such as leagues featuring various divisions, that greatest contact was originally made and maintained over the years.

Alexis watched a doubles match being played under floodlights and was always amazed by the politeness of the participants with the word 'sorry' being mentioned perhaps as often as the ball crossed the net. On the face of it they seemed happy and content. Were they aware of the nationalistic feeling brewing amongst the suppressed Arab population, wondered Alexis? What sort of future lay ahead, particularly as most were born in Egypt and regarded it, as he did, as their only home? Would President Nasser's speech affect some ethnic minorities, reflected the young man?

"Great shot," whispered Alexis as one of the players smashed a high top-spinning lob.

"Did you say something?" asked his mother from the kitchen window adjacent to the balcony. Alexis slowly approached the window and glanced at the couple of primus stoves standing on the thick marble worktable. He liked the noise emanating from the stoves and when younger he had spent endless hours boiling water while working out his maths homework by these odd-looking pressurised-burner paraffin cooking appliances. Alexis was still troubled by the day's events. He looked at his mum.

"Assume," he uttered in a quivering voice betraying a genuine struggle to formulate his argument, "that somebody decides to confiscate Mr Notiyan's numerous properties to sell and distribute the proceeds to the poor. Would that be morally right?" Mr Notiyan was a prominent Armenian, occupying the adjacent penthouse and owner of the whole apartment block as well as some factories and shops in the neighbourhood.

"Well, you are treading on dangerous ground by making such simplistic comparisons," replied his mum as she was mixing the ingredients for the French dressing, "but I see the point you are making. Of course, Mr Notiyan would be very unhappy and fight tooth and nail for the properties he possesses and has built over the good old days of colonialism. But it will be interesting how Britain and France react to Nasser's proclamation. Legally, after all is said and done, it is their property. All I can say is food for thought for Mr Eden – and talking about food, would you call Pavlos? Dinner is ready."

Alexis called his brother and returned to the window only to hear his mum concluding, "It is only a question of time until the expatriate communities bear the full brunt of the President's speech."

They laid the table on the balcony and enjoyed a pleasant meal in this tranquil and peaceful part of suburbia. The food was washed down with Stella beer, a local favourite, and the meal was rounded up with a cold sweet made up of peeled guavas soaked in rich syrup, mashed out of the guava skins, mixed with sugar and a generous dollop of cognac. The conversation swung back and forth over many topics with Mary commanding the central role but always allowing her sons to freely express their thoughts in support of their arguments.

As they were about to clear up Mrs Mani turned to Alexis. "I met Mrs Voras at the bazaar yesterday and had a quick chat. Mona and her brother will have to take extra lessons at the conservatoire because apparently," continued Mrs Mani amongst the clutter of cutlery and plates, "the annual end-of-year concert has been put forward a couple of months and will now be held in early October. Mona is on tenterhooks as she is petrified of concerts whereas her brother is very much looking forward to the occasion."

"When are the lessons resuming?" asked Alexis.

"Next week I think," replied his mum who disappeared behind a pile of plates and pans.

Alexis was overwhelmed at the thought of Nina possibly having more lessons. He did not play any instrument himself but lots of his school pals did so he was aware of the comings and goings within the local conservatoire. It would be relatively easy to get hold of a timetable and find the time when Nina might be attending so that he could arrange a seemingly coincidental rendezvous after disembarking the tram at Camp de César. He stood on the balcony and glanced at the darkness below which enveloped Italy's little paradise. As Alexis stared at the emptiness of the abandoned tennis court, he saw an image resembling the slim figure of Nina rising from the shadows with her neat fringe and her disarming smile. Although she appeared confident, behind that façade he perceived an innate reserve which rendered her very difficult to approach. Perhaps he was wrong: deep down, he longed to be wrong.

5

August 1956

During the summer months Alexandrians often took a stroll late in the afternoon along the Corniche stretching 20 km from the western port to the Palace of ex-King Farouk at Montazah in the East. They shared similar thoughts with the inhabitants of Upper Egypt who longed to visit Alexandria to feel the cool Mediterranean breeze.

Since the abdication of the King in 1952 the authorities deigned to open the magnificent gardens of the Summer Palace to the public and put plans in place to turn the once-royal quarters into a hotel, including numerous restaurants and a casino. Alexis was ten years old when the Free Officers movement, using Major General Naguib as the frontman, staged a coup d'état. He clearly remembered running to the Corniche with his brother Pavlos to catch a glimpse of the deposed playboy King. However, all they saw were armoured vehicles parading down the Corniche towards the Palace. Four years later this royal enclave was further commercialised by the building of a series of luxurious cabins along its magnificent harbour only to be afforded by the better-off Alexandrians.

Behind the winding Corniche lay a thin strip of land

a few kilometres wide forming the Alexandrian suburbia. City commuters made use of the double-decker trams which stretched some 32 km from Ramleh station in the city to Victoria terminus next to the Summer Palace. What was so characteristic about this particular area was its cosmopolitan expatriate community comprising mainly Europeans, Armenians and Jews including some Arabs, both Copts and Muslims, who were professionals holding positions in Government, the Judiciary and high-ranking military officers. The Greeks living in Egypt in the 1950's, referred to colloquially as *Egyptiotes*, far outnumbered any other expatriate community and numbered over 200,000 in Alexandria alone. Other Arabs living in this suburb were servants to European families, caretakers of apartment blocks and merchants in the buzzing bazaars such the one between the tramway stations of Camp de César and Ibrahimieh. Their families often occupied a single or rarely a double room at the top of apartment blocks and were regarded as very fortunate to be able to share the same upper airs of Alexandria as their expatriate masters. The heads of these families were often seen loitering barefoot in entrance porches of apartment blocks, wearing their long cotton *galabiehs*, or seated in nearby cafes drawing smoke through elegant shisha pipes, while listening to a background of monotonous Arabian music. Their children, shabbily dressed, played aimlessly in the streets, every now and then begging for some *baksheesh* from residents of the expatriate community, only to be chided by their proud parents.

Alexis was born in the capital city Cairo but had only a scant recollection of that great metropolis since his family moved to Alexandria when he was young. With the summer beckoning he looked forward to spending many days on Alexandria's sandy beaches along the Corniche, his favourite being Sidi Bishr with its calm crystal-clear waters sheltered from the open sea by a bare oblong-shaped island, some 100 metres from the shore. He looked upon this island as his guardian angel in that it protected him from the rough waters that lay beyond.

The conservatoire where Nina had enrolled for piano lessons comprised a charming two-storey villa, built at the turn of the century, in Rue Holbitine, running parallel to Rue Canope in Camp de César. Petros Kalos, the closest of his school pals, was taking advance piano lessons while another school pal, Christos Papas, was the best young violinist of his generation. Together with Yanis Lotas the four youngsters formed a close-knit grouping, rather elitist as some thought. The strength of the group lay in the fact that they shared common interests, for example, apart from Petros the other three formed the nucleus of the school's basketball and tennis teams and were also members of the local Greek basketball team at Ibrahimieh to the strong disapproval of the school's Headmaster, a classics graduate from the University of Athens. He was austere, stern and unrelenting, especially in the assertion of authority and exercise of discipline. Although he somehow accepted the fact that the three pals were far better than any of the other school basketball players he continuously tried to discourage their involvement in the Club because the other first team players were semi-professionals and the notion of the youngsters rubbing shoulders with such characters filled him with abhorrence. It took all the eloquence and powers of persuasion of Alexis' mum to convince the Headmaster of the benefits that such membership might accrue. The turning point was when the top coach moved Alexis and Christos from the juniors to the first team, thus bypassing two other teams on their way to the top tier, to strengthen the team for the pending National Championships. The Headmaster, despite his reservations and grave misgivings, finally relented.

Petros' and Yanis' families were members of Alexandria's Yachting Club which lay at the Eastern port overlooking the Citadel of Qaitbay. The two boys were therefore very comfortable with all water pursuits both for leisure and competition. Yanis, the son of a wealthy industrialist, lived in fashionable Quartier Latin while Petros lived near Alexis further along Rue Canope. Christos' family, on the other hand, occupied a luxurious six-floor apartment overlooking the racecourse at Sporting. Alexis and Petros first met when they progressed from the elementary school near their homes to the Averofeio Gymnasium and, as fate had it, sat at the same double desk during the first day at school. What started as a casual acquaintance had by now developed into the strongest of friendships.

Alexis found out from Petros that Nina's next lesson

was due on the first Saturday afternoon in August and plotted his scheme for a seemingly accidental encounter. Since they first met at Palma at Easter almost six months ago his affection for her had grown steadily and by now she was constantly in his thoughts.

It was very likely that she would disembark from the tram at Camp de César, walk up the steps and proceed along Rue Elevsis then cross a succession of many streets running parallel to the tramline first Rue Memphis, then Rue Heliopolis, followed by Rue Canope before reaching the conservatoire. There were several spots where he could wait for Nina's arrival. He could pretend to gaze at the posters outside the Odeon Cinema next to the station, or perhaps by the Jewish Synagogue a little further on, but would he be too conspicuous in these places? Well, there was always Carabet's little shoe-polish shop near the intersection between Rue Elevsis and Rue Canope where he could sit for as long as he wished without drawing much attention from passers-by.

Carabet, a shabby Armenian in his fifties, had rugged features rendering his furrowed and wrinkly-lined face more distinct. He had a unique squint which confused his customers who were unable to perceive whom he was addressing at any time. He was as far from the technological age of the 20th century as he was from its permissiveness. Alexis and his friends used the little shop as an alternative meeting place, to the consternation of the owner who saw his business fade away as the three high-level customer chairs for polishing shoes were invariably occupied by the young intruders. However, being that they were also his best customers he couldn't really be very angry with them. Scruffily adorned, with a grubby apron, he loitered outside his shop or lounged at the café bar opposite contaminating his lungs with frequent puffs from an imposing *narguileh*.

The weather in early August was scorching hot as Alexis approached the little shoe-polish shop at around four o'clock. He judged that the best option was to speak to her before the lesson, hoping that she may be alone. What if Mirto, her closest friend from school, was with her? She was the sister of Michalis who attended a class above Alexis and was very friendly with Christos as their homes were in the same apartment block near the Sporting Club. He may have to abandon his little 'accidental' meeting if she was not alone.

Carabet's shop was equidistant from the tram station and the conservatoire. He judged that he needed a bit more time with Nina than just the shorter distance between the shop and the conservatoire. So, he made his way towards the tram station at Camp de César, arrived at the Odeon cinema and glanced at the posters. The film *Student Prince* was on, featuring Edmund Purdon. He reflected what he might say to Nina when they met.

The decision to speak to her was overwhelming and he felt nervous – perhaps best to let chance take its course and not plan anything specific. He glanced at his watch: it was nearly time for Nina's arrival. What if she misunderstood his motives and reacted in an unexpected or unsympathetic way? But he figured, he was not a total stranger and although he had no idea of the nature of her feelings towards him, he felt something, albeit tenuous, existed between them. He paced up and down the entrance hall of the Odeon periodically glancing at the staircase leading up from the tram station every time a Victoria tram stopped at the station. Finally, he saw her coming up the steps. Mirto was not with her: here was his chance. Alexis hid behind one of the large marble columns supporting the Odeon's façade and watched Nina's reflection on the glass-fronted poster frames as she crossed the street and passed him by. "Well, Mani, it is now or never," he whispered to himself. He started following her, gathering courage as he went along. He increased his pace until he was right behind her while she stopped to glance at the traffic as she was about to cross Rue Memphis. He took a deep breath and said,

"Hello Nina."

"Hello," she replied in surprise as she turned towards him. These greetings were not uttered in their native Greek but in English. Amongst the youngsters of Alexandria, it was not uncommon to switch from one language to another, often from Greek to English or French or indeed Arabic as all these languages were part of the school curriculum, and what could be better practice than to slip from one to another as often as one could. In view of the daunting task confronting Alexis, he thought it would be better to express himself in a foreign language, thus emulating the myriad of American films that dominated the Alexandrian cinemas at the time. They walked side by side approaching the Synagogue. Nina turned to Alexis and said,

"Is there a post box nearby?" pointing to a letter she was holding.

"Yes, there is one past the conservatoire."

"How are you?" went on Nina after a brief pause.

Alexis seized the opportunity and replied, "Not so good."

"What is the matter?" Nina asked anxiously as she turned and looked at him.

"I feel very mixed up," said Alexis hesitantly.

"Why?"

They had arrived at the Jewish Synagogue which lay opposite yet another English school, the St George's. Alexis turned and looked at the imposing façade of the synagogue and felt as though he was physically trapped between this Jewish place of worship and Nina's inaccessibility. He was holding a rolled-up piece of paper between his trembling hands and squeezed it more and more without knowing why he was doing so. Finally, he uttered softly, "Because..." And after a brief hesitation he unburdened his affection for her.

It was as though the words were pushed out against his better judgement. Nina remained silent. Alexis turned towards her and saw her reddened countenance as she lowered her eyes and stared straight down at the pavement obviously having been taken completely by surprise. Alexis felt utterly relieved, as though a great burden had suddenly been lifted from his shoulders. He regained his composure and was first to break this uncomfortable silence.

"I am sorry if I startled you?" he continued while reverting to the familiarity of his native language. It seemed important after taking the courage to express his deep feelings for her to now wish to appear sincere. This was real, not some game he was playing, he was not acting.

Nina momentarily turned and looked at Alexis then switched back staring at the pavement and remained silent trying to make sense of what had just happened. They crossed Rue Canope without uttering a word, both deep in thought. Alexis did not press Nina to unveil her own feelings as he felt it was up to her to do so if she so wished. He had gone as far as he desired. Having overcome his natural reticence and the shyness that existed between them he hoped to pave the way for a future deeper relationship. However, Nina was so taken aback by Alexis' revelation that she became more and more withdrawn. Alexis pointed to the post box and after posting the letter they made their way towards the conservatoire. On arrival, Alexis stopped by the pavement as she continued towards the entrance. She turned towards him, looked at him fleetingly, and smiled. As her slim figure receded in the distance Alexis could not distinguish her countenance but she looked very attractive before finally vanishing into the picturesque building of the music academy. He stood for a few minutes staring at the Conservatoire entrance hoping miraculously for her to reappear and throw her arms towards him. Alas, no such luck, so he slowly made his way towards the nearby Boy Scout grounds. He sat on a bench, utterly exhausted but at the same time exhilarated that he had achieved his goal no matter what the consequences. Suddenly he needed to be alone, away from the bustling activity at the Scouts and his friends, so he started to walk away from the scene of such personal emotional turmoil, crossed the tramlines and within minutes arrived at the Corniche, where he often found much-needed solace. He stared at the vastness of the Mediterranean and felt very relieved. A few tears of joy ran down his smooth face.

6

September – October 1956

At the rear of the Scout grounds lay a long narrow dirt track running parallel to Rue Canope. It had numerous ramshackle little houses, occupied mainly by less well-off Alexandrian families, Arab to a large extent, some of whom worked in the European sector while others were engaged in low-paid municipality jobs. Amongst these neglected buildings lay the service entrances at the back of the more salubrious apartments and individual villas of the expatriate community. The lane was usually very quiet, as though the joy of living had been somehow erased from the people living in these rundown dwellings.

One of these houses was occupied by the Palestinian family of Ismail el Kefr. They had come to Alexandria from the Jabal el-Hussein camp, one of four refugee camps established in Jordan shortly after the outbreak of the hostilities with Israel in 1948. The camps housed a quarter of a million Palestinians who either fled in panic or were forcibly expelled from their homes in Palestine. Although they formed part of 700,000 refugees that fled Palestine after the establishment of the State of Israel, they were more fortunate than many other families not to remain in a refugee camp. With the help of relatives in Egypt they were able to leave the camp and settle in Alexandria. Young Ismail felt strongly about the loss of his homeland in Lydda, often in his younger days acting with blind emotion by regarding all foreigners as responsible for the misfortune that had befallen the family.

Opposite Ismail's house and within the grounds of the Scouts lay a massive tree with numerous branches extending in all directions. The tree was the pride and joy of many young Cubs and Scouts who spent hour upon hour climbing up and down via a makeshift ladder building a raft, exploring the hidden wildlife within the tree and acting as a Robinson Crusoe family. It was during these innocent activities that Alexis first came to notice Ismail who watched his young neighbours inquisitively as they went about their enterprising pursuits, no-doubt disturbing the quietness of the little lane. From the outset Ismail and his young Arab neighbours were very suspicious of his young counterparts and often the suppressed feelings of all the youngsters surfaced, resulting in small skirmishes of throwing stones at each other. The intervention of Ismail's parents, or indeed the caretaker Abu-Ahmet, was often necessary to defuse the situation and to prevent some minor fracas from developing into full-scale gang warfare.

Following the expulsion of King Farouk in 1952 a fervent nationalistic feeling spread amongst a wide cross-section of the indigenous populace. Although the relationship between Ismail and his mates and Alexis and his fellow Boy Scouts strained even further during the months and years after the King's expulsion, Alexis was oblivious about the extent of Ismail's enmity for all Europeans and their various religious denominations until an accidental meeting between the two on a wintry afternoon in the lane not far from Ismail's house. Alexis, in one of his rare truancy acts from the Averofeio Gymnasium, was seeking refuge in the Scout grounds. He was shooting his ball at a basket strategically framed at one of the low-level buildings when, as a result of a wild shot, he directed the ball over the two-metre high wall at the boundary where it landed near Ismail's little house. Although the lane was regarded by all as no-mans-land, he decided to climb over, carefully avoiding the fragments of thick broken glass glued to the top, and jumped to the other side. He landed safely in the lane but to his great consternation Ismail was standing a few paces away, the ball coming to rest halfway between the two.

The sight of the crouched young Alexis staring alternately at the ball and the youthful Palestinian offered a glimpse of a menacing confrontation that could have had dire consequences and scarred their young lives for ever. After recovering from the initial shock Alexis regained his composure, stood and faced Ismail. For the next minute they stared at each other as though trying to penetrate each other's young minds. To Ismail, Alexis represented the epitome of Alexandria's privileged class, the embodiment of a European identity, the blossoming of a generation that would replace the old elite. Indeed, the generation he needed to fight if the Arab culture was to prevail and be allowed to thrive. To Alexis, Ismail was the epitome of a subdued and servile Arab population. Alexis stepped forward and picked up his ball. Ismail muttered a few words in Arabic which he did not understand. Ismail continued to spout what appeared to be some sort of verbal abuse but as it was obvious that Alexis was not very fluent in Arabic, he proceeded to demonstrate pictorially the essence of his mutterings. He grabbed a long baton lying nearby and using the loose grit of the dry soil of the alley he drew a large cross and stepped on it becoming more and more agitated in the process.

The penny dropped: although Alexis did not have a strong religious upbringing, he was taken aback by such acute irreverence and blasphemy. He was momentarily at a loss as to how to respond but soon he felt the need for revenge and to defend the beliefs of the majority of the expatriate population. As words failed him, he too resorted to a pictorial expression of his hurt feelings. He picked up another baton and drew an open thick book, scribbled on one side something in Arabic and stamped on it. The significance was all too obvious: he was stamping on a sacred book. The two youngsters stood defiantly in front of the sacred pictorial images ready to pounce at each other given the slightest extra provocation. Fortunately, Ismail's mother appeared on the doorstep of her house and, sensing that a confrontation was imminent, called her son to come home thus avoiding a fight, to the bitter consternation of the two youngsters. Had his mother been unaware of his whereabouts, a squabble would have taken place but the transient physical wounds that would have ensued would have been insignificant compared to the long-term psychological scars. If truth be told, however, the youngsters were only expressing deep-rooted emotions ingrained in them by their elders.

Many years had passed since this incident and time had supplied a vital ingredient healing their strained relationship. The proximity of Ismail's house to the Scout grounds resulted initially in a delicate coexistence but gradually an appreciation of their respective culture and ethics developed. They were eventually formally introduced by Panos Yeoryadis, a stocky individual who although was not a member of the Boy Scouts was living in the neighbourhood and knew both Alexis and the other patrol leader Yeorgis. Presently, Panos and Ismail were now students at the University in Alexandria and were seeing a lot of each other, thus bringing the young Palestinian closer to Alexis and others in the Boy Scout movement. As a result, Ismail was by now taking part in many of the group's recreational activities. Alexis and Ismail learned to respect each other and while differences of opinion still existed, they became close.

Following the move of Alexis' family to Alexandria two distinct friendship groups were formed with Alexis being the link. The group originating at school met during the academic year, while the other at the Scouts met all the year round, its strong bond derived from the fact that they were all locals. Apart from Ismail they were of Greek origin but with diverse educational background. Panos had attended the British Boy's School, where Yeorgis was currently a pupil, while Thanos Metis who lived in Rue Canope near Carabet's shoe-shop was attending Victoria College, a private school affording exceptionally high-quality teaching, an example of the long-standing British connection with Egypt. With its high fees it was only afforded by a minority of the expatriate community. Victoria College's pupillage was readily identified by the characteristic uniform comprising dark blue-blazer, grey trousers and dark blue cap with sky-blue stripes emanating from a central button at the top.

The boys from the Averofeio Gymnasium came from all over Alexandria. From such a motley group gradually unfolded a cluster of a few individuals seeking similar interests forming a closer clan. Its continuity was disrupted during the summer months, as each family had their own vacation plans. It was remarkable how at the beginning of the new academic year, their friendships resumed as though time stood still.

This scout grouping met frequently in the dying days of the summer of 1956. After family outings the youngsters would meet late in the afternoon at the Scouts. They were all at an impressionable age ready to be confronted by a major regional event which was to shape their adolescence.

7

Gaza Strip, Palestine, January 2018

Numerous interconnected tunnels deep under the Gaza Strip were dug over the years. As soon as one was discovered by the IDF and blocked, other tunnels emerged.

A new deeper and recently excavated tunnel leads to a set of small rooms housing the latest communication equipment enabling the leadership of Hamas to contact their military sections, agents and other associates in Istanbul, Beirut, Damascus, Cairo and other capital cities throughout the Middle East. Hamas, a Sunni-Islamic Palestinian political organisation, formed in 1987, has stated repeatedly, and has enshrined in its 1988 Charter, that its purpose is to liberate Palestine from Israeli occupation, which includes the West Bank, the Gaza Strip and the modern State of Israel itself. Its military wing is the Izz ad-Din al-Qassam Brigades.

Great care is taken by Hamas to avoid being bugged by Mossad, the Israeli agency responsible for intelligence collection, covert operations, and counterterrorism. Every major operation, such as the killing of undesirables within Palestine's hierarchy first identified by Mossad agents, would have to be ratified by Varash, the Committee of all the Chiefs of Israeli Intelligence Organisations. Bugging the Hamas communication centre was Mossad's and its agents' chief goal although Hamas had employed highly skilled counter-surveillance operatives and experts in bug-sweeping to design and install electronically detecting surveillance devices, including covert listening devices. Mossad had also recently established a working relationship with Morocco, Jordan and Saudi Arabia, the latter because of its pro-Sunni stance and anti-Shia Iranian factions which support the civil war in Syria. A great schism in the Palestinian Liberation Organisation set up by Yasser Arafat occurred a few years after his death in 2004 when inter-party rivalry mushroomed with two dominant factions, Fatah and Hamas, gaining centre ground.

Following the second Palestinian Legislative Council parliamentary elections of the Palestinian National Authority on 25 January 2006, a majority of the seats were gained by Hamas and, in 2007, this Palestinian Sunni Islamic fundamentalist organisation assumed control of the Gaza Strip. Fatah, under the guise of the Palestinian Authority, was confined to parts of the West Bank with its headquarters at Ramallah. Following attempts towards reconciliation, Fatah and Hamas formed a unity government which for a few years ruled over the Strip, West Bank and East Jerusalem, but mistrust led to renewed clashes and as from 2016 Hamas governed Gaza while the Palestinian Authority took control of parts of the occupied West Bank. The aspiration of the two factions at present do not differ that much in that Hamas, after much procrastination, accepted in May 2017 the

Palestinian Authority's espousal of a two-state solution, with the border as it existed before the 1967 Six Day War with Israel and the capital of the new Palestinian State to be in East Jerusalem.

The leader of Hamas, Ali Al Hakimi, was in contact with his Adjutant Abdul.

"Could you inform the section heads that I would like to hold a meeting to discuss the announcement of the US President regarding their Embassy move to Jerusalem?" He could not bring himself to utter the word Israel even though he accepted its de facto recognition.

"Will do. When do you wish to hold the meeting?" replied Abdul.

"Within a few days," replied the Hamas leader.

The meeting has been arranged for 2pm a week later at location X, Abdul informed his boss a few days later.

To avoid pinpointing this location by agents of Mossad, letters had been assigned designating meeting points. An elaborate scheme was devised to change the designation frequently to confuse the agents. Designation X this time was identified as the Shatila Refugee Camp in southern Beirut, which was established in 1949 and housed tens of thousands of Palestinian refugees forcibly displaced from Palestine after Israel came into existence. Ali and his close associates made their way in the dead of night to a remote beach near Al Mawasi at the southern end of the Strip to board a Nor Tech 390 quad racing boat fitted with 4, 400R motors , to travel to a quiet inlet off the village of Douha about 15 km to the south of Beirut. The 200-km-odd crossing was fraught with danger as the Mediterranean shores between Israel and Lebanon were regularly patrolled by the Israeli navy. They also had to avoid underwater listening devices. That evening they managed to evade the patrol boats and arrived safely at their destination. They were met by a car driven by a fellow Hamas operative and were taken to the Shatila Camp. This location was also chosen because colleagues from Istanbul and Damascus would be attending, thus facilitating their passage without arousing Mossad's suspicion. Upon arrival at Shatila, it was decided to move the meeting to a safe house in Ashrafiyeh where its cafés and impressive buildings would offer an excellent camouflage concealing the occurrence of a top-level Hamas meeting.

Sombre faces greeted Ali and his entourage as they met to consider their response to the President's announcement.

"We must fight it tooth and nail," pronounced the newest recruit to the Hamas leadership, Qasim Al-Jazari, who had travelled from Istanbul. Young Qasim was born in 1980 in the Jerash refugee camp in Jordan, just north of Amman, of parents who were expelled from Nablus in the West Bank after the 1967 war with Israel. As he grew up in the camp, he observed the misery that his parents had endured not being able to return to their home which was now part of the Yitzhar settlement, a Jewish Orthodox community, south of the city of Nablus. Qasim's parents were ordinary civilians not fighters and accepted their fate but their son was full of anger and hate towards the major powers but especially the USA, Europe, and some rich Arab states including Saudi Arabia, for allowing such an injustice to persist for such a long time. His parents were living on international aid, oddly as it may seem provided by the USA, as well as on handouts from friends and relatives and some sympathetic Arab countries. He attended UN-run schools and graduated from the Islamic University of Gaza with a degree in Politics. He grew to become an angry young person wishing to overthrow the State of Israel, often expressing strong views about the Israeli government and IDF's brutal response to random and frequently ineffective attacks from Palestinians in the Gaza Strip on Tel Aviv or Jerusalem. He was therefore a prime target to join the Islamic Jihad Movement which was an offshoot of the Muslim Brotherhood in Egypt. The declared aim of this terrorist group was the total destruction of the Jewish state and the establishment of a Palestinian State with pre-1948 borders. However, within a few years and under the influence of some moderate university pals, Qasim realised that the aims of Islamic Jihad were wholly unrealistic and, in fact, detrimental to the aspirations of both Fatah and Hamas in reaching a just settlement with Israel. When Hamas in 2012 expelled the Islamic Jihad from the Gaza Strip, Qasim decided to distance himself from their ranks and at the age of 23 he was recruited as a foot-soldier for Hamas where he was given tasks such as supervising the building of numerous tunnels that connect the Gaza Strip to Israel and Egypt and often led raids into Israel. As such, at the age of 30 he came to be noticed by Hamas' leadership who eventually asked him to join its Inner Council as coordinator of the many activities of Hamas. In his new role he attempted to influence other members of Islamic Jihad to leave and join the struggle as members of Hamas. The Islamic Jihad movement was then withdrawn from Gaza and set up its headquarters in Damascus, and even though its members were predominantly Sunni the movement was so desperate for support that it accepted funding from Shia's military Council in Iran and Hezbollah.

"What are you suggesting?" asked Asim Al Balawi, the Head of the Izz ad-Din al-Qassam Brigades, who was in charge of all insurrections against Israel and deputy Head of Hamas.

"First we instruct our people in Gaza to protest," replied young Qasim.

"Our people in Gaza will protest out of their own volition without waiting for our call. But is it really what we wish?" started Ali. "A mass protest at the border will give the IDF the excuse to fire at our people on the pretext that they need to defend the border and prevent our people crossing it. Attacking the border guards with slingshots throwing stones may be a noble act but totally ineffective and may result in the death of many of our citizens as Israeli military will exercise their shoot-to-kill policy at the slightest provocation as they have done on many previous intifadas."

"What other options do we have? Do we know the reaction of the Palestinian Authority?" queried Qasim.

"They are contacting some nations at the UN who are supportive of our cause and urging them to make a statement on the issue," replied Ali. Ever since the failed attempt to gain full membership of the UN, because of the US voting against such a move at the Security Council, the Palestinian Authority was given non-member observer status.

"That will not get us anywhere. How about unleashing a few rockets towards Israel?" replied an angry Qasim who, when cornered, always suggested resorting to violence, acts of which terrorised the Jewish inhabitants of towns and settlements near the border with the Gaza Strip but were militarily practically ineffectual, as casualties were negligible.

Ali Hakimi was used to such a reaction, particularly by young Palestinian militants. He took over as Head of Hamas from his predecessor who was targeted by Mossad and supplied its findings to Varash. They in turn discussed the rationale for killing the Hamas leader and passed its findings to the Prime Minister of Israel who had to authorise the execution. The Prime Minister, who on principle did not wish to get involved, passed the information to two of his ministers, one of whom was the Minister of Defence, who approved the killing. Mossad then instructed its sleeper operatives to go ahead with the execution which was carried out by the aid of a drone which targeted the ex-Hamas leader as he was leaving a regional meeting south of Amman. The present leader, Al Hakimi, was all too aware that he too was a target and took extra precautions regarding his whereabouts and movements.

One of the major problems regarding the issue of Palestine has been the uncoordinated activities of a number of organisations throughout the world by Palestinians of the Diaspora. Apart from the huge number of refugees that fled their homes, forcibly or otherwise after the 1948 and 1967 wars, there has been a continuous exodus of young Palestinians who now live all over the world. There are well documented reports that after the 1967 war thousands of Palestinians were forced to flee from Israeli-controlled areas. As a result, these Palestinians of the Diaspora have formed organisations and associations, some linked to each other, while others operate quite autonomously. Being a minority in their new place of abode they assimilated with their way of life whilst still harbouring a longing to occasionally visit their old stomping grounds in Palestine.

The discussion continued for a considerable time, putting forward a variety of suggestions from peaceful protests at the border to acts of terror aimed at specific targets over the border and in Israel itself.

Ismail el Kefr returned to his home in Camp de César after meeting some friends in downtown Alexandria. He tried in vain to contact his 44-year-old son Mustafa, a graduate of politics and economics from the University in Alexandria. His son followed his undergraduate degree with a Master's at the Islamic University of Gaza. There he met Qasim when they were both involved in student activities and thus forged strong links with Palestinian politicians both in the West Bank and the Gaza Strip.

The adjutant Abdul approached Qasim and gave him a piece of paper informing him that Mustafa el Kefr had tried in vain to contact him over the past few days. Since the days at the University in Gaza they had kept in touch but as Qasim was heavily involved with Hamas he did not have much time to contact his young friend in Alexandria. Their meetings were sporadic and impromptu and of course clandestine in order not to raise any suspicion of the security forces, both in Israel and Egypt, that their friendship had endured. Mustafa had not joined Hamas or any Islamic organisation but occasionally offered assistance in running errands or ferrying key personnel to various locations in Alexandria or beyond.

Qasim nodded in acknowledgment and wondered if Mustafa had something important that he wished to discuss. He was scheduled to meet two operatives in Cairo in the next few days so perhaps he could signal to his friend that they could meet somewhere in Egypt's capital city.

Days later Qasim and Mustafa met in a house off Al Bustan Street in the centre of Cairo. They greeted each other warmly and briefly discussed family news.

"How are your parents?" asked Qasim his friend who knew them well from his frequent visits to Alexandria.

"Mother has passed away, but dad is fine. He spends endless days meeting old friends downtown. He also travels to Europe and particularly to Athens to meet some Greek friends he met when he was young and joins their reunions." After discussing the whereabouts of mutual acquaintances, they switched their talk to the President's intention about the Israeli Embassy.

"I am so appalled by such a deliberate provocative suggestion. Most of my friends and colleagues are at a loss as to what the immediate future will bring," said Mustafa.

"Well, for a start there will be strong condemnation from us, and I assume Fatah, but most worrying is the situation in the Strip where any protest risks a brutal response from the IDF with considerable loss of life."

"Then why don't you stop mass protests at the border?" asked Mustafa.

"Whatever we say, the people will protest. It is in their blood," responded Qasim, who was now happy to echo the words of his leader Ali.

"But after Al-Nakba how do you see the future?" asked Mustafa. He was right to refer to the Catastrophe that befell the Palestinians all those years ago.

"Our population is growing at an ever-increasing rate and one day our sheer numbers will be such that they will not be able to stop our revolution. Look what has happened in South Africa," said Qasim.

Mustafa, primarily under the influence of his dad Ismail, had always approached the issue of the Palestinian-Israeli conflict with a more conciliatory attitude. He went on. "But Qasim, there is a massive difference between apartheid in South Africa and the situation you are confronted with in Palestine. Apart from one or two countries, apartheid was opposed by practically the rest of the world, whereas Israel has been recognised by the majority of the countries within the UN and is supported by a mighty superpower."

Qasim looked at his friend squarely in the eyes searching for a counter-argument. Indeed, he was all too aware that there were some 30-odd countries that did not recognise Israel, but the stark reality was that most of the major countries did. He had to convince his university pal that Hamas had moved considerably from the original charter of non-recognition of Israel and armed struggle towards achieving their main objective of establishing a state in the whole of the old Palestine as it existed during the British Mandate.

After an uncomfortable pause he continued. "The statement in Doha last year by our leaders has clearly shifted our position in that Hamas will accept a two-state solution with borders based on the pre-1967 war accompanied by the return of our displaced people from the refugee camps back into Palestine and compensation for the loss of their original homes."

"But Hamas has not explicitly recognised the State of Israel," rebuffed Mustafa, "and I say this because successive Israeli PMs state forcibly that Hamas does not recognise their country, frequently stating 'they wish to throw us into the sea by force.' By not recognising Israel, Hamas is playing into the hands of the Israeli Government who welcome the status quo. Hamas should call their bluff and openly and incontrovertibly recognise the State of Israel."

"But our statement in Doha implicitly accepts the existence of the State of Israel because by accepting a two-state solution, one being Palestine with borders which existed pre-1967 War, it is obvious which is the other state," replied Qasim without wishing to utter Israel by name, "and what is more, the statement in Doha clearly states, unequivocally, my friend," stressing the last word to emphasize the point, "that the Hamas conflict is with the Zionists and not with the people who live presently in that other country who continue to expand their occupancy in the West Bank by building new and extending existing settlements. It has been said many times that eventually they would like to occupy all the remaining Palestinian territories and it seems that the major powers are accepting this scenario or are not doing anything to object to such a blatant expansionist policy."

The two friends continued their discussion in that little semi-dark room in the metropolis not far from the Nile, surrounded by empty walls and rickety furniture, each putting forward powerful arguments in an attempt to offer a solution to this intractable problem: how to force representatives from both factions to the negotiating table.

"Look at the situation in Gaza", prompted Mustafa. “It is like living in a cage, starved of basic resources, like electricity and water and with an economic blockade that puts a stranglehold on the whole wellbeing of that strip of land. The livelihood of your Gazan people has been crushed by the economic blockade, allowing them to grow very little produce and exporting practically nothing. Could you put your hand on your heart and tell me that Ali is doing all that is required to end such a miserable existence, if it means that he goes against the Hamas Charter drafted 32 years ago?”

“If Ali goes against the Charter, it will be a betrayal of our principles, the realisation that the end game will not offer a solution which will be acceptable to most of our people, most of our supporters,” replied Qasim.

A message came shortly, interrupting the discussion, reminding Qasim that he was to meet the two operatives in a safe house at a remote district of Dahshur west of Helwan in the south of the city.

The Direction Générale des Etudes et de la Documentation, DGED, the external intelligence agency in Morocco, were alerted by an informant in Cairo that Qasim was in Egypt to meet some operatives and was now talking to Mustafa at Al Bustan Street. DGED immediately informed Mossad agents who passed the information to Varash who in turn sanctioned the execution of Qasim. Mossad assets in Cairo were put on alert and made their way to the address where Qasim was to meet the two operatives. Mossad agents followed Qasim as he entered the block of flats at Al Bustan Street. They kept in constant touch with Mossad's assets who were to execute Qasim. As they did not consider Mustapha a threat to security, they kept their distance, observing Qasim's movements remotely. After two hours Qasim left Mustapha at Al Bustan Street and was driven at speed to the safe house in Dahshur. The Israeli agents, upon reaching that destination, observed the main entrance at a distance. They did not notice the two Hamas operatives entering the safe house so assumed that there was another entrance.

A small drone, fitted with a miniature video camera, was carefully guided from an open window onto the ceiling of the meeting place in Dahshur, thus offering the Israeli intelligence officers a magnificent vantage-point from which to observe the movements of Qasim and his fellow operatives. An hour later, Qasim left the house in Dahshur and was being driven towards Cairo in an old Opel. The Mossad agents instructed the Israeli assets on a Harley-Davidson to pursue Qasim and left the scene, leaving the assets to fulfil their mission. The car sped up the Aswan Western Agricultural Road turning right onto the southern ringroad making its way towards Ismailia, bypassing Cairo southwards. It joined the Saad el Din al Shasly Road and veered towards the Ismailia Desert Road. At the next traffic lights, the two assets on the motorcycle drew alongside the stationary Opel. Qasim, eyes shut, was reflecting on his chat with Mustafa when, as the traffic lights changed from red to red-amber, the second passenger on the motorcycle and designated shooter drew a small Rossi 352 revolver, cocked back the trigger and fired three shots towards Qasim, leaving him dead at the scene. The driver of the Harley-Davidson revved up his powerful engine, thrusting forward at an accelerating speed, tyres squealing, and turned immediately left heading northwards towards El Odour City. Within tens of seconds he was lost in its narrow streets.

The Egyptian authorities could not hide the execution of Qasim from the outside world as it was carried out in full view of passers-by and other traffic. There were no tears or recriminations back at the Hamas headquarters as they accepted that their lives were constantly at risk from the hunting operatives of Mossad and their local assets. With the pending move of the US embassy to Jerusalem there was a lot to be done in a short time. Mustafa, distraught at the death of his university pal, wondered whether he too was a target, albeit by association, since he had never been a Hamas operative nor ever involved in any insurrection against Israel or the occupying IDF.

8

Alexandria, October 1956

Another glorious summer was over. The first day of the new academic year was always very exciting as Alexis met once again with other school pals who were not part of his Boy Scouts group. They exchanged notes about the summer and planned for the social activities that lay ahead. Amongst the myriad of girls in their sky-blue uniforms leaving the school that first afternoon there would hopefully be the slim figure of Nina whom he longed to see. Ever since their last encounter before her lessons at the conservatoire, circumstances were such that their paths had not crossed. At the completion of the last lesson the boys walked steadily towards the tram station and sat opposite on the knee-high wall of the Salvayios, the commercial branch of the schools. From that vantage point they had a good look at the comings and goings of the boys and girls waiting to board incoming trams. Finally, Alexis noticed Nina's figure in the far distance accompanied by Mirto. After a short walk they arrived on the platform. Although she smiled as they came close, Alexis still perceived something that was driving her away from him. His premonition in early August when he opened his heart to her seemed to be correct. A Victoria-bound tram approached, stopped, Nina and

Mirto embarked and the double-decked carriages soon trundled towards the depths of Alexandria's suburbia to the east of the city.

"Well you Romeos, it is about time you went home," shouted the school supervisor for tram embarkation. The boys soon dispersed. Such were the events on the first day back at the schools at Shatby that fateful autumn.

Parents and friends congregated at the concert hall in Rue Sultan Hussein on Friday 19th October 1956. Alexis' close friends were performing at their annual concert of the conservatoire. The younger members appeared first, often for no more than five minutes, gradually working up to the more advanced and accomplished students to whom a career linked to music beckoned. It was impressive that some pupils who were not musically gifted managed to give a solid performance. Mona's younger brother, unaware of the importance of the occasion, gave a good display of musical skill which pleasantly surprised his parents who did not expect anything special. They were anxiously waiting Mona's turn as on their way to the music hall they sensed all was not well. Halfway through the proceedings she entered the stage, bowed to the audience and sat on the lean stool. From striking the first note it became obvious she was very nervous and struggled to play her chosen piece, confidence ebbing away with every key she pressed. What made it worse were the murmurs from the audience, initially a few whispers but within a very short span becoming more and more audible which contributed to the downfall of poor Mona. She suddenly stopped, lowered her head towards the keyboard, stood up and disappeared off stage sobbing inconsolably. Although such a poor performance was the result of Mona's own nervousness, it did reflect badly on the music teacher whose sole aim was to impress the parents and advance the standing of the conservatoire. A look of concern appeared on the countenance of the music teacher as the next pupil started her piece which, to his great relief, was flawless and played with great gusto.

Alexis was sitting in the last row and had a perfect view of the auditorium and its stage. From such a vantage point he was able to observe the comings and goings of the pupils and analyse the various characters. He was present because Nina was performing and to some extent to support his pals, Petros and Christos. After what seemed an eternity, smiling disarmingly Nina entered, stared at the audience, and bowed gracefully. Her lean figure stood elegantly in the surrounding emptiness of an otherwise dull background. Her presence had a dynamic and electrifying impact on him. She approached the piano, adjusted the height of the stool and, allowing seconds to compose herself, started her adagio, pressing the keys softly but deliberately to gather confidence and avoid early faults. Within minutes she was in her stride and gave a virtuoso performance. To Alexis the scales conveyed a message, not related to the composer's metric structure, but it appeared that Nina was communicating with him in a strange language, whose *ipsissima verba* he did not understand but which sounded most beautiful. Alexis was listening, eyes shut, reflecting on the circumstances in which he now found himself. The finale was given by Christos who as usual gave a splendid performance of Brahms' Hungarian Dance No 1.

At the end of the concert Alexis and his friends gathered in the courtyard outside the building, gossiping about the afternoon's events while proud parents and their offspring passed by on their way home. Mr Voras' face was drawn, having witnessed his daughter's disastrous performance, and with eyes facing straight ahead walked by the youngsters without uttering a word. No doubt Mona would be withdrawn from the conservatoire unless the music master could offer words of consolation and a sound reason why she could not cope. Nina and Mirto emerged from the Concert Hall making their way towards Nina's chauffeur-driven family car waiting around the corner. Nina's mother insisted that her daughter be driven there and back, thus avoiding the hustle and bustle of the journey using the tram. As they approached Alexis' little group, they were congratulated on their splendid performances only in return to be lavished with similar complimentary remarks for their solo performances that afternoon.

"Well, all over for another year," prompted Christos, "What we need now is a party to unwind, which, as it happens, I am organising next Saturday."

"Is that the 27th?" asked Petros.

"It is," said Christos.

The boys readily acquiesced; however, the two girls muttered something to the effect that permission was needed from their parents but as Christos' family was very well known there was little doubt of their agreeing to let their children attend the party. Petros and Nina were exchanging viewpoints about their mutual performances while Christos asked Mirto to pass the word to other girls in their form about his pending party. Alexis stood close to Petros throughout his self-criticism about his performance while occasionally looking at Nina without participating in their post-concert deliberations. Gradually Nina became aware of Alexis' closeness and reflected on how serious his countenance looked. He in turn tried in vain to gauge her attitude following their momentous meeting a few months ago but perceived a sangfroid which disturbed him. She could not ignore that there was a bond between them but there was no obvious reciprocation regarding her feelings, although she still seemed to be interested in the attention he was paying her. He wondered whether her attentiveness to Petros' minor peroration was waning in view of his constant but silent interest in her. Petros soon realised that his conversation with Nina had turned into a soliloquy as she seemed to be more interested in Alexis' presence and brought his musical musings abruptly to a close.

There followed a reticent goodbye and Alexis watched her chauffeur-driven car draw away towards

Rue Saad Zaghloul on its meandering journey along the Corniche and eventually Glymenopoulo.

By nine o'clock on Saturday 27th of October the party at Christos' was in full swing. There were about 20 pupils from the Averofeio Gymnasium School and a similar number from the girls' school as well as some of Alexis' close friends from the scout movement. Christos' apartment facing the Sporting Club racecourse was quite spacious, comprising a number of high-ceiling living rooms of great opulence branching off a wide corridor. Antique furniture adorned many of the rooms and an imposing chandelier hung in the spacious drawing room with its multiple spider-like branches holding pointed electric bulbs, giving a bright atmosphere in the space below. Christos' parents appeared at regular intervals from the inner quarters of the apartment to add a modicum of respectability but after a sharp look of disapproval from their son they quietly made themselves scarce.

Youngsters formed clusters of familiarity while reticent pupils were left to fend for themselves, standing awkwardly in corners or sitting in chairs and sofas reluctant, or not knowing how, to mix in. Alexis meandered through the clusters listening to the latest gossip, exchanging the odd comment and moving along. He noticed Nina's group by the grand piano, an elegant Steinway which had been handed down by Christos' grandfather, a prominent industrialist. Nina wore a narrow-waisted, full-skirted brown dress with moccasin shoes while Mirto was dressed in a black jumper, grey skirt and black flat shoes. They seemed quite happy, every now and then accepting an invitation to a slow tango or the cha-cha.

Rock 'n' Roll was starting to catch the imagination of the youngsters, given the worldwide fame of Chuck Berry's hits, with Alexis being by far the most accomplished dancer of their milieu. Alexis tagged along to his older brothers' parties, possibly at the instigation of Mary Mani, although Pavlos never objected to having his younger brother amongst his peers. As Alexis hardly knew anybody, he spent most of the time observing couples dancing and started imitating their moves, particularly when they jived and danced the Rock 'n' Roll. On occasions he was encouraged to participate and to his great surprise he realised that not only could he follow the various steps but soon started to improvise and formulate he own brand of Rock 'n' Roll. So, when years later he went to his pals' parties he quickly established himself as the top dancer, his dancing partner being Marika, Christos' girlfriend. It was customary, therefore, at least once during the evening, for the pair to perform in front of their jubilant peers who formed a circle around them, clapping and rejoicing every new spectacular move.

However, that night the group sprang Alexis an unpleasant surprise when somebody, who remained anonymous throughout, invited a top amateur dancer to the party with the sole purpose of challenging Alexis' dancing prowess. Although Alexis realised immediately the consequence of such an invite, he did not shy away from the inevitable contest even though the outcome was strikingly obvious. The murmurs intensified when, as Bill Haley's voice sounded loud and clear over the turn table, "One o'clock, two o'clock...", the top amateur sauntered to the centre of the lounge giving an extraordinary exhibition of Rock 'n' Roll with his imported partner. Suddenly Alexis noticed that practically all his mates were staring at him, making it impossible not to accept the challenge. As Marika and Alexis started their accomplished and novel routine, including some skilful pirouettes, their friends encouraged them by vigorously clapping and urging them on but, alas, they were no match for the other pair, who, it transpired, were Alexandria's amateur champions. As soon as the record finished and both pairs stopped amidst robust and persistent clapping, a girl from school approached Alexis and stated without equivocation, "You know you were no match at all for him," to which Alexis, looking straight at her, replied, "I am well aware of that", which took her by total surprise and she avoided him throughout the rest of the evening.

Alexis withdrew to the comfort of a sofa in a corner of one of the rooms, sipped a beer and pondered about the profundity of it all. Was he upset that such a challenge was schemed against him? Not really, he reflected, it was bound to happen sooner or later at subsequent parties as apart from his immediate milieu odd couples seemed to infiltrate their gatherings. He glanced around: Ismail was chatting to Petros and Yeorgis while Panos and Thanos were engaged in an animated conversation, hands frequently waving about, with two girls he did not recognise, probably from the Lycée Français. Lots of couples were now dancing cheek to cheek following a slow rhythmic tango; Nina was nowhere to be seen. He stood up and walked into the dining room. Feeling peckish he approached the large table where all sorts of foodstuffs and delicacies were laid and picked some. He turned toward the balcony and saw a couple standing near each other by the railings. At first sight it appeared as though they were admiring the fine October evening and its star-littered sky, watching the horizon unfold beyond the Sporting Club racecourse. But soon Alexis perceived something deeper on both their profiles as they turned and faced each other. The slim figure of the girl was unmistakably that of Nina's and her tall companion was Tasos Phoundas, a close friend and school pal of Michalis, Mirto's elder brother. Tasos was born and brought up in Johannesburg, South Africa and the excellent reputation of the Averofeio Gymnasium had compelled his father to send him to Alexandria to complete the last two scholastic years. He lodged with his cousin Rea Loizithou at their apartment in Camp de César. Alexis, distraught at what he had just seen, turned to the dining table and continued to nibble without being conscious of what he picked. He went to the lounge and sank into the comfortable sofa. He shut his eyes and reflected on the balcony scene. When he reopened his eyes Tasos was standing nearby chatting to Yeorgis while Ismail was dancing with Nina and Petros with Mirto.

"That Rock 'n' Roll must have exhausted you," said Tasos to Alexis. "Where did you learn such amazing moves?" Alexis opened his eyes and was momentarily startled by Tasos' unexpected reference to his dancing skills.

"Well, I gradually picked these up over the years at parties that my brother Pavlos took me to and adapted them to suit myself and my partner Marika. When one is enjoying oneself, tiredness does not come into it," he replied.

Alexis stood up and, approaching the boys, said to Tasos, "Have you settled in Alexandria?"

"I arrived mid-June and thanks to Michalis I haven't been without friends. We spent practically the remainder of the summer at Montazah where Michalis' parents have a chalet. It was enormous fun." As Michalis was in a form one year ahead of Alexis', no wonder he had not come across Tasos earlier at school.

Although Alexis gave the impression of listening very attentively, he let his mind reflect on what Tasos had just revealed. Balmy summer days at Montazah with Mirto and Michalis meant that Nina was often present and therefore it was natural that something may have developed between the two. Would that explain Nina's attitude during their brief encounter some months ago?

Quite possibly, he reflected.

"I believe you are the captain of the basketball team at school. I do enjoy the game and would not mind a few games now and then," went on Tasos.

"He is a pseudo-professional," interrupted Yeoryis smilingly, "He and Christos are members of the Greek Club at Ibrahmieh and as from next season they will be playing for the top team, having been elevated from the fourth team to the consternation of many members of the other teams they bypassed."

"I am sure there would be a place for you in the school team," replied Alexis who felt somewhat embarrassed by the praise afforded him by Yeoryis.

By now Ismail and Nina had joined the group and the conversation swerved from topic to topic. Ismail was recounting his experiences during the past few months. Being a few years older than his pals he had just started his first year at Alexandria's university after having spent the best part of his summer vacation at an army training camp near Port Said. The military training was not compulsory, but he felt he owed it to his adopted country having given shelter to his family following the loss of their home in Palestine during the 1947 skirmishes with Jewish paramilitary groups. Alexis cast his thoughts back to the first encounter with Ismail when they nearly came to blows in the lane separating the scouts from Ismail's little house. Ismail often referred to his house as his little heaven compared to the tents in the refugee camp the family had left behind.

"The worst part of the training was waking up early in the morning. So, I am glad I am back at university where the regime is somewhat more relaxed," he went on smilingly.

"Come on you guys," retorted Christos as he approached the group, "you have not eaten much – look, there is still plenty," pointing to the large table where numerous ornate round silver serving platters were still half full.

"If I eat any more, I will burst," exclaimed Panos. "Did your mother cook all these?" As Christos nodded Panos went straight towards the back of the apartment where Christos' parents were sitting and offered his hearty congratulations.

Tasos turned to Mirto and, offering his hand, moved her to the dance floor. Alexis approached Nina and asked her if she would like to dance. She readily acquiesced. Alexis and Nina approached the other couples and joined in. They remained silent as though they both felt uncomfortable with the uneasy atmosphere that enveloped them. Alexis drew Nina close to him; she did not offer any resistance. As their bodies touched Alexis felt a continuous quiver emanating from his dancing partner. She seemed as though she was trembling. Alexis glanced at her.

"Did you have an enjoyable summer?" he asked.

"Yes," answered Nina in a tone which betrayed her unwillingness to elaborate.

"Did you often go to the beach?" continued Alexis without stating which of the myriad of Alexandrian beaches along the Corniche he was alluding to.

"Yes, I did."

"I often went to the beach at Sidi Bishr but did not see you there," went on Alexis.

"I hardly went to that beach."

"Why not?"

"Mirto was kind enough to invite me to their family chalet at Montazah, overlooking the beautiful bay. I do not really like to tackle the waves one finds at the other more exposed beaches. You see the –"

As Nina described the serene beauty of the ex-Palace grounds, the picturesque bay with its unending rows of identical chalets following the curvature of the waterfront, Alexis felt a strong pang, almost a strong pain which he was able to sustain with fortitude. His suspicions were justified. Nina finally concluded

"Otherwise if I fancied a quick dip, I nipped down to my local beach at Glymenopoulo and found sanctuary under an umbrella."

"To avoid the sun no doubt."

"I find it too hot and besides it does not appeal to me to spend endless hours worshipping this volume of fire."

"It is a bit more than that surely," retorted Alexis.

"Than what?"

"A volume of fire."

"Oh, really? Enlighten me," continued Nina disparagingly.

"I read an article in a science magazine which stated that there are some very interesting processes taking place up there."

"Such as?" interrupted Nina.

"Well, lighter elements, such as hydrogen, join together under very high temperatures, forming heavier elements such as helium, and in the process release enormous amounts of energy which eventually reaches the sun's surface and a good deal of it in the form of electromagnetic waves are emanated into space. After travelling some 150 million kilometres, these waves find us here on earth and a portion, called ultraviolet energy, crosses the earth's atmosphere and reaches us down below and may cause us harm, that is, burn the skin. So next time you find yourself on a sun-soaked beach, do reflect at the amazing processes taking place up there," concluded Alexis as though he was lecturing a child.

"You are trying to blind me with science, but you have convinced me even more not to sunbathe," said Nina.

They went on dancing. Alexis wished he could mention their last encounter on her way to the conservatoire when he revealed his true fondness, but he held back. The tension from the ensuing silence was finally relaxed when Yanis, dancing with Irini Samara, came by them and mentioned something inconsequential. Irini was attending the same form as Nina and lived in the same apartment block as Thanos Metis in Rue Canope and knew Alexis and the other Scouts well. She was introduced to Alexis by Thanos and eventually she attended many of the functions and parties of the youngsters. Her chubby cheeks, thick lips and enigmatic eyes gave her a welcoming countenance. She was of average height, nicely built with chestnut hair which she often swept back in a ponytail. She was extremely comfortable in jeans and slacks especially when she was riding her horse in her father's farm, the epitome of an outdoor girl.

Finally, Yanis turned to Alexis and said, "Have you heard the good news?"

Alexis hadn't the faintest idea what news Yanis was referring to but was immensely relieved for the interruption.

"What news?"

"Our application for taking part in the league tennis competition amongst all the schools has been accepted. Our first match is against the Victoria College sometime next month."

"Good," replied Alexis, and he and Nina stopped dancing. He continued to discuss the winter's tennis fixtures with Yanis as Nina joined Tasos in another group.

It was past one o'clock in the morning. Christos' parents' frequent appearances from their hide-out convinced the youngsters it was time to call it a day. Nina's and Irini's chauffeurs were waiting to take the two teenagers to their respective homes. Thanos went back with Irini as he lived in the same apartment block in Rue Canope while Michalis and his sister Mirto were in no hurry to depart as they lived in the same apartment block as Christos, just a few staircases further up. Alexis, Tasos, Ismail and the other scout friends decided to go back to Camp de César via the Corniche. As they walked beside the railings of the winding coastal road, Alexis reflected on the events at the party and cast his mind to the balcony scene, where Tasos and Nina stood and looked very sincerely towards each other. Alexis wished he could confide in his two closest friends, Yeorgis and Petros, but he couldn't as Tasos was with them. He glanced at Tasos who was tall and very athletic and then instinctively turned towards the Mediterranean. The sea was unusually rough. The flickering lights of distant fishing boats bobbing between the waves brought home to Alexis the hardship of fishermen trying to earn their living. The sound of waves had a profound impression on Alexis as though they brought messages from faraway lands.

9

29th October 1956

The morning after the party Alexis overslept. As he awoke, his eyes fully open and hands across his chest, he was the epitome of a dispirited young man whose fate was written all over his face as he cast his thoughts to the events of the party. He was perplexed by Nina's attitude as he realised that she was seeking both his and Tasos' attentions. Alexis' reflections had turned into a soliloquy as he was muttering words like, "Strange", "Time will show," and "Intriguing."

"What is intriguing?" asked his mother as she pushed open the bedroom door which he had left ajar.

"Oh, morning," replied Alexis, ignoring her question. "Have you been up long?"

"I have," replied his mum as she proceeded to the kitchen.

Alexis joined her and started eating a bowl of goat's yogurt laced with honey.

"How was the party?" she asked while she toasted two pieces of bread.

After a brief reflection Alexis started describing the party atmosphere: the flamboyant youngster who could not stop boasting about various artistic achievements; the reticent adolescent who couldn't find enough places to hide; the randy youngster who should have known better and was not satisfied with the limited opportunities that were on offer. All these characters were finely scrutinised by Alexis as he mingled with his peers at the party. Lengthy conversations and arguments were abridged to a couple of sentences focusing on key points. And yet he refrained from mentioning the balcony scene and wished to find out more before he could assess the significance of what might turn out to be a seemingly innocent encounter. He did of course mention Nina's presence at the party but in the same context as all the other girls in the group.

Although she firmly believed that her son was perfectly capable of handling his interactions with other youngsters, she wished to keep abreast of developments at a crucial stage of his adolescence. Platonic relationships, and for the present these were no more than that, could become much more intimate and intense and she felt that being close to her son, without being overpowering, would make it easier for him to confide in her should he find the need. Brief and succinct advice was Mrs Mani's greatest asset, a quality which stemmed from her natural gift of perception.

Although she presented a convenient outlet for Alexis' mixed feelings it was not at all obvious where she turned for recharging her own emotional batteries. She had attended Cairo's *Deutsche Schule der Borromäerinnen*, run by a congregation of the Nuns of Saint Karl Borromäus. The school, founded in the dying days of the

19th century, was housed in a building in the districts of Bab El-Louk and Maadi. The reason Mrs Mani had attended that school fell on her Swiss mother, Gilda, who was born in a little village near Solothurn and met Alexis' grandfather while he was studying catering and hotel management in Switzerland and married just before the outbreak of WWI. Mary Mani got a first-class scholastic education and showed a remarkable thirst for knowledge and in particular all aspects medical which convinced her teachers that she should proceed to study medicine. However, just after graduation from school she fell in love, at the tender age of 17, with Mr Mani and allowed matrimony to shroud her unexploited talents. It was a decision that she would deeply regret later in life often blaming her mum Gilda with her European attitude for giving her fullest consent for her daughter's wish to marry young, rather than a dismissive reprimand and a one-way ticket to Zurich to pursue her medical studies.

However, as time passed, she came to terms with her fate and resolved to self-educate by reading volume upon volume of history, philosophy and literature to compensate for her lack of further education. In her quest to achieve her goal she followed some basic rules: prepare a convenient environment, get a dictionary, read widely, follow-up with references and talk to knowledgeable and interesting people. Her bedside had stacks of books, at present focusing on Mauriac, Sartre, Proust, Kafka, Gorki, Chekhov, but also probing into obscure writers such the working-class Romanian, Istrati. Alexis and his brother would return home late in the evening and invariably find their mum lying in bed with a book in her hands and with notes strewn all over the bed beside her. She derived the greatest enjoyment and fulfilment from the written word. Numerous pages in these books had bits of loose notepaper with scribblings highlighting something she had read and found intriguing, using these as an *aide-mémoire* for future reference. It was a new word, a phrase or a well-constructed sentence which delighted and fulfilled her insatiable thirst for knowledge, eventually establishing her erudition.

Living in Alexandria she became familiar with the works of the Greek poet Cavafy whose family had moved to the city in the middle of the 19th century, after spells at Liverpool and Constantinople returning to Alexandria where he developed his poetry while working as a public servant. Mrs Mani found his poems, published in local newspapers, pamphlets or given to her privately by friends complex, difficult to comprehend, esoteric, full of idiosyncrasies and written in a flat uninspiring style. Her scant knowledge of Greek was initially a handicap but gradually, having mastered the language, she was able to move to prose, reading the works of Kazantzakis and Venezis.

Monday the 29th October, 1956, marked another day in the turbulent history of the Averofeio Gymnasium. Alexis came straight back from school and after a quick snack withdrew to his room to tackle a problem in trigonometry involving the theme of loci. Having read the relevant section on the subject in his book by Tonga he sketched the relevant information on a blank piece of paper and was so absorbed that he did not hear his mother at the door talking to him. She paused for a moment or two and then repeated the statement a bit louder.

"I just heard on the radio that Israel has attacked Egypt."

"I see," replied Alexis, not fully realising the significance of his mother's statement. Suddenly, the last few words seemed to strike a chord and turning to his mother said, "War?", sounding rather alarmed.

"At 4 o'clock this afternoon Israel attacked Egypt and war was declared," responded Mary Mani. Alexis, eyes fixed towards his mum, remained silent. A chill ran down his spine and he felt frightened. The front at Sinai was only 450km east of Alexandria and he readily visualised the Israeli tanks thrusting forward apace, being very effective in annihilating the opposing Egyptian army who almost certainly would have been taken completely by surprise.

"I wonder what it feels to be out there at the front?" muttered Alexis in a quivering voice. "Will there be any air raids here?"

Mrs Mani sensing Alexis' anxiety added a few comforting words and stressed that there was really nothing to worry about. However, there was an urgent job to be done in filling the gaps in the French shutters with newspapers and other scraps of paper they could find to ensure the camouflage was effective to comply with any forthcoming blackout orders. They both got down to the job and soon ran out of paper. Alexis even used the paper he had scribbled his trigonometry question on. “No hard feelings, little problem, it is for a good cause,” he muttered. That evening wastepaper must have been the most sought-after commodity in Alexandria and soon the residents resorted to cloth or anything pliable they could find to ensure an effective blackout in anticipation of any Israeli air raids.

Within hours Alexandria’s air raid sirens sounded loud and clear. It soon became obvious that it was merely an exercise as no planes passed by nor bombs fell. It was the first time that Alexis was conscious of sirens although he had been subjected to similar sounds in Cairo during the latter part of the Alamein offensive when German motorcyclists reached the outskirts of Alexandria and the threat of ensuing air raids was real. Presently, he felt the tension mounting, no doubt very conscious that this was no war movie but all too real.

Later that evening, Alexis, walking towards the Scouts along Rue Canope, sensed a strange atmosphere with residents rushing to stock up with provisions in case of a prolonged war and the consequent shortage of imported food due to blockades. On arrival he found Thanos, Yeorgis and Petros trying to calm down the caretaker, Abu-Ahmet. They bought bottles of Coca-Cola out of his icebox which gave the old man some comfort.

“Bloody Yehudim,” he uttered repeatedly, referring

to the Jewish forces pounding the Arab fortifications at the border.

"Don't worry Abu-Ahmet, the Israeli forces are far away," replied Alexis reassuringly, who all of a sudden had gained strength from the old man's pitiful countenance.

The news of the war had a different effect on the various communities of Alexandria. The Arabs in Egypt feared total occupation by the Israeli force while the Jewish community feared reprisals by their frightened neighbours and practically barricaded themselves in their homes. The rest of the expatriate communities wondered about how this latest war with Israel would affect them but feared that a prolonged conflict would brand all as undesirables and hold them responsible for the consequences of a disastrous outcome. During the ensuing days there was bound to exist an unstable equilibrium pivoted firmly on the solid foundations created between the expatriate communities and the Arabs after many years of peaceful coexistence. These very foundations had stood the test of time, two world wars, and the first Arab-Israeli conflict in 1948. Could these now begin to crumble following prolonged hostilities?

The thought of war had a deep effect on Alexis and his friends, none of whom had so far being exposed to such a real and dangerous situation. At a stroke, the tranquillity of the Alexandrian expatriate community had been shattered without being able to assess with certainty what the consequences might be. Alexis and his friends were trying to make sense of what was happening as rumours were flying around as to what had triggered this conflict, with some suggesting nationalisation of the Suez Canal was the cause. Others attempted to find links with the 1948 Arab-Israeli war which had had its origins in the establishment of the State of Israel and the loss of Palestine with the creation of hundreds of thousands of refugees being displaced from the homes they had lived in over centuries, Ismail and his family being a prime example. To some this was justified as the Jewish people had to establish a lasting homeland, but others foresaw problems emanating from the local Palestinian people.

It soon became fairly obvious to Alexis and his mates that they were all too ignorant about the complex facts surrounding the Arab-Israeli conflict. The next day they all met again at the Scouts and continued to discuss the unfolding situation. Alexis noticed that Ismail was missing and had not been seen since war broke out. They decided to go to his house behind the Scout grounds to ask his mum when they saw Panos, who was the closest to Ismail, heading towards them in Rue Canope. His face was drawn and he obviously did not have good news to relate.

"Ismail was called to the army headquarters and left for Cairo an hour ago," said Panos. The boys looked at each other expressing anxiety without being able to add anything sensible. They returned to the Scouts where the only audible sound was that of Abu-Ahmet's who kept murmuring, "Bloody Yehudim." As Panos and Alexis bent down to tell him about Ismail, the old man's face became even sadder, if that was at all possible, with his eyes becoming more and more watery until a tear ran down his cheek. Such a miserable appearance had a deep effect on Alexis which remained with him for months after the hostilities had long ceased.

The first to react to such news was Yeorgis.

"Look, almost certainly as a reservist he will be the last to be called to the war zone," he concluded reassuringly.

"Let us hope so," replied Petros.

"Well guys, we have work to do," went on Yeorgis.

All pairs of eyes turned to Yeorgis wondering what on earth he was referring to. The astonishment was so graphic on their young faces that Yeorgis could not keep the suspense any longer.

"I suggest we take to the streets in turn and inspect the camouflage of the balcony doors and windows making sure that no light escapes from the narrow slits of the French shutters," said Yeorgis.

"What a brilliant idea," exclaimed Petros, who was getting very excited at the prospect of policing the streets and narrow lanes of the fashionable expatriate neighbourhood. The five youngsters, after succeeding to calm down Abu-Ahmet, set off on their task walking down Rue Canope towards Ibrahimieh and observing some residents still hard at work masking their shutters. The local community had come together in this hour of crisis and did their best to effectively conceal the one part that united everyone irrespective of race or creed: Alexandria itself. When the boys came across an apartment where the shutters were shoddily camouflaged, they promptly let the owners know by gently unleashing a bundle of light stones in the direction of the window. To their surprise this was very effective indeed, with leaks disappearing almost instantly.

At the end of Rue Canope Petros nipped into his house and informed his parents what he was up to. He re-joined the others progressing down towards Ibrahimieh passing the Cinéma Gaieté featuring *Casablanca* with Humphrey Bogart, crossing the tramway and heading towards the Corniche. Upon reaching the coastal road they crossed it and turned left back towards Camp de César. The tall lights illuminating the Corniche were switched off and the Casino, an imposing edifice extending into the sea, was eerily dark and silent. The boys stood by the railings and gazed out onto the pitch-black open sea, their thoughts oscillating between tank battles in Sinai to imminent air raids and dogfights in the skies above. Yeorgis reminded them sharply that they had important work to do. After they continued along the Corniche towards the city, they soon cut inland heading for the tramline and resumed their home-guard duties.

It was around 11 when they reached the tram station at Camp de César and bid farewell to Yeorgis. They proceeded towards Rue Canope and upon passing Cabaret's little shoeshine shop they reached the apartment block where both Panos and Thanos lived.

"Ismail will be alright," said Panos to Alexis and stood outside the apartment block chatting to Thanos. Alexis and Petros continued to walk, turning into Rue Canope while reflecting on the events of the most extraordinary day of their young lives. Before proceeding much further, Alexis stopped, turned back and said to Petros, "Follow me?"

A bewildered Petros followed Alexis as they reached the crossroads and turned right. Alexis stopped and signalled to Petros to hide behind a large tree outside the café opposite Carabet's shoeshine shop. Panos and Thanos were still chatting. Within a few minutes Thanos entered his apartment block but Panos proceeded towards the Synagogue and turned into Rue Heliopolis. The boys followed him. As they in turn turned into Rue Heliopolis, Panos reached an elegant-looking bungalow, walked into its front garden and pressed the bell. The door opened and a middle-aged lady let him in.

"I knew it," he whispered to his young friend.

"What is going on?" asked Petros.

"I have heard that some boys, and I do not know any more details or other names, have been visiting widows and well-to-do ladies living on their own."

"Visiting widows?"

"Well, you know, keeping them happy," replied a hesitant Alexis.

"You mean sexually?"

"What do you think?" replied Alexis condescendingly.

"Give over," exclaimed an astonished Petros.

"Our friends, Panos and Thanos, are after all a few years older than us so it fits."

"Well, no wonder these two are always immaculately dressed."

"We do not know whether Thanos too is part of such a scheme, but I wonder what they were chatting about a few minutes ago."

They left the scene and went back to Rue Canope, soon reaching the Italian Club Palestra, and parted company.

"See you tomorrow at school," shouted Alexis with a broad grin on his face as he entered the large gate of his apartment block, leaving Petros totally stupefied by what he had just witnessed. He continued along Rue Canope towards his home not knowing what to think.

10

30th October – mid-November 1956

The following day the pupils at the Averofeio Gymnasium were sent home as the Headmaster and his staff decided that the school would remain shut until the hostilities were over. It was a decision which, despite its gravity, pleased the youngsters. Alexis, taking advantage of the cessation of classes, and no doubt prompted by his mum, decided that it was about time he delved into the history of Palestine and how it tied up with the establishment of the State of Israel. His first port of call was the family's *Encyclopedia Britannica* which gave a summary of the history of the Middle East, giving references to more specialised books on the subject. After reading a couple of pages he realised the enormity of the task he had set himself. Every now and then he had to refer to other tomes of the home Encyclopaedia to clarify a point which was crucial to the historical argument. But, unfortunately, the abbreviations 'qv' which appeared after a special name meant going through another section of several pages. These concerned Arabs, Christians and Jews living in the region, Zionism and Judaism, Moses and the Old Testament, the New Testament and Septuagint, Theodor Herzl and the Balfour Declaration. The historical aspects behind these topics were unknown to

Alexis and his pals, as at school they covered the Byzantine Empire with emphasis on the fall of Constantinople in May 1453 by the Ottoman armies, commanded by the 22-year-old Sultan Mehmet II, and their eventual overthrow in 1821. However well-versed Alexis was in the atrocities inflicted on the Greeks during their almost four-hundred-year domination by the Turks, and the heroism of Kolokotronis and other heroic figures, it did not help in his present task of untangling what he came to refer to as the 'Palestinian Conundrum' and the plight of its peoples. Be that as it may, he did not flinch facing such a seemingly insurmountable task and ploughed along encouraged by his mother who often joined her son in his research by feeding him with old books and relevant newspaper cuttings she had amassed over the years. Alexis kept notes and slowly but surely was beginning to form a somewhat coherent picture of the turbulent times of the region and the plight of its inhabitants, both Jews and Palestinians.

The news from the front was scant and confused. By listening to local and foreign radio broadcasts it was apparent that the fighting was fierce in Sinai, especially around the Mitla Pass where Israeli parachutists had landed and were engaged in an all-out attack to capture this strategic post. The Egyptian forces were taken by complete surprise and were pushed back towards the Canal Zone. The Egyptian high command deemed it essential to concentrate their main forces on the eastern bank of the Canal since there was no sign of a major confrontation on the west side of the Canal.

Although two major European allies were incensed by Nasser's decision to nationalise the Canal, France had an extra axe to grind against Nasser because he openly supported the rebels in Algeria. So, although after Nasser's speech Britain was attempting to solve the Canal crisis with Egypt by diplomatic means, they were alerted to a plan by France to occupy the Canal Zone. In utter secrecy, even from high government ministers in their respective countries, a series of meetings took place from the 22nd to the 24th of October at Sèvres, a leafy suburb near Paris, between representatives of the governments of France, Britain and Israel, barely a week before Israel attacked Egypt. The plan, spelled out in the so-called Sèvres Protocol, entailed Israel attacking Egypt and, on the pretext of wishing to end the hostilities, Britain and France would issue an ultimatum to both countries to stop the fighting. At Sèvres, it was agreed that Israel would ignore the ultimatum, hoping that Egypt would also follow suit which would then allow France and Britain to intervene on the pretext of ending the hostilities and occupy the Canal Zone, their ultimate goal.

A second front was thus established when at dusk on October 31st a combined force of parachutists landed and occupied strategic positions between the towns of Port Said and Suez. Operation Musketeer was launched, whereby Egypt was confronted by the might of two major European powers aided by the fledgling but very determined Jewish State.

The air-raids brought the harsh realities of a bloody war close to Alexandria's port and the airport, two sites Egypt's enemies had earmarked as potential targets. As fighting had intensified, the air raids were not only confined to dawn's greyness or twilight's duskiness but later that week there was a midday attack aimed at the seaport. Alexis and his mates roaming the streets, not fully appreciating the perils of the situation, ran to the Corniche where they heard the terrifying thunder of anti-aircraft missiles, but could not see any attacking fighting aircraft. They made their way back to the Scout grounds where they found an excited Abu-Ahmet convinced that the Russians were about to land in Alexandria. The youngsters in vain tried to explain to him that they had just returned from the Corniche and saw no landing craft, nor any Russians. However, Abu-Ahmet was adamant of a Russian involvement and quickly dismissed the arguments of his young Scouts by stating that the coast extended for many kilometres and the landings were taking place beyond the Corniche. Although it was impossible to evaluate the credibility of Abu-Ahmet's pronouncements, these rumours, and there was no reason to suppose that these were anything but rumours, added a new dimension to the already confused events which had led to war. This stemmed from the fact that the pupils of the Averofeio Gymnasium had over the past few years been subjected to a relentless brainwashing by their Headmaster against anything to do with Russia. With his Ciceronian oratorical skills, he related the events that had taken place between the borders of Greece and its Balkan neighbours, particularly Bulgaria, which plunged Greece into a bloody civil war characterised by fierce bloodshed and cruelty. "These communists," he declared, "had forcefully transferred many Greek infants across the border into Bulgaria,brought them up not to speak their native language, to hate their country of birth and eventually to fight against it." The Headmaster trembled with emotion as he related these events as though he had first-hand experience of such episodes. The fact that Russia itself may not have been directly involved in these incidents was irrelevant; the communist dogma was condemned outright. His attitude and prolonged denunciation of anything to do with communism had convinced Alexis' entourage that these attacks were directed at two brothers in their classroom whose parents were known to be communists. The two brothers endured the frequent unrestrained utterances of the Headmaster with serene equanimity, never reacting despite constant provocation. Such consistent condemnation by the Headmaster had the ultimate effect of convincing the youngsters that everything relating to communism was bad and caused many to flinch as soon as the subject arose. It was not therefore a surprise that Abu-Ahmet's revelations about a Russian involvement caused deep consternation to both Alexis and Petros who had the misfortune to be seated in the first row and were subjected to the full force of the Headmasters' convoluted dicta.

The most dramatic air offensive the Alexandrians were subjected to took place the following Sunday evening. Alexis and his mother were at home when the sirens sounded and hurriedly switched off the lights and went to the balcony. The sky was clear, the night cool, but the drone of an approaching aircraft sounded ominous. Suddenly flares were fired into the dark sky illuminating the massive 12-storey apartment block to the east of the Italian club Palestra thereby projecting it vulnerably above the low-level surrounding dwellings. A lone figure of an Arab stood at the top of this large edifice and from such vantage point was able to observe the ensuing air raid. He was not satisfied with the aim of the anti-aircraft fire, gesticulating for better control and direct hits, but soon his actions were smothered by strong clatter of more anti-aircraft fire. Although the target was once again the port it now appeared that the aerial warfare was conducted closer to the city centre at Ramleh and the suburbs. Members of Palestra were crowding around their darkened windows to catch a glimpse of the ongoing action but were too low to observe anything. Suddenly a thundering noise was heard as a bomb exploded nearby, shaking the apartment blocks and causing windows to vibrate and smash, throwing fragments of glass in all directions. The Arab was at last petrified and remained motionless, eyes fixed in the direction of the Corniche near the Ramleh tramway terminus. Mrs Mani was the first to react from the shock.

"Come along Alexis, it would be safer downstairs,"

she urged. They hurriedly left the balcony and proceeded down the steps of the winding marble staircase meeting the Armenian landlady, Mrs Notiyan, going up to her apartment.

"It does not sound good," she said to the landlady as they crossed.

"Don't worry Mrs Mani, our building is very well constructed," replied Mrs Notiyan reassuringly as she continued her way up.

Alexis and his mother stopped at the landing near the entrance hall not really knowing where to proceed as there were no air-raid shelters in the vicinity. The residents were left to their own devices to fend off any danger from such attacks, the last of which was nowhere near a military target. As they stood in one corner of the landing Alexis got the distinct impression that Mrs Mani was afraid, anxious and tense, as her usual equanimity had momentarily abandoned her. Her anxiety was justifiable as she was confronted with a situation that was not familiar to her and was afraid not only for both of them but for her elder son Pavlos, who earlier that morning had gone to the city to meet his girlfriend and was therefore much closer to where the bomb fell. Her state of nervousness was gradually transferred to her younger son who became more thoughtful and anxious.

After an interminable state of confusion and indecisiveness it soon appeared that the worst of the offensive was over with the sirens sounding the all-clear. Having witnessed his mother in an unprecedented state of anxiety he now saw the rapidity with which she regained her composure and, turning to Alexis said, "The worst is over; we can go back up." She put her arm around Alexis' shoulder and they mounted one by one the innumerable marble steps leading to the top apartment. Alexandria was gradually emerging from an uncomfortable experience not seen since Rommel's Panzers were at El Alamein and elements of German motorcycle units reached the outskirts of Egypt's second city.

Later that evening Joshua Schumann came unexpectedly to the Mani apartment holding what appeared to be a large heavy parcel wrapped up in brown paper.

"My dear Joshua, what a pleasant surprise!" said Mrs Mani as she let him in the apartment. He seemed pale and exhausted. Joshua placed the box on the low table and, turning to Mrs Mani, replied:

"I am afraid this is not a social call, Mary, and I do apologise for the inconvenience I am causing you by calling this late. I am in a jam and I think you may be able to help me."

"Of course, come and sit down," she replied.

Joshua approached a large armchair and sat down. He opened his silver cigarette case and extended his quivering arm, offering one to Mrs Mani, who accepted. Promptly, he searched for his lighter, fumbling through his pockets. Alexis sat diagonally across from him and looked at him as he lit both cigarettes. Joshua was tall with dark hair and large brown eyes.

"This parcel," he began in a low drone, "contains

what one might describe as an unexpected present." Alexis and his mother glanced at the solitary parcel at the table.

"It is an army radio transmitter that belongs to a friend," went on Joshua, "and under the present situation we feel it is unwise to keep it in his house. It is only a precautionary measure as thus far the authorities do not seem to suspect my friend. However, there have been reports that the police are starting to search some Jewish homes and therefore it would be most helpful if you could hide it here for a while until the present tense situation eases. It is highly unlikely that your apartment will be searched. Isn't that so?"

"Of course, there is no fear of that," replied Mrs Mani, "but are you sure you and your family are alright?"

Joshua searched for an ashtray to get rid of the bending cylinder of ash at the end of his cigarette. His demeanour betrayed an uneasiness which was so uncharacteristic of his usual urbane self.

"Yes, we are alright at least for the time being, but if I appear sad it is because I feel so," he went on in a broken voice. "This is the second time that war has broken out between Israel and Egypt in the past eight years and the relationship between the two countries is bound to deteriorate, presenting us with a very uncertain future. My whole family feels home is in Egypt as we were all born here and as you know there is a great affinity between our communities; but since war was declared I have felt a stranger in a transformed environment. My close friends, Arabs and expatriates alike, do still support us but there is a nervousness all around which cannot be ignored and puts into question our continuing existence here in Alexandria. You must feel the same Mary, although I must admit not to the same extent as we do in the Jewish fraternity."

Alexis was listening to Joshua's trembling voice with alarm. His words made a deep impression on the young adolescent's mind, sensing Joshua's deep anxiety as he talked about his fear for the future. He glanced at his mother, always a patient listener, who was very attentive and understanding, adding now and then words of comfort and empathy. As the conversation progressed, she deliberately attempted to divert the essence of the discussion away from the war and the tension it created. Gradually she succeeded in her task and Joshua eventually regained his composure.

"It is good to talk to you Mary," said Joshua, who stood up and addressed Alexis. "All this must be a very new experience to you, young man."

"It is," replied Alexis. "What I find intriguing is the origin of the Arab-Israeli conflict which, I must admit, is difficult to unravel."

"Alexis is reading about Palestine and its history," butted in his mother.

"Very interesting. We must have a chat about the issues involved after the present situation calms down," said Joshua.

"I would love that," replied Alexis eagerly.

"I must be going," said Joshua, and made his way towards the door. He apologised once again for the trouble he had put on them, thanked them for agreeing to keep the transmitter, and left.

That night Alexis could not sleep easily. He remained awake for long periods. Vivid in his thoughts were the air raid, the flares, the sound of the bomb crashing somewhere near Ramleh and the respondent anti-aircraft fire. Vivid too was the frightened state of his mother during the latter part of the air raid. Graphic were the pallid features of Joshua's countenance and of course Nina was not very far from his thoughts. Through the sound of silence in his darkened bedroom he thought he heard her whisper and imagined her pervasive smile which he so longed for at these uncertain times.

Alexis and his pals spent much of the next few days at the Scout grounds. There were conflicting reports about the landings of the British and French parachutists at Port Said where the fighting was at its most intense. Abu-Ahmet was very solemn and was getting more miserable by the hour, blaming Egypt's neighbouring countries for not coming to the rescue and joining in the fight. Seated on a long wooden bench outside the Scout grounds he was puffing the *narguileh* he had purchased from the café opposite Carabet's shoeshine shop. He was often surrounded by his numerous young children who had somehow sensed the enveloping crisis and were crouching near their father seeking comfort. The sight of this seemingly motherless family epitomised the huge problem that faced the government in their attempt to raise the standards of the majority of Egyptian folk. Abu-Ahmet did not expect any more out of life than a peaceful existence towards old age but there was little such hope for his children. The present war was bad enough for those at the front and their families as casualties mounted by the hour but equally the diversion of resources towards the war effort and away from needy social and economic infrastructure was bound to have devastating consequences for Egypt's future. Abu-Ahmet showed a sense of aloofness for the future problems facing his country but amidst the random puffing one could perceive an inveterate abhorrence for the outbreak of the current hostilities by the constant mutterings of "Bloody Yehudim".

Alarming reports reached Alexis and his group that, following the landings, the parachutists, finding little resistance, had advanced towards the city of Suez. Against all odds, Ismail had found himself in the thick of the battle and the young Palestinian became the constant preoccupation of his friends. Yeorgis was trying to instil some confidence in the downhearted group of adolescents while Panos was in constant touch with Ismail's parents in case there was news from the front.

The end of hostilities came as suddenly as its outbreak ten days earlier. Once the plot between France, Britain and Israel was unravelled, the US President unleashed a scathing attack on PM Anthony Eden, forcing him to an immediate ceasefire and withdrawal of troops.

Britain and France were faced with a humiliating retreat resulting in the eventual downfall of the British PM.

The ceasefire was welcomed by most of the expatriate communities and Alexandria soon reverted back to its tranquil lifestyle, belying the worrying undertones that recent events had brought momentarily to the fore. The schools were swiftly reopened and life in this very ancient city, at least outwardly, returned to some normality. The Corniche was soon buzzing with Alexandrians rambling amidst the prevailing littoral atmosphere. The double-decked trams were once again full of youngsters going to and from their homes to the various schools. The bazaar between Camp de César and Ibrahimieh sprung back to life with the familiar sight of guavas, bananas and other indigenous fruits geometrically piled up high on their rickety stalls.

Despite the return to normality of daily life, the war marked the beginning of the end of an era characteristic of the sustained exploitation by the expatriate minority of the indigenous majority. Scant references were made as to why one's grandparents had emigrated to Egypt during the last century, what caused such large-scale immigration and what were the reasons for choosing Egypt. But they came, settled and exploited to the full the opportunities that had been presented to them. As a result, they enjoyed a good standard of living affording all the mod cons and acting as veritable colonialists without a scintilla of guilt. The silent majority continued to be dominated without rebelling, their ineffectual leaders prior to Nasser having been suitably bribed by the expatriates. However, following the ousting and abdication of King Farouk by the group of young officers, the dormant nationalistic sentiment began to rise amongst the wider indigenous populace wishing to rid themselves of the chains that had kept them subdued over hundreds of years and longing to discover their identity. As a result, the expatriate settlers had limited time left and they knew it.

11

November 1956

On the Saturday afternoon after the ceasefire the Scout grounds at Ramleh were buzzing with excitement. Alexis and his mates met at just before six o'clock attired in their khaki uniforms, blue neckties and brown hats. Each group assembled outside their headquarters and after some preliminary announcements Scout Group No. 3 played the bat-and-ball game under the artificial floodlights precariously fixed on wooden poles placed at the top of surrounding buildings. After the game the Scouts withdrew into their huts. It was usual to start with songs, the first of which was 'Ging Gang Gooly':

> Ging gang gooly gooly gooly gooly
> Watcha, ging gang goo, ging gang goo.
> Ging gang gooly gooly gooly gooly
> Watcha, ging gang goo, ging gang, goo.
> Haila! Oh Haila Shaila. Haila Shaila. Haila whooo.
> Haila! Oh Haila Shaila. Haila Shaila. Haila whooo.
> Shallywally Shallywally Shallywally Shallywally.
> Umpa Umpa Umpa Umpa.........

The voices of the youngsters sounded loud and clear. The scouts in the adjacent unit reciprocated and sang another song even louder. Urged by the respective patrol leaders Scout Group No. 3 responded by singing even louder only to be imitated by the adjacent group. The enjoyment that the young scouts derived from such trivial pursuits was graphic: they simply loved every minute of it.

Next there followed many outdoor and indoor activities carried out individually by each group. The patrol leaders Yeorgis and Alexis thrived on setting the standard and assigning their younger members various tasks. The previous Saturday each member of the various patrols had been assigned a mini-project and they had come with graphs and other tools ready to describe the progress made. There were also collective tasks, such as learning the various techniques of knot-tying. For example, if ropes of dissimilar material needed to be tied the scouts resorted to the sheet bend knot as this ensured that they would not slip when entwined. If two ropes needed to stay together at all cost, then a double sheet bend technique was used. Finally, it was time for another outdoor activity followed by a period free for each patrol to spend as they pleased.

At precisely eight o'clock, as was customary, the whole Scout movement assembled in formation depicting the Greek letter pi outside the headquarters of the Scout Master, Mr Notaras. Alexis stared at him without paying much attention to what he was stating. He turned towards the wide-open gate and noticed the chubby figure of Panos standing at the entrance staring straight at him. The main floodlights were switched off and the centre of the congregation was lit by a solitary spotlight high above Mr Notaras' office. The only other light was that by the wall at the entrance next to Panos. Abu-Ahmet, standing next to his icebox, watched the proceedings unfold. The Greek anthem, sung with gusto, brought matters to a close and the youngsters dispersed. As Alexis and Yeorgis started walking towards Panos, he in turn stepped back to clear the way for the flocks of Scouts leaving the grounds via its narrow gate. Alexis and Yeorgis stopped barely a couple of metres from Panos to let the Scouts through. They stared straight at his forlorn face, illuminated by the solitary light near the entrance. It was obvious that something was amiss. The procession of the young Scouts leaving the grounds was endless and without being able to come any closer the three friends stood there immersed in a myriad of thoughts for what seemed to be an eternity.

The way was now clear and Alexis approached Panos, "Do you have news about Ismail?"

"Yes," replied Panos with a trembling voice, "his parents just received the news that he was gravely injured at Port Said after the landing of the parachutists."

Yeorgis remained silent. It was one of those rare occasions when he ran out of words, not being able to say anything appropriate. There was no need to sympathise with Panos as the news affected equally the three of them. Alexis too felt very uncommunicative and handled his feelings with a touch of taciturnity. He turned and glanced at the massive tree in the corner of the grounds opposite Ismail's little tottering house and reflected on his first tense meeting with Ismail and their subsequent blossoming friendship.

Abu-Ahmet, sensing the sorrow that befell all three, passed them by on his way to his house and switched off the light by the gate. Through the prevailing darkness and silence of the warm Alexandrian evening, the three youngsters cast their thoughts towards the hospital where Ismail had been transferred hoping that he would soon recover. They each had their own reminiscences of the young Palestinian as they stood just barely one hundred metres from his humble abode.

12

December 1956

Ismail el Kefr's injury at Port Said at such a young age had a profound emotional effect on Alexis and his friends. His *hors de combat* was so sudden when a few weeks back he was mixing happily with all the youngsters at Christos' party. News filtered through that he was out of danger but was kept in as his injuries were quite extensive.

Many weeks had passed since the ceasefire in early November and as Christmas was drawing close the Mani family prepared to spend the festivities at home as Mr Mani telegraphed to state that by the middle of December he would be back from Sudan. The Saturday three weeks before Christmas was Alexis' birthday. It was customary to spend the evening at home with friends of the Manis and of course with his own close friends. Ismail was missing as he was recovering from his injuries.

The youngsters withdrew to Alexis' large bedroom and amused themselves with various games or indulged in chit-chat over the latest news from school or the Scouts. As was often the case on such occasions in the Levant, a series of meze were offered comprising small triangular cheese-pies, spicy sausages, assortment of fish and meat dishes, rounded off with *mille-feuille*, a layered cream and puff pastry sweet or *petits éclairs*, their oblong shape brimming with *pâte à choux*. Alexis had purchased the pastries from Patisserie Delices at Saad Zaghloul, the fashionable café in the heart of the city, next to the Ramleh tramway terminus. The youngsters kept going to the lounge, grabbing a plate, filling it with assortments of food and returning to Alexis' room.

It was past eight o'clock and some of the older guests had departed. Alexis and Petros were engaged in a game of chess while Yeorgis and Panos, who both attended English-speaking schools, were testing each other's knowledge of English using *Nelson's Royal English Dictionary*. Alexis was quite good at chess, having watched many close games between his parents. It required a considerable effort to follow his parents' respective moves which often baffled Alexis, not seeing immediately the subtlety involved, but he persevered and was fast learning the intricacies of the game. Often, he witnessed a not-too-noble endgame when the loser would express their frustration by throwing about one or two pieces resulting in minor damage such as the beheading of the black queen, a deformed white king and only half of a white bishop surviving.

"What on earth happened to this set?" exclaimed Petros the first time he saw the battered state of the pieces.

"Parental differences," replied Alexis, mockingly.

"Check," uttered Alexis as he moved his queen across to a face Petros' exposed king. Petros proceeded to castle his king.

"You cannot do that while you are being checked," prompted Alexis, looking at Panos, who nodded in approval.

"Oh, sorry," muttered Petros and buried his head between his hands in deep thought.

"Has he cornered you again?" said Yeorgis as he was leafing through the section of letter *e* in *Nelson's Dictionary*. "Elision!" he shouted with delight. Panos muttered the word once or twice and obviously he did not understand its meaning.

"Not a clue," said Panos.

"Well," replied Yeorgis with excitement, "listen to its definition," and he quoted, "'the act of striking out or cutting off, especially,'" Yeorgis emphasized the last word as he glanced at a bewildered Panos, "'a syllable at the end of the word'. That is fascinating, is it not?"

"Mm, what an interesting word," replied Panos.

"In fact, our English teacher at school does exhibit a slight elision," continued Yeorgis, "he has a very public-school accent, very posh indeed." And to emphasize the point he was making, he proceeded to imitate his teacher by quoting verbatim a sentence he had heard him state the previous day while accentuating the teacher's elision.

"Boys, you will never grasp the essence of English literature unless you devote a considerable effort and study carefully the texts I recommended at the beginning of the term." Panos roared with laughter and after his friend stopped, he proceeded with his own imitation of elision.

Alexis was unaware of the literary effusions of his friends as he was concentrating on an all-out attack to bring the game to a close.

"What are you babbling about?" said Petros turning to the other two. "Babbling," replied Yeorgis hastily, "what a cheek," he added, and they all burst out laughing.

As Mrs Mani approached Alexis' room the apartment's bell sounded so she turned and made for the door.

"I give up," stated Petros who obviously could not respond to Alexis' last move.

"Your basic weakness," continued Alexis as he was putting the pieces back in the old wooden box "is that you concentrate wholly on your game without paying much attention to the opponent's game."

Mrs Mani appeared at the bedroom door with Joshua Schumann, his wife Hannah and their two children, Avi and sister Rivka. Greetings were exchanged. Mrs Mani took the visitors to the lounge to offer them some refreshments.

"Who is Mr Schumann?" whispered Yeorgis to Alexis.

"He is an old family friend from Cairo and a very prominent member of the Jewish community here in Alexandria, having moved up from the capital a few years ago," replied Alexis. "He studied architecture in Paris."

At that moment, Pavlos and his girlfriend entered the bedroom and sat at the edge of Alexis' bed.

"Are you looking forward to going to England?" asked Petros, still sitting at the table opposite Alexis.

Pavlos was very excited about going to London, but sad, however, that he was leaving his girlfriend behind.

"Yes," he replied hesitantly and looked at his girlfriend who looked rather miserable at the thought of their separation. He glanced at his watch and quickly added, "We promised to meet some friends down at Pastroudis so we must be off." Almost certainly this was an excuse as he wished to be alone with his girlfriend rather than spend time with Alexis' friends. They bade their farewells, left the apartment and made their way towards Atarin on the eastern side of the city where the girlfriend lived with her parents.

Soon afterwards Joshua and his son entered the bedroom and the two of them sat at the square table with Alexis and Petros forming a quartet as though a game of poker was about to begin.

"It is a long time since I played a game of chess. Do you all play?" asked Joshua.

"I believe so," prompted Alexis and turning to Panos he went on: "Do you play?"

"Not very well," replied Panos, "I learned some time ago when Ismail and I played a few times at the university."

Panos suddenly stopped talking and the boys exchanged hasty and subdued glances at each other as though their thoughts were swiftly focused on the state of their absent friend. Joshua quickly perceived the prevailing uneasiness amongst the youngsters all of whom suddenly seemed much less communicative. He slowly sipped his cognac, allowing some time to alleviate the tense atmosphere that had emerged.

"Our close friend and neighbour, Ismail, was injured in the recent hostilities at Port Said. He is recovering at a hospital in Cairo and we all are waiting anxiously for more news," explained Alexis.

"I am sorry to hear that," replied Joshua, and looked at Avi who remained silent.

"He is a Palestinian refugee," started Panos in a low voice, "whose family were given asylum in Egypt after the 1948 war. With the aid of some other Arabs and the Government his parents were able to bring the family here to settle. Ismail and I are attending the university in Alexandria. He is studying law."

"What about yourself? What are you studying?" asked Joshua.

"Economics," he replied and went on, "Ismail was not meant to be at the front line. After the hostilities broke out, he was sent to an army camp near Port Said..."

"I see," whispered Joshua with a sigh, "and it was the full onslaught of the English and French forces that his unit sustained." Panos nodded.

"I do sincerely hope that after this latest conflict sense will prevail and some kind of peaceful coexistence may emerge," went on Joshua.

Alexis grabbed the moment and pressed Joshua. "How realistic, though, do you think the prospect of peace is?"

"It is very early days," replied Joshua. "It depends on the reaction of the Arabs in the Levant and attitude of the Jewish people in the area."

"It appears," butted in Yeorgis, "that at present the Arabs and the Jews do not see eye to eye at all."

"Why is this?" asked Petros innocently.

"The Arabs resent the loss of their homeland in Palestine," replied Panos hastily.

"And as long as this persists the Israelis feel that they must be on their guard against any future attack by the Arabs," stated Avi, who felt confident enough by now to take part in this sensitive discussion.

Mary Mani walked in with Joshua's wife Hannah and their daughter Rivka, as Yeorgis and Panos plunged deeper into arguments about the rights and wrongs of the Arab-Israeli conflict. Hannah was a plump lady with puppy-dog eyes and thick eyelashes and short blonde hair. It was evident that the youngsters were not putting forward a coherent argument, but simply repeating what they may have heard from their parents or gathered by glancing at headlines in newspapers. To comprehend the circumstances behind the creation of the State of Israel from Mandatory Palestine required a thorough grasp of historical events in the region. Mary pointed to two empty chairs by the window for Hannah and her daughter to sit. She drew another chair and sat near Alexis at the corner of the table. Joshua glanced at her and they exchanged a few understanding smiles and in so doing acknowledged the enormous task of trying to elucidate the origins of the present hostilities linked to Palestine and the eventual creation of the State of Israel. They both knew that amidst the haphazard arguments uttered by the youngsters lay many half-truths, rumours and innuendos. A more systematic approach was required.

Joshua took advantage of a break in the exchange of views between Panos and Yeorgis and steered the divergent discussion to a more fundamental premise.

"It seems to me," he started addressing Panos, "that the history of Palestine from earlier times to the present may throw some light on some of the points you have just alluded to with Yeorgis." And turning to Alexis he went on: "Your mum tells me that you have recently done some reading on the subject. What aspects of Palestine's history have made an impression on you thus far?"

"Its turbulence," responded Alexis instinctively, but went on. "Don't ask me to elaborate further because I doubt if I could. I kept notes, jotted down important dates and names of protagonists. I have got my notes here." He stood up, approached an old teak bookcase, rummaged through some books stacked on various shelves and tried to locate his set of pencil notes he had made over the past month.

"By the way," interrupted Mary Mani, "Palestine is a relatively modern name for the region we are about to discuss. If we go back to about 1200 BC during the twentieth dynasty in Egypt, archaeologists found several references to *Peleset* which was transliterated from hieroglyphics as p, r, s, t in a number of inscriptions..."

"Transliterated?" asked Petros with bewilderment.

"The process of converting text written in the Egyptian language to alphabetic symbols," replied Hannah.

"Oh, I see," exclaimed Yeorgis as he turned and grimaced at Petros who was chuckling away.

"And this term," continued Mrs Mani, "apparently referred to people living in neighbouring lands which we may assume to be the region west of the river Jordan between modern Lebanon and the Sinai or Negev desert."

"But the first time that a name resembling the present one was alluded to was by Herodotus in his books *The Histories*, where he mentioned a place called *Palaistinê*, situated between Phoenicia and Egypt," said Joshua.

"Which period are we talking about now?" asked Panos, full of pride of his Greek ancestry now that an ancient Greek historian was mentioned.

"Fifth century BC," replied Hannah. Alexis finally amassed his voluminous notes, brought them to the table and attempted to put them in chronological order. A puff of smoke eddied above the table as Mary Mani lit a cigarette while Alexis leafed through his rough notes. His mum stood up and opened the window to let in a waft of fresh air and regained her place. Before Alexis started narrating what he had found in his searches his mother said:

"Having established some ancient connection with the region we are about to discuss, we will also find out that it was a Roman emperor that first coined the name *Palestina*, but for the sake of simplicity for this discussion let us refer it as Palestine."

"Fair enough," replied Alexis, and started. "During the Mesolithic period the region where Palestine is situated today was inhabited by indigenous Neolithic and other immigrants all of which were given the name Natufians."

"Natufians, what period would that be?" asked Petros.

"Around 7800 BC," replied Alexis, consulting his notes and going on: "The next notable inhabitants were the Ghassulians around the year 4000 BC who were immigrants but very little is known about them. Apparently, excavations revealed their origin only a few years ago. I got some information on these from a university professor who gave a lecture recently at the museum in town. Then we move into the Bronze Age where an assemblage of previous civilisations inhabited Palestine, such as Neolithic-Chalcolithic, immigrant Ghassulians and other immigrant proto-urban groups. At this stage there seemed to be a lot of connection between Palestine and the old Kingdom of Egypt and its pharaohs with some evidence that they exercised some tenuous political control over its neighbour." Alexis paused.

"Perhaps we should make a note of this old Egyptian connection," butted in Mrs Mani, whose poignant interventions signalled first a sound knowledge of the relevant history and secondly a desire to concentrate on the crucial facts which eventually would lead one to establish claims of sovereignty.

"But," interrupted Joshua, "the people who inhabited Egypt at that time were not Muslim as Islam doesn't make its appearance before the sixth or seventh century AD."

"*Touché*," replied Alexis' mum while looking at both Joshua and Hannah with a wry smile.

"Have the Jewish people appeared yet?" asked Yeorgis eagerly.

"Not yet," replied Alexis, and continued his narrative while frequently consulting his notes. "Around 2300 BC, Palestine's civilisation was destroyed by the invasion of nomadic tribes thought by some scholars to be the Amorites. At the same period Egypt was invaded by an Asiatic group who brought the old kingdom to an end. In the middle of the Bronze Age the Canaanite culture is introduced into Palestine, a culture which was still flourishing when the Israelites infiltrated into Palestine in the 14th and 13th centuries BC."

"By Israelites, do we mean Jewish people, and from where did they originate?" asked Panos. Alexis looked baffled not being able to respond. Hannah came to the rescue.

"For the sake of this discussion it is sufficient to assume that the Israelites were an Iron Age Semitic-speaking tribe which branched out of the Canaanite peoples that inhabited the Southern Levant, and it is prudent to assume that they adhered to the Jewish faith. Let us not delve into what the Hebrew Bible states as it becomes exceedingly complicated," Hannah concluded.

"Ah, so this is the first time that Jewish people appear on the scene?" pressed Yeorgis.

"Indeed", interrupted Joshua, "and incidentally it is this period in the Bronze Age which has provided the background for the Old Testament which is based on the writings of the Jewish Bible, the so called Tanakh, and which many Christians and Jews believe to be the word of God."

"How true are the stories in the Old Testament?" asked Petros. Joshua sighed and replied slowly, "Well, as in every story, fact and fiction are intermingled to produce a feasible interpretation of some events. A historian once said that the early history of the Israelites cannot be confirmed from any source other than the Old Testament and it is impossible to know at what point it ceases to be legendary."

"Let us say that the Bible is a mixture of true episodes, some fictional events, wishful thinking, poetry and some events which were obviously not true," said Mrs Mani, wishing to keep the discussion on track.

"The Hyksos rule of Egypt and its influence over Palestine's history is often referred to in connection with the history of Palestine prior to the consolidation of the Jews," continued Alexis who was by now constantly consulting his notes. "Many scholars believe that it was during the Hyksos rule that a group of people emerged, largely Semitic, called the Habiru, from which perhaps the modern name of Hebrew has its origin. These people were very knowledgeable in military methods and introduced novel methods of town fortifications. During the Amarna Age in the 14th century BC, Palestine was ruled by Egyptian vassals but by then the Egyptian Kingdom was so weakened that the infiltrating Israelites had established themselves in Palestine."

"So, the Jews originated from the Habiru?" prompted Petros.

"Partly," replied Alexis. "At the same time there were other groups who had settled in the Levant and were regarded by Israelites as fellow Hebrews. These were the Ammonites near the Syrian border, the Edomites in the South and the Moabites, East of the Dead Sea. We then have many centuries of a flourishing Kingdom of Israel where the era of Solomon represents the highest point of political history for the Hebrews. A Syrian and Babylonian rule follows only to be surpassed by the dominance of the Persian Empire during which many exiled Jews returned to Jerusalem from Babylonia and started to work on the restoration of Judah and the building of the Temple which had previously been destroyed."

"Let me hasten to add," prompted Hannah, "some modern historians do not believe in the connection between the Jews and the Habiru. But let us not go down that route and assume that the connection with peoples living in Canaan is more accurate."

Alexis paused, flicked a couple of pages of his notes and continued. "OK, I understand," he replied looking at Hannah and went on. "The next notable period in the history of Palestine is the Hellenistic rule under Alexander's successors, the Ptolemaic dynasty, followed by the Seleucids which lasted about three and a half centuries and then Palestine fell under the spell of the Romans during the Arab conquest."

"You have just described a thousand years covering the history of Palestine in a few sentences," said Mary to her son with a wry smile.

"I know," replied Alexis, "it is quite difficult to extract the salient points from of all this," pointing to his thick wad of hand-written notes.

"Quite," replied his mother. "However, before we leave the Hellenistic period behind us, it is perhaps important to add that there was intense opposition to the programme of Hellenization imposed by the Seleucids on the inhabitants of Palestine resulting in the notorious revolt of the Maccabees." The youngsters all stared at Mrs Mani in awe at her timely intervention as she lit another Craven A cigarette. It was obvious she was au fait with what Alexis was recounting, revealing an in-depth knowledge of the history of the Levant.

"Was there any emigration of the Jewish people from Palestine during those thousand years of Greek and Roman rule?" asked Panos.

"This is referred to as the Diaspora," butted in Hannah, who also had a good grasp of the historical events surrounding that period. She went on, "In all the great cities of antiquity there emerged Jewish settlements, starting with the Babylonian conquest of Palestine where large number of Jews were sent to Babylon, some of which were allowed to return to Palestine under the leadership of Nehemiah and Ezra after Babylon fell to Cyrus, the King of Medes and Persians. Well, the Jews dispersed themselves, so to speak, in many cities in the region. The Jews of Alexandria, for example, became much more Hellenized than those of Judea and they began to lose contact with their native language, Hebrew. It became necessary to translate the Old Testament into Greek..."

"The Septuagint," interrupted Alexis.

"Indeed," replied Hannah, who by now was very impressed by the young man's research into the history of that region, albeit still at a very superficial level. Hannah went on.

"It was not only in other countries of the Levant that the Jews found refuge as the Diaspora also spread into Western Europe. Even before the decay of the Roman Empire, the Jews had settled in many Roman cities and around the first century AD we see the makings of an interesting phenomenon which at first may be seen as insignificant but in retrospect will appear very important to this discussion." Hannah's intervention developed into a soliloquy. She went on: "This has to do with the schism between Judaism and Christianity. In all the cities to which they emigrated, the Jews influenced all those that were dissatisfied with the established religious dogmas put forward by Rome and Constantinople. Many converted to Judaism and it appears that it was in Jewish circles that Christians were first attracted. But Orthodox

Judaism became more orthodox and narrow after the fall of Jerusalem and, following the consolidation of the Christians, relations between Judaism and Christianity deteriorated, stimulating antisemitism. Throughout the Middle Ages the Jews in Christian countries were not allowed to participate much in their culture or exercise their traditions and were thus oppressed. In fact, during the Crusades there were many pogroms; however, paradoxically in the context of the present Arab-Israeli conflict, is the fact that during the Middle Ages the Mohammedans were more humane towards the Jews , especially in Spain where they contributed significantly to culture and philosophy."

"Pogroms?" asked a startled Yeorgis.

"Simplistically, it is the deliberate persecution of an ethnic or religious group," answered Hannah. Alexis then resumed his narrative.

"The Arab conquest of Palestine began during the seventh century AD and lasted nearly seven hundred years and, if I understand correctly, the important feature of this was..." He paused, checking carefully his notes and continued, "...an intense process of Islamisation."

"Another thousand years gone," murmured a frustrated Petros.

"Pardon?" said Alexis turning to Petros.

"Nothing," replied Petros, slightly embarrassed.

"Finally," continued the youngster, "Palestine fell to the Ottoman Empire and remained under its jurisdiction for four centuries until the British occupied it at the end of the First World War."

"General Allenby was in command during the defeat of the Ottoman/German Empires by the British Empire", interjected Panos, who had just covered the Sinai and Palestine campaign of the Middle Eastern part of the Great War at his school, the Victoria College. Alexis nodded.

"Has there been an Empire which has not at one time or another occupied Palestine?" asked Petros innocently.

"The Chinese dynasties," replied Yeorgis, laughingly.

Mrs Mani, sensing that the concentration of the youngsters was on the wane, took the opportunity, following Yeorgis' flippant utterance, for a break by offering pastries and soft drinks to the youngsters and to adults a glass of Remy Martin, her favourite tipple. Joshua sipped his cognac and reflected on what had been discussed thus far. He turned to Petros.

"Do you now appreciate how difficult it is to answer your question about Palestine's sovereignty? To whom does Mandatory Palestine really belong was your question, if I remember correctly?" Petros nodded.

"Why do you insist on calling it Mandatory Palestine and not just Palestine?" interrupted Alexis.

"Simply because there wasn't a recognised nation called Palestine, merely a region in the Levant occupied for many centuries by the Ottomans," replied Joshua, and went on, "The answer really depends upon what one considers to be the essential element inherent in the definition of a country's sovereignty. If the right to sovereignty of a piece of land lies on who were the first inhabitants, then surely Palestine belongs to the Natufians and who knows, they may have even originated from China," said Joshua chuckling while turning to Yeorgis, "but if it rests with the first lasting civilisation..." (Joshua accentuated the word "lasting") "...then Palestine belongs to the Jewish people; and finally if sovereignty is determined solely by the majority of its people or is decided by the longest rule then Jewish legitimacy of Palestine is questionable and Palestine can be argued to belong to the Arab Muslims."

"But surely, some would argue," interjected Mary, "that who first inhabited a piece of land should not be the only crucial factor in determining who should occupy the same land in the twentieth century. So, let us agree that both Arabs and Jews can claim a good measure of sovereignty on the piece of land called Palestine."

"Why do we exclude the Christian Greeks in this analysis?" asked Yeorgis.

"Well, because their main influence centres on Jerusalem and not in the villages within the Levant," said Hannah.

"Why don't they divide Palestine into two halves?" retorted Petros who appeared very pleased with offering such a simple solution.

"Before your question can be answered," replied Mrs Mani while looking at Petros, "it is important to examine the modern period of Palestine's history during the British Mandate spanning some 40 years or so." Petros was on the verge of losing his patience with the three grown-ups who avoided answering his questions directly, but he bore their digressions with fortitude.

"Perhaps it is appropriate to start with the Balfour Declaration," continued Mrs Mani, signalling to her son to continue with his notes.

"Oh yes, I scribbled it down here somewhere," he said, hurriedly flicking a few pages; "it cropped up time and time again in practically all the sources and references about Palestine or Israel."

"Arthur Balfour," interjected Mrs Mani as Alexis was struggling to find this most significant statement regarding the fate of Palestine, "was the British Foreign Secretary during the latter part of the Great War. He wrote to Lord Rothschild, the leader of the British Jewish Society in England, describing the view of the British Government regarding the future of Palestine with respect to the Arabs and Jewish people living in Palestine at that time."

"Here we go, I found it. The statement in a letter was, I quote, 'His Majesty's Government view with favour the establishment in Palestine of a national home for the Jewish people and will use their best endeavour to facilitate the achievement of this object, it being clearly understood that nothing shall be done which may prejudice the civil and religious rights of existing non-Jewish communities in Palestine or the rights and political status enjoyed by the Jews in any other country'," concluded Alexis.

"Before we continue a short introduction to Zionism would I think be very helpful to put everything in context," butted in Joshua.

"Zionism?" exclaimed Petros in bewilderment.

"Indeed," replied Joshua, "the Jews of the Diaspora that Hannah alluded to earlier had hardly assimilated and integrated successfully within the European communities in which they lived. The Jews who had settled in Eastern Europe, such as the Soviet Union or Poland, fared the worst because they lived in ghettos that could hardly be considered civilised and, moreover, were never given equal rights, political or otherwise. In short, there was considerable discontent in all aspects of their lives and indeed with the quality of life amongst most Jews living in the Diaspora. Even in countries where they seemed to have been treated better, antisemitism was exercised by a small minority of people who refused to accept the Jews as equal in their societies. Such antisemitism was used in some countries for deliberate exploitation by some elements towards achieving their political aims."

"The Dreyfus affair in France for example," interjected Mary Mani. Joshua nodded and went on.

"So, for centuries the Jewish discontent grew, and many prominent Jews expressed the desire to establish a national home for their own people, preferably in Palestine, the Holy Land, where there were ancient ties. This movement, which came to be known as Zionism, started with a small group in Odessa, under the physician Leo Pinsker, who called themselves *Hovevei Zion*...",

"Incidentally that means lovers of Zion," interjected Hannah.

"Mm," murmured Joshua, nodding his head and continuing, "...who tried to do everything possible to promote the formation of Jewish agricultural settlements in Palestine. Although it was the Rothschild family that supported these early settlements, that group paved the way towards Jewish emigration to Palestine. However, it was an Austro-Hungarian journalist, Theodor Herzl, who renewed the vigour of Zionism because antisemitism was rife and regarded as the main obstacle towards assimilation of the Jews in Austrian society. He published a pamphlet toward the end of the 19th century called *Der Judenstaat*, in which he expressed his views about the difficulty of assimilation and emancipation thus forcing the Jews to consider establishing a home of their own. He devoted an enormous effort promoting Zionism in Vienna, the movement's headquarters, but he also found considerable support in England where he was able to establish the financial backup for the movement."

"Wasn't it at that time that Britain offered some four thousand square miles of uninhabited land in the highlands of Uganda to the Zionists?" asked Alexis.

"Yes, after the turn of the century," replied Joshua, "but that was not the first time that such an offer had been made and eventually rejected by the Jews. Around

1825, an American Jew, Mordecai Noah, the playwright, journalist and diplomat, acquired the Grand Island in Niagara River and invited the Jews of the world to form a home there which he called Ararat. Later, however, he realised the inveterate feeling of the Jews for Palestine and advocated helping them instead to establish a home there. Similarly, with the Ugandan offer, there were some minority Jewish groups, for example that led by Israel Zangwill, who were willing to accept such an offer, but the ties of the Jews with Palestine were too strong so establishing a home elsewhere was a non-starter."

The youngsters were by now all ears as questions were coming thick and fast.

"You have mentioned these agricultural settlements in Palestine," said Alexis looking at Joshua. "What sort of relationship existed between the Jews and the indigenous Arabs? I ask this because I read somewhere that there was opposition towards employing Arab labour in their settlements and that they insisted on Hebrew as the spoken language?"

"This is a very old and delicate point which is raised time and time again when discussing Palestine," said Mrs Mani, "the question of Jewish insularity."

"That question," replied Joshua smilingly, "reminds me of the riddle of the chicken and the egg, only applied to a community. Was it Jewish insularity and isolation that aroused suspicion and distrust amongst the native population or was it the persecution and dislike for the Jews in the first place that forced them to cling together in a tight group for survival and consequently prevent a successful assimilation? It is not an easy question to answer; however, I see the point you are making," said Joshua, addressing Alexis, "such isolation would have raised the suspicion of the Arabs surrounding these settlements. By the way it is worth stressing that such settlements occupied such a minute part of Palestine that one can assume that there was scant contact with their Arab neighbours..."

"The settlements were often attacked by the Palestinians, who had to employ guards at night for their defence," interrupted Hannah.

"That is correct," replied Joshua and went on. "Anyhow, to come back to Zionism, Herzl died prematurely and later the leadership moved to Germany. At the outbreak of the Great War it was swiftly decided to move the headquarters to London since Turkey and Germany were allies against, amongst others, Britain. The leadership was therefore passed to Jews of Russian origin living in London, such as Chaim Weizmann and Nahum Sokolow. This connection of Zionism with Britain sowed the seeds for the subsequent Balfour declaration."

"Very noble of Britain," said Petros innocently.

"Well" replied Mary Mani cynically, "the establishment of a Jewish state, which by all accounts would be friendly to Britain, would have effectively secured the passage of ships though the Suez Canal on their way to the lucrative markets in India. However, the official reason was supposed to be with the European discontent of the Jews."

"How did the Balfour Declaration go down with the Arabs in Palestine?" asked Panos.

"From the outset the Arabs opposed the creation of a Jewish State there because they feared that one day, they would exert control over all Palestine", went on Mrs Mani.

"What was the proportion of the Jewish population in Palestine at the time of the Declaration?" asked Yeorgis.

"I have some figures here," replied Alexis, swiftly rummaging through his notes. "In 1922 there were 589,000 Arabs, 71,000 Christian Arabs..."

"Are they known as the Copts?" asked Panos looking around at the adults in the room, all of whom who nodded. Alexis glanced at his pal and turning back to his notes continued, "... and 84,000 Jews. The latest figures I was able to find were for the year 1947, where there were 630,000 Jews and 1.181 million Arabs. Further, at that time the Jewish land holdings were eight per cent of Palestine."

"So, during the period between the two world wars, the ratio of Arabs to Jews was reduced from seven to one to just less than two to one," concluded Mrs Mani, who wished to focus on the gradual but systematic immigration of Jews into Palestine before delving into the rights and wrongs of the various powers and administrations.

"Perhaps it is important to stress here," butted in Hannah, "that even before the Balfour Declaration, land owned by Arabs was sold to Jewish settlers, simply because some well-off families had moved either to Syria or Jordan and did not wish to retain any ties with Palestine. So, between the late 19th century and early twentieth century, land sales continued, enabling some settlers to legitimately claim to own a piece of land rather than having acquired it by subterfuge or clandestine means."

"It was not necessarily an individual who bought the land but in many instances purchases were made through a number of organisations such as the National Jewish Fund and the Palestine Jewish Colonisation Association," interjected Joshua.

"Surely," said Panos, "the Arabs could have formed similar organisations to protect land owned by their people."

"The Arabs were on the whole less sophisticated and there are reports that the leaders were offered bribes and were involved secretly themselves in land deals with the Jews. In essence they were outwitted by the more savvy Jewish settlers and their organisations," replied Mary "however, in percentage terms just before the creation of the State of Israel the transfer of land ownership to Jews was quite small, of the order of eight per cent, and the majority of the purchases were made in coastal areas such as the Jezreel Valley or Jordan Valley and to a smaller extent the Galilee. These were sparsely populated areas, not least because the soil was such that it was unsuitable for growing the staple crop of Palestine, corn. Also, Jews buying land in these areas meant that no large Arab population had to be evicted as there were very few living there."

"To give you an idea," said Joshua, "Jezreel Valley lies some 20 km south of Haifa and Jordan Valley stretches from the Sea of Galilee to the Dead Sea and is essentially the border between Jordan and Mandatory Palestine."

"Did the British remain in charge in Palestine throughout this period?" asked Yeorgis.

"In effect, yes," replied Mary. "After the First World War, there was an article of the covenant in the League of Nations signed in 1919..."

"Article 22," interrupted Alexis glancing at his notes.

Mrs Mani glanced at her son, acknowledged his comment and went on, "This article recognised the provisional independence of the Arab provinces previously under Ottoman rule subject to a mandatory power which would be selected after consulting the various communities."

"How was the Balfour Declaration implemented?" asked Panos.

"The Declaration was incorporated into the Mandate by close cooperation between the British in charge and the Zionists. In 1920 a quota of some 16,500 Jewish immigrants was announced for the first year: an announcement which the Arabs bitterly resented. In 1921 in Jaffa there were anti-Zionist riots where around 50 Jews were killed and nearly the same number of Arabs also died and many more injured from both sides. However, the British Government continued with its policies inherent in the Mandate and in June 1922 Winston Churchill..."

"The guy who smoked cigars and drunk a bottle of champagne a day," announced Panos whose history lessons at Victoria College covered the legendary British leader during WWII.

Mrs Mani smiled at Panos and continued: "... assured that the Declaration did not mean the imposition of Jewish nationality upon the inhabitants of Palestine as a whole but it meant the further development of the existing Jewish community with the assistance of the Jews from other parts of the world. This would ensure, slowly but surely, the creation of a centre in Palestine where Jewish people would feel at home on grounds of religion and race, without ever seeking the disappearance or the subordination of the Arab populace, their language or their culture."

Alexis' mum was in her element as she had followed these events closely during the past few years and was pretty sure of the facts. She continued.

"There followed a relatively quiet period with the Arab protests being subdued mainly because of the reduction in the number of immigrants coming into Palestine. For example, it was reported that in 1927 emigrants exceeded immigrants and in the following year the two flows were nullified."

"Well," interrupted Joshua, "I would question the word 'quiet' because in 1929 there was a massacre in Hebron where over 60 Jews were murdered and nearly that number again wounded and indeed days later a similar massacre occurred in the village of Safed."

"It was reported at the time that the reason given for these massacres was the fear that the Jews were planning to seize control of the Temple Mount in Jerusalem," butted in Mary.

"What is the significance of this Temple?" asked Petros.

"The Temple Mount or *Har HaBáyit*, to the Jews..." said Joshua while Mary interjected.

"Of course, to the Muslims it is known as *Haram esh-Sharif* or Noble Sanctuary."

"Indeed," continued Joshua, "it is a prominent elevation situated in Old Jerusalem and has been worshipped for thousands of years by many of the religions of the Levant."

"Do you mean Christianity, Judaism and Islam?" asked Panos.

"Quite so," replied Joshua.

"How then did Palestine manage to acquire so many Jews by 1946?" interjected Petros.

"That is where Herr Hitler comes into the equation," said Yeorgis triumphantly.

"Quite so," replied Mary Mani while looking at Yeorgis and continued. "A new impetus to Jewish immigration in Palestine was given after the fate of the European Jewry in Germany's concentration camps started to leak. After the Nazis came to power in 1933 there were some 80,000 Jewish immigrants to Palestine and two years later nearly 60,000, although not all came from Germany. It is fair to say, however, that a few years before the Nazis came to power the British Government realised that it was their responsibility to accord some priority to some of the promises made to the Arabs which were inherent in the Balfour Declaration. The Zionists bitterly resented what they viewed as a pro-Arab stance and their fears were only put to rest when Ramsey McDonald, the then Prime Minister, assured Weizmann that the British Government was still in favour of the Balfour Declaration and its subsequent 1922 Mandate. The Arabs were not at all happy with such a policy and regarded it effectively as Jews being able to dictate and control Palestine's destiny. The Arab attitude towards the Zionists therefore hardened particularly after some 20-odd countries attended an Arab conference in Jerusalem to discuss the dangers imposed on them by the emergence of the Zionists in Palestine."

"So, can we surmise that if it was not for Hitler's final solution of the Jewish problem as he saw it, Zionism would have never consolidated in Palestine and Israel would not have been born?" asked Panos.

"Well, that is a hypothetical question," replied Mary nonchalantly. "What is more certain is that the establishment of Jewish settlements would have been much slower and consequently this would have rendered the fulfilment of Zionism that much more difficult."

"I believe that," intervened Joshua, "if it was not for Hitler and his final solution, as Panos has just stated, there would by now have been a final agreement in Palestine acceptable to all the factions, in fact not partition but peaceful coexistence. After all I see it as the only solution even today."

"That maniac Hitler," muttered Petros with youthful anger.

"Your suggestion," said Mrs Mani addressing Joshua and ignoring Petros' mild utterance, "is highly controversial and indeed very debatable. There is no evidence that the Zionists would have been satisfied with anything less than a full National Jewish State. Their reaction to the British policy in 1939 is enough evidence of their expectations."

The boys had by now lost track of the arguments while Alexis was searching his notes feverishly to catch up with his mother's latest intervention. Suddenly he found what he was looking for.

"Are you referring to the White Paper of 1939?" Alexis asked his mother.

"Yes I am. This was the culmination of a series of events which started in the mid-1930s highlighting the numerous bloody clashes in Palestine between the Arabs and the British military forces as a direct result of Arab opposition to the growing Jewish immigration into Palestine. A commission of enquiry was set up which ultimately proposed partition of Palestine which was bitterly opposed by the Arabs while the Zionists were indecisive about it. As the Arabs rebelled further the British military forces had to take drastic steps to prevent further bloodshed and exiled most of the Arab leaders to the Seychelles. In the process they crushed any prominent Arab force that existed in Palestine at the time. The

British Government concluded that partition was not practicable and called for further negotiations to be held in London in early 1939 between the two factions, but alas no agreement was reached. It was after that conference that the White Paper was published which in effect declared that the Balfour Declaration was largely fulfilled and insisted in curbing Jewish immigration to a maximum of 12,000 per annum for five years, adding that any further immigration was to have Arab acquiescence. Finally, the White Paper stated that there were to be restrictions as to which specific bits of land were to be transferred to the Jews and that Palestine would become independent within ten years."

"Do you mean a combined Palestinian state?" asked Panos.

"Exactly that," replied Mrs Mani. "But the Zionists were greatly disturbed by such a policy and regarded it as a betrayal of the Balfour Declaration."

The discussion was now being conducted predominantly by the two elders present, with Hannah taking a back seat.

"Be that as it may," went on Joshua, "what we ought to stress is that the attitude of the Zionists must be seen from the point of view of the suffering of European Jewry. It was difficult to accept such drastic change in Palestine's immigration policy at the time when thousands of Jews were being exterminated in Hitler's concentration camps."

"Surely," interrupted Mary, "the British Government

couldn't have known the sheer scale of the annihilation of the Jewish people."

"I agree," went on Joshua, "the extent was perhaps not known but the peoples of Germany, Russia, Austria, Poland, Hungary were witnessing the depletion of the Jewish population irrespective of whether they knew where there were being transferred to and this information must have somehow been transmitted to the British Government in London."

"At that time there was still hope that peace would prevail between Germany and England and its allies, thus preventing another world war," continued Mary.

"Yes," replied Joshua, "but one can understand the frustration and panic of the Zionist leaders when they encountered extermination from the Nazis without the consolation of whole-hearted sympathy from the British."

"This is as far as I have been able to find out about this subject," stated Alexis while collecting his notes into a neat bundle.

"When did the State of Israel come into being?" asked Yeorgis eager to find out more about the genesis of one of the newest countries in the Middle East. Mary glanced at Joshua and Hannah and although it was getting late all three adults recognised the significance of Yeorgis' question which must have puzzled the youngsters that evening all sitting comfortably in a large bedroom in an Alexandrian apartment. Mary, with all eyes looking at her, took the initiative and continued.

"The Second World War intervened, and both the Jews and Arabs fought the common enemy, the Germans and their allies. Some tens of thousands of Arabs and an equally large number of Jewish settlers were enlisted in the British army and fought in various war zones."

"I read somewhere about the formation of the Jewish Brigade," butted in Alexis.

"The Jewish Brigade was formed comprising some tens of thousands of soldiers who had enlisted in the British army. Moreover, the Jewish situation in Palestine was vastly strengthened towards the end of the war because many more Jews were allowed immigration certificates especially after the horrors of the concentration camps were revealed. Ammunition was manufactured in Palestine for the British war effort but I daresay the Zionists capitalised on this opportunity by amassing a large stock which was used against the Arabs and the British after the war." Mary Mani stopped and after a little reflection continued. "So, you can understand that the situation which existed in Palestine immediately after WWII ended was very tense with renewed hostilities between the two factions. The Arabs trying to hold on to the land they had occupied for some thirteen-hundred years and the Zionists trying to consolidate in the land of their ancient forefathers. The Arab countries formed the League of Arab States..."

"Known in Arabic as the *Jami'at ad-Duwal al-'Arabiyah*," butted in Hannah.

Ms Mani nodded and continued: "... which was

created in Cairo in 1945 comprising some six regional countries to promote the notion of Pan-Arabism and safeguard their sovereignty and interests which inevitably supported the fellow Palestinian Arabs and boycotted Zionist goods. The British who were in charge of the Mandate found themselves in the most awkward position of trying to reconcile the aspirations of both factions and resented the fact that their forces were being mercilessly attacked by the underground organisations which one report claimed totalled around 65,000 strong."

"The Haganah," uttered Panos whose parents of some Jewish school pals at Victoria College had been members of that underground organisation.

"The Irgun and the Sternists were splinter groups also involved in underground activities," added Mary.

"Tell us more about these groups," urged Petros eagerly, who envisaged all sorts of heroic activities in Palestine at the time.

Mrs Mani glanced at Joshua and Hannah who were silent and very thoughtful. Joshua's face attained an uncharacteristic seriousness and it was obvious that he was desperately trying to formulate the right and fair answer to a question he anticipated and was about to be confronted with. Mrs Mani took a deep breath and went on.

"The aim of these groups was to establish a national home for the Jewish people in Palestine and they fought very hard against the one body that stood in their way: the British administration backed by their army. Lord

Moyne, the British Minister in Cairo, was murdered in 1944 by members of the Lehi group who had split from Irgun..."

"Lord Moyne was after all against the formation of a home for the Jewish people," interjected Hannah.

"Be that as it may, surely his assassination inflamed an already dangerous situation," replied Mary, "and two years later there was utter condemnation by the whole world when the King David Hotel, which housed government officers and military personnel, was sabotaged by members of the Jewish underground groups killing over 90 people. In addition, there were also a number of small-scale attacks on the occupying forces which helped the Zionist cause and threatened the Mandate which hardened the attitude of the British." Mrs Mani realised that Joshua wished to intervene and paused.

"It is ironic," started Joshua in a low but deliberate voice, "when one considers the attitude of most observers towards these underground groupings." He paused and then continued. "The origins of the Haganah as we know it now goes back many decades when small groups were formed in the 1920s to protect some Jewish settlements from Arab extremists. Initially they were very small, used small boys to pass messages along to other groups and hid their basic weapons in underground tunnels and other hideouts. Their consolidation into a fighting force became more substantial after the Hebron and Safed massacres when it became obvious that a military style unit had to be born. These were the same groups that were also actively attempting to liberate as many Jews from being sent to the concentration camps and were regarded as heroes and admired for their bravery and gallantry. After the war the emphasis shifted towards the British occupying forces in Palestine who stood in the way of achieving their long-standing goal of a national home…" Hannah interrupted her husband by adding: "And in order to put behind them the years of misery and humiliation they had endured in the concentration camps." Joshua nodded and continued.

"Regrettably there would be casualties, some innocent ones too, but after the war Palestine was in turmoil and an amicable solution to the Palestinian problem was frankly quite unrealistic."

"But how can one justify targeting innocent people?" interjected Petros.

"Of course, amidst the people occupying the hotel at that time there were civilians, some of the administration and other simply bystanders of other nationalities. But the underground targeted the military which after all represented the occupying force and thus the hotel was deemed as a legitimate target," replied Joshua.

"The end justifies the means," uttered Mrs Mani reflectively.

"To the Jews living in Palestine at the time, particularly the Haganah and their more militant splinter groupings, the Irgun and Stern…"

"You mean the terrorist groups," butted in Panos.

Joshua looked at Panos and continued. "It was justifiable because their actions helped to bring nearer the fulfilment of their ambitions: a national home and the ensuing stability and peacefulness which had long been denied them by most European states," said Joshua.

"The fulfilment of Zionism was soon to be accomplished," continued Mrs Mani as she explained the last few years of the existence of the Palestinian state as an entity. "The British, unable to find any workable solution, referred the problem to the United Nations which ultimately decided on partition. This suited the Zionists because by that time they totalled half of the people living in Palestine while only occupying 8% of the land and if partition was to go ahead, they would be given half of Palestine. All the Islamic countries voted against partition and the British refused to implement a policy that did not carry the approval of both sides and slowly but unmistakably civil war broke out with many thousands of casualties, both Jews and Arabs. The United Nations Commission in Palestine was prevented by Arab resistance from implementing partition and it appeared that a workable solution could only be achieved if both the Arabs and Jews cooperated. The Zionists, after their success at Nachshon in April of 1948..."

"What happened there?" butted in Petros.

"This was the successful offensive of the Jews against the Arabs who had blocked the Jerusalem to Tel Aviv Road," answered Mrs Mani and went on, "and pressed for partition because they feared a change of policy by the United Nations. As soon as the British Mandate was over in May 1948 the State of Israel was proclaimed with Ben-Gurion as its first President. Not surprisingly it gained immediate de-facto recognition by America."

"Palestine was no more," announced Alexis.

"That is not a straightforward way of answering your question," said Mrs Mani addressing Petros, "but a diversion was necessary in order to understand why the partition plan never materialised. But it is questionable whether that particular partition plan would have offered the long-term stability which both sides craved, because, looking at the detailed division of Palestine given that six areas each alternately was being allocated to the Arabs and Jews, would pose an enormous task of each faction securing its borders from one another. The Swedish UN Peace Mediator Count Folke Bernadotte was aware of the problems with the partition plan and was attempting to modify it and wrote a report advocating the issue of borders between the two newly created states should be carefully drawn up and adhered to, together with allowing the return of the Palestinian refugees and the Internationalisation of the city of Jerusalem. That was a step too far for the Stern Group who ordered his assassination and he was killed in West Jerusalem the day after his report was published. He had in effect stated that it would be an affront to the principle of elementary justice if the refugees were not allowed to return to their homes. Not surprisingly the neighbouring Arab countries declared war on Israel without achieving anything substantial regarding the aspirations of the

Palestinian Arabs."

"Presumably," asked Panos, "it was just before the creation of the State of Israel that the mass of Palestinian refugees came into being."

"The Palestinian Conundrum," uttered Alexis.

"What is so puzzling about the Palestinian refugees?" asked Petros who did not quite understand what exactly Alexis meant when he referred to the Palestinian refugee problem as a conundrum.

"Well," went on Mrs Mani, "one is not talking here about a few hundred or even a few thousand families. Reports claim that close to a million people abandoned their homes in Palestine. These refugees were given shelter and protection in neighbouring countries such as Syria, Lebanon and Jordan. That number then represented about two thirds of the entire population of Palestine. What, one may ask, caused such a massive exodus of a whole community?"

"Perhaps panic," exclaimed Yeorgis.

"Panic is certainly a contributing factor," replied Mrs Mani and looked at Joshua.

"You think there was terror involved and forced eviction?" replied Joshua in a low voice.

"How can we exclude it?" pressed Mary in a voice which sounded almost apologetic, "when one is confronted with such a mass of people fleeing their own homes and losing everything they possessed?"

Mary paused and appeared thoughtful. Silence ensued. Clearly, she had not finished her argument, but it was apparent that she faced a dilemma. On one hand lay the factual evidence of atrocities, terror and in some instances massacre of the Palestinian people and the destruction of hundreds of villages which had to be aired for a balanced view of the problem but facts which evidently would hurt Joshua and Hannah and indeed their children. She glanced at the youngsters all of whom had their eyes fixed on her waiting spellbound for what she was about to say next. As it happens in many such instances she acted intuitively and continued.

"We have friends of the family that have met Arab refugees living presently in the Transjordan valley who had told them of the massacre by the underground movement Irgun of hundreds of civilians at the village of Deir Yassin. The refugees also stated that there were hundreds of villages that had met a similar fate of terror and eviction, for example, the massacre of some 20 villages one being at Nasir ad-Din on the shore of the Sea of Galilee. Of course, it is difficult to know all the facts behind such a ruthless action and similar psychological warfare which must have spread panic amongst Palestinian Arabs."

"Ismail told us," said Alexis, "that while his family was living in a refugee camp they met other families who had related similar stories of panic, forceful eviction, rape and mass killings by the Israeli forces in order to capture villages that apparently were not assigned to them during the apportioning of Palestine into Jewish and Arab parts, the cities of Haifa and Jaffa for example."

"Every country," replied Joshua, "has in its history its black pages. The events at Deir Yassin and at other villages should be condemned by all Jews in normal circumstances," he paused as he struggled to formulate his next sentence.

"As should the massacre of the Jews at Hebron," interrupted Panos.

"Indeed," replied Joshua who had regained his composure and continued, "but I am afraid the circumstances surrounding the creation of the State of Israel were far from normal. The feelings of the majority of the Jews were running very high, they were hungry for freedom and deeply resented the way they had been treated for centuries. They were tired of being made pawns of the major powers and when the opportunity arose to acquire a piece of land, especially with biblical connotations, which they could call their own, they grasped it without much attention to the consequences of their actions. Every Jew sympathises with the plight of the refugees which in part was the root of the 1948 war as well as this last war between Israel and the neighbouring Arab countries that you have all witnessed."

"Talking about the recent war," intervened Alexis, "is it not a bit strange that eight years ago the British were trying to defend the Arabs and themselves in Palestine from the Zionists and now the British and the French have fought side by side with Israel against another Arab country?"

"The British claim that they were only protecting their own interests in the Canal Zone," replied his mum and, turning to Joshua, she went on. "I accept what you say about the feelings of the Jews during such turmoil eight years ago but the fact remains that incidents like that at Deir Yassin and in countless other villages have remained vividly in the minds of the refugees, who I daresay will relate these to their children and grandchildren, and instead of healing old wounds they will exacerbate the situation for the future unless the Palestinian Conundrum, as Alexis puts it, is sorted out."

"Could you elaborate this point?" pressed Alexis.

"You see, during the past eight years the refugees have been kept in makeshift camps with no real hope for the future except for those few for whom passage has been granted to go to neighbouring countries."

"Like Ismail's family," butted in Alexis.

"Yes," continued Mrs Mani, "Ismail's family was more fortunate, but there are sound reasons why this has not been extended to many more Palestinian refugees. First, this will require huge funds and a great effort because there are close to a million or so refugees and that is no mean task. Second, there is the question whether the refugees wish to go anywhere else except return to their homeland in Palestine. After all we saw how adamant the Jews were against establishing a new home in Long Island or the Ugandan highlands so why should the Arabs accept an alternative proposition to what for many centuries was their home in Palestine? And thirdly,

I read a newspaper report suggesting that the leaders of the neighbouring countries wished to maintain the refugee camps in their present basic state in order to remind the world of the plight of the refugees and the unfair way they have been treated."

"But surely some countries could really afford to take many more refugees?" exclaimed Petros.

"There are other issues at stake. Take this country here," retorted Mrs Mani, "it is only a few years ago that they ousted the King and a charismatic leader has emerged. The first priority of Egypt's leaders is raising the standard of living of its own population who have been disadvantaged for many years. How can anybody expect the neighbouring countries to rally all their support to the Palestinian cause to the detriment and welfare of their own indigenous people?" Mary paused momentarily to collect her thoughts and, addressing Alexis, went on. "What I am afraid is that assuming that the condition of the Palestinian refugees remains the same for years to come then one wonders how their offspring will react. The older generation would probably accept their fate because the fire which drives one to achieve the impossible task..."

"Such as returning to Palestine," butted in Yeorgis.

"...has long ceased to burn," continued Mrs Mani after having acknowledged Yeorgis' intervention. "Furthermore, the middle generation remembers all too well what happened in 1948 and are reluctant to do anything about improving their situation, so Palestinian hopes are pinned on the younger generation who do not remember much and are continuously reminded..."

"Brainwashed," butted in Avi.

"Yes, I daresay you are correct, brainwashed indeed," replied Mary and pressed on, "about past atrocities so eventually they will rebel against those that caused such misery to their grandparents. What sort of future is there for these youngsters who live in these camps and are subjected to pitiful conditions while watching the newer Jewish State flourishing and expanding its borders? We have this potentially explosive situation which will always be on the brink of eruption at the slightest provocation."

"Let us also not forget that consequent to the 1948 war some Jews living in neighbouring countries did suffer and in some cases were expelled. And who knows how this last war will affect Jews presently living in Arab countries?" said Joshua, he and his family being a living embodiment of such a predicament.

"How does one attempt to solve such a tragic situation?" asked Yeorgis in a voice which betrayed a heavy dose of desperation.

"I firmly believe in peaceful coexistence," replied Hannah, "after all the Jews and Arabs coexisted peacefully in Palestine for many decades and what is more, we do coexist here alright, do we not?"

"With one important difference," replied Mary. "Before the new impetus of Zionism and the subsequent Balfour Declaration, the Jews in Palestine and indeed here were the minority. Although there are always ethnic differences in multiracial countries between the separate communities these differences accelerate once the numbers emigrating become significant. This is the trend that the Arabs were fighting against but failed to curb or were not allowed to bring under control."

"What about another attempt at partition which may result in a lasting solution?" said Alexis.

"Such a partition will have to be radically different from the one proposed in 1947," responded Mary. "It is not practical to divide the country into several parts and allocate the proceeds on the basis of its ethnic majority within each of these. This would create many Jewish and Arbs states not just two. For that reason, I think partition is impossible so the only ultimate solution I foresee is that of peaceful coexistence."

"Do you expect Israel to open its doors and accept back all the refugees and let bygones be bygones?" exclaimed Hannah.

"I am afraid I do not see an alternative viable solution but do not ask me how this should be implemented. One is dealing here with an extraordinary set of events over the past 38 years since Balfour which created the status quo so why not hope for an equally exceptional set of circumstances in the future which will create a unified Arab-Israeli State? Incidentally, after the ceasefire the border between Israel and the remaining Palestinian land was marked in green on UN maps and was agreed by Israel and its neighbouring countries. The stark reality is that the new state controlled nearly 80% of Mandatory Palestine compared to just 55% allocated to them in the UN partition plan in 1947," concluded Mary Marni and went on. "Boys, it is past midnight."

After the discussion Alexis and his mates headed towards the scout grounds. They found the gate locked so without hesitation jumped the wall and meandered aimlessly in the courtyard. They felt as though they were the only boys in the whole of Alexandria who knew so much about the turbulent history of Palestine, a notion which made them feel close and somehow bonded them.

The cloudless Alexandrian sky was full of stars gleaming merrily away, each with its own turbulent world, rubbing along complacently with their neighbours and keeping their own secrets firmly in their mists amongst the vast cosmic separations.

It was a stimulating evening for the youngsters, the arguments of which would remain with them for a very long time and have dramatic consequences in the years ahead. What was ingrained in their youthful minds was the notion that an honourable and fair solution to the Palestinian Conundrum had to be found if peace was to prevail in that troubled region. They soon dispersed to their respective homes, their minds full of arguments and counter-arguments relating to the ethnic peoples of Palestine.

13

Jerusalem, January 2018

The Staff at the White House communicated directly with the PM of Israel assuring him that the President's announcement was genuine and that it would come to pass in the fullness of time.

This bit of news was music to the ears of the right-wing leader of the Likud Party and Head of the coalition. On his last trip to the USA the previous summer the President's idea about the Embassy's move was mooted but without specifying dates and it was left as something to consider in the future. Now that it had become a reality Israel's PM was keen to discuss its implications and the reaction of countries within the European Union as well as those in the Middle East. From his private residence at Beit Aghion in Smolenski Street in the affluent neighbourhood of Rehavia in Jerusalem the PM called a meeting of the Security Cabinet which formulates and executes the Government's foreign and defence policies. Present were the Vice PM, the Heads of the Defence, Foreign and Treasury Ministries, the Chief of General Staff, the Military Secretary to the PM and the Head of Shin Bet, the Israeli Security Agency. Instead of meeting as usual at the Kiryat Ben-Gurion Government complex in Givat Ram area of the city, they would on this occasion meet at the PM's residence. All those attending the meeting were members of the coalition that Likud had had to form after the last election. Likud and the last party to join the coalition, Yisrael Beiteinu, were secular parties but the PM had to seek the support of the Orthodox Jewish Home party and the two Ultra-Orthodox parties of United Torah Judaism and Shas as well as Kulanu in order to reach a working majority of seats in the Knesset.

"We must stand firm and united," said the PM accentuating the last word to impress upon his coalition partners and went on, "despite any opposition to the Presidents' announcement that will inevitably emerge from the usual countries in the UN". Following graduation from a university in Israel he had spent some time in the USA for further studies, working in an investment bank in Boston. He had thus cultivated numerous links with prominent Jewish factions in the USA and members of AIPAC to which group he had addressed at one of his recent visits to the USA.

"We must strengthen our security at the borders particularly around the Gaza Strip as I am anticipating large scale protests," continued the PM.

"I will see to that," replied the Chief of General Staff, who as effective Head of IDF had overall responsibility for keeping the borders secure from infiltrators.

The Head of Shin Bet looked at the PM and said quietly, "PM, do we exercise a shoot to maim policy or perhaps?" and stopped short of spelling out a more drastic action. The PM pondered for a while and turning to the Head of Shin Bet replied, "I leave that for consideration of the operational commanders in the field to exercise their initiative and judge what appropriate action is necessary to safeguard our villages and settlements beyond the separation wall."

The head of Shin Bet nodded in approval.

The assassination of young Qasim was not mentioned in the Israeli media. It was an operation well-conceived and executed and the fewer people who knew the better. The main objective was to eliminate young Qasim from the scene, so reducing the likelihood of violent acts against the inhabitants of Israel and their government. It was inevitable that Qasim would be replaced by another operative so the cycle of violent insurrections would continue ad infinitum unless a settlement was reached.

14

Port Said, May 1957

It was the last Christmas the Mani family would spend altogether, as Pavlos had signalled his intention to leave for London in mid-April now that he had completed his schooling and had spent a few years working in the city for an import-export business owned by the Benaki family. A close friend of the family who had long emigrated to London kept sending Pavlos pages upon pages of the *Daily Telegraph* job advertisements section.

Early in the New Year Alexis' dad decided to chance his luck and gamble a few pounds on the roulette tables at Mantazah. Ever since the abdication of King Farouk, the palace and its extensive gardens at Montazah had become a fashionable summer resort. The carefully landscaped meandering gardens occupied a huge acreage surrounding the imposing Moorish-like palace, similar to the gothic church of St Mark at Ramleh, and included a tower similar to that of the Palazzo Vecchio in Florence. The palace, turned into a casino and night club, comprised a magnificent mosaic structure lavishly decorated with priceless ornaments of antiquity. Its frontage was spanned by an array of tall trees overlooking a semi-secluded bay off the Mediterranean. An array of well over 50 self-contained chalets occupied one side of the bay while a huge diving board dominated the other side. One such chalet belonged to Myrto's parents and it must have been there that Nina and Tasos had met during the dying days of the previous summer.

Late one evening Alexis' family caught a taxi to Montazah. As Alexis was under 18, he was not allowed at the roulette tables so Mr Mani booked a table at the adjoining restaurant where he could have a drink while waiting for his parents and Pavlos to return following a bet or two. The restaurant was dimly lit as Alexis scanned the other tables. Only a few were occupied. On one table diametrically opposite his sat a fat Arab with a young lady, obviously his mistress judging by the disparity of their ages. He seemed to be all over her without paying much attention to any onlookers. She, on the other hand, although not very pretty had some attractive features, and seemed content enough with her catch. Alexis pretended not to be interested in that odd couple although he often glanced in their direction and was fully aware of every move they made. On another table, a family of four sat enjoying a leisurely meal. After about half an hour Mr Mani showed up rather excitedly, hotly pursued by Pavlos and his mum, approached Alexis' table and showed him his winnings.

"It was my lucky night," he exclaimed. "A bet of three pounds on a couple of individual numbers came up after half a dozen spins and that is all it took to win over two hundred Egyptian pounds. I would have won more had your mum not dragged me out of the room."

"Wow," exclaimed Alexis.

They sat at the table still chatting about the bets and ordered some drinks. Such a windfall of course would secure Pavlos' ticket to England. Alexis' mum knew fully well that the longer one continued betting at the roulette tables the more likely it would be to come out the loser as the odds were stacked against punters.

"Do you really believe that your luck would have continued?" replied Mary with a hint of sarcasm. Her husband looked at her without really wishing to debate the issue knowing that she was right. She sipped her glass of champagne and continued looking at her husband.

"Well, I propose tomorrow morning we go and book Pavlos' boat passage to England." Alexis looked at his dad with a question. "What would have happened had you lost?"

"Surely, that is now academic," replied his dad as he downed a glass of bubbly.

They remained at this picturesque restaurant, chatting about Pavlos' pending trip while consuming a lavish meal, and returned home by midnight. The following day the family caught the tram to the city terminus and off they trotted to the city's Thomas Cook Offices to secure Pavlos' one-way ticket to England. The luxury liner was scheduled to arrive from Sydney and after a day's stop-over at Port Said head to Southampton. Because the Canal was blocked by sunken destroyers and other naval casualties during the recent war the Agency promised to book Pavlos' passage immediately after the Canal was cleared. That took many months but eventually in early May the Canal was cleared and allowed the shipping line from Southampton to Sydney to function again.

Alexis volunteered to accompany Pavlos to Port Said and was thrilled to spend a couple of days away from home exploring other parts of Egypt. Preparations were finalised and all the necessary documents such as a passport and pounds sterling were obtained. Although their parents were sad at seeing the elder son leave Alexandria they were convinced that it was the best option as the situation in Egypt was getting more uncertain by the month.

The brothers boarded the train at Sidi Gaber and sat opposite each other in a large compartment. Alexis glanced at Pavlos and saw tears streaming down his young face as he realised that he was separating not only from his family but also his long-standing girlfriend. He felt wretched and let his emotions overpower him. Alexis, not knowing how to react, gazed out of the window. The train ploughed the undulating sand dunes of Mandara at the outskirts of Alexandria, then came across the endless white-speckled cotton plantations of the Nile Delta, a commodity vital to the economy and harvested in early autumn by an army of turbaned pickers. During its traverse through the Nile Delta the train stopped in the towns of Damahur, Tanta and Zagazig where passengers got off and on and finally made tracks toward the Canal Zone and the town of Ismailia. After Zagazig, the plantations gave way to endless wave-like sand dunes.

Alexis was excited to be witnessing such mesmerising scenery which although familiar to him nevertheless conjured up images of past experiences and childhood reminiscences.

"You look hypnotised," said Pavlos.

"I feel at home. I somehow come alive when I come across such a barren landscape as this desert," said Alexis, sweeping his hand across the window. "I feel as though an invisible force is being exerted on me, a magnetism drawing me closer trying to whisper something secretive, something sublime..."

"Here we go again, you are philosophising," interrupted Pavlos, "You know what, forget about engineering or maths – you should study philosophy." Alexis smiled at his brother's comment and continued to be absorbed by the desert-like scenery.

"Certainly I regard the desert as a huge reserve of resources," continued Pavlos, "such as minerals, gas or oil and of course one can understand Nasser's intention to irrigate large parts of the shores of the Nile to render it fertile, which will be hugely beneficial to the local economy."

The train applied its brakes as it approached the town of Ismailia which was situated halfway between Suez in the south and Port Said to the north. There was little to stare at as the train stood at the station, the voice of an Arab *passatempo* vendor trudging the platform came loud and clear as he approached the open window of the compartment where the two brothers sat. They bought a couple of piastres worth of dried fruit and nut mixture and mechanically started picking at the packets to pass the time, while immersed in their respective impressions of life in Alexandria. After Ismailia the train veered northwards and for the remainder of the journey the brothers witnessed the magnificence of the Canal, that awe-inspiring waterway connecting the Red and Mediterranean seas, with all its splendour and grandiose appearance. Alexis was mesmerised to be so close to the Canal where war had been waged so recently and was transfixed with astonishment at the scale and wonder of this artificial project. Because of his recent research of the history of Palestine, Alexis was quite familiar with the history of the Canal. It was conceived by the French diplomat de Lesseps after he was invited to do so by Said-Pasha, Egypt's ruler and very much a Francophile having studied in Paris. The brothers saw the relics of the battle, numerous burned-out tanks and a myriad of barrels, some intact, others crushed to smithereens by armoured vehicles. Instances of the war as experienced in Alexandria came flooding into Alexis' mind, accentuated by the thought of Ismail being injured around that region. The misery of war was real, the deaths, the horrendous injuries flashed by Alexis who had only to look beyond the Canal and catch a glimpse of the Sinai Peninsula to compound his depressing thoughts. He longed for much-needed solace.

Soon after they arrived at Port Said they found a small hotel as Alexis was staying overnight. They dumped their stuff and sauntered towards the town in search of a restaurant. Suddenly they came across Yanis who apparently had spent a few days in Port Said with his father who was having talks with a local representative of his import-export company. Yanis' father was extremely successful in running his business headquartered in Alexandria but with branches all over Egypt and other parts of the Levant. He knew France and England fairly well as he cooperated with some major companies.

"Why don't you join us for a spot of lunch? I am meeting father shortly and he knows a few good local eateries," said Yanis.

They met Mr Lotas who directed them to a scenic restaurant overlooking the harbour. The liner that Pavlos was to catch had already arrived and was departing later that evening. They sat at an oval table on the spacious pavement underneath an arched terrace, characteristic of the main street in town. They left the choice of the food to Mr Lotas who seemed to have an intimate knowledge of the restaurant's fine cuisine.

The discussion centred on Pavlos' imminent trip to London, which Mr Lotas seemed to know well following his frequent trips involving his company.

"Are you staying long in town?" asked Pavlos.

"No, we are heading back to Alexandria this afternoon having discussed aspects of a recent assignment with a colleague who is stationed here." He glanced at the menu, then anticipating Pavlos' next question went on. "It is a difficult period for me and my associates because recent events have disrupted the flow of goods in and out of the country. Business has picked up as of late, but I am most concerned with the long-term prospects and indeed for our future in this country especially after the ensuing antagonism of most Arabs against the Europeans. Already some of my acquaintances in the trade have left and others are in the process of doing so." Mr Lotas paused, looked around him to make sure he was not being overheard and leaning forward whispered, "They are mostly Jews and Copts."

Alexis thought of Joshua and his family and wondered what lay ahead for them.

"Eventually," continued Mr Lotas while leaning back on his chair, "many Europeans will be affected by the changing attitude of the Nasser administration. Already new laws have been drafted in order to ensure that Arabs are absorbed in businesses run by the expatriate communities which can only mean that in the long run the owners will lose control."

"Do you mean nationalisation?" asked Yanis.

"Not quite," replied his father confidently. He lit a large cigar, puffed away some undulating smoke causing a visible suspension of particles to ebb and while looking at this contaminated stream of air receding from him continued, "I believe there will be some nationalisation. Well, after seizing the Canal one can nationalise pretty much everything else, but in the cases I just mentioned there will be the slow but systematic infiltration of Egyptians into private enterprises with the view of eventually acquiring the skill to run such businesses by themselves and hence oust their European owners or bosses. Some stand to lose everything as they have invested all their capital into their businesses and other ventures. It is very sad."

"It is rumoured that many Europeans have already transferred most of their wealth to Swiss banks and others are in the process of doing so," uttered Alexis innocently.

Mr Lotas was clearly taken aback by such a blunt statement, especially coming from a youngster. How dare such a youth refer to a practice that was widely being used by most well-off expatriates, including himself. However, his annoyance was short-lived. He quickly regained his composure and, addressing Alexis, stayed clear of Swiss banks and money transfers.

"Well, I daresay some may have done. This whole business will be bad for Egypt; they simply do not have the experience and knowhow to run their own country. The foreigners have run their economy for centuries and wishing to change the status quo overnight is simply not on. The economy will grind to a halt and they will have to seek assistance from other countries, notably the Soviet Union."

The young Arab waiter brought the food and Alexis watched him closely as he served the party in turn. What future lay ahead for this young man now that years of expatriate exploitation was on the wane, precipitating its imminent collapse?

The conversation switched from topic to topic but kept in part reverting back to Pavlos' trip to England. After they finished their meal, Yanis and his father drove straight back to Alexandria while the two brothers strolled through the various streets of Port Said.

"Beautiful watches for effendi," shouted a street vendor attired in his cotton *gallabiyah* and bearing a striking red *tarbush*. He stood behind the brothers holding a large tray with a variety of watches. One or two looked quite pricey.

"Let's ignore him," uttered Alexis, but Pavlos was keen to buy a new watch as he wore a battered old one that was losing minutes as fast as they ticked away. He stepped forward and scrutinised some of the watches but could not make up his mind. The vendor then produced another one from a hidden pocket of his long dress and said,

"This one is a special one, 18 carats effendi. For you only five pounds. It costs at least 50 in the shops."

"It is obviously stolen," whispered Pavlos to Alexis while examining the watch closely. Then suddenly he gave the watch back and said, "Five pounds is too much," and started walking away followed by a bewildered Alexis who had never before seen his brother haggle for anything. The vendor followed them and smilingly said, "For you, effendi, four pounds, but that is my final offer."

Pavlos, who thought he had struck a bargain, bought it without hesitation. "You will not regret it, effendi," replied a happy vendor as he pocketed the money and vanished to the back streets. Pavlos put his new watch on and gave the old one to Alexis to dispose of. They went to the hotel, rested for a while, and went for another walk to kill a few more hours as the liner was due to depart at midnight.

All of a sudden Pavlos screamed, "Heck, my new watch has stopped." He took it off shaking it with some force. After several minutes of trying to force it to go his disappointment turned into anger.

"Just let me lay my hands on that bastard. I will blow his head off," said Pavlos defiantly.

"Let us first have the watch examined before you make a fuss," uttered Alexis trying to pacify his elder brother. "It might be something simple that can be easily fixed." They proceeded to look for a jeweller's shop and finding one went straight in and asked for the watch to be examined. After less than a minute the shop assistant confirmed that the watch was a fake and that it was not even worth a few piastres let alone the four hundred piastres Pavlos had paid for it.

Pavlos was furious and as soon as they left the shop was hell bent on finding the street vendor. But where could they start their search?

"He must be somewhere nearby. You saw the number of watches he had for sale. Let us go back to where we met him."

They hurried back to the main street of Port Said and looked around but could not find anybody resembling the Arab vendor. Pavlos was very pensive, trying to focus his mind on the task ahead while Alexis treated the whole thing much more lightly, convinced that Pavlos had lost the plot but prepared to stick it out.

"Now, first let us turn left into that side street," said Pavlos with conviction. "Follow me." Pavlos started walking towards the side street hotly pursued by an amused Alexis who was becoming concerned that Pavlos was prepared to devote every remaining second on African soil tracking down the rogue vendor. Pavlos walked down the side street which ended in a tee junction. He lingered, looked left, then right, then left again, not really knowing which route to follow. As by instinct he turned left and strode along the narrow street which in turn gave way to a small square adorned with a number of fruit and vegetable stalls along its perimeter. There were two roads leading off either side of the square. Pavlos paced up and down, back and forth glancing at the shops and then looked around for some clue or divine inspiration to guide him.

"We have lost him," uttered Alexis, "and unless we are very careful, we shall lose ourselves too in these strange surroundings."

"Let me think," replied Pavlos, "there is still time. Let us go this way." The two brothers followed the right turn which led to another major street parallel to the street where they started and pressed on. They searched thoroughly the area and finally returned to the spot where the vendor first met them. It was in vain as they evidently had lost him.

"We are going around and round in circles," uttered Alexis impatiently, knowing fully well that it was a hopeless task. Pavlos, however, was persistent.

"Let us return to the little square and take the other street," he said as they approached the same tee junction. They did so and finally reached a busy road leading to a road junction. In the corner sat an aged Arab on a low stool staring abstractly on his shoe-shine box. Pavlos, contemplating his next move, stepped toward the old man and placed his right shoe on his shoe-box. The old man started mechanically to apply some polish.

"We were here a moment ago – we came from the opposite direction, remember?" said Alexis moodily.

"Are you looking for something?" asked the old man in Arabic.

"Have you seen a street vendor with a white *gallabiyah* and a red *tarbush* passing through here?" asked Pavlos.

"Why do you want him?" asked the old man.

"He sold me a fake watch for four pounds and it is worthless," replied Pavlos angrily. The Arab remained silent for a moment while polishing Pavlos' second shoe. Then without looking at the two brothers he said, "That will be two piastres, effendi". As Pavlos gave him the coins the Arab stood up, amassed his shoebox and brush, placed them in his frail box, picked it up and said in a low voice as he left:

"You might care to look in the café opposite."

The boys were astonished at their luck. Pavlos turned and scrutinised the café. It comprised a square room, but the clientele could not be discerned from such a distance. The two brothers approached the entrance and saw a few tables and chairs placed randomly in this room. At one table sat the very Arab with the red *tarbush* sipping his *narguileh* and chatting to his mates. All the tables were occupied. Pavlos' face lit up with great satisfaction, eyes gleaming with revenge while Alexis froze with fright at the prospect of such an encounter.

"You cannot go in there," uttered Alexis, who was petrified at the sight of such a bunch of hostile Arabs.

"Want a bet?" replied Pavlos defiantly.

"Pavlos, be sensible – let us forget the whole affair. They will lynch you if you step in and start accusing him..." pleaded Alexis.

"Follow me and witness for yourself," replied Pavlos and stepped inside heading straight in the direction of the Arab.

Deathly silence ensued as Pavlos stepped in while his terrified brother was caught in two minds. Was he to follow him or was he to go and call for help? There was precious little time to make up his mind. "Brother, give me a break," he whispered to himself as he followed his brother. The action was irreversible: they had to face the music.

"That watch is a fake!" shouted Pavlos, defiantly pointing his hand towards the watch.

The Arab showed a moment's hesitation not knowing how to react.

"Come with me to the Police Station," Pavlos continued, facing squarely toward the Arab. Some of the Arabs in the café flinched on hearing the word 'Police', there being a noticeable concern on their faces. Alexis stood by his brother hoping for a miracle.

"Give him back the money!" shouted another Arab to the *tarbushed* guy. "Give him the money back and let him go," others repeated.

As if Alexis' prayers had been answered the Arab produced the four pounds from his inner pocket and took the watch back. Pavlos took the money and resorted to a lecture of morals and ethics.

"This is not the way to treat visitors to your city..."

However, he did not finish the sentence as Alexis dragged him out of the café. Pavlos was still muttering to himself as they left the area and spent the remainder of the evening chatting excitedly about the evening's episode. Alexis expressed his admiration for his brother's daring attitude which was the antithesis of his own phlegmatic character while his brother was justifiably brimming with pride. As the departure time of the liner drew nearer Pavlos was getting very excited while Alexis felt sad at separating from his brother. Deep down however he was happy at the prospect of his brother's start of a new life in cosmopolitan London.

"See you in London after you finish school," said Pavlos, kissing his brother, and headed towards the customs. Alexis soon lost sight of him but stayed there for a few moments staring alternately at the customs entrance and the huge liner. The quayside was heaving with relatives exchanging presents and delicacies while bidding farewell to their loved ones on that calm, moonless and warm night.

Sleep did not come easily to Alexis that evening and even when it did he remained restless. He dreamt of being mixed up in Port Said's underworld and kept seeing apparitions of the Arab with the red *tarbush* while the gold watches gleamed in the surrounding darkness – he and his brother were arrested by the police and his parents had to travel to Port Said to bail them out. What a relief it was when he woke up and realised that it was all a nightmare, no doubt triggered by the intense emotions he had experienced the previous day. Pavlos had departed blissfully unaware of Alexis' trauma who hurriedly proceeded to the station to catch the train back to Alexandria. The two-hundred-odd-kilometre journey was uneventful and as the train approached the outskirts of Alexandria and trundled on to the platform Alexis jotted down in his notepad a few lines which read:

Dear pristine Alexandria
I wish you were eternal
Tell me about Nina
Even though it may be final

Alexis stepped out at Sidi Gaber station and sauntered towards the tram terminus.

15

Alexandria, May – June 1957

Although Alexis and his immediate entourage were following the science stream at Averofeio School, their curriculum included options in art subjects such as history, geography and the classics. Alexis' abhorrence of Ancient Greek stemmed from the very first lesson he attended, purportedly to learn the various dialects and idioms of the language of his forefathers. Most of his schoolmates shared a similar dislike for the ancient language but curiously they all looked forward to the twice-weekly lessons. This was readily explained when one got to know the classics teacher, the inimitable Mr Pateras, a middle-aged gentleman, receding at the temples, slim and with a characteristic swagger. He was a graduate from the University in Athens but had also spent some time at the Sorbonne, carrying out some further studies in Greek literature. He was confident, known for his wit, erudition and unusual teaching methods which distinguished him from the rank-and-file teachers at the school. He divided his teaching between the Averofeio School and the University of Cairo where he taught classics to degree-level undergraduates.

Despite his immense knowledge of the subject, as he could recount parts of the epic poems of Homer's

Iliad and *Odyssey* extempore, his failure as a teacher in the conventional sense was indisputable. He was a born orator or indeed storyteller, not a teacher. He treated his pupils as university undergraduates having a carefree attitude to conventional teaching which was diametrically opposite to the pedantic Headmaster who ruled with an iron fist and succeeded in frightening the life out of most pupils. Mr Pateras' laxity in his teaching methods resulted in his pupils not appreciating the complexities of grammar or intricacies of syntax relating to the ancient language. It was left to the resourcefulness of the pupils to find out for themselves the set of rules that govern the usage of Ancient Greek and the study of the sentences and their structure. Mr Pateras shied away from the task of teaching Ancient Greek and instead entered his fanciful little cosmos by describing his time in Paris and the exciting times he had experienced in the metropolis while researching at the Sorbonne. His storytelling was breath-taking and awe-inspiring. A recurring theme was related to stories connected to dreams and the subconscious. Was Mr Pateras psychoanalysing his young listeners by observing their reactions to his constant but equivocal bewitchery, thought Mary Mani, who was kept fully aware of the teacher's eccentricities by her son? The pupils were transfixed listening to the stories which he ensured would be most exciting by ending in a sentence such as, "and the door opened and what did he observe..." and of course that coincided with the bell signalling the end of the lesson. The pupils were left with the impression that during the next lesson the intrigue behind 'the opening of the door' would be revealed – but, alas, it never was. A new tale ensued, only to culminate in more intrigue and innuendo. Although his teaching methods could quite justifiably be criticised, Mary Mani came to condone his actions in that one could consider his modus operandi as a lesson in life as it existed outside school and complemented the routine lessons that the pupils were subjected to by the rest of the teachers.

It was therefore no surprise that the pupils in Alexis' class relished the thought of spending an hour in the unpredictable moods of Mr Pateras. However, a particular lesson had special significance as the teacher had to set each pupil's semi-semester marks. This was an important task as the marks formed part of the aggregate mark at the end of the year and as such could make all the difference between a good and a mediocre performance.

Mr Pateras had already allocated marks to a number of pupils. As he turned the page of his enormous brown mark-book he came across the next pupil.

"Petros Kalos," he said without looking at the pupil.

Alexis' closest friend, pale-faced and clearly very nervous, stood up, looked at the teacher and waited for his mark with trepidation.

"Let us see now," said the teacher. "I have recorded a mark of 14 and that should stand," he concluded. As the marks were allocated out of 20, that was a good mark, so Petros sighed with relief and glanced at the Prefect whose comments and suggestions Mr Pateras often consulted. The Prefect's facial expression signalled to Petros that all was well and he sat down. Soon it was Alexis' turn.

"Alas, I haven't as yet set a mark for you Mani," said the teacher. "What sort of mark do you think I should award you?"

Alexis, who treated such a procedure with a measure of youthful arrogance, mixed with some scorn, replied that he did not know, implying that it was the teacher's headache and not his. Mr Pateras was clearly annoyed that this student chose not to participate in his charade.

"Judging by past performances I think the mark for you should be eight," went on the teacher.

Alexis without flinching continued to look at Mr Pateras and did not respond. Such a low mark, in fact below the pass mark, had been chosen in order to study Alexis' reaction, which to the teacher's consternation was not forthcoming. A psychological game was in progress between Mr Pateras and Alexis, viewed with relish by the other pupils. The Prefect sensing the ensuing deadlock decided it was time to intervene and said, "Sir, there are extenuating circumstances."

The teacher raised his head from the brown markbook and looking at the Prefect through his small metal rimmed glasses said, "Well, I am all ears." Clearly the teacher's countenance revealed a measure of satisfaction by the intervention of the Prefect as student participation was essential for a successful outcome.

"Well, Sir, he excels in a particular sport," replied the Prefect.

"Mm, I see, do enlighten us," he asked without showing any signs that there was room for negotiation.

"He is by far the best basketball player of his generation. He plays for the first team at the private Hellenic club, Ibrahimieh, having been spotted while playing for the junior team, and was elevated to the top team thus bypassing two other teams. This is unprecedented," concluded the Prefect.

"Mm," murmured Mr Pateras and pondered for a while before adding, "perhaps a mark of 11 may be more appropriate."

"But Sir," continued the Prefect, "he had performed exceptionally well in the recent champions final between his Club in Alexandria and Zamalek, the champions of Cairo. More to the point, Sir, towards the end of the match he managed to intercept the ball and started dribbling towards the basket on the other side of the court followed by his fellow forward on his right while the guy from Zamalek who had lost possession of the ball hastily retreated trying to defend his basket area but staying close to Alexis."

"So?" went on a bewildered Mr Pateras without a hint that he understood the intricacies of that game or more to the point of what the Prefect was referring to.

"Then Sir, Alexis did an extraordinary manoeuvre while holding the ball. He stopped dribbling near the free shot area, jumped up while turning and faced his mate on his right. His mate, together with Zamalek's defender and practically every one of the 10,000 or so spectators thought that the only option left to Alexis was to pass the ball to his mate before landing, so the defender stopped chasing him, left him in mid-air so to speak and closed in on the other attacker. However, to the astonishment of all present, Sir, Alexis continued to rotate and carried out a 360-degree pirouette in the air, ending up on the surface facing the basket and with two further steps guided the ball gracefully into the basket for two most valuable points." Those pupils in the class who had gone to the match and witnessed this spectacular sequence of events nodded in agreement while all the other pupils looked open-mouthed at Alexis in admiration. "The spectators, friends or foe," continued the Prefect, "leapt up and burst into tumultuous applause. Even Zamalek's players on the court clapped in disbelief at what they had just witnessed. The newspapers the following day hailed Alexis as the most exciting prospect in men's basketball for a generation."

The teacher's countenance shone, clearly revealing a measure of satisfaction that his farcical way of awarding marks for Ancient Greek was being played by his class.

"Let us also not forget," continued the Prefect, "that Alexis is the heart and soul of Group Three at the Boy Scouts and is very helpful to some of the younger scouts."

"I see. All this sounds quite impressive, young

Mani," replied the teacher with a grin. "Such a talent warrants an overall mark of 13."

Alexis smiled at the Prefect, murmured a reluctant 'thank you' and sat down.

Such machinations, however unfair and inappropriate, had to be endured and indeed played at by the pupils of Mr Pateras' Ancient Greek class. Surprisingly, and despite the irrationality of such a procedure, the marks were in broad agreement with marks that the pupils received for other subjects. There was one occasion, however, that irked Mr Pateras for a considerable time after he had introduced such a ludicrous scheme. This involved awarding a ridiculously low mark, that of seven, to a pupil who readily argued vehemently with Mr Pateras' outrageous assertions on a specific issue and stood his ground. Unbeknown to Mr Pateras the pupil concerned was at the top of the class and when his final report came out there was quite an embarrassment as the mark for Ancient Greek stood out like a sore thumb compared to the 18/20 marks the pupil was awarded in all other subjects. Mr Pateras was furious for not having been warned of his monumental blunder and subsequently encouraged student participation especially from the elected Prefect.

The bell sounded the end of the lessons for the day. A new system had just been introduced of having lessons from eight o'clock in the morning until two o' clock which proved very popular as it ensured a long and welcomed break during the afternoon. The pupils flocked towards the tramway at Shatby and waited on the platform. As soon as a tram stopped, they made a dash for the entrance to the carriages, causing a mild commotion while embarking as queueing was not something they were taught to observe. Alexis and his mates were standing near a short wall opposite the platform destined for trams heading east. They observed the comings and goings with characteristic casualness. Petros seemed very excited.

"There she is," he whispered to the others.

"Who?" replied Alexis.

"Rea."

"Oh yes I see," retorted Alexis who saw Rea walking towards them chatting to Irini and Myrto. Petros had singled out Rea who was Tasos' cousin and whose family apartment he was able to share when he arrived from South Africa. She was short and rather stocky with long black hair falling down her back, well beyond her well-proportioned shoulders. As the girls passed by Alexis' group, she gave them a wry smile and proceeded towards the platform. Petros smiled back while Tasos as soon as he saw his cousin followed her having heard Petros' remark and smiled. As they were both going back home, Tasos decided to accompany his cousin back to Camp de César.

"We must make sure we stay in contact during the summer and arrange a few outings," went on Petros who longed for the end of the exams and the beginning of the summer vacation. Alexis was ready to respond to

Petros' remark when he heard Yanis' addressing them.

"After the exams are over, we have to play the final of the tennis league against the British Boys' School at the Sporting Club. They too are undefeated and therefore it will be the decider. I hear they have a player equivalent to a county player in England."

"I feel the tension already," butted in Alexis who was the second-best player after Yanis at the Averofeio. "Is the match to be held at the Sporting Club?"

"I think so," replied Yanis.

"Will there be many attending the match?" asked Petros and on realising that there were very few who promised to go he took it upon himself to galvanise some support. Addressing Christos, he said:

"The Sporting Club is not far from where you live so we can use your home as a base for meeting just before the match." Finally, the whole gang were persuaded to attend which pleased Petros in that somehow he had achieved keeping the group together, at least as the summer months began before family arrangements took priority over all other activities.

"I bet Yeorgis will be there supporting his school," said Alexis. "I will make sure that Panos and his pals from Victoria college come too even though his school lost the semi-finals rubber."

The tramway station was by now practically empty. Alexis and his mates stepped forward towards the platform and embarked on the next tram that drew in. As it pulled away, Alexis stood on the open-air platform at the rear and glanced at the receding façade of the imposing school. How peaceful it all seemed that sun-soaked afternoon compared to the daily chaos following the school's gong.

With the exams over, the youngsters looked forward to the much-anticipated tennis final against the British Boys' School. The Sporting Club occupied a magnificent setting in Alexandria's suburbia. Founded in 1890, it is the oldest racecourse in Africa and held flat as well as jump racing throughout the year. Its green racecourse amidst the barren desert-like landscape of the surrounding area gave notoriety and loftiness very much longed for by would-be members. Membership was usually achieved by recommendation and a payment of an annual subscription of 100 Egyptian pounds, a sum which most middle-income European families would not be able to afford and thus increased its exclusivity. Apart from enjoying the races, the Club offered other recreational activities such as basketball, an array of well-maintained clay tennis courts and a large swimming pool.

The match was in progress with Alexis and Yanis representing the Averofeio School while the British Boys' School featured the notorious Toni who was the outstanding player Yanis had alluded to. Having lost the first set, Yanis, who was the senior player, kept advising Alexis on tactics, such as concentrating on Toni's partner who was the weaker of the two. The tactic worked well as the Greek boys wiped out their early deficit of two one games down and finally squared the match.

The young spectators, although clapping at the occasional good shot, paid scant attention to the match. Petros and Rea were sitting a little further from the group chatting and giggling away while occasionally glancing at some close rallies. Nina and Myrto were chatting nineteen to the dozen, almost certainly discussing plans to continue visiting Myrto's cabin at Montazah throughout the summer. Yeorgis sat next to his mates from the British Boys' School supporting his team while Panos attained a neutral stance and clapped winning shots from both teams.

Michalis and Tasos were discussing with Christos and Thanos what they would do after graduation. Michalis and Tasos would take their final exams the following June and Michalis having taken part in many school theatre productions, and was instrumental in forming a young dramatic society, fancied himself as an actor and contemplated a career on stage. Given that Alexandria did not offer any serious training in this area it was mooted that London's RADA or a similar academy in Athens offered better opportunities. His well-off parents disapproved of his acting aspirations and had other hopes for their son, such as encouraging him to join the family's import-export business. Tasos, persuaded by Michalis, was beginning to show an interest in taking part in school plays but this was more due to convenience than a desire or ability to act.

Thanos had already explained that because of the

close ties of Victoria College with many institutions of higher education in Great Britain, he had applied and was offered a provisional place at Pembroke College, Cambridge to read Theology. The subject matter was not a surprise as his father was the Averofeio's teacher in religious studies. Ismail, who was ostensibly watching the match, was sitting next to the boys and was able to listen to these exchanges. Ismail had recovered, and except for mostly hidden scars, seemed fine.

"Why not attend Farouk University you guys?" he said and went on to stress that he was attending classes there and that it had a good reputation for most disciplines so would they contemplate staying in Alexandria?

The youngsters looked at each other. Ismail had asked an innocent but penetrating question that required a delicate answer. Ever since King Farouk's abdication and especially after last year's war with Israel there was uncertainty as to where the future lay for the expatriate communities in Egypt and although there was no immediate danger or possibility of expulsion, most of the people reflected as to where they might end up should the situation in their adopted country take a turn for the worse. It was evident that Thanos, with his Victoria School connection, Alexis, prompted by his brother settling in London and Michalis' aspirations for the theatre, possibly enrolling at RADA, had mapped out a firm future for themselves. Great uncertainty faced other contemporaries to Alexis and his pals whose future direction after school was insecure. They may have to follow Ismail's suggestion and join Farouk University or find employment in Alexandria.

Christos explained that in two years after graduating he hoped to enter the University in Athens and went on, "Alas, I shall have to sit an entrance examination as the Certificate from our School is not fully recognised. Apparently many more apply every year than there are places available, hence some method of deciding who is admitted is essential. But I do not preclude starting at Farouk University if the circumstances require it." The situation with Tasos was quite different from the other three. He turned to Ismail and said:

"I have no roots in Alexandria so apart from the friends I have made since I arrived last year there is very little to keep me here after graduating next June. Alexandria is a temporary home, albeit a very nice one," he said, glancing in Nina's direction and went on, "it is where I was sent by my dad as the Greek School in Johannesburg was no match against the Averofeio."

"Fair enough," replied Ismail.

The others muttered half-baked answers to Ismail's question and while Ismail shrugged his shoulders in bewilderment they swiftly moved to other subjects.

Alas, the pair representing the British Boys' School got their act together and won the final set quite easily. After brief speeches by the Captains and the presentation of the trophy, Alexis suggested they go for a dip by the sandy beach at Sporting. Most of the boys thought it a grand idea and convinced the reluctant girls to join in.

They crossed the tram tracks, passed by Christos' apartment block, reached the Corniche and descended on to the beach. The boys without hesitation stripped to their trunks and plunged into the warm waters of the Mediterranean while watched by the girls who preferred to sit by the shore and gossip about this and that. Ismail's livid scars went uncommented on, as he entered the water, and he seemed oblivious to any impact seeing them may have had on his friends.

They had a great time, diving from the little springboard, splashing each other and seeming liberated from thoughts of the rigours of swotting for the exams and enjoying everything with youthful abandon. The craze was to defy the waves by diving into the heart of the mountainous volume of water coming towards them and emerging victorious in the wave's wake.

"Look out, there is a big one coming along!" shouted Thanos to his fellow swimmers while pointing at the next wave. They all looked up transfixed by this seemingly mini-tsunami making its menacing way to their frail silhouettes and looked upon by the girls who were terrified at the prospect of the ensuing mêlée. One false move or misjudgement at the time of the dive downwards towards the heart of the incoming wave and the swirling breaker would carry the unfortunate youngster tumbling up and down in its cyclonic eddies as the wave reached the shallows. Some dived expertly, some were panic-stricken and bore the consequences and some were able to ride the wave if caught just at the correct time. Having dried their bathing costumes in the warm atmosphere they adjourned at Christos' nearby apartment for some refreshment which Mrs Papas was only too pleased to provide. It was getting late in the night when they all decided to disperse and head for their respective homes. Nina's chauffeur-driven car was waiting by the front entrance while most of the others headed for the station and boarded the first tram that came along. Irini and her cousin Thanos, who lived in Rue Canope, joined Alexis and his mates on their way back to Camp de César. On arrival at her apartment block Irini bid them farewell while the boys headed for the Scouts.

"Another medal for your fine collection," said Yeorgis to Alexis. Most of Alexis' medals were for basketball so the odd one for tennis pleased him no end.

16

July 1957

The first movement of Tchaikovsky's first piano concerto was nearing its end and the whole orchestra joined the piano in a thunderous finale.

"Wow," exclaimed Alexis and went on. "When I listen to classical music, I experience feelings that are difficult to describe," he said to his mum as they sat late one afternoon in mid-July on their balcony in Rue Canope.

"I expect Rock 'n' Roll gives you an altogether different experience?" pressed his mother as she continued to read Franz Kafka's *Die Verwandlung* where the protagonist metamorphoses himself into a monstrous vermin. When months ago, his mum tried to explain the essence of this novella to Alexis he failed to understand her fascination with the author's dark fantasy and sheer lowliness.

"I should say so. Rock 'n' roll brings animal instincts to the fore. I cannot stay still for too long, feeling impelled to dance and invariably innovate to increase my repertoire of routines. On the other hand, folk and easy-listening type of music, well, makes me more romantic," he concluded blushing as he uttered the last few words.

"Mm," replied his mum without really taking in

what he had just alluded to.

Alexis disappeared into the apartment to turn the record over. He reappeared, glanced on the street below, watching a few passers-by and stared at Palestra's court where four members were playing a leisurely doubles tennis match. He regained his seat. Mary resting the book on the small table turned and faced her son.

"Have you seen Nina lately?" she asked.

"The whole gang was at the tennis final the other day and she was there with other girls from the school," he replied looking straight across the tall buildings of the Italian club to avoid his mother's inquisitive gaze.

"How is she?" she pressed on.

"OK I suppose but I didn't have an opportunity to talk to her at the Sporting Club," and as if anticipating her next question continued, "I still find her very attractive. I do not know what it is, her face with her signature fringe, her slim figure; her wholeness I suppose without really being able to pin it down to anything specific. However, I have the suspicion that she is seeing another boy from our school, so I am keeping a low profile," concluded Alexis truthfully. His mum sensing that all was not well between Nina and Alexis avoided probing any further.

Such sensitive chats were not unusual because Mary Mani wished to remain close to her son and kept abreast of developments, ready, when needed, to offer advice. Alexis welcomed his mum's closeness and found her attitude stimulating rather than intrusive. She had probed into Alexis' relations with previous girlfriends so why not at present when he showed intense interest in Nina but was reassured that so far all affections were platonic. Adolescent sexuality was playing havoc with all of Alexis' contemporaries, some of whom were able to transit into adulthood much easier than others. Some boys who were older than Alexis were involved with middle-aged and lonely women of the expatriate community, as Alexis and Petros had discovered a little while ago, whose circumstances were such that seeking a willing adolescent proved the only recourse to pleasure. Mrs Mani had already delved into Pavlos' steady relationship with his girlfriend who seemed to have progressed to an intimate liaison.

The tranquillity of Rue Canope was interrupted by the sirens of a police car as it raced by their apartment block and headed towards Ibrahimieh. Alexis stood and looked down the street catching a glimpse of the police car as it faded to the distance.

"I saw Hannah Schumann yesterday in the bazaar down below. It appears that the police are keeping a close eye on prominent Jews," said Mrs Mani.

Although the conflict with Israel had long ceased, the scars of war lingered and showed no signs of abatement. It was evident that one was witnessing the beginning of the end of a long period where the expatriates enjoyed a very comfortable life at the expense of the supressed indigenous Arab population.

"What did Hannah have to say?" asked Alexis.

"That is the point, nothing much. She couldn't stop and chat because she thought she was being followed and I guess she did not wish to put us in a spot of bother."

"You mean hiding the transmitter here?" said Alexis hastily.

"Quite," she replied. "When do you think you could take it to the Scouts?"

"Soon, I hope. I will have a word with Yeorgis," said Alexis. "We will store it with the other camping equipment. So, Joshua's fears about his family's future in Alexandria are justified?"

His mother nodded.

"Are the secret police tailing the whole family?" asked Alexis.

"I am not sure who they are tailing. Although Joshua was not directly implicated in any sabotage activity, I believe he was asked to get rid of the transmitter which no doubt was used by some for espionage during the war and being a prominent Jew the police will keep a close eye on him. There are rumours that some Jews have been rounded up. Who knows, Hannah may have been imagining being followed but one thing is for sure: we must get rid of the transmitter because sooner or later they will find out that we know the Schumann family personally."

"Don't worry, I will see to it soon," he replied reassuringly.

The anniversary of Nasser's speech was fast approaching. A turbulent year had passed that every Alexandrian expatriate or Arab would never forget. Mother and son cast their thoughts back to the long discussion with Joshua and his family and in the presence of some of his close friends to get to the bottom of the Palestinian Conundrum. There were no outward signs that the expatriate community were unduly suffering as a result of the nationalistic feeling aroused after last October's war. However, industry was starting to feel the consequences as owners of companies were obliged by law to employ an Arab as Assistant Manager or in other prominent positions, regardless of whether they were fully qualified for the job. The rationale behind such a practice was allegedly in order to gain experience and, it was claimed, to look after the interests of the Arab labour force within the company. But the owners saw it as the first step towards nationalisation and eventual takeover of the business with minimum compensation. Mary Mani related a few examples where that was already happening. She went on:

"You remember Mr Sophianos who owns the biscuit factory?" Alexis nodded and she continued. "I met his son a few days ago who told me that an Arab had joined them as Assistant Production Manager, without the slightest knowhow of production techniques; but alas Mr Sophianos had no power whatsoever to stop such an appointment."

"During the next few years, we will witness a steady repatriation of the expatriate communities as the Arabs gain more control not only of the economy but in the judicial, government posts and other sectors," said Mary Mani. "Your brother and I had a good chat about his future, and I am pleased that he finally decided to follow the advice of his friend and join him in England rather than stay here even though he had a decent job. I suspect his girlfriend will eventually meet him in England or Greece after he settles down in England. Such arrangements are happening at all levels. I know families who have travelled to Greece with the intention of settling there for good although officially they were supposedly going for a holiday. They are simply discarding their re-entry visas and staying put. As soon as you complete your school in two years, I daresay we will leave Egypt hoping that your dad can secure another assignment abroad," concluded Mrs Mani.

The music had stopped. Mother and son remained on the balcony enjoying some refreshments in the warmth of the unfolding evening. Alexis was pondering about his ancestry and ethnicity as he knew that both his parents' families originated from different backgrounds in culture, customs and language.

"Why did our families, I mean yours and dad's, come to Egypt in the first place?" asked Alexis after some further reflection.

It was the first time that Alexis had delved seriously into the origins of his ancestry. The recent war had disturbed the serenity with which he viewed his own presence in Africa and the calmness of his existence. Egypt was the only home he knew but at his fathers' insistence he went to Greek schools. He was born in Cairo and had attended the Ambetios School until the age of eight when the family moved to Alexandria, that mercurial city of memories that had seduced so many travellers and writers in the past, where he was spending his adolescent years and where he had truly fallen in love, or so he thought. He had fond recollections of his two years at Davarakios School near the tram terminus at Ibrahimieh prior to joining his present School at Averofeio. Massive change lay ahead. The prospect of leaving Alexandria for good had disturbed him. Within the span of a few years his carefree and happy life in this city would end and vivid recollections of his adolescence would follow him to distant lands. Her reply required careful consideration.

"In the past," started his mum in a voice which betrayed her desire to be truthful but fair, "people who were dissatisfied with living conditions in their native lands looked elsewhere for new horizons, new prospects to build a new and better life. The obvious places at that time were the underdeveloped countries where hard work and determination would assure success. Emigration to such places led to the emergence of distinct communities which over a fairly short time became much more affluent compared to the suppressed, and to a large extent poorly educated, indigenous population. Years of detached coexistence cultivated the roots of a proud expatriate community surrounded by an inferior native populace. Nevertheless, such parochial expatriate communities kept some ties with their countries of origin. They enjoyed a reasonably high standard of living and developed a progressive educational system which was based on private tuition. Many of these early settlers, having started from scratch, were successful in building large businesses, held key positions which secured their complete dominance over the powerless and often leaderless majority. My father originated from Southern Greece and your dad's father came from Asia Minor via Cyprus. Prompted by cousins and other family ties who had emigrated earlier they decided that the opportunities here in Egypt were far greater than they would have been had they remained behind, assuming of course that they were allowed to do so. After the First World War there was a systematic expulsion of the Greek population who had lived in Anatolia by the Ottoman Turks and there are reports that several hundred thousand Greeks, Armenians and other races were forcibly expelled, killed or massacred. Your grandfather's family realised early on, way before the Asia Minor Crisis had erupted, that their future lay elsewhere and headed for Cyprus and from there they eventually, during the 1880s, moved to Cairo. That makes us certainly part of the Diaspora associated with the countries of the Levant."

Alexis was holding on to every word that his mother was relating. He and his family were not alone facing eventual uprooting putting an end to decades of a privileged existence. Most of his friends' families faced the same dilemma. Could they all afford to uproot and head from whence they had come? Could mother countries welcome them back with open arms particularly as years of living apart forged an uneasy distrust with those who left to seek a life elsewhere? Could they go to another country, such as Rhodesia or Southern Africa, where history would repeat itself and settle as foreigners only to start all over again?"

"Was it a mistake for our forefathers to uproot themselves and settle here?" asked Alexis tentatively.

"Hindsight is a great virtue," continued his mother. "If only one could predict the future we would all have been much wiser. At the time that they settled here there were many other places where expatriate communities had been established and flourished. As you have learned at school there is a long tradition of Greeks in Egypt..."

"Alexander the Great and the Ptolemaic dynasty," butted in Alexis.

"Exactly, and let us not forget of course Herodotus many centuries before them, but even after that early period the Greeks continued to live in Egypt and exert strong influence during the Medieval and Ottoman periods where many politicians of Greek ancestry ruled over parts of the Ottoman Empire which included Egypt. When your grandfathers came to Cairo around the end of last century there was already a well-established Greek community dating from the middle of the 19th century. Those settlers encouraged emigration from mainland Greece, and particularly from Crete and Asia

Minor, to come and settle in Cairo. So, to answer your question directly, it was not a mistake because, at that time, Egypt was largely a feudal country with a large portion of its uneducated population being fellahins who were farmers working as agricultural labourers. In fact, it was some enterprising Greeks who established the cotton and tobacco fields in the Nile Delta and Upper Egypt where these fellahins found work. Coupled with feeble leadership and puppet rulers during the dying days of the Ottoman Empire, Egypt was a fertile country where these settlers, not just Greeks, but Armenians, Italians, Jews, would make their home. It was a land of opportunity which looked very attractive."

"I see now why so many foreign nationalities came to live here," said Alexis who was beginning to grasp the reasons for the influx of so many different sets of peoples into Egypt.

"But of course," continued his mother, "some one hundred years after the Greeks established their flourishing community in Cairo, and of course subsequently here in Alexandria and in other parts of Egypt, we now have the emergence of a powerful, and by all accounts a charismatic, leader whose first task seems to be to redress the balance and seek social justice and equality for the indigenous Arabs forcing many expatriates, Greek and others, to think carefully about their future."

The bell of their apartment rang interrupting Mrs Mani's deliberation.

"That must be Petros. We thought we would continue with our German lessons," said Alexis, and on his way to open the door, turned the gramophone's volume way down. A couple of years ago the two youngsters had decided to teach themselves German to the whole-hearted approval of Mary Mani who curiously enough had not instigated it. It was his mother's library which contained many books in German that had prompted Alexis to learn his mum's mother tongue. They bought a little book of the series, *La Methode Quotidienne "Assimil"* entitled, *L'Allmand Sans Peine* which taught German through French which helped to improve that language too.

Alexis came in with Petros and after exchanging greetings Mrs Mani pointed to an empty chair by her for Petros.

"How is your German coming along?" she asked the young man.

"I haven't done any for a couple of months due to our school exams, but we have covered quite a bit over the past year."

Petros handed her the little book and she leafed through its pages. She handed it back to Petros and went on. "Judging by how much you have covered thus far it may be a good idea to start reading a book in German. You will need a dictionary of course but progressively less so." As the boys showed keen interest in the idea she went inside and fetched a large brown book from the tall bookcase in the lounge and handed it to Petros.

"*El Hakim. Roman aus dem Heutigen Ägypten*, written by John Kittle," whispered Petros.

"A novel," exclaimed Alexis as he was filled with excitement at the prospect of reading his first German novel in its original language. On the first page there was an inscription by Alexis' mother dedicating the book to her mother, Gilda, for her birthday citing *Unserer lieben muti zum geburstag. Cairo den 14/7/1937*. Alexis glanced at his mother who was thoughtful.

"Shall I read aloud the first chapter and translate it as we go along?" said Mrs Mani. The boys agreed.

"Mein Freund, verweile und *höre mir zu: Ich will dir mein Leben* erzählen. Ich, der yunge Kopte Ibrahim aus Assiut in Oberägypten..." she started in a monotone. Her German sounded so natural showing no hesitancy as she effortlessly read the text. The youngsters listened to her hardly believing that a foreign language could be read so beautifully. The first couple of paragraphs were self-explanatory, hardly needing any translation, however, as the chapter progressed, the boys came across more and more unknown words which Mrs Mani paused and translated. They made copious notes, consulted the dictionary and went on listening to Mary Mani who related the story of a young Copt, Ibrahim, from Assiut in Upper Egypt.

The time passed quickly. Mrs Mani read the last sentence of the chapter.

"There we call a halt for now. Keep your notes with the book so that you can refer to some of the translations," she said and handed the book back to Alexis.

"A novel, mm," murmured Petros to himself. He

opened the relevant page in Nelson's dictionary where some pages were partly torn or dishevelled, evidence of its continuous usage by Alexis' mum, and read: "Novel: a story made up or founded on fact to show the working of human passions." He stopped and looked at Mrs Mani for inspiration.

"Oh, that is one way of defining it." She paused to collect her thoughts and continued. "Another would be a fictitious prose narrative portraying characters and actions in a continuous plot."

They continued to discuss the essence of novels with Mrs Mani making most of the comments while the two youngsters listened attentively.

"Let us have something to drink," said Mrs Mani as she disappeared inside the apartment and reappeared at the window of the kitchen facing the balcony.

"Refreshments and some pastries?" she asked. The youngsters nodded. The sun slowly disappeared below the horizon, setting in the twilight in an otherwise cloudless sky. After an hour and some more German the youngsters decided to stroll to the Scouts and found Panos and Yeorgis talking to Abu-Ahmet.

17

July 1957

Having promised his mum to hide the transmitter at the Scouts, Alexis decided to break the news to Yeorgis' and invited him home.

"Hi Yeorgis," said Mrs Mani as she greeted the youngster.

"Hello Mrs Mani," replied Yeorgis. Alexis' mother left them on their own knowing full well what they were about to discuss. Casting back to before Christmas when Joshua and his family visited Alexis on his birthday, the youngster turned to Yeorgis and said:

"Do you remember Joshua and his family?"

"Yes, I do," replied Yeorgis.

"I have a small favour to ask you. I wonder whether there is any room up in the loft in our Scout's hut where we keep all our camping gear."

"Room for what?" asked Yeorgis inquisitively.

"A small item, not too big, that Joshua brought here a few months ago," replied Alexis and proceeded to indicate the volume it would occupy. As Yeorgis was in charge of what was kept up in the loft, he replied that there would be room but asked:

"What is it?"

Alexis hesitated but had to tell Yeorgis as he needed

his friend's acquiescence if he was going to make use of the space available.

"A portable army transmitter," he uttered.

Yeorgis was taken completely by surprise.

"You mean a functional transmitter?" Alexis nodded. "You must be kidding?" he exclaimed.

Alexis proceeded to relate the whole saga of Joshua's visit and the transmitter.

"Up there in the loft, together with all the other camping gear it may go unnoticed," said Alexis imploringly.

"Mm, do you realise the implications if it were ever found?" went on Yeorgis anxiously.

"I know but surely it is wiser than leaving it lying around in our apartment for much longer. As the authorities follow the movements of prominent Jews they may find out of our connections with Joshua and could pay us a surprise visit. If they find the transmitter here my mum would have some explaining to do," replied Alexis.

Yeorgis pondered for a bit but quickly his adventurous and daring spirit came to the fore and to Alexis' huge relief agreed to hide the transmitter in the loft. The boys decided to transfer the transmitter that evening. Alexis went to his room and brought the portable transmitter wrapped up in a few pages from a recent issue of the *Tachidromos*, Alexandria's daily Greek newspaper. Alexis' mother joined them in the lounge.

"Alexis told you of our little problem," she said to Yeorgis.

"He has," he replied and turning to Alexis went on.

"Let us have a look at it," he asked Alexis eagerly.

Alexis unfolded the half-wrapped parcel and revealed a greenish metal box comprising two compartments. One housed the transmitter antennae bulb mounted on a pointed metal rod for easy fixing to soft, clay-like ground while the other housed the transmitter itself. Yeorgis was examining every part of the compact equipment with keen interest as he was looking forward to the pseudo-spy activity he was about to engage in with his friend.

They rewrapped the transmitter in newspaper and were ready to go.

"Apologies to get you involved in all this," Mrs Mani continued.

"Come to think of it Mrs Mani, it will be quite fun," replied Yeorgis excitedly.

"Do not treat this so lightly. It could turn out to be very dangerous," she went on.

"We are well aware of that mother," butted in Alexis. "Let us go."

The Scouts' hut lay some 400m from Alexis' apartment block. The two youngsters descended the flights of stairs, turned right onto Rue Canope and headed for the Boy Scout grounds. The parcel was tightly wound with heavy duty string which enabled the youngsters to carry it together, Yeorgis in his right hand and Alexis in his left. They walked in a slow but deliberate pace avoiding the glances of any onlookers sitting on their balconies or fellow passers-by. They turned and glanced at each other, with Alexis being the more nervous of the two. As they approached the road junction, they saw a uniformed policeman chatting to Carabet outside his shoeshine shop. Alexis froze. Yeorgis sensed Alexis' anxiety by the awkward jerk transferred to his hand from Alexis' side through the string.

"Keep walking and relax," said Yeorgis briskly. They continued and crossed the road by which time the policeman having passed Carabet's shop came face to face with the youngsters under a tall lamppost. The light shone dimly through the faces of the two friends and the policemen automatically glanced down at their parcel and said,

"As Salam Alaikum."

"Wa Alaikum Assalam," replied the youngsters smiling back, and without stopping speeding up towards the Scouts.

"I told you it would be alright," said Yeorgis to Alexis triumphantly.

"Well hold on, it is not over," replied Alexis despondently as he glanced back and saw the policemen staring at them. However, to their great relief the policemen lost interest and headed the other way. They arrived at the Scouts, headed for the hut of Group Three, unlocked it and took the wrapping off. As such it would be less conspicuous conforming to the other camping gear stored up in the loft. They hid it behind some old tents which had hardly been used for decades and were to remain so if Yeorgis had anything to do with it.

"Let us celebrate," uttered a jubilant Alexis.

They made for Abu-Ahmet's ice box and removed two bottles of Spathis lemonade.

"Good work," said Yeorgis as he raised his bottle and knocked it against his friend's.

18

Summer 1957 – April 1958

The summer was over. The youngsters were back at the Averofeio Gymnasium and the other expatriate schools. It was a particularly cold December, rare by Egyptian standards. Christmas soon passed and carried with it all the usual festivities and adolescent parties. During the following year most expatriate families contemplated whether to leave Alexandria to seek alternative homes or stay and assimilate. Days at Averofeio followed by afternoons in the Boy Scouts with sport and group gatherings consumed most of the time of the young adolescents. Ismail was by now part of Alexis' group that met at the Scout grounds and other favoured parts of Alexandria's suburbia. Alexis met with Nina and Tasos at parties and excursions, always civil to one another but realising the awkwardness of the situation; Alexis kept his distance wishing to allow time to settle their fragmented relationship. The curious aspect of this human triangle was that Nina seemed to seek both Tasos' and Alexis' attention whenever they were together at various functions. It happened on a couple of occasions when Myrto invited the group to her cabin at Montazah. For their part Tasos and Nina did not outwardly show great affection towards each other, keeping their relationship as discreet as circumstances allowed.

Irini was seeing more of the Rue Canope guys which was inevitable as they were neighbours, although her fling with Yanis seemed to still be going strong.

One evening in early April, Joshua and Hannah came to the Mani apartment. Hannah looked a bit forlorn.

"Hannah, are you alright?" asked Mary.

"I have been feeling rather tired of late and saw our doctor who has recommended that I visit a specialist clinic in Zürich."

"I am so sorry. When are you leaving?"

"As soon as I can arrange my visas and make the necessary bookings."

"We decided," continued Joshua, "that it would be prudent if Avi and Rivka go with her and stay with some friends while Hannah visits the clinic. In that way, she will have some family with her while awaiting news about her condition."

Mrs Mani turned to Joshua and asked, "What about yourself?"

"Unfortunately, I will not be able to go along as I anticipate the authorities will make it very difficult for me to leave Egypt even for a genuine reason such as this," replied Joshua.

"Pity," replied Mary and turning to Hannah continued, "I do hope whatever they find it is not too serious."

Mrs Mani went to prepare some tea while Alexis was chatting to the Schumanns about school and his aspirations for the future. She returned with a tray and placed it on a small metal-top table adorned with large number of engravings depicting life in ancient Egypt. Joshua and Hannah were sitting in two large armchairs in front of the colourful concertina room-divider.

"How about spending next Sunday on our boat?" said Hannah to Mary. "Avi and Rivka have arranged to be out with their friends so Joshua and I will be on our own relaxing at the Yachting Club."

Joshua was taken aback by Hannah's offer, but he quickly recovered his composure and butted in.

"Indeed, we would be delighted if you and Alexis could join us. The weather is supposed to be fair this time of the year."

"You have a boat?" asked Mrs Mani rather perplexed.

"Ah well, this is Joshua's new hobby. Yachting, you know," replied Hannah quickly realising that perhaps she was too hasty in issuing an invitation without first consulting her husband. "He has already spent hours modifying this or that," she went on.

"It is not new, so a number of the fixtures needed fixing to make it really seaworthy," said Joshua.

"What a lovely idea," replied Mrs Mani, "we would be delighted," and turned to Alexis who nodded. "What type is it?" she asked.

"A speed boat," replied Joshua.

"Good," exclaimed Alexis who fancied a trip on a fast boat.

That evening Mary was in a rather pensive mood. She had sensed that Joshua and Hannah were not being very truthful earlier. Her suspicion was based on the fact that the Greek Hospital, Kotzikion in Rue d'Aboukir had a very good reputation and was run by competent surgeons and nursing staff. Patients of all nationalities have been admitted in the past so Hannah would have had no problem being treated there. But, perhaps, on reflection she thought it would indeed be safer to have the opinion of specialists in Switzerland. Joshua had amassed a considerable fortune from his business activities and from inheritance so meeting the cost of flying Hannah and the children to Zürich and paying for private consultations would be no big deal.

There was another aspect which troubled Mary. His reason for not accompanying his wife to Zürich was not totally plausible as Joshua had many Arab friends in influential places in government and the judiciary so getting an exit and re-entry visa would not have been that much of a problem either. Besides Joshua's considerable fortune was his guarantee of return. There was something which did not make sense as though a sixth sense was warning her that all was not what it seemed.

Joshua and Hannah were punctual. They picked Alexis and his mum up on time and soon headed for the western part of the Corniche and in no time reached the Yachting Club. The ground floor of the impressive square edifice housed the sweeps and scull rowing boats. On the top lay a spacious veranda filled with small oblong or round tables and comfortable chairs. Joshua signed in his visitors and after a brief tour of the boathouse the party headed for the veranda.

"Guess which is our boat?" asked Hannah.

Alexis and his mum glanced down at the quayside along which lay a variety of sailing and speed boats. After a few abortive attempts at guessing, Joshua pointed out his boat which was of a fair size and anchored at the far side of the marina.

"I am off for a bit of angling," said Joshua, and addressing Alexis continued: "Come along and keep me company."

"Great," replied Alexis, while looking at his mother who nodded her approval.

"How about you two ladies?" asked Joshua.

"We will have a spot of lunch on the veranda," suggested Hannah. "The sea may be a bit rough outside the harbour which I do not really fancy," she concluded.

Joshua's boat was one of the newest models comprising an enclosed deck saloon area giving all-year usability despite adverse weather conditions with a cabin which comfortably slept four passengers. On one corner was a table with all the latest navigational aid equipment while at the opposite corner next to the cabin there was provision for on-board cooking. Joshua was explaining the functions of the various gadgets with Alexis keenly absorbing it all and asking more questions.

"How about my new angling equipment?" went on Joshua, removing a new rod from its hold and passing it to young Alexis.

"I suppose it is no good fishing in the harbour,"

murmured Alexis inquisitively.

"You will be surprised how much fish there are down below here in the harbour; however, the catch is considerably better further out so I normally anchor a kilometre or two from the shore."

Joshua and Alexis headed for the boat and the two ladies found a table, settled and ordered lunch: Mediterranean prawns, bean salad and octopus for mezes. As they chatted while gazing at the boat, a thunderous noise reached them as the boat's powerful engine was switched on. Within minutes the boat was leaving the harbour's narrow entrance with Alexis unaware that they were crossing over the area at the bottom of the sea where the remnants of Cleopatra's palace and Alexandria's old lighthouse had lain for centuries. Joshua headed for the open sea, switched off the engine and dropped anchor at just short of the 3km limit designating Egyptian territorial waters. He secured his 2m rod and reel with line on one edge and pointed Alexis to the cooler where drinks were kept. Alexis fetched two ice-cooled Cokes, handed one to Joshua and sat by him. Joshua started fishing. They felt the heat of the late April sun and resorted to wearing sunglasses and hats. Despite Hannah's fears the sea was calm only with the occasional wave from a passing ship at a distance reaching them, causing the anchored speedboat momentarily to bob several times and eventually turning it to face the shore. The Yachting Club's veranda was a speck in the distance but what impressed Alexis was the magnificent panorama of the Corniche spanning the silhouette of Alexandria's coast, a sight which he had not experienced before, with vistas of the old fort in the west and countless minarets, Christian church spires and illuminated billboards in a repeated fashion extending from west to east along the meandering coastal road. Alexandria's history with its multi-ethnic peoples was there before his eyes. Alexis' rumination was interrupted by the sound of another speedboat approaching from the east and keeping a constant distance from the shore. As the speedboat came closer Alexis perceived a machine gun and two maritime police officers on deck.

"The patrol boat," uttered Joshua and glanced at his watch, "on time," he went on. The patrol boat veered towards Joshua's boat and idled its engine when a few tens of metres away. Joshua handed the fishing rod to Alexis and went to the other side of the boat.

"Hello Mr Joshua," shouted one of the police officers.

"Hello Halil," replied Joshua as he approached the stern. "All calm today?"

"Yes, no problem. Have you caught anything?" asked the Arab.

"Early days yet, I've just started. I have my young friend here helping me," went on Joshua pointing to Alexis who waved to the Arab.

"OK I'll leave you to it, good luck."

"Thanks," replied Joshua waving at the speeding patrol boat. He regained his place and resumed the task of catching something to impress the ladies back on the veranda.

"I thought for a second that they would board our boat for an inspection," said Alexis with relief.

Joshua laughed out loud.

"Oh no, not Halil. Although there are other patrol boats, invariably I meet Halil when I am out here. He did come on board at first when we met, when I had the smaller boat, but nowadays he is friendly and very accommodating."

Meanwhile on the veranda Hannah and Mrs Mani were relaxing after lunch finishing off an *appellation d'origine contrôlée* of dry Bordeaux. Mary Mani was in her usual reflective mood.

"Is Joshua worried about your condition?"

"When I first told him he was worried, however, he has calmed down but is eager to see what the specialists in Zürich come up with," replied Hannah. Mary looked around to make sure they could not be overheard and whispered.

"Do you think you are still been followed?"

"They certainly kept us under observation for months after the war. Don't forget that initially the authorities suspected that Joshua helped some compatriots escape Egypt and kept a close eye on our movements. Matters are a bit calmer nowadays but who knows?" said Hannah while staring at the open sea in the direction of the anchored boat. "However, Joshua suspects that they will make it very difficult for us the leave the country."

"They are letting you go to Zürich?"

"Yes, but I have a good reason. They are not letting Joshua join me. They gave all sorts of excuses when he applied for a visa and refused to give him one. This is surprising despite his contacts. Fortunately, we have some funds abroad so we can meet the medical bills," she said.

"As there are so many restrictions these days in transferring money abroad, I would have thought the authorities would allow you both to travel to Zürich as you would almost certainly return to protect your assets. Surely, the authorities would not care much if the whole family left the country with just 80 Egyptian pounds each, would they?" retorted Mrs Mani.

"Well, this is the reason why Joshua bought this expensive boat. He might as well enjoy his wealth while he can. As you know the mood of many expatriates living in Alexandria has changed for the worse," said Hannah regretfully.

"I see what you mean," replied Mrs Mani.

"This boat will occupy Joshua's mind for a while until I come back by which time things may have calmed down and who knows the authorities realising that we are not connected to any covert operation may let us go to Europe for a while," concluded Hannah.

"Good afternoon Mrs Mani," said a young man approaching their table. Mrs Mani turned and saw Yanis Lotas standing at the edge of the balcony by their table.

"Hello Yanis, have you met Hannah?" she replied.

"No I haven't," replied Yanis extending his hand in greeting.

"Is Alexis about?" he asked.

"He went fishing with Joshua in his lovely new boat," she replied while turning towards the horizon without being able to spot the boat.

"I am about to have a rowing practice, so I must go and get ready."

I will tell Alexis that you are here."

"Ok, I hope to see him later. Goodbye." Yanis disappeared down a flight of steps. A little while later Joshua's boat approached the harbour with Alexis standing at the bow holding a net with their catch and waving towards the veranda. They waved back and shortly afterwards Joshua moored the boat in its usual spot.

"Alexis!" shouted Yanis from the other side of the quay. Alexis turned towards his direction and Yanis started walking towards him.

"I saw your mother a little earlier and she said you went fishing. How was it?"

"Great experience. Have a look at our catch!" replied Alexis pointing the net at Yanis.

"Looks impressive but I've never had the desire to go angling although I envy you catching a ride in that luxurious boat. By the way, Irini is organising an outing at her father's farm," said Yanis.

"When?"

"Sometime in early July after the exams."

"Good show, I'm looking forward to that outing."

"Was it a fun row or practice?" asked Alexis as Yanis made his way back to his skull.

"Hard practice," retorted Yanis. "See you tomorrow at school."

"See you," replied Alexis and joined the others on the veranda. They exchanged pleasantries, related Halil's appearance and examined the catch. Joshua ordered some snacks for the two of them and after another couple of hours Joshua dropped Alexis and his mum at Rue Canope.

Alexandria's airport was situated a few kilometres outside the city. It was tiny as it only handled a few scheduled flights per day. Hannah and her children were to board the Super Constellation aircraft of Misr Air, Egyptian's national carrier, bound for Athens, and from there she was scheduled to fly to Zürich via Swiss Air. Alexis and his mum offered to accompany Joshua and Hannah to the airport, and they all arrived with time to spare.

"Don't you worry about Joshua," said Mary to Hannah, "He will be in good hands. Make sure you rest after your arrival at Zürich."

"I will not worry about Joshua."

"You all seem to worry about me unnecessarily. I can look after myself," he pronounced emphatically.

"Misr-Air announces the departure of Flight Number 81 to Athens. Will all passengers proceed to gate number one?" announced a voice on the public-address system.

"We will say our goodbyes here," said Mrs Mani warmly embracing Hannah and their children while Alexis shook hands with all of them. Joshua followed the three passengers to the gate. Soon the Super Constellation was climbing the cloudless Alexandrian sky and disappeared well above the distant horizon.

"I am confident that nothing serious will be found," uttered Mary.

"I hope you are right," murmured Joshua as they drove back to Camp de César and dropped Alexis and his mum at their apartment.

19

May 1958

Irini's father managed a cotton farm which lay about an hour's drive south of Alexandria. One Sunday morning in May the youngsters crammed into four cars and headed towards the town of Damanhour crossing numerous cotton farms set up a century ago by prominent Greeks of the diaspora such as the Benaki and Choremi families. At the end of their journey the farm stood like an oddity amongst the vastness of the green fields. They soon split into small groups and explored the farm and its surroundings. An array of tall date trees either side of a bare clay-soil path led to the stables where Irini kept her favourite horse. Opposite the stables at a distance stood a two-storey white building where Mr Samaras stayed overnight on his frequent visits to the farm. Alexis' and Petros' Boy Scout training came in very handy assisting Mr Samara in lighting up the charcoal for the barbeque and setting up the equipment for roasting a hog for the occasion. Mrs Samara, a tall elegant lady, stayed in the background and prepared additional foods, ably assisted by the other parents who had offered to drive the youngsters to the farm. Alongside the white building lay a large veranda, strewn with chairs, large sofas and a table in one corner on which stood the latest Argosy mod-el record player playing records at 35 rpm and capable of stacking up to ten records for the continuous spewing out of tunes by the Platters, Frankie Lane or Elvis. An ad hoc picnic area was set up in front of the veranda where blankets were laid for the youngsters to relax and it formed their base from which to explore and return to after their escapades. There was hardly any wind and the temperature reached over 20 degrees centigrade.

"Come and see my Little Treasure," shouted Irini to her friends.

Little Treasure turned out to be her favourite horse which she rode every time she visited the farm. It was a brown horse adorned with a rich dark mane and had two large floppy ears. Although Irini had reassured her guests that the horse was usually fit and strong that Sunday morning the animal appeared tired and subdued owing to some arduous work it was put through the previous day and all it wished was to return to the stables.

"Does anybody want a ride?" asked Irini.

Some youngsters had a go, but it was quite obvious that the poor horse was utterly exhausted and was only interested in going back to his stables. Every time he sighted the entrance to the stable building his floppy ears stood on end and his whole body quivered with excitement and anticipation. However, as Irini wished to please her young guests she kept guiding the horse away from the stables against its wishes but to the delight of her friends. When she got to the end of the long drive, she stopped looking for a volunteer rider. She looked at

Alexis and said, "You haven't had a go?"

"He is so slow it is hardly worth the bother," he replied disinterestedly.

"If wishes were horses, beggars would ride," shouted Panos laughingly, quoting the good old Scottish proverb and nursery rhyme.

"Come on, have a go, show Panos he is wrong quoting this proverb," shouted Yeorgis. Alexis glanced at both his friends and turning to Irini he reluctantly agreed.

"OK," he said and climbed on the saddleless horse. Irini tried to move the horse but Little Treasure would not budge. He had obviously reached the end of his tether.

"Oh well," muttered Alexis looking at a disgruntled Irini. "I told you he is not interested".

"Perhaps he will go the other way," suggested Panos.

"OK, let us try," replied Irini and turned the horse round facing down the path leading to the horse's stables.

"That is better," exclaimed Alexis sensing some positive response from Little Treasure as his muscles tightened up and turning to Irini he said, "Let go of him."

"Are you sure you can manage?" she asked rather anxiously.

"Oh yes no problem, let go," he replied.

She did. Little Treasure was instantly liberated by the sight of the stables in the distance and started moving forward as though rejuvenated by divine intervention. His initial trot gave way to a canter which in turn became a gallop. Alexis was petrified. There was no saddle to grab, nor any reins with which to guide the horse. He was thrown from the near to the offside while at the same time desperately trying to regain his balance as he was jolted up and down following the horse's gallop. Meanwhile the horse was heading at an accelerated pace along the path towards the stables watched by the jubilant youngsters who urged the stallion on.

"Grab the mane!" shouted Irini to Alexis.

Alexis, after a few seconds of being galloped forcibly forward, managed to get hold of the stallion's mane and miraculously remained on the horse even though he was halfway down his off-side. The cries and shouts of the youngsters alarmed Mr Samaras who suddenly appeared on the scene and managed to slow down the horse's gallop and eventually bring it to a halt.

"I thought you said you could manage!" said Irini with a touch of irony to a shattered Alexis as he dismounted the horse. Alexis sighed with relief while ignoring her comment.

"Good show, that was a magnificent ride. Can I have a go?" exclaimed Panos showing full admiration for Alexis' dexterity in holding on and not falling off.

"Nobody else has another go. This horse is extremely tired and should be left well alone in the stables," answered a stern Mr Samaras as he led the horse away.

Lunch followed. The youngsters gathered around

Mr Samaras ready to carve the spit-roasted pig. It soon became apparent to the mesmerised onlookers that he was following a well-established procedure of carrying out such a task by first laying the pig on a table carefully covered in a cotton cloth, removing the centre rod and other supporting metallic parts and getting rid of the numerous string ties around the beast which held it together. With a large sharp knife, he chopped the head off and proceeded to apportion the remaining body in manageable circular cuts which could be easily subdivided further into small portions. The meat was eaten alongside various green and bean salads with warm pitta bread freshly baked in the farm's wood-burning balady-type oven. The combination of such a mouth-watering lunch coupled with a few cans of Stella beer made the youngsters quite lethargic as they settled down in twos and threes in various nooks and crannies for some peace and quiet.

Petros was in a bad mood. He turned to Alexis.

"After the holidays we shall have to prepare for our final exams – what a dull prospect. No parties, no outings – I do not know how I will get through all this," he said and stared ahead into the distance. Alexis looked at him and replied.

"You are being miserable again. Why don't you try and enjoy today and start thinking about the exams when the time comes?" Petros remained silent but it was obvious that he was feeling sorry for himself because Rea had not turned up today as she was not feeling very well. As if by coincidence or by desire Nina and Tasos were also absent.

By mid-afternoon the group had split up. Christos and Marika were taking a stroll with Panos and Myrto just beyond the farm while Yanis and Irini kept emerging and disappearing from the roof of the white house wishing to reassure her parents that she was close by even though they kept losing sight of her. All in all, the youngsters had a great day at Irini's farm and were quite ready to face the end of the year exams that Petros was so dreading.

With the exams over, the youngsters looked forward to another summer vacation of spending time at beaches, feeling the cool breeze on the water's edge and organising other outings. That summer was particularly hot, and inhabitants of Upper Egypt flocked to the coast to immerse themselves in the cool air at the Corniche. By mid-July, Michalis had arranged a party to say farewell to some of his close friends. All the gang was there, and as usual Marika and Alexis obliged with their latest exhibition of Rock 'n' Roll routines. Alexis went to the party with his near neighbours Irini, Petros, Yeorgis, Thanos and Panos. Ismail made his own way to the party, following a lecture at the University. Michalis and Tasos were discussing their pending trips to Athens with Thanos.

"When are you flying to Athens?" asked Thanos.

"In a couple of weeks," replied Tasos.

"Actually, early August," butted in Michalis.

"I thought you were joining RADA in London?" asked a bewildered Thanos looking at Michalis.

"First, we are flying to Athens where my parents have a flat and then after a month or so I will proceed to London," replied Michalis. Tasos approached Alexis and said:

"I am leaving for Athens in a few days and will not return to Alexandria. I am leaving a bit earlier than expected as I need to find lodgings in Athens and enrol for some lessons to prepare for the entrance exams."

"Our basketball team will miss you. It has been nice knowing you. I wish you all the best," said Alexis genuinely as they shook hands. They stared at each other as if they tried to read each other's minds. Was Tasos conveying a message to Alexis? Was he asking him to look after Nina in his absence perhaps guessing what Alexis felt for her?

"My pleasure too for having met you," declared Tasos genuinely. "I hear that you intend to go to England after school next year."

"That is the plan, so let us see how things unfold," replied Alexis.

As Tasos withdrew towards the others, Alexis glanced at Nina who had observed their parting words and continued to stare in Alexis' direction. Alexis felt a quiver down his spine. Was there an ulterior motive for why Tasos singled him out for an individual goodbye? Could it be that Tasos recognised the inevitability of the situation he was leaving behind as he was well aware of Alexis' deep feelings for Nina and that she might well hold reciprocal feelings towards Alexis? But how could Tasos have known how he felt? Perhaps Nina had discussed with him how she had met Alexis and their somewhat mercurial relationship that followed? All these mixed feelings enveloped young Alexis as he tried to find answers to his questions.

It was getting late and the group dispersed. Alexis and his close mates made their way to the Scout grounds and sat on a bench by the imposing fig tree.

"Penny for your thoughts," uttered Yeorgis.

"He is thinking about Nina again," pressed Panos.

"Now that Tasos is leaving I feel so helpless. I do not know what course to follow," replied Alexis.

"Let events take their natural course," said Petros.

"I suppose so," whispered Alexis unconvincingly and all four remained silent while gradually sinking into their private worlds.

20

Alexandria, September 1958

Before the start of the next academic year, Myrto signalled her intention to invite the youngsters to the family cabin at Montazah. Whether it was at Nina's instigation Alexis could not tell but it seemed odd that weeks after Tasos had left for Athens, another outing was arranged when Nina and Alexis would find themselves in each other's company. He reflected on the last meeting he had had with Tasos and the look he gave him. It spoke volumes.

The youngsters made their way to the resort in twos or threes. When Alexis and Yeorgis arrived at the cabin most of the youngsters had scattered about.

"Hi," said Myrto, "they have gone for a swim." Yeorgis sat on the edge of a long concrete jetty in front of the cabin.

"Alexis, would you give me a hand to set up the record player and speakers?" said Myrto. While Alexis went into the cabin, Yeorgis admired the magnificent view that lay in front of him, wondering whether King Farouk used that little jetty in the bay to leave Egypt when he was forced to abdicate by the Free Officers' coup d'état some six years ago. He was promptly reminded by Thanos that King Farouk, his wife Nariman, their children and their entourage made a dignified exit from Ras el Tin Palace at the other side of the Corniche in his luxurious royal yacht, *El Mahrousa*, and sailed to Italy, landing at the island of Capri. However, it was a beautiful spot and no doubt the royal family spent many happy relaxing times in this bay almost certainly shielded by his entourage of advisors and government officers who did not wish him to find out the extent of the brewing discontent throughout his country.

"It was about time you turned up, you two," said Yanis as he emerged from the calm waters of the bay accompanied by Irini who was by now constantly by his side.

"The traffic at the Corniche was quite slow and our bus crawled in the congestion," explained Alexis.

"Myrto," shouted Rea who was sunbathing with Petros at the other side of the jetty, "do please lend me some of that sun spray, my back is burning fiercely."

"Catch," shouted Myrto who went ahead and threw the little can down Rea's way. She caught it gracefully and started spraying herself on her exposed skin.

"Wake up!" shouted Alexis to Petros who was half-asleep near the water's edge, eyes shut and oblivious of his surroundings. Panos approached Alexis, whispered something in his ear, they chuckled, and with mischievous expressions on their faces proceeded to tip-toe towards Petros and push him in the bay. After resurfacing he mumbled something incomprehensible, got out of the water and made for Alexis. Alexis started running but soon realised that his only sanctuary was the bay's calm waters. He ran towards the cabin but Petros was catching up fast behind him, so he veered to the right where Yanis and Irini were laying down drying themselves, jumped over them and dived in the bay. Petros stopped and yelled at him quite angrily. "I will get you later, you scum."

Alexis looked around him and noticed a small square raft some 50 metres ahead anchored in the middle of the bay and started swimming towards it. He swam on his back by kicking his legs to propel himself forwards, stopped to regain his breath and, changing stroke to freestyle, continued to the raft until he was close enough to make out the silhouettes of two girls of the gang. He resumed his swim and was soon on the raft. One of the girls was Christos' girlfriend, Alexis' dancing partner, and the other was Nina.

"Hi there," said Marika to Alexis. Nina had not heard her.

"Hello," replied Alexis, "Have you been here long?"

"I have and I've had enough of the sun. I will go back as I feel a bit peckish," she replied and leapt, feet first, to swim towards the jetty.

"Are you really worshipping the sun?" said Alexis as he approached Nina.

"I did not realise that you were here," replied Nina defensively. "I must have somehow dropped off."

"I seem to remember you did not really like the sun," he pressed on.

"I do not like sunbathing for hours but I do for a bit." Alexis sat at the edge of the raft gazing ahead at the Mediterranean, splashing his feet aimlessly in the warm waters.

Alexis turned and looked at her. She wore a sky-blue bathing costume which contrasted well with her tanned, lithe body.

"It's a beautiful day," he continued. "It is so picturesque and calm here, just as you described it to me at Christos' party." Nina remained silent. Alexis laid down on the wooden raft and faced the blazing sun. Occasionally the calmness of the water surrounding the raft was disturbed by a passing speedboat creating undulating waves which bobbed the little raft, creating yo-yoing oscillations only to be dampened as the speedboat receded in the distance.

"Are you joining me?" said Alexis as he stood and got ready to dive off the raft. She turned, looked at Alexis hesitantly, and without replying stood up and dived in. Alexis watched her as she swam rhythmically away towards the opening of the bay adjoining the Mediterranean. Alexis dived after her, caught her up and they both continued in unison until they reached the entrance to the little bay. They stopped, seemingly breathless and buoyed on the salty waters facing the cloudless sky to regain their strength. They bobbed, moving their hands in the water to remain afloat, and suddenly came face to face hardly a metre apart. Words did not come easily despite the myriad of past instances that flashed through their young minds. As Tasos' departure to Athens was so recent Alexis remained silent and allowed her to break the silence.

"They will be worried about us," she said. Alexis agreed, and they swam back to the raft, climbed and lay down rather exhausted. After a few minutes Alexis heard some splatter behind the raft. He turned and to his horror he saw Petros climbing the little raft.

"Let bygones be bygones," exclaimed Alexis apologetically to a defiant Petros who was now standing next to Alexis like a heroic Roman gladiator.

"What is up?" uttered Nina, rather surprised.

"Settling a recent score," muttered Petros and then as if by a miracle he continued: "Well, I forgive you. It is my kind-hearted nature. In truth I have been sent out here to search for you two. Myrto is worried that you may be foolish enough to swim far away beyond the harbour's entrance and be swept away by the hidden current lurking in these waters never to be seen again..."

"Very poetically put," said Alexis with a hint of sarcasm.

"Everybody is having a bite to eat, and we would not want you to miss out," went on Petros as he dived and swam towards the jetty.

"Let us swim back," replied Nina to a reluctant Alexis.

After lunch Nina was sitting outside the cabin on the little wall listening to some bouzouki songs while Alexis was leaning against a tree not far from her. Most of the others had scattered in various directions exploring the Palace grounds. It was the first time that Alexis was feeling comfortable in Nina's presence without being hampered or intimidated by past events. Tasos had left for Greece and Nina didn't seem unduly sad at his recent departure.

"Are you fond of rebetico urban Greek music?" asked Alexis as the record was playing folk songs using a thrichordo type of bouzouki instrument.

"I am," responded Nina.

"Do you prefer it to European pop songs?" he went on.

"Isn't Greece part of Europe?" she retorted.

Alexis swallowed quickly realising his blunder. He looked at Nina and caught her enigmatic smile which was so disarming.

"*Touché*," he responded, acknowledging that this was not one of those times where one would attempt to wriggle out of a sticky situation.

"You know what I mean," he went on.

Nina gave him a wry smile and went on.

"I like both and of course it depends on the occasion."

"Mm," went on Alexis, "There are some songs which appeal to me enormously, those full of pathos which generate feelings of regret and sadness, such as those which may have been experienced by our forefathers under the long Turkish occupation. Somehow, they appeal to my inner self and given the right mood they also inspire me to think and ruminate, to ponder about this or that. This is not to say that I do not like the pop type, but when I am jiving with Marika to an Elvis Rock 'n' Roll my animal instincts come to the fore but afterwards I feel exhausted in contrast to feeling nostalgic as I do when I listen to urban Greek themes."

"Perhaps this proves that deep down you are more Greek than you pretend to be even though your four grandparents originated from Cyprus, Greece, Switzerland..." she hesitated.

"And Italy," he butted in.

"Yes, I see. Often in the past, you gave the impression you wished to renounce your Greekness but deep down it seems that there is a lot of Greek in you. *N'est-ce pas?*" she uttered inquisitively ending up with a little French to emphasize her point.

Nina was surreptitiously alluding to Alexis' family background which was known to many of his pals but rarely spoken about in the open. She wanted to find out more about Alexis without encroaching too much on aspects of his private life he may not have wished to discuss. She was fascinated by Alexis' idiosyncrasies, one of which was his aloofness and his delving into serious topics, an attribute not often seen in many adolescents.

"More so for you Nina, because you have attended a French elementary school, although I have only attended Greek schools from a very young age."

"Upbringing," interrupted Nina, "engulfs much more than schooling."

"True," responded Alexis and withdrew pondering where the discussion was leading.

Nina and Alexis continued to discuss very personal aspects of their young lives as though they wished to probe their respective inner feelings, grasp at mutual aspirations and come close to something that seemed unattainable. They did not allude to their fragmented relationship of the past few years, each wishing to go so far; but something prevented them reaching that undefinable invisible barrier which separated them. However, time was running out.

In the afternoon, the youngsters decided to explore the surrounding area at the back of Montazah grounds. As they left the Palace grounds they turned left and proceeded towards Mamoura beach and walked on the sandy beach in twos and threes. This was one of Alexandria's fine sandy beaches, without any commercialisation and with its clean waters brushing the sand in shallow rhythmical waves. There was a spectacular sight witnessed at dawn. As the water receded flocks of frogs would come to light only to hide again as another wave approached the shore and be absorbed by the sand.

Reaching midway along the beach, the youngsters came across a path on their right leading to cultivated fields in the distance. They followed it and soon met some fellahin working in the fields while across a little dried out stream an ageing cow was circling blindfolded around an ancient well, providing precious water, its bells clanging merrily. A mule-drawn cart trotted along the narrow path carrying fruit and vegetables.

Marika and Christos were leading the group. Although to a bystander it may have appeared that they meandered haphazardly through the fields, some partnerships had already been formed: Petros and Rea, Yanis and Irini, Panos and Myrto. They chatted, laughed, giggled or teased each other with youthful innocence and a carefree attitude.

Alexis and Nina were not walking together. She was chatting to Thanos while Alexis and Yeorgis, bringing up the rear, were discussing their respective futures. Yeorgis had confided to Alexis his wish to become a game hunter in Tanganyika, the territory in East Africa that was seized from Germany in 1916 by the Royal Navy with the help of British Indian infantry. Yeorgis had approached the British Consulate in Alexandria with the view to enquire about the possibility of settling in that country. However, Tanganyika was in the process of changing from a colony to acquiring a sovereign status and, as such, the authorities were reluctant to allow unlimited access to any foreigner who wished to emigrate. He was therefore granted a one-year visa and was looking forward to exploring its possibilities after he had completed his schooling.

Late in the afternoon, the group returned to the chalet at Montazah. Some dived in the bay's warm waters, some listened to records, while others danced or chatted endlessly away. All through the latter part of that beautiful summer's day Alexis and Nina kept in close proximity to one another. The other youngsters were aware of the situation between Tasos and Nina and were somewhat perplexed by the unfolding saga between Nina and Alexis. To their friends it was as though nothing ever happened between them and yet a myriad of things might have happened. Alexis was reticent in expressing his strong feelings to Nina so soon after Tasos had left the scene. Would she ever express her feelings to him, he pondered? In truth his hesitancy stemmed from his inability, after almost two years, to read her feelings towards him. Nina was always keen to be near Alexis although her aloofness baffled, while at the same time intrigued, Alexis. Did she enjoy the attention she was getting from Alexis particularly as he was quite well known for his sporting prowess and his company was very much sought after by other youngsters in their milieu? Did she tolerate him because of his obvious popularity and relative notoriety? He would have to wait and see how matters developed during the following year which incidentally was the last he would stay on Egyptian soil.

The group dispersed, with several of them catching the tram from Victoria station back to Camp de César. Petros was in a pensive mood.

"Did you enjoy yourself, Mani?" he asked his friend with a wry grin as they sat on two highchairs in Carabet's shoeshine shop.

"I am about to close the shop," complained the old man.

"Don't worry, we will not be long," replied Petros. Carabet withdrew to his tiny workshop at the back to continue to repair a pair of shoes he was given earlier while mumbling something in Turkish.

"Today was a good day," said Alexis.

"You seemed to get along very nicely with Nina."

"You were very observant," replied Alexis. Petros gave him an inquisitive grimace as though he implied that he understood what was going on. They sauntered off towards Rue Canope on their way to their respective homes to the relief of old Carabet.

21

Alexandria, October 1958 – Easter 1959

The final year of Alexis at the Averofeio would pass like a whirlwind. More concerts at the conservatoire, numerous parties, close-fought basketball and tennis matches and intense studies occupying the lives of the young Alexandrians amidst an unprecedented upheaval within the expatriate communities. The boys and girls organised outings and often visited en masse the cinemas downtown to see the inevitable American films.

Easter festivities were widely celebrated by the Alexandrian expatriates mainly from habit rather than deep religious beliefs. Easter weekend was eagerly awaited as most teenagers looked forward to meeting their boyfriends and girlfriends away from prying parental eyes. Worshipping God was an afterthought only observed by a selected few who had been brought up within very religious families.

Easter week bore special significance to Alexis and his Scout mates. The Greek Orthodox Church at Camp de César in the grounds of the Davarakion and Pratsikion schools had arranged with Mr Segal to assist in crowd-control by forming a central aisle within the church so that worshippers who entered the church shuffled all the way either side of that aisle toward the altar. While meandering slowly forwards towards the priest, they glanced at the sacred pictures, followed by a short prayer and taking communion. They then turned and exited through this central alley formed by the uniformed Scouts who stood tirelessly hour after hour as the crowds slowly strolled either side towards the altar.

Despite the stuffy atmosphere, Alexis enjoyed such duties as it allowed him ample time to reflect on what was going on around him and to analyse the characters of a large mass of people during their most humble and dignified action. After a few years he knew intimately every detail inside the church, its icons, sacred pictures, mosaics, the impressive chandeliers. Occasionally he joined with the choir and sang the psalms or turned towards Yeorgis and they would whisper a few flippant comments to each other. Yeorgis, however, was much more religious than any of Alexis' fellow Scouts and treated the whole procedure much more reverently.

It was Easter Friday. Businesses were officially shut on Monday after Easter and many Europeans cherished the thought of a long weekend especially as it appeared that the weather would hold its usual fineness. As Alexis had been on church duty throughout that week he was released earlier that evening. As soon as he entered his apartment he made straight for his room and took off his Scout uniform. He was changing when his mother appeared at the door.

"Was it crowded today at church?" she asked.

"Rather," he replied.

"Of course, Easter Friday is particularly busy."

"It always is."

"I was thinking," went on Mrs Mani, "it would be rather nice if we invite Joshua to spend Easter Sunday here with us and have lunch. He can tell us news about Hannah's condition. The last I heard was that she was receiving more treatment."

"Sure," replied Alexis, "that will be a great idea. I rather fancy a trip to Rushdi. I will jump on the tram and be there in a jiffy. Having spent a few hours standing in the church I need a bit of a stroll. I will surprise him."

"Alright, I will pop down to the bazaar and get some shopping."

Soon afterwards Alexis left the apartment. He reached the tram station and waited for the Victoria Line tram with its triangular insignia, as Rushdi was one station before Stanley Bay on the coastal route rather than the inland route which was served by the Bacos Line. He boarded the first Victoria Line tram and instead of going to the first-class section he climbed the little winding staircase leading to the upstairs section and sat in the open-air space at the rear. It was a bit breezy but his black woollen jumper kept him quite comfortably warm. He took a few deep breaths of fresh air. Rushdi was not far away from Glymenopoulo where Nina lived. The tram crossed Sidi Gaber station and soon reached Rushdi where Joshua lived. He left the tram, crossed the tram tracks and headed towards the coast. Just before he reached the Corniche he turned right into a narrow lane which led to a spacious site, elevated from its surroundings, where Joshua had built his impressive villa, in a style quite different from neighbouring dwellings. The bungalow was surrounded by well-maintained lawns and tall trees which added to its seclusion. Alexis stood in the middle of the lawn and glanced at the Mediterranean Sea to his left. The sea was calm and the evening sky filled by a myriad of glittering stars, while the tranquillity of the place was every now and then interrupted by a few passing cars and taxis following the winding Corniche below.

Alexis glanced at the bungalow. All the curtains were drawn and if it wasn't for an occasional faint thumping noise, the origin of which Alexis could not discern, he would have guessed that the bungalow was not occupied. The garage was locked and there was no sign of Joshua's car in its usual place opposite the front door. Alexis started walking on the paving stones leading to the main door and rang the bell. Suddenly all went very quiet: the faint noise stopped. Alexis turned towards the sea but could not see anything in the dark. With his back to the house he missed the slow movement of the front window curtains. He turned around and rang the bell again. Some minutes passed which seemed like an eternity before the front door opened and Joshua appeared. He looked tired with sweat running down his face; his youthful features had abandoned him.

"Alexis, what are you doing here?" he asked cuttingly.

Alexis was taken aback by such an obvious inhospitable greeting which was so uncharacteristic of Joshua. They stared at each other momentarily.

"My mother asked me to invite you for lunch on Easter Sunday," uttered Alexis.

"On Sunday," whispered Joshua. "Mm, well?" he hesitated and seemed indecisive. Alexis, very perplexed, stood gazing at Joshua with stupefaction.

Finally, Joshua having regained his composure said, "You have obviously sensed that something is amiss here."

Alexis nodded.

"Come in," went on Joshua and shut the door behind him. Alexis felt hot and took his jumper off. Joshua led Alexis into the spacious lounge through a narrow passage and an alcove. Alexis, on reaching the lounge, took one look at it and exclaimed:

"Wow."

The lounge was in a state of complete disarray. Alexis noticed a large metal bar on the table. Joshua picked it up and approached the other end of the lounge which was adorned by a pair of large French Empire Period gilt ground porcelain vases, delicately decorated with pictures of angels carrying musical instruments or old manuscripts. Joshua lifted the iron bar and taking a measured swing smashed one vase to pieces. A few more hits and the vase was reduced to porcelain crumbs strewn on the carpet floor. He then smashed the other vase.

"Joshua," said Alexis in a quivering voice, "what is going on?"

"Come and sit down and I will tell you what all this is about," replied Joshua.

Joshua bought two cans of imported Dutch beer and offered one to Alexis who sat in one of the remaining intact armchairs. Joshua sipped his beer, took the long iron bar from where he had left it and continued to destroy valuable paintings and precious antique ornaments.

"Why do you have to destroy such personal items?" asked a perplexed Alexis who was still oblivious of Joshua's motives.

"I cannot bear the thought of some government official acquiring these private possessions," uttered Joshua.

"I don't understand," said Alexis whose confusion and curiosity had reached its apogee. Joshua paused momentarily, turned, looked at Alexis and said:

"On Sunday, I plan to escape from Alexandria."

"Escape?" repeated Alexis, "How?"

"By boat."

Of course, the speedboat, thought Alexis; suddenly all was being unveiled.

"Surely that is dangerous."

"Extremely," replied Joshua, "but it is the only way out."

"Where will you head for?"

"Israel."

"Does Hannah know?"

"No, it is best that she does not know."

Alexis was lost for words and did not know how to react. Joshua went on.

"It has taken a long time and effort to build and furnish this villa. Hannah and I brought these vases from Shanghai, the other ornaments and everything else from our various trips abroad. Some of the paintings are rare and I acquired them while I was living in Paris." Joshua stared momentarily at a small painting which appeared to be a reproduction of a Rembrandt depicting a little boy wearing a large hat. His countenance was so real and the whole painting looked like a photograph.

"I witnessed the creation of this painting," went on Joshua. "I was living at the time in Montmartre when a friend asked me to join him for dinner. We went to a bistro nearby where a young painter with fair hair and a large mouth with a moustache was in the process of painting a little boy. The boy was attired in period clothes and what I remember most was the boy's sad face which is depicted so vividly in this picture." Joshua still looking at the picture turned to Alexis and said:

"Will you take it with you and cherish it? You will do me a great favour. It has no real value, but its sentimental value is immense. I do not have the heart to destroy it." Joshua took the picture off the wall and handed it to Alexis.

"This is very sudden," exclaimed Alexis.

"Well, with Hannah's illness looming ahead I took

the opportunity to get her and the children safely out of the country before I thought of my escape."

It was too much for Alexis to digest all this in one go. He felt awkward, as though he was going to faint. Joshua sensing this fetched some water and gave it to Alexis who gradually sipped it while staring at the smashed pieces strewn all over the floor. He regained his composure and resumed his questioning.

"Will you not be the loser as most of your money is tied up in this house?"

"Not anymore," replied Joshua with his face radiating with achievement. "After I conceived this escape I have been amassing quite a few gold bars which I bought for cash on the black market."

"Gold bars, on the black market?" said Alexis. "I don't understand."

"There is a lot of such secret trading these days as the authorities have imposed great restrictions on moving money and items freely about," explained Joshua.

"I see," uttered Alexis. "Surely the gold bars are heavy."

"Indeed, they are. I only hope the boat is still afloat," he answered smilingly. Joshua went on to explain that after he exchanged his cash for gold bars, he transferred these to the boat and had hidden them in various compartments even without the knowledge of Hannah and the children.

"It is all very sad," murmured Joshua in a low voice. "I never thought it would come to this as both Hannah and I love Alexandria and feel happy here. But I realise that this country's future lies in the hands of the Arabs and not us, the expatriates," pointing to himself and Alexis, and went on. "If you think about it, we are paying for the mistakes of our forefathers who ignored the plight of the indigenous populace, making it comfortable for themselves and their families with some of course amassing fortunes." Joshua stopped talking as he was exhausted.

"I am glad you turned up this evening," he said to Alexis. "I wanted to talk to somebody. I wish your mum was here as she would understand my motives better than anybody. I want you to explain it all to her after I have gone, preferably by Sunday late morning at the earliest. By then, hopefully, I will be truly gone." It was obvious why he had chosen Easter Sunday to escape. Easter Monday was a holiday and the earliest anybody would have realised would have been Tuesday when he would not have arrived at the office for the usual weekly briefing to his staff.

"You had better be going now," said Joshua in a wearied voice.

"Ok, I wish you all the best on Sunday," whispered Alexis as he put his jumper back on and shook Joshua's hand.

"I hope one day we shall meet, in the not-too-distant future, under happier circumstances," said Joshua finally.

"I wish you luck," said Alexis holding the small picture, and was soon on his way back home. As soon as he entered the apartment, he went straight to his room to hide the picture. His mother was lying in bed reading Pittigrilli's *Cocaïne*, a novel which was banned by the Catholic Church for its daring approach to drug use and sex.

"Is Joshua joining us on Sunday?" she shouted.

"Yes, he is due here at noon," he shouted back and remained in his room to avoid further questions.

The following day Alexis was going about in a haze. He went to the Scouts in the morning and was glad not to meet any of his close friends. He returned home, had a snack and went for a short siesta, mainly to avoid close contact with his mum. Later, after lunch, she said to Alexis, "Shall we go to the pictures tomorrow evening? We always do on Easter Sunday so if we decide to do so we must pre-book." Amir, Metro and Rialto were the most salubrious of Alexandria's dozen or so cinemas. On Sunday evenings the cinemas were packed because it offered a very popular family entertainment and was particularly popular on holiday weekends.

"Pictures," uttered Alexis hesitantly who was dying to relate to his mum the news of Joshua's pending escape but dared not.

"Let us see what is on," she replied as she opened the *Tachidromos*' entertainment section. "Metro, Rialto, Amir," she murmured as she went through Alexandria's long list of cinemas all showing the latest Hollywood releases. "Amir's film is *Stop-Over Tokyo*, a spy thriller with

Robert Wagner and Joan Collins, while Metro's film is *Gone with the Wind* with Clark Gable, but we have already seen it, and at the Rialto there is *Sayonara* with Marlon Brando. What do you fancy?"

"Let us go for the spy thriller," replied Alexis, not really fancying any of these but, not wishing to start a dialogue with his mum, he opted for the first that came to mind.

"I will go and reserve the seats."

His mum went into the bedroom and fetched a one-pound Egyptian note.

"There you are. Three tickets at 25 piastres each, remember Joshua will be with us."

"Of course," replied Alexis and disappeared down the flight of steps.

The seats at 25 piastres each were the most expensive in the mezzanine section of these cinemas affording a panoramic view of the large imposing screen.

Joshua meanwhile had spent Saturday morning barricaded in his villa not wishing to attract the attention of his neighbours. The following day at noon he locked the bungalow and started driving west in his opulent Buick along the Corniche towards the Yachting Club. So far everything was working to plan. He was dressed in his usual angling attire complete with a white cap. The Corniche was gradually filling up with promenaders and holiday makers enjoying the fine Sunday midday balmy weather. He soon passed Chatby and arrived at the Ramleh tram station. He was only a few hundred metres from the Yachting Club but decided not to park the car there. Instead he reached the restaurant-nightclub Calithea and parked the car behind in its secluded spot. He left the car unlocked and made for the nearest taxi rank. He carried with him a small overnight bag with some provisions such as bread and cheese. He took a taxi and arrived at the Yachting Club. Forcing himself to appear as natural and jovial as usual he went to the veranda and ordered some late lunch.

"Good morning Mr Schumann," said the head waiter.

"Hello Max," replied Joshua. Max, a stocky fellow of Maltese decent, served Joshua's brunch.

"Are you fishing today? It is a fine afternoon," asked Max.

Joshua nodded.

"Will you be having dinner here this evening? I have some nice entrecote if you fancy it."

"That depends," replied Joshua, trying to appear natural. "I will start fishing just north of here but if I have no luck I may head along the coast eastwards towards Mantazah in search of a richer catch. I may spend the night at Sidi Bishr so do not count on me for dinner," replied Joshua and proceeded to finish a strong cup of black coffee.

"Fair enough, good luck with your catch," replied Max.

"Thanks," uttered Joshua and sighed with relief as the waiter headed for the kitchen. An hour later following brunch he boarded his boat and made for the open sea. On approaching the 3 kilometres limit he switched the engine off and dropped anchor. He got his angling gear out and started fishing.

Alexis went to Amir and booked two seats for the six to nine screening for Sunday evening. On his way back to Ramleh to catch the tram he crossed the Corniche and stared at the Yachting Club in the far distance. He turned and fixed his eyes on the open sea where Joshua had taken him fishing a few months ago. "Good luck for tomorrow," he muttered silently and turned back towards the tram terminus.

Joshua fished for about two hours with a moderate catch. The patrol boat made its appearance from the far distance and was soon by Joshua's boat.

"Hey Joshua, are you going to spend all weekend fishing?" shouted Halil from the patrol boat. He had a wide smile and was in good spirits.

"It looks likely if I want a decent catch," replied Joshua and smiled back. "After a while I may try my luck a little further afield, say at Aboukir."

"You are getting ambitious," replied Halil, "There are many professional anglers at Aboukir. Of course, you always have the Red Sea as a last resort."

"Oh no, that is a bit too far, besides after a while it will be dusk."

"Anyway, the coast is yours," said Halil as he signalled to his Egyptian mate to rev the engine and head westwards. Joshua followed the patrol's boat course until its diminished silhouette disappeared behind Alexandria's western port. Joshua knew that on Sundays the next patrol boat was not due until late in the evening. He continued mechanically to fish without really paying much attention to anything he caught. After an hour dusk was drawing in. He put away his rods and basket with his catch, lifted the anchor and hesitated. A few hundred metres ahead lay international waters and freedom. He was well aware that his engine was much more powerful than any of the patrol boats' engines, which gave him added comfort as he contemplated his next move. He took out his binoculars and examined carefully his surroundings, left and right, to see if there was any other boat in the vicinity. He found no sign of any life as dusk continued to set in. Suddenly as if by instinct he set his course east and put on full throttle. The potent engine thrust the heavy boat forwards, destination Israel. As the boat gained speed a cold chill ran down his spine; he realised he was at the point of no return. He glanced astern toward the shore, left and right, but there was nobody. It looked as though he had made it.

Having spent Saturday evening avoiding his mum for fear of spilling the beans on Sunday morning Alexis walked into his mothers' bedroom and gave her 50 piastres change.

"Why did you only buy two tickets?" questioned his mum.

"Joshua is not joining us. Later today he will escape on his boat from the Yachting Club. He will head for Israel and eventually will join Hannah in Zürich and reveal all." Alexis went on to explain Friday's unexpected encounter with Joshua. Mary Mani realised that her suspicions had been justified.

On Sunday late in the afternoon Mary Mani and her son went to the cinema having spent the best part of the day discussing Joshua's escape and its implications. Alexis did not really enjoy the film, even though the story was gripping, as his mind was set on Joshua's escape. After the film ended, they sat at an outside table at the Patisserie Elite facing the cinema Rialto. Flocks passed by heading for the tram station. It was quite a spectacle to experience this *va-et-vient* as all the cinemas finished their mid-performances at around the same time. Alexis ordered an ice cream while his mother a cognac. They sat there in silence, amidst this human traffic observing, studying and scrutinising such an assemblage of characters, Europeans and Arabs, young and old, happy and sad, rich and poor. What future lay in front of them in view of the tumultuous times of political unrest and world events? They started walking towards the tram terminus.

"Let us have a bite to eat" said his mum pointing at the Brasserie Alakefak in the direction opposite the Ramleh tram terminus, "they serve some delicious rolls of gigot d'agneau," she concluded. They headed towards the brasserie's bar, ordered the rolls and started picking at some pickled gherkins and black olives which lay in front of them. They sat at a table near the entrance and watched the comings and goings by Alakefak's impressive façade. Thoughts enveloped them of happier times when they met Joshua and his family at the Yachting Club or at other functions and remained there for a considerable time after having consumed their rolls, both silently contemplating their own family's future and casting a thought on Joshua's daring escape and his present whereabouts.

22

April 1959

A week after Joshua escaped from Alexandria there was a knock at the Manis' apartment. Mary opened the door only to be confronted by two well-dressed but stern-looking Arabs. They showed her their identification cards.

"Secret police," uttered Mrs Mani as she glanced at their cards.

"May we come in?" asked the elder of the two.

"Of course," she replied and made way for them to enter.

They entered the apartment with Mrs Mani shutting the door behind them. She led them to the lounge and pointed to the two large armchairs. She sat on a settee opposite and opened a cigarette case.

"Allow me," prompted the elder of the two Arabs and offered her one from his own case. "Craven A," he added smilingly.

"Thank you," replied Mrs Mani and bent slightly forward to reach the Arab's cigarette lighter. She remained silent; the ball was evidently in their court.

"Do you know Mr Joshua Schumann?" said the senior of the two Arabs in a slow but deliberate voice and looked at her to see if there was a facial reaction. The question did not startle her as she was half-expecting such a visitation.

"I do."

"How well do you know him?"

"Fairly well, he and his wife are friends of ours. We know them from our time in Cairo when we all lived there and now here in Alexandria the families visit one another every so often."

"Are you aware that a week ago he escaped from Egypt?"

"Yes, a mutual friend informed me a few days ago."

"Did Mr Schumann confide in you that he intended to leave the country?" The Arab was conversing in Arabic but ever so slowly to make sure that Mrs Mani could follow him. However, having been born and having lived in Egypt for all her life she knew the language fairly well and could easily follow him.

"No, he did not mention anything to me," she replied with conviction.

"How strange since your two families were so close?" went on the Arab.

"Perhaps Joshua would have mentioned something had the circumstances been normal."

"Would you care to elaborate Mrs Mani?" pressed the Arab.

"May I be frank?" she said. He nodded and she continued. "Egypt is undergoing a transitional period at this very moment. Quite naturally after the 1956 War there flourished a nationalistic feeling amongst your people…" She hesitated to collect her thoughts and continued. "Ordinarily there is an urge, a mood by your own people to stand up and be counted and not be dictated by some European fortune hunters or their inheritors." Putting it as bluntly as that convinced the Secret Police officers that she accepted that a huge injustice had been allowed to exist for decades and so realised that she sympathized with the plight of the Arabs. Although Mrs Mani firmly believed that an injustice had been done, by declaring her thoughts so bluntly at the beginning of the discussion she hoped to somewhat mellow the interrogative approach of the two officers and render the atmosphere more congenial for an exchange of ideas. She went on.

"This may be putting it quite harshly, but this is how the person in the street is feeling right now. The crucial question is what happens to the many expatriates and their families who control and indeed own key industries and a century ago chose to make Egypt, and particularly Cairo and Alexandria, their home?" She paused, took a couple of puffs of her Craven A.

"The obvious answer is that they should make way for the indigenous population to take over. But how fast should this transition take? I suggest it should take place gradually to avoid the obvious anxiety that many of my compatriots face in these uncertain times. And let me hasten to add that it is not only the rich that such a change may affect but it may reach all levels down to the grass roots and add to the insecurity that many already feel. I call this a transitional period because after a few years those who chose to remain will have learned to adapt to the changing conditions while the majority of the expatriates will have left, thus creating another diaspora..."

"Or may perhaps return to their country of origin," interrupted the Arab who was conversing with Mary Mani while the younger officer listened obediently to the exchange.

"That is not as easy as it sounds," she went on. "Take the Greek community for example. My husband and myself and our children were born in Egypt while my father came from mainland Greece and my mother from Switzerland. If our family settle in Greece or Switzerland, we would be treated as foreigners as other Europeans living in those countries. You see, great numbers are involved so absorbing such a large ethnic community in another country makes matters very difficult. It is this kind of anxiety and insecurity which causes many expatriates to feel stressed and despairing about the immediate future. This is what I meant by abnormal conditions where rationality has been thrown out of the window and helplessness has engulfed many expatriates."

"Mm, you paint quite a desperate picture, Mrs Mani. Besides, the authorities have not asked any communities to leave: it appears that some are doing so regardless of any government pronouncements or other decrees and what is more, it is indeed sad and quite damaging to the relations between the Arab and the expatriate communities if some, like Mr Schumann, resort to daring attempts to leave the country, especially when they defy the laws," concluded the Arab.

"Indeed, it is sad, but have prominent people been given any option? What alternative has been left open to them?"

"To work together with the resurgent Arab population for the attainment of better conditions and fairness for all, European and indigenous, communities."

"Do you really believe that there is room at the top for both Europeans and Arabs?" asked Mrs Mani penetratingly.

"Doesn't it all depend, Mrs Mani, on the attitude of both factions as to what future lies ahead for all concerned? Mr Schumann's actions are bound to irritate the authorities who, quite naturally, will tighten the grip and impose stricter rules and restrictions which quite apart from inflicting heavy blows to intercommunal relations would also damage business confidence," he concluded. Mrs Mani looked at him squarely in the eyes because in a sense he was part of the emerging ruling elite.

"Well, allow me to return to the point I made earlier. What really drove Mr Schumann to suddenly leave Alexandria – " she did not use the word escape as that may have conjured unfortunate connotations, "– a town that I know for sure he and his wife regarded as home and loved very much? Surely one must assume that it was the prevailing attitude of the Egyptian Government with its recent policies which must have convinced Joshua that there was no real future in Egypt for him and his family."

"It is indeed the most difficult situation that any country has been confronted with in recent times," said the Arab having conceded some of the arguments that Mrs Mani was levelling at him.

"Do not misunderstand me," went on Mrs Mani, "I fully appreciate the difficulties facing your country. Events are happening very fast and there is a kind of contagious fever that is sweeping the mass of the expatriates, a fever that it is still not very potent, but might nevertheless turn into panic and then it would be extremely difficult to foresee their actions and in turn would be impossible to predict how the authorities would react. I am trying, as an expatriate, to explain the dilemmas that face all of us at the present juncture. The prospects of the expatriates look very bleak in the foreseeable future given that they have attained a reasonable standard of living...."

"To the detriment of the indigenous population," butted in the Arab.

"No doubt, and I have alluded to that already," she replied. "However, were most of the expatriates aware of such exploitation, and if they were, what could they have done about it? One is powerless however well one understands the unfairness and basically we have to look at the situation facing each individual and their families. Every expatriate family stands to lose a great deal from their eventual expulsion..."

"The government has not so far advocated expulsion

of the Europeans from Egypt and does not intend to do so in the near future," said the Arab reassuringly using the words expatriates and Europeans interchangeably.

"Not in such clear terms," said Mrs Mani who was by now in full control of her arguments and enjoyed immensely the conversation with the Senior Secret Service Agent. He was well educated, and no doubt destined for higher office in the years ahead. She went on: "But one feels that conditions are made very difficult for lots of expatriates when their jobs are becoming more and more insecure and their livelihood threatened with the consequent result that many choose to leave on their own accord rather than be forced to accept lower-paid positions or eventual redundancies. Expulsion or not it really amounts to the same thing. Having talked to a lot of my friends I sense a kind of bitterness that there is no mercy, that is that there is nothing to be done to alleviate their situation, that each family is on its own which may lead to panic-stricken and desperate attempts such as that of Joshua's."

"You talk of mercy, Mrs Mani, but for a very long time the indigenous population was supressed and that was done mercilessly. I accept that the individual may not have been able to change the situation much; however, there is much change in the air and this cannot be reversed: one cannot stem the tide of history and at such a momentous turn of events, when Egypt's future is at stake, priority must be given to the majority of the suppressed populace rather than the various ethnic minorities that had it so good for such a long time and lived here for over a century and longer."

"These ethnic minorities, as you put it, will suffer a great deal," interrupted Mrs Mani, "and what is more those that will suffer most will be the ones that can least afford it. Uprooting such a family will cause a lot of hardship as it means that they will have to build, from scratch, some sort of life elsewhere and the older amongst us will feel the pressure even more, to breaking point I daresay."

"The irony of all this is that we do not wish to hurt the ordinary expatriate family," the Arab went on. "The authorities are more interested in the assets of the rich industrialists who seem to own half of Egypt and have a firm grip on the economy. Unfortunately, any new measures we announce will not hurt these people as they have already moved fortunes outside Egypt in secret Swiss bank accounts or other safe havens."

"They may of course be deeply hurt morally and personally when they realise that the empire they built is gradually being taken over, out of their own control and jurisdiction. Do you blame them directly for Egypt's status quo?" asked Alexis' mum.

"We do not blame these people for what they have amassed, what we resent is the fact that these people may still be in control of key industries, such as cotton and food, and unless steps are taken they will be reluctant to relinquish their stranglehold," said the Arab.

"Certainly," said Mrs Mani, "this transitional period

will be seen as the slow and painful ending of an era. We are witnessing the disentanglement of an entire expatriate community which could flourish for a century or more and although some will be reluctant to surrender what they regard as their own they are often powerless to protect their interests. On reflection," continued Mrs Mani as she got rid of a fraction of curving ash from the tip of her third cigarette in the ashtray, "it is good that such a transition doesn't appear to have led to any violence or bloodshed between the various communities. The expatriates cannot defend their assets in any meaningful way really except in some special cases by persuading you and the authorities that their continued presence in a new Egypt would be for the good of the country. But for most of the expatriates nothing can really be done, and they must accept the new laws magnanimously. After all, some observers have already remarked that the expatriates have extended their welcome by a long shot and time has come to disappear into the wilderness," concluded Mrs Mani, waving her hands to simulate far and beyond.

"That is putting it a bit harshly," commented the Arab, "I would not call Europe a wilderness."

"But for many expatriates who have only known Alexandria and Cairo as their home it will be just that. You know, coming to terms with the unknown as the expatriates will sooner or later have to be confronted with, will be a terrifying experience. Our forefathers had to face just that when they first settled here..."

"Ah, but at least they knew that they had to compete with a silent supressed majority which were no match in terms of education, shrewdness and cunning," retorted the Arab decisively.

"Yes, but now, barring a few that would end up in other African countries, the others would be forced to return to Europe and would have to compete with equals which would be a frightening experience to many. Is it not tantamount to heading towards a wilderness where the chances of success are very slim? However, I must stop prophesying chaos and ask you how you view Egypt's future in view of the formidable task that lies ahead?" concluded Mrs Mani as she wished to change the direction of the dialogue towards the future of the country rather than continue on the plight of the expatriate community.

"Formidable," replied the Arab, "is precisely how we view the task ahead. We would advocate a gradual transition where initially there is a partnership between the Europeans and the Arabs in many industries but as matters are moving very fast we may have to face running the economy without the expatriates and in some key industries that may pose a problem to say the least."

"Because of the lack of skilled personnel and graduates?" added Mrs Mani.

"Yes of course," conceded the Arab, "but also because of the lack of people with management experience and decision-making which obviously cannot be gained overnight. So in a way we will be thrown in the deep end and who knows, it could turn out to be an advantage because we shall have to somehow move forward and succeed come what may, otherwise the alternative will be a complete collapse which doesn't bear thinking about."

"That is a very frank answer," said Mrs Mani.

"I believe that frankness and candidness have been the essence throughout our conversation. I hope we may have many more such discussions: it's the fundamental aspects of some of the points we discussed that especially appeal to me."

"I too have enjoyed our conversation, but realistically I do not see many other occasions where we could resume such conversation."

"Is it that time may be running out?"

"Precisely."

"I thought so. However, I do regret that," he added sincerely. They shook hands and the two officers were soon going down the marble winding staircase leading to the main entrance hall.

A few weeks later Alexis had asked his mum whether his closest friends, Yeorgis, Panos and Petros could come to dine with them one evening. She readily acquiesced as she enjoyed the banter between Alexis' friends. It was a mild evening in early May and Mrs Mani had prepared dinner outside on the balcony. The four youngsters were chatting away during dinner and were switching from topic to topic.

"My dad told me the other day that the authorities have imposed a maximum limit of 20 Egyptian pounds per person leaving Egypt," said Panos after a lull in their conversation.

"A fat lot of good this sum will do for those who leave," answered Yeorgis.

Mrs Mani reflected on the recent visitation of the two Secret Service men and the fact that the senior of the two insisted that no special restrictions had been imposed but gradually more curtailments were being announced thus restricting the movement of people and currency out of the country.

"I can tell you some stories that my father heard that would make you laugh," continued Panos.

"Go on," said Alexis.

"What stories?" murmured a perplexed Petros.

"There is this story of an old man who wanted to smuggle out some jewellery. He put one of his legs in plaster and tipped, anonymously of course, the police, who duly broke the plaster as he arrived at the customs only to find nothing. They apologised profusely and days later when he arrived back at the port with a fresh plaster he was allowed to proceed without any problem. Little did the customs men realise that his leg was now stuffed with lots of jewels." The boys laughed.

"I like that, very classy," retorted Yeorgis.

"Ingenious," shouted Petros.

How sad, thought Mrs Mani as she lingered while clearing the dishes from the table and listening to the conversation between the four boys. Panos was in his element being the focus of his friends' attention. He continued:

"And there are other stories about jewels hidden in toothpaste or diamonds being swallowed."

"Swallowed?" asked Petros in amazement. "How do they retrieve them afterwards?"

"Naturally, I suppose," butted in Alexis.

"Ouch," flinched Petros.

"Not all attempts were apparently successful," continued Panos, "A woman had hidden gold coins in freshly cooked pies and was caught only after the persistent and suspicious cries of her relatives to 'look after the pies'."

"Silly relatives," said Yeorgis.

Panos went on to relate other desperate measures used by expatriates. Mrs Mani cast her thoughts to those of her compatriots who were forced to resort to this sort of subterfuge but was amused by the way Panos was describing such grim realities. How was the external world viewing the situation in Egypt? she wondered, a thought that preoccupied her for some months until her own family's departure from the country of her birth.

23

Egyptian and Israeli coast, April 1959

After an arduous trip across the Mediterranean, not venturing further than a few kilometres from Africa's coast, Joshua reached Bardawil Lake about 50 km east off Port Said, having passed by Ras El-Bar north of Damietta, the eastern tributary of the Nile. He carefully navigated through an opening into the lake and found a deserted inlet where he spent the night and got some much-needed sleep.

The next day he lingered for the whole day not wishing to travel before sunset, so he set off early in the evening heading east past the town of Arish in the distance before he continued northwards toward his intended destination of the Israeli port of Ashdod. Next, he reached the Gaza Strip and saw the flickering lights of Al Mawasi, the district on the shore west of Khan Yunis in the far distance. He continued past the whole of the Strip and soon entered the border region of Israel with the Mediterranean Sea. All was quiet as he sailed passed the city of Ashkelon in the distance and continued northwards, finally reaching the coastal town of Ashdod. As the main port grew nearer, he made for a prearranged remote location and was met by a friend who had been tipped off regarding his pending arrival. He knew he would be welcomed in Israel following the Law of Return which was passed in 1950 and guaranteed, after issuing a three month certificate, immediate citizenship to any Jewish person who wished to settle in Israel. A similar law for the Palestinians was never enacted even though some Palestinian refugees had documented evidence of their ancestral homes in Palestine, the issue being described as demographic engineering by an economic forum of the United Nations. Joshua, with the help of his Jewish contacts, soon visited the various departments in Tel Aviv and Jerusalem, secured all the appropriate papers and went through the necessary formalities to become a permanent citizen and resident of Israel.

Joshua sent a telegram to Hannah in Zürich informing her and the children of his successful escape from Alexandria. With the formalities over and his citizenship assured he arranged for Hannah and the children to come to Israel where they established their home in a fashionable part of West Jerusalem. He soon settled in his new country and set up his architectural practice in the heart of the city. He hired several licensed architects but during the first eight years of his arrival in Israel Joshua's practice only just ticked over. Following the 1967 Six-Day War, the government under the leadership of Golda Meir gradually gave permission for scores of settlements to be established in the occupied territories which was so opportune as Joshua's practice was at the point of much-needed expansion and benefitted from a large number of government-funded contracts. Further, the need for new housing, factories and other major projects throughout Israel itself was great. His son Avi completed his schooling and enrolled at the Ben-Gurion University to study architecture with the intention of following in the footsteps of his father. He proceeded to a PhD in Architecture at the University of Manchester in the UK studying the transformation of the urban order in early Christian Jerusalem with particular emphasis on the natural and artificial physical features of the ancient city and the connection with its rituals. He returned to Jerusalem and was immediately employed by his father in his practice.

His daughter Rivka completed her schooling and on the advice of her grandfather enrolled to study law at the Sorbonne in Paris. Upon graduating Rivka practised law in France for a few years and carried out a postgraduate degree in international relations. She did not wish to return to Israel but settled in France working for a number of conglomerates. She then joined the staff at the French Embassy and gradually ascended to head its fledgling security section.

Avi upon his return to Israel married Golda, a young girl he was introduced to by relatives, and after setting up home in West Jerusalem the family was expanded by the birth of his son Shimon. From an early age Shimon showed an aptitude towards the classics. His bar mitzvah was held on the first Shabbat after his 13th birthday, followed by a great celebration in Joshua's luxurious house in West Jerusalem.

Hannah on the other hand, having fully recovered from her illness, ran the household and helped Golda bring up young Shimon. A few years after she arrived in Israel she set up a goat farm in the foothills of the region that latterly became known as the Jerusalem Corridor, a quasi-triangle with its apex in Jerusalem; its northern border was the old road to Jerusalem, while its southern border was the Elah Valley. In the early days there were no trees and shrubs in the area but with the help of the Jewish National Fund, established by Theodor Herzl in 1901, planting a tree became a Jewish mantra, part of Jewish folklore and ethos for the survival of the new State of Israel. Gradually agricultural fields and fine vineyards were established, and Hannah would spend a considerable time cultivating her farm with the help of other ladies. In the fullness of time the farm expanded its raison d'être by making and selling a host of other merchandise.

24

Alexandria, June 1959

Today was Graduation Day for the boys at the Averofeio Gymnasium. The youngsters viewed such a day with excitement but also with some trepidation.

The ceremony took place in the courtyard of a smaller school behind the cinema Rialto, on an afternoon in late June. Pupils and their parents were attired in Sunday best with some youngsters proudly wearing monogrammed shirts. They sat in chairs arranged in a semicircle facing a long table displaying all the diplomas and special prizes of merit. Mrs Mani sat at the back, next to Alexis, listening to the speeches by the headmaster and the teachers who in turn sat behind the long table facing the motley assembly of parents.

At the end of the long row of teachers sat Mr Pateras who had his usual detached demeanour as he regarded such a conformist and habitual ritual as Graduation Day with derision. Needless to say, he did not contribute to the speeches of his fellow teachers but exhibited an aloofness characteristic of someone who frankly wished to be elsewhere. The two Arab teachers sat silently, not comprehending a word of what was said, as literally, it was all Greek to them.

The male-dominated assemblage of teachers was

interspersed by three women teaching French, English and History. The French teacher had a pleasant personality and was very much liked by the boys to the extent that she was invited to, and often accepted, excursions outside school. The English teacher was dainty with boyish features and was heavily made-up. She was hemiplegic with her affected leg extended and rotated in a wide arc giving her a characteristic gait. She remained distant and gave the impression of being disinterested in reaching out to the minds of her pupils. The History teacher was a stern lady in her mid-forties, with an austere outlook who spread terror amongst her pupils. She was allegedly the ex-lover of the headmaster, their fraught relationship coming to the fore every so often, but with neither willing to quash any talk of their recurrent affair, the rumours persisted and spread like wildfire. Together these 12 teachers epitomised the exceptional calibre of teaching at the Averofeio as each one was carefully selected from the large number who aspired to teach at this prestigious school.

Alexis glanced around and saw Yanis who sat between his parents, Mr and Mrs Lotas. They gleamed with pride as their son had performed exceptionally well and was in line for some of the special prizes. A little further back sat Petros with his parents and behind him sat Christos on his own, away from his parents. They sat two rows behind Christos, highlighting the frequent fracas that had taken place between Christos and his father as the two of them did not see eye to eye on a number of issues. They often quarrelled but as Mr Papas was not strong enough to impose any discipline or his authority on his son he was often seen trotting along to the headmaster's office to report on his son's misdemeanours and to seek his advice.

With speeches completed it was time to present the individual diplomas which stated two marks, both out of 20. The first referred to the pupil's conduct which invariably was the highest unless he was involved in a serious breach of discipline which could be very detrimental for future employment or further study. The second mark was an aggregate of the pupil's performance in all the 13 subjects of the final year. This mark varied between 10, a bare pass to 18 for exceptionally gifted pupils. Below 10 would mean a pupil taking the examinations again in a few topics before the start of the next academic year or, rarely, having to repeat the final year. The names of the pupils were announced alphabetically, and a long procession followed as each pupil shook hands with the Headmaster and collected his well-earned diploma. Alexis received an overall mark of 14, Petros 15 and Christos 16. Yanis Lotas, however, had amassed the very respectable mark of 17 and was extremely pleased as he went back to his seat, with the surrounding parents offering their hearty congratulations for his exceptional performance. Despite the difference in the marks between the four school pals, it was evident that there was not a scintilla of jealously between them. During the past six years at the senior school they had experienced a lot of happiness and camaraderie especially at functions outside school.

The highest mark, however, that of 18, was rewarded to a reticent pupil, who came from a humbler background. He proceeded rather hurriedly towards the Headmaster, not feeling comfortable with being in the limelight, shook his hand, clutched his diploma and returned to his seat amidst tumultuous applause and a standing ovation. After the handing out of the diplomas the Headmaster proceeded to award the special prizes with the humble boy receiving five merits, mostly for the sciences. Yanis, who was very good at languages, also received two awards for English and Arabic while Christos received his for French. The Headmaster gave a short speech thanking the parents for attending and wishing the pupils all the best for the future. Refreshments were on offer while pupils and parents mingled amongst the teachers to bid their farewells.

"Nice to see you again, Mrs Mani."

Alexis' mother turned around and saw Mr Pateras standing behind her.

"Good afternoon to you," replied Mrs Mani.

"Are you pleased to see a number of your pupils graduating with high marks?" she went on.

"Indeed, I am always happy for them; however, whether I agree with such a send-off is another matter," he replied. "Getting high marks at school is of course encouraging but whether they will do well in their further studies or indeed in employment is hard to say. Some disciplinarian parents do push their children very hard while at school and this may have a detrimental effect in the years ahead. We are experiencing interesting times, as you well appreciate, Mrs Mani; with the future so uncertain, families splitting up, siblings leaving home all creates added tension which is bound to affect some of these boys. Some will cope well with all the challenges that will face them while others will not and that saddens me, but let us hope that the majority will handle their new circumstances without many problems."

"You mean some boys may show signs of a burn-out?"

"Physical and emotional exhaustion is difficult to handle. Some pupils may be exhausted, mentally too tired to cope with minor incidences. Frankly they may feel totally spent."

"That is putting it a bit harshly. Are you a pessimist at heart?"

"As you may be aware I spend a few days per week in Cairo giving a course on Classics to students at the university and I regret to say that some students, when they arrive, are emotionally drained which is evidence of parental domination during their formative years. Away from home the student needs all the reserves they can muster and if these have been exhausted during schooling, problems may arise which are extremely difficult to handle."

"When all is said and done, however, a good school Diploma should assist in securing a university placement particularly if a scholarship is also required," said Mrs Mani.

"Of course, but I hope that the pupil attained it by self-discipline and not undue parental pressure."

Alexis approached them.

"Are you looking forward to new challenges, young man?" asked Mr Pateras.

"I am, and also relieved that school is over, but sad that after the summer I will lose touch with many of my pals. It seems that we are all scattering in different directions," replied Alexis.

"What lies ahead?"

"I intend to follow a course in engineering. My brother lives in London and is sending me the prospectuses for the universities there."

"Why London?" pressed Mr Pateras. Alexis hesitated and his mother butted in.

"Alexis is a British National." Mr Pateras frowned, not quite understanding how one of his pupils did not possess a Greek nationality.

The question of Alexis' nationality arose when he reached 16. He could have applied for and almost certainly have secured Egyptian nationality on account of his place of birth; however, being that his grandfather's original home was Cyprus, the route to acquiring British nationality beckoned. Following Cyprus becoming a Crown Colony in 1925, a law was subsequently passed in 1948 stating that persons of Cypriot origin could become citizens of the UK and Colonies. There were further possibilities to explore, such as becoming a Swiss national following his maternal grandmother's origin or indeed opting for Greek nationality given that Alexis' other grandfather was born in a small town near Sparta in the Peloponnesus peninsula in southern Greece. Mrs Mani considered carefully all these options, weighing the pros and the cons, and after much deliberation she decided that the most favourable option for Alexis was to obtain a British passport. A visit to the British Consulate in Alexandria with his birth certificate was all that was needed and within days Alexis had acquired his impressive looking black passport.

"Well, the whole family possesses British passports. My father-in-law came from Cyprus to settle in Cairo just before the end of the century and through him we are all endowed with British nationality so it makes sense for Alexis to study in England rather than, say, Switzerland where my mother was born. As his brother is at present in London it is best for Alexis to head for England where he will have some family support."

"And yourself, what are the plans?"

"My husband is arriving back from Khartoum in a couple of months and there is a possibility of a further assignment in Benghazi. So, for the next few years I may still be on African soil, alas not for Alexis. What about your plans?" asked Mrs Mani.

"I will remain here for a few more years and divide my time between Cairo University and the Averofeio but with our future here in Egypt being so uncertain I may have to think again. As you may be aware the placements of every teacher at the Averofeio are administered from Athens, so I could be seconded to another country or indeed return to Greece."

What their conversation had alluded to was another example of the fabric of society in Egypt gradually being torn apart after hundreds of years of relative peace and tranquillity. Mrs Mani reflected on the conversation that had taken place a few months previously with the two Secret Agents after Joshua's escape. Every expatriate family was facing an uncertain future as happened to the British in India after independence and no doubt will happen to a host of other colonised countries in the future. It was something that should have occupied the minds of many settlers, but they put such thoughts aside not willing to face reality. But the political situation in Egypt was changing, giving rise to an ominous wake-up call which was the cause for much distress and nervousness.

The Headmaster and teachers meandered amongst the parents while the youngsters had gathered together to discuss plans for the next couple of weeks.

"My cousin and I are giving a party," announced Petros, "a sort of farewell party for you guys," as he gestured to his three closest friends.

A few days later Mrs Mani received a telegram from her husband informing her of his return to Alexandria from his assignment in Khartoum. His new assignment in Benghazi was confirmed, so Mrs Mani started making preparations to leave the apartment and gave notice to Ms Nottiyan, the landlady, of their pending departure in a few weeks. No doubt, she reflected, the stay in Benghazi will be another sojourn thus heralding a period of nomadic life where permanency was difficult to contemplate and only to dream about. It was something that would preoccupy her for some months to come.

25

September 1959

It was the afternoon prior to Petros' party. Alexis was having a lukewarm bath, eyes closed, letting his mind reflect on events since Graduation Day. He hadn't seen Nina and wandered whether she had left for Athens with her mother for the vacation. He was busy helping his mum with preparations for their pending relocation to Benghazi. The furniture in the apartment had to be sold, and a few sentimental glassware pieces had to be carefully packed. Their papers had to be in order, including exit and re-entry visas. The latter of course was irrelevant as the family, unbeknown to the Egyptian authorities, had no intention of returning to Alexandria. They would not have been allowed to leave unless their return visa was stamped in their passports.

A few days earlier Alexis and his mum stuffed two large suitcases with her main collection of German books that she had amassed in her library and could not possibly carry with her on her way to Benghazi in a small minibus. They headed for the Deutsche Schüle der Borromäerinnen in the city, the 77-year-old German school that had acquired a great reputation for learning and was the brainchild of Pater Ladislaus Schneider, a priest who wished to educate German and Austrian children living in Alexandria. The librarian was immensely grateful for Mrs Mani's gesture when she handed over this priceless collection of rare books without requiring any recompense.

"I just wished to find a safe home for these books that mean so much to me and my family," she stated to an overwhelmed librarian.

She did however keep a few books that she was not willing to let go and these were packed together with the novel that Alexis and Petros had used for learning German.

His friends' families went through similar deliberations regarding their future so after Graduation Day the group was quite disrupted and only occasionally met at Sidi Bishr or at other beaches along Alexandria's winding Corniche.

Alexis stood up and using a large loofah started scrubbing himself vigorously. Come to think of it, he reflected, the last time he and Nina were together was at Myrto's cabin although in the intervening months they had met at various functions, what with Hanna's illness, Joshua's escape, swotting for the school examinations, Graduation Day and their preparation for their departure there had been little chance to meet. Surely, had she gone to Athens she would have attempted to see him one last time to wish him well in his new life in London. That would have been nice, reflected Alexis, but there again, where and how? They both seemed to have preferred not to delve deeper into their tenuous liaison. They were reluctant to take the first step needed to break the impasse that enveloped them.

Petros insisted on casual wear so Alexis opted for his red open-neck shirt, brown slacks and matching brown moccasin shoes. He hoped that the dance floor would not be too slippery otherwise his customary rock-n-roll display with Marika may be a touch hazardous. As he was a bit early, he went to the balcony and gazed down on Palestra's ground where there was a basket-ball match in progress between the local team and St Mark's. It was a fast game, the ball being passed with great speed and accuracy between the competitors. The few hundred spectators following the match roared and clapped each time a team managed to score. He glanced at his watch: 8.30, still early, he thought. Every now and then he looked down at the passers-by in Rue Canope. He distinguished Irini and Rea coming from the cross-roads on his right heading towards the other end of Rue Canope where Petros and his cousin lived. The girls, as they sauntered by Alexis' apartment block, gave furtive glances up at his balcony and continued on their way to the party. Alexis went inside, splashed some eau de cologne and regained his excellent vantage point on the balcony.

"I am back!" yelled his mother as she entered the apartment and joined him on the balcony. "Good match?"

"It is a close one," replied Alexis, "How was town?"

"I must have chosen the wrong day to go to the La

Galerie Lafayette as it was extremely busy, but I did buy what I wanted." Alexis did not respond as his thoughts were really on Nina and whether he would see her again before his imminent departure. Just past nine o'clock he stepped back into the flat and sat opposite his mother who was reading Albert Camus' *The Plague*.

"You will be late for the party," she said without looking at Alexis.

"I had to see the end of the match. It was close: St Mark won by two points. The poor Italians will be devastated as they led practically all the way."

"Who is at the top of the league?" she asked.

"St Mark," he replied.

"Ah, well, they deserve to win," she responded smilingly. Alexis remained silent as his mother continued with her reading. Suddenly after a pause he said:

"Are you sad we are leaving Egypt for good in a few days?" Mrs Mani stopped reading and looked up at Alexis reflecting on his insightful question. After some deliberation she replied:

"I am not sure whether sadness is the right way to describe my feelings. After the last war it gradually became quite obvious that our future, well indeed not just for us but for many living in Egypt, would be uncertain. I cannot deny that I look towards the future with some trepidation but on the other hand I am looking on our departure from Egypt positively in that at least your dad has another well-paid assignment so we will be in a much better position compared to many other families. Soon you will join Pavlos in England and embark on your university studies and hopefully your dad will be able to meet your fees and lodgings during your studies. There is much to look forward to. How do you feel?"

"Sad that I will miss so many friends also excited to be going to England," replied Alexis. She paused; then, looking down at the book, she asked Alexis:

"Is Nina going to the party?"

"I do not really know. I seem to remember that her family were planning a holiday in Greece, not sure when though." Then, not wishing to discuss Nina, further he quickly excused himself and set off for Petros' house. He spiralled down the marbled staircase and turned left down Rue Canope. This was the last party in Alexandria. Did he feel sorry? Not quite – perhaps a touch of nostalgia? Possibly! He walked slowly towards Petros' house, his pensive thoughts turning into a mild soliloquy while trying in vain to explain his perplexed feelings.

He approached the two-storey white house and heard the unmistakable sound of a blue tango. He knocked on the door and all of a sudden the door opened and Nina was standing there as large as life. What a relief, she was there. His fear of not seeing her melted away in an instant. She wore a green dress with a wide black belt around her waist and flat black shoes. Her straight-across fringe covered the top of her forehead. Instantly this party acquired an altogether more poignant significance and it was exciting being close to Nina once more. She greeted him affectionately with a prolonged and irresistible smile and stepped aside making way for Alexis to enter the spacious lounge. He immediately recognised many Scout friends and school pals from Averofeio.

"We thought you wouldn't turn up," said Petros as he approached him.

"I was watching a close match at Palestra," he replied without having fully recovered his composure after realising that Nina was present.

"Who won?" asked Petros.

"St Mark," replied Alexis and proceeded to the adjoining dining room which was laid with all sorts of food and drinks. Petros' and his cousin's parents were sitting in the dining room entertaining some other friends and close relatives. As soon as Petros' father saw Alexis he stood up and approached him.

"Alexis, I hope you're going to dance with Marika this evening. All of us," pointing to his brother and sister-in-law and other elders in the room, "are expecting something really extraordinary."

Alexis smiled and reassured him that he would at some stage do his usual routine with his dancing partner. He then turned towards Petros' mother, a very nice, welcoming lady whom he had come to know quite well over the years, and shook her hand. He had by now regained his full composure and talked freely with Mrs Kalos about all the preparations for their pending move from Alexandria to Benghazi.

"Petros will miss you terribly," she confided in Alexis

in a low voice. "He is already a bit miserable even though he does not wish to admit it."

"The feelings are mutual, Mrs Kalos," replied Alexis genuinely. "I am trying to avoid thinking about it. In fact, I have just had a chat with mum about us leaving Egypt because I wanted to know how she felt."

"I suppose with your father already working away there isn't much to keep you in Alexandria. Although all you young people have happy memories of a carefree life in Alexandria, you realise that it is coming to an end and this is bound to hurt. However, you ought to think of the future, your new life in England and the new friends you will be making."

"That is exactly what my mum said," replied Alexis as he was dragged out of the dining room by Petros and Yanis and ushered onto the centre of the dance floor only to be greeted by a sympathetic Marika. She herself, moments before, had been led there by some youngsters who derived great joy from seeing Alexis and Marika swivelling, gyrating and pirouetting to the sounds of a fast beat. Alexis smiled back at Marika, took hold of her hands and grimaced to signal that although they were forced to perform their routine prematurely, he was intimating, 'what the heck, let us not disappoint them.' They started moving rhythmically wishing to get into the mood of Elvis' *Jailhouse Rock* and, gradually gaining confidence, increased the speed of rotation and gyration and performed some amazing routines, at times locked in an embrace to prevent Marika from flying off uncontrollably and hurting herself in the process. The boys and girls formed a circle around the dance floor and clapped with utter disbelief at some of the dangerous but at the same time elegant moves they were witnessing. The elders, hearing the ecstatic sounds, came out of the dining room and watched with amazement this performance justifying the notoriety these two had acquired over the years. Nina watched too, at a distance from the circle of the jubilant youngsters and remained slightly aloof, her natural reticence never far away. After five minutes of pure hurly-burly and pandemonium the record player came to a stop followed by euphoric clapping and stamping of feet in approval of this great display of dance routines. Although at every party such a performance was not only expected but demanded, in the final analysis both Marika and Alexis enjoyed entertaining their friends and derived a lot of satisfaction themselves from expressing their feelings so freely on the dance floor.

"Let's have something to drink," said Alexis and escorted Marika into the dining room. There they were congratulated by the adults and endured their wholehearted approval humbly, every now and then smiling politely and nodding their sweating heads in acknowledgment of further compliments.

"You must follow me to London," said Alexis smilingly as he opened two cans of Pepsi. "Nobody will be able to follow my routines as you do."

"You flatter me," replied Marika as she sipped the cool drink.

"It is the truth," said Alexis with a smile and downed his Pepsi all in one go. They parted and went their separate ways because in truth apart from dancing there was very little in common.

The party was now in full swing and having consumed a number of Stella beers most youngsters lost their natural shyness and became more jovial. Petros and Rea were dancing cheek-to-cheek quietly in one corner. For them there was no farewell as Rea had to complete her final year at school and Petros had to stay in Alexandria for another year until his younger brother had completed his final year at the Averofeio. He had thus enrolled at the University of Farouk in Alexandria for a one-year foundation course which was a pre-requisite should he wish to continue his university studies in Egypt. As most lectures were in Arabic, such a course was essential for a smooth transition to a degree course. The family therefore postponed the upheaval of uprooting to another country, in their case almost certainly to Greece for a year. Similarly, there was no farewell between Panos and Myrto. Panos was making good progress at the university and hoped to complete his studies in four years and Myrto had to complete another year at school. He nevertheless lamented the fact that most of his close friends were leaving Alexandria for good.

"In the end I will be the only one left behind," he kept saying jokingly; however, through his constant references it was not too difficult to discern a deep sorrow that he would be the only one left behind in Egypt. Alexis glanced at Petros and they exchanged a sympathetic smile.

"Who is he kidding?" whispered Alexis to Petros. "He has the company of some very well-established ladies, so let us take with a pinch of salt his comment about all of us leaving."

"Do you mean there are more than one? Are you sure?" asked Petros.

"Who knows," retorted Alexis as he glanced at Panos. He wasn't a good dancer, but he enjoyed pop music and translated his feelings on the dance floor quite adequately, particularly in the presence of Myrto. The records that the youngsters played were at the top of Europe's hit parade and every time a new one hit the top spot it was bought by the more affluent of Alexis' bunch and played repeatedly at the parties. 'Petite Fleur' was Alexis' favourite which was recorded by an ex-jazzman in Chris Barber's band. Its melody appealed enormously to Alexis whose romanticism came to the fore as soon as its sweet-sounding tunes emanated from the record player. Instinctively he looked around for Nina, saw her talking to a couple of girlfriends, approached her and asked her to dance. They moved onto the floor without uttering a word. Alexis was unaware of anybody else sharing the dance floor with them. The short record came to an end and Alexis and Nina joined another group. After a while 'Petite Fleur' was once again being played and as another youngster pipped Alexis to a dance with Nina, he continued to gossip with the others. After a while Nina returned and when the next record sounded Alexis and Nina made their way to the dance floor. They zigzagged through the other couples still without saying much, just exchanging pleasantries. When their eyes met, they did not flinch. Alexis perceived a sincere expression in Nina's face. He wanted to believe that that was remorse but was not sure. As he stared into Nina's beautiful eyes a myriad of memories enveloped him of the turbulent few years since they had first set their eyes on each other at Palma. The record stopped and they approached Yeorgis.

"Nina, you look lovely tonight," complimented Yeorgis.

"Thank you," she replied, blushing slightly.

"By the way, I have been granted permission by the British Government to visit Tanganyika," went on Yeorgis addressing Alexis.

"Tanganyika?" exclaimed Nina.

"Yeorgis is hell-bent on joining the big game hunters," and turning to Yeorgis he went on, "How long is your visa permit for?"

"Unfortunately for only one year. Apparently, it is extremely difficult to get permanent residency in Tanganyika for a foreigner such as myself. I was only able to obtain a one-year visa after some strings were pulled by my Headmaster and of course having some cousins living there must have helped."

"What will you hunt?" asked Nina in amazement.

"The big five: you know, lions, elephants, rhinos,

buffalos or leopards," answered Yeorgis in an aggressive manner and raised his hands towards Nina to emphasize his statement.

"Oh don't, you frighten me," let out Nina as she backed off.

"Sorry," replied Yeorgis regretfully.

"Is he frightening you with his fearsome animal act?" butted in Panos who approach them with Myrto by his side.

"Isn't that exciting to be going to Tanganyika for game hunting?" said Myrto to Nina.

"It may be exciting to you, but it sounds scary to me. I hope you will not do anything foolish," said Nina.

"Don't worry," replied Panos, "He will only be devoured by a hungry lion or a leopard. You know lions are very proud and given the right circumstances they do not attack humans, but one has no chance with a leopard."

Panos went on to explain very graphically how a leopard treats his bait and had the two girls on the verge of tears. Yeorgis, on the other hand, remained calm and seemed unperturbed by the possible fate that may await him. He appeared fearless and in no way would Panos' minor utterance to emphasize the dangers of big game hunting dent his confidence. Yeorgis was a strong believer and perhaps he had convinced himself that a divine force would look after him and always guide him to follow the correct course. He was due to leave Alexandria at the end of September and fly via Cairo to Dar-el-Salam where he would be met by some of his cousins in the capital of Tanganyika. After a few weeks of training in a village, not far from the capital, he would join a professional hunter's group deep within the African bush. This trip was really a consolation that he too was losing many of his Scout and school pals. Panos had by now finished his graphic description of Yeorgis' pending life as a hunter.

"Don't forget to send us a picture or two after one of your expeditions," said Petros who had joined the group.

"Of course, I will."

Alexis remained silent throughout Panos' description of life as a hunter. He wondered what prompted his fellow Scout patrol leader to choose a future in Tanganyika. No doubt he possessed a sense of adventure and a will to tackle the most dangerous of situations but was Tanganyika the right place? Perhaps it was, as his cousins lived there, after all he would be leaving one expatriate community to join another so no major change in his way of life. He would remain on African soil which pleased him no end as he was wedded to this continent as he felt at home: the place of his birth. But, reflected Alexis, as it was only for a year, it would be another transitory place thus prolonging the day when a decision would have to be made to secure a permanent residence somewhere else.

"A penny for your thoughts," whispered Nina softly to Alexis.

"I am always in a reflective mood when I am about

to lose one of my closest friends. We have known each other since we both joined the Scouts at the age of eight. Let us dance."

They left Yeorgis' youthful gathering and joined the other dancers.

"I thought you were not coming tonight."

"Really, why?" she replied.

"I thought you had gone to Greece for the summer holidays."

"It fell through."

As Alexis and Nina danced round and round to the tunes of a slow waltz, Alexis sensed that Nina was not as unapproachable as she had felt in the past; her unattainability was perhaps a shallow pretence. Her readiness to communicate, her seemingly positive response towards him was solely perceived by Alexis who was physically close to her while to others she continued to maintain her usual non-committal attitude. However, there was nothing concrete or tangible in her attitude which would beckon a change of approach. The music had stopped and Petros signalled to his friends that it was time for a bite to eat.

Food could not have been further from Alexis' mind. Rea and Myrto had already approached Nina and all three made their way to the dining room where the youngsters were busily serving themselves from the large oval table at the centre. Alexis having replenished his empty glass made for the record player and started sifting through the records that were strewn about the low side table. He came across 'Petite Fleur', placed it on the turntable and sat on a comfortable sofa. Yanis came out of the dining room, sat next to him, plate full in one hand and a Stella beer in the other.

"Are you not indulging?" he asked pointing to the assortment of food on his plate.

"Will do in a minute, I could not get anywhere near the table as all of you were surrounding it."

They sat in silence listening to 'Petite Fleur' while the others emerged from the dining room with their plates and drinks and sat on nearby chairs or cross-legged on the floor. Alexis eventually fetched something to eat and regained his place on the sofa. The youngsters trifled and mocked at each other as they became more and more talkative. Alexis felt restless. This party was his last chance to have a chat with Nina and time was pressing on. He half-picked at his snacks and was not fully aware of the conversation around him.

"When are you leaving, Alexis?" asked Christos.

"In a few days," he replied and quickly glanced at Nina who sat nearby. Although it was obvious that she had heard Christos' question she appeared to ignore Alexis' reply and went on nibbling at her food.

"How about you?" went on Christos, addressing Yanis.

"I will spend the summer in Alexandria and fly to London sometime in late September. I cannot face the English winter without stocking up on a good deal of sunshine beforehand."

"Remind me to give you my brother's address in London," said Alexis. "I will be staying with him when I arrive so you could contact us. I believe it is somewhere near South Kensington."

Irini was clearly very sad at Yanis' pending departure and made no attempt to hide her feelings. Throughout the party she stayed close to him and they looked forward to making the most of each other's company for the remainder of the summer.

"When are you leaving for Greece?" Alexis asked Christos.

"In a couple of weeks."

"What are your plans there?"

"I wish to enrol at the polytechnic in Athens but I need first to prepare for an entrance examination which I have been told is quite tough. Apparently, there are too few places available for too many candidates."

"What topic?" asked Myrto

"Physics."

"That sounds quite tough. History for me," replied Myrto.

"Why is History easier than Physics?" went on Alexis. "We are governed by history and although its study is more straight forward than Physics, its interpretation could be very subtle. To master history and the ability to interpret it correctly requires intrinsic intuition and a rare gift..."

"Rubbish," interrupted Yeorgis, "You are philosophising again."

Alexis shrugged off Yeorgis' comment.

"Well," continued Christos, "I am not really interested in studying History."

"There is a great need for Physics and Engineering graduates," said Panos. "Even at Farouk University there is fierce competition to secure places for the sciences whereas one can enrol for Law or Classics without any entrance examination following the prelim year."

"I am dying of thirst," said Yanis and headed for the dining room.

"Come on, let us dance," said Panos to Myrto and coached her to the dancing floor. Other couples followed suit. Then 'Petite Fleur' sounded loud and clear. Instinctively Alexis turned and looked at Nina who returned his glance. For the next few seconds, they remained motionless and kept staring at each other. Alexis approached her, offered her his hands and she complied. They started dancing.

"So finally, you are leaving for good," said Nina softly.

"Yes," replied Alexis, "but I know where my heart will always be. Here in Alexandria."

"Why are you so fond of this place?"

"I have fond memories and besides there is this young girl with a fringe that I will leave behind."

Nina looked at Alexis and smiled.

"A lot has happened since I met you that afternoon at Camp de César when you were on your way to the conservatoire. Do you remember?"

"I do."

"You ran away from me when we got to the conservatoire. You did look back though, just before you disappeared inside."

"I did not know how to react after what you had said, and running without responding was the best defence mechanism, I suppose," she said genuinely.

"You have had a lot of time to reflect on what I said to you, and I still feel the same, which I hope does not surprise you?" She turned and looked at him.

"Well," pressed Alexis, "I do not mind a belated answer."

Such was their emotional state that they did not realise that the record player had stopped. They went on dancing and passed by the other couples who were eagerly waiting the start of the next record. Their absent-mindedness had gone unnoticed. Alexis pressed on.

"Then, I could not stop you running away but tonight circumstances are different. I am holding you tight and you are trapped...", Alexis jokingly put emphasis on the last word as he squeezed her slim body towards his "... so you cannot run away in silence."

"I do not wish to run away," whispered Nina.

Alexis relaxed his hold on Nina and watched her beautiful, enigmatic brown eyes. Evidently the secrets deeply embedded in her mind were not released readily. The record player was now playing 'Vaya Con Dios', the top song in 1953 sung by Les Paul and Mary Ford. Alexis drew Nina close to him and his athletic body touched her frail figure once more. Alexis felt very excited to be near to Nina and their cheeks came close. He bent and gave her a hurried kiss on her lips. She shut her eyes while he kept watching her face. After a few glorious moments Alexis put his head over her shoulder and held her very tightly. He realised that he may have inadvertently hurt her.

"Sorry," he whispered.

"It's all right."

The record player was now playing a Charles Aznavour song sung with great pathos and emotion.

"I like this song very much," he said

"More than 'Petite Fleur'?"

"Oh, so you have noticed?"

"How could I have not noticed? Every time it is played you made a beeline for me."

"I am still waiting for an answer to what I said to you back then on your way to the Conservatoire. Don't you think that you owe me an explanation?" She nodded.

"Well then?"

"As much as I like this party and I am enjoying it a great deal, I do not think it presents the right ambience for what I wish to say. I feel somewhat exposed for something that it is so private to me. Can we meet in some other place, some other time?"

"Where do you suggest?"

"As you are leaving quite soon let us say tomorrow evening at Glymenopoulo beach near my home."

"I know it; I will be there at seven."

She acknowledged and they went on dancing. It was not a surprise that she chose that beach as it was near her home and that would make her feel more comfortable and put her mind at rest. He was surprised at the way Nina had handled the situation. She evidently felt very strongly about what she wished to say but felt uncomfortable doing so at the party. Alexis had lots of questions that he wanted to put to her but held back. He deemed it important to let her express her feelings first without putting any pressure on her. He glanced at his watch. It was nearly 11 o'clock. Only two more hours at the last ever Alexandrian party he was attending. He wanted to prolong his stay at the party but on the other hand he wished it was already the following evening when they would meet. He somehow tried to reconcile these two seemingly incompatible wishes and was daunted by the emotional state that he knew would envelop him until his assignation with Nina.

The sound of a hasapiko, which originated from Constantinople in the Middle Ages, emanating from the record player interrupted his thoughts. The couples on the dance floor stopped dancing and allowed space for Christos and Marika to take centre-stage and show a typical side by side exhibition of Greek folk dancing, placing one arm around the other's shoulders and at first followed the slow rhythm of the sorrowful folk tune. Feet forward, then back, then bending to the left and to the right, torsos bent backwards then forwards. As the youngsters watched, Marika and Christos absorbed in this ethereal music continued repeating various routines. Gradually the tempo stepped up and with it their steps. At the end, the music attained a superfast tempo and the two dancers performed some amazing steps until the record came to an abrupt stop. The youngsters stood there motionless at the edge of the dancing area and as if by some divine order they burst into a rapturous applause while Christos and Marika bowed and bobbed accepting this unprecedented accolade with serene dignity.

Another folk record was placed on the turntable. Once again there were no words as such just monosyllables echoing melodiously, la, la, la, la, la, and gradually many of the youngsters joined shoulder to shoulder singing the repetitive la, la, la. A long chain had formed with the boys and girls moving rhythmically and trying their best to produce the right steps so as not to disturb the harmony that prevailed all along the chain. Nina joined in and was now between Alexis and Yeorgis. Alexis turned towards his fellow patrol leader and smiled. How many times had the two of them talked about Nina and now this elusive girl was firmly anchored between them also absorbed by that stirring Syrtaki sound? Christos and Marika confidently led this frail and delicate human chain of youngsters along its meandering path in the lounge, back and forth, to and fro they all proceeded carefully watching their guides at the helm who seemed in a world of their own. Marika waved a red handkerchief about as though a fast beat metronome was orchestrating her movements. Myrto was the other side of Alexis and beyond her Panos, Petros and Rea followed by Yanis and Irini. That human chain was a symbol of the bond they had formed over the years which none wished to break as that would signal the end of a co-existence so pure, so innocent. However, dark political clouds ahead dictated otherwise. Oh, how they wished to remain as they were but in truth within days the breakup would commence; a process which would continue for months, even years, and scatter them throughout the Levant and beyond. They reluctantly came to accept that the Alexandrian sojourn was on the wane and that they would have to return to countries of origin of their forefathers, places so unfamiliar to them. They had reluctantly accepted that they could not substitute the Alexandria they knew and grew up in with any other place. Their minds seesawed between hope and despair. As soon as the record came to an end the exhausted youngsters clapped and slumped breathless on sofas and chairs, eyes shut and legs stretched. There followed a string of slower records on the turntable. Alexis approached Nina who sat wearily on a corner armchair.

"Tired?" he whispered. She looked up at him.

"I haven't done such exercise for months," she replied.

"It is good for you and besides I saw you swimming in Montazah a few weeks back. That was quite arduous."

"Mm," she whispered.

"How are you getting home tonight? Don't tell me, the blue Ford." Nina grinned. The end of the party loomed and tearful youngsters in twos or threes gathered together hugging and embracing and uttering reluctant farewells.

"Nina, I see your chauffeur has arrived," said Alexis glancing out of the window. "See you tomorrow." They exchanged a smile and parted.

26

September 1959

The cloudless sky on the horizon merged seamlessly with the calm blue Mediterranean waters. Alexis took off his canvas espadrilles, folded back his slim-fit black trousers and began splashing the shallow waters of Glymenoloulo's sandy beach. The sand was still warm, having been exposed to the ubiquitous sun for all of that September Sunday. The beach was deserted. The meandering Corniche towered a good few metres above and afforded a vantage point of the beach and the sea beyond. The high wall added to the beach's seclusion more characteristic of the remote beaches beyond the Palace at Montazah. Alexis checked his watch. It was nearly seven o'clock. He turned and glanced at the natural stone steps leading to the beach: there was no sign of Nina. He turned towards the emptiness that hung over the surface of the still sea. He started walking along the edge of the water away from the steps picking up small pebbles with his right hand and, stooping slightly to gain a more advantageous throwing position, he turned and launched them over the water while holding his espadrilles in the other. Thrown at the correct angle the pebbles bounced numerous times scudding on the surface of the shallow waters only to sink in the distance.

After a while he returned, dried his feet, put back his rope-soled sandals and adjusted his trousers. He sat on the sand and tried to relax.

"Sorry I am late," said Nina as she approached him from behind.

"Hi," replied Alexis and stood up, extending his arms in welcome. They joined hands and stared at each other, their expressions full of sincerity. Nina appeared as sublime as ever. She turned to look at the sea and gently withdrawing her hands took a few paces forward.

"I love this spot," she said.

"Why?" he enquired.

"Because it is so peaceful."

"Peaceful?"

"Well, let me put it this way. True peace is not simply the absence of tension: it is the presence of justice."

"That is quite a profound statement," said Alexis.

"You do like profound statements, don't you?" asserted Nina and turned towards him.

"Mm, I do," replied Alexis.

"I was aware of that, which is why I just mentioned the bit about peace. I knew you would appreciate it." Nina paused momentarily, nervously adjusting her fringe and she continued.

"Why are you always so serious Alexis?"

Alexis looked straight at Nina without replying while his jaw tensed, accepting, nevertheless, that her question had a modicum of truth. Nina sensing that Alexis was taken aback went on.

"You know, all these years I have known you I never remember ever hearing a wholehearted laugh."

"Perhaps because I do not wish to appear frivolous."

"But I also noticed it when in the company of others, with our mutual friends," she declared.

"I suppose," went on Alexis hesitatingly as though he struggled to formulate his response, "I am serious because I like analysing complex situations and tend to dig deeply into facts." Alexis stopped and sat on the sand cross-legged. He continued. "Take for example the war that Britain, France and Israel waged against Egypt a few years ago. It sparked my curiosity as to why it happened and the issues underlying it."

"Oh yes," Nina exclaimed and sat next to him, both staring straight at the blue Mediterranean waters.

"It is such a complex situation which involves displaced people, such as the Jews in Europe arriving en masse in Palestine after world war two, the termination of the British Mandate in Palestine, the creation of the State of Israel resulting in the expatriation of many Palestinian Arabs...", and turning to face Nina, "...with Ismail's family being a prime example."

"I was aware of Ismail's circumstances but never knew precisely his family background. It is such a sensitive issue and I was never sure whether he wanted any of us delving into his past," she replied not expecting to get involved in such a weighty discussion on the eve of Alexis' departure from Alexandria.

"Some of us, a few years back, had a very interesting

discussion in our apartment about the Arab-Israeli conflict with my mother and a Jewish family who we knew well when we lived in Cairo. I had already carried out some research into the matter and came across some key aspects, such as the Balfour Declaration..."

"Balfour Declaration?" she asked inquisitively.

"Putting it simply it was the desire to establish a home in Palestine for Jewish people alongside the Palestinian Arabs who had lived there for centuries but without affecting their future or aspirations. Alas, it never worked out that way and gradually many Palestinian Arab families fled or were forcibly displaced and as a consequence are living in refugee camps in the West Bank of the River Jordan or indeed in neighbouring countries such as here, Lebanon, Jordan and Syria." Alexis paused as he realised that although this issue was raised as an explanation of him appearing to be serious, it was not what the two of them had met to discuss. He turned towards Nina and said:

"Do you think that I should not get involved in such matters?"

"No not at all, I just wandered why you appeared sometimes to be so humourless," she replied defensively and went on.

"Last night you said that I owed you some explanation or words to that effect." Alexis nodded. She continued.

"Don't you think we both owe ourselves an explanation?"

"Yes, but I have tried..."

"How hard have you tried?" interrupted Nina.

Alexis paused to collect his thoughts. How hard had he indeed tried to convince Nina of his affection? He had expressed his love but had he not purposely remained aloof after that? Was it that he had accomplished what he had longed for and withdrawn from the scene, awaiting developments to unfold without exerting any influence one way or another? Did he enjoy this stage more than the previous angst of having to find ways of opening his heart to her?

"Perhaps not very hard, but you see, Nina, deeply entrenched in all of us there is this feeling of one's own worth..." he hesitated for a moment to find the right words, then continued, "...which we value dearly and which often prevents one from freely expressing one's deep emotions. Do I make sense?"

"Do you mean pride?"

"I suppose I do."

"Let us walk," she said, pointing to the water's edge. The sun had just disappeared, and they walked in the twilight.

"That afternoon at Camp de César, almost three years ago," started Nina, "has remained vividly with me and will do so for a very long time. I did not at the time realise how strong your feelings were. As you know I behaved a bit irrationally. I was taken aback."

"I am so sorry if I made you nervous. Did you tell anybody what happened on your way back from the conservatoire?"

"No, I did not as our lessons finished at different times. I returned to Camp de César station alone and was sure you would be waiting for me."

"I wanted to give you time to think it over. In fact, physically I was not very far but mentally I was right there with you."

"After that afternoon I did not see you for a long time. Were you avoiding me?"

"I thought it was the best not to press the issue and the next time we saw each other was at the end of the year concert." They remained silent then Alexis went on.

"Did you have a good time that summer?" Alexis did not look at Nina but gazed at the sea. He realised it was a loaded question, but he had to ask it. Surprisingly, Nina appeared to expect such a question.

"That was the time that I met Tasos," she said, starting in a low voice without looking at Alexis, eyes fixed in the darkness in front of her. "He was very friendly with Michalis and I was often invited to their chalet at Montazah. It took a lot of cunning tactics by Myrto and Christos amongst others to bring us together. Finally, they succeeded. I like him as he is very genuine."

"Yes, that is what struck me about him," murmured Alexis.

"I suppose it was a kind of reaction on my part that I gave in to Myrto's and Cristos' persuasions. I hadn't seen you after we first met at Palma for the Sham el-Nessim celebrations that Easter. After the afternoon when you met me on my way to the conservatoire you disappeared for quite a while. Now I know why. So perhaps it was not a surprise that I reacted the way I did." Nina paused. They had walked far enough in one direction. Alexis turned, putting his arms round her frail shoulders.

"Nina, let us not blame ourselves for what has happened."

"Who else is there to blame?"

"Should there be anyone?"

The Alexandrian twilight evanesced, giving way to darkness. Alexis kissed Nina, her eyes wide open. He slowly combed her fringe.

"I am very, very fond of you," she whispered

These were the words that Alexis longed for. He stood gazing at Nina, unable to utter anything without spoiling the everlasting echo of her enchanting words. It appeared as though the huge differences and prejudices that had for such a long time kept them apart were all of a sudden non-existent. The stubborn feeling of pride which was deeply ingrained in them both had mellowed and had given way to forgiveness and understanding. It was as though her seemingly nonchalant demeanour gave way to genuine care, coolness to warmth. But as Alexis stared at Nina's face, he perceived an expression which revealed the complexity of their relationship. He realised that her apparent transformation, and the joy they now shared, was fugacious and was brought about by the desire to explain the past. Alexis sensed a mountainous store of emotions and complex feelings which had formed an insurmountable barrier and cast doubts on their future relationship.

Alexis embraced Nina and in vain tried to cast away his inner turmoil. Momentarily, as he held Nina close, he was able to overcome such scepticisms. However, as these glorious moments evolved into stark reality, he became aware of the large gap that epitomised their inability to come to terms with each other. The similarity of their characters stood defiantly between them as a huge iceberg in a sea of emotions. For Alexis there was no need to battle away against his shattering realisation as he sensed a potent force driving them apart. Nevertheless, the oscillatory nature of his feelings continued, and he was able for the present to ascend to heights of unimaginable happiness only to reluctantly descend to depths of absolute despair and inconceivable emptiness. The bare truth was that he was about to leave Alexandria for good and within another year after completing her school she too would also be leaving, but to Greece, not to England. As they stood there in an embrace at the edge of her beloved local beach an invisible energy enveloped them enabling them to face a separate future with fortitude.

"Alexis," whispered Nina, "you are deep in thought."

"I think of the happiness that has momentarily enveloped me and the despair that awaits me. Do you understand?"

"I do," she replied.

They slowly started walking back towards the steps entrenched in a turmoil of mixed emotions. They stopped at the bottom of the steps and with hands locked they smiled at each other, sensing the end of a brief chapter in their young lives in this most magnetic and ethereal of ancient cities, Alexandria, a city steeped in memory.

As they bade farewell, they let their hands slip gradually away and Alexis watched her climb the steps and fade away into the darkened Corniche.

Two days later Alexis and his parents left for Benghazi. The little minibus contained their clothes, a few priceless possessions and three persons whose souls were left behind in Alexandria. Although they could not imagine it at the time, Nina and Alexis would be reunited far, far in the future in yet another period of momentous regional upheaval.

27

Benghazi, London, Athens 1959-1973

Although Alexis looked forward to his pending trip to London, parting from his mother filled him with great sadness. It was her role as a mentor and confidante that he would most miss. Mum too was apprehensive at losing her son knowing full well that, apart from brief holidays, the separation would be permanent, a stage after all that every mother must face when children fly the nest. It was natural therefore to spend a good part of the remaining days in each other's company discussing everything and anything under the sun. It was Alexis' way of charging his batteries and getting used to the new chapter of his life that lay ahead. The spacious veranda at Berenice, Benghazi's most salubrious Grand Hotel, was a favourite haunt for the two of them to sit while Mr Mani looked forward to betting a few Libyan pounds at the hotel's roulette tables. Mr Mani had a habit of entering the roulette hall while announcing his bet to the croupiers who knew him well. Although the next round of betting had started with the little ball spinning merrily around the wheel he would shout, irrespective of whether the '*rien ne va plus*' announcement had been made by the croupier signalling that no more bets were allowed.

"*Alphonse, deux livres à chaque* Numero *de la séquence neuf jusqu'à zero.*"

"*Bien sûr, Monsieur Mani,*" the croupier would respond, placing two-pound chips on each number between zero and nine before the little ball came to rest in a given slot. By betting on the sequence 9, 22, 18, 29, 7, 28, 12, 35, 3, 26, Mr Mani covered a quarter of the wheel numbers that lay next to one another on the roulette wheel so increasing the likelihood of a hit. Despite such smart methods the likely outcome at the end of the evening was the habitual loss.

Alexis' departure day had arrived. His last glimpse of Africa, as the boat drew away from the now almost deserted quay, was the lone figure of Mary Mani looking towards him, waving and sending a few last messages of goodwill. As Africa gradually faded away in the distance Alexis, exchanging glances between the sea and the vanishing shoreline, pondered about the profundity of it all. He remained on deck a considerable time enveloped by a myriad of memories and thoughts about Alexandria, Nina, his mum, the school and the Boy Scout friends he was leaving behind. The twilight gave way to darkness, as the ship's silhouette mingled amidst the waves turning them into transient frail undulations.

Africa was no more.

A voice interrupted his thoughts.

"Are you travelling far?"

He turned and saw a tall middle-aged gentleman

standing by the rails next to him. He appeared sincere.

"London," replied Alexis.

"We live in London too. What are your plans?"

"To pursue my studies."

"Which university will you attend?"

"I am not really sure. My brother who moved to London a few years ago has some information about possible places."

"How long have you lived in Libya?"

"I was in Benghazi, only in transit from Alexandria."

"I bet you were glad to leave Alexandria. From what I gather things are tough in Egypt these days. I believe this Nasser fellow seems a nasty character?"

This was Alexis' first encounter with what the outside world thought of Egypt's youthful leader. It did not shake him as he was forewarned by his mum to expect such hostile comments. He did not wish at that time to enter a prolonged conversation with this stranger about Egypt and their new leader but, there again, he could not stay silent. He turned looking at the gentleman and said:

"All the riches in the world will not force me to become a lotus eater." The Englishman looked at him with stupefaction. He was obviously not aware of the ancient legend surrounding the fruit of the lotus tree which grew in North Africa and fabled to make those who ate it forget their home.

"Charles, I am putting the kids to bed," sounded a voice from the upper deck. "It is story-time."

"My wife," whispered the Englishman who thought

it a God-sent opportunity to distance himself from this strange young man. "I wish you all the best in London," he said before disappearing up the staircase.

Alexis' boat made a short stop at Valletta before reaching Naples and finally Rome. After a short lunch in Rome he boarded the overnight train to Paris. He decided to spend a couple of days in the capital and headed straight for Montmartre in the 18th *arrondissement*, where in vain did he try to trace the little café where Joshua's picture had its origin and Alexis had brought with him in his suitcase. He sat at a nondescript café in the area and reflected on the scene as it might have been in Joshua's student days. Young aspiring artists were busily drawing images or profiles of some of the customers. After walking aimlessly throughout Paris' centre visiting historic sites, he continued his trip by train and ferry and finally arrived at his destination, London. Yanis Lotas, who had arrived weeks earlier, had already made contact with Pavlos so the three met and were able to plan their approach for enrolling at a college where they would study for their A-levels in order to fulfil the entrance requirements to a British university. This they did and within months of arriving Alexis and Yanis started their long university education in the UK.

For the next ten years while in London, Alexis kept in touch with his mum as well as his close Boy Scout and school pals. He wrote copious letters about his experiences in London, often visiting the heart of the city discovering narrow cobbled alleys, trying to come to terms with the fact that he was living in the city that he had only previously known through the eyes of Pathé News at Alexandria's cinemas. At first, he found digs on the outskirts, eventually settling in Barons Court, a stone's throw from Imperial College, where following his first degree at London University he was now researching for his Doctorate. For the final year he managed to secure a room at the student hostel in Exhibition Road in South Kensington, just walking distance from his department.

Alexis would spend many summer vacations in Benghazi but by 1970 his parents had left and settled in Athens. They had started a translation business using their extensive knowledge of many languages which spanned Greek, Arabic, Italian, German and English. Alexis' father's assignment in Benghazi, although very lucrative, had only lasted a few years as the political situation in Libya deteriorated. The modern state of Libya came into being by the amalgamation of three provinces, Tripolitania in the West, Cyrenaica in the East and Fezzan in the south. The Algerian Mahammad Ibn Ali Senussi founded the Sufi Muslim religious order and eventually established the Senussi movement. This family helped the British oust the Italians and the British allowed Senussi's grandson, Idris, unite the three provinces into the Libya of the late forties with Idris proclaiming himself king in 1949. Because he was desperate for inward investment, he aligned himself too strongly with Western powers such as the USA and Britain, allowing them to build bases and exploit the country's vast oil reserves. This was resented by young nationalist army officers who made a move in 1969 while the king was visiting Turkey to oust him, prominent amongst them being Colonel Muammar Gaddafi. Sensing the animosity between the new ruling party and the expatriate communities living in Libya alerted Alexis' parents and they hastily decided once more to uproot and eventually settled in Athens.

Petros' and Christos' parents too had also moved to Athens and so when Alexis arrived in the metropolis in 1962, after a few weeks holidaying in Benghazi with his parents, he made sure to meet up with his old pals and reminisce about good old Alexandria. One sunny afternoon, on the fashionable beach resort of Asteria, Alexis and Petros were enjoying a leisurely swim when they came across Tasos and Nina who had reunited after Nina had completed her schooling. She too had by now settled in Athens with her mum. Tasos introduced Nina as his fiancée and Alexis and Petros offered their hearty congratulations. To overcome any awkward moments Alexis did say that he too had met a young English girl, Erica, with whom he was becoming increasingly involved. Time it seemed had healed the wounds of his separation from Nina, who was in the process of enrolling at the University of Athens to study medicine. The young Alexandrians spent some time at Asteria reminiscing about their outings and parties, and trying to locate the whereabouts of some of their contemporaries who had scattered all over the world. They promised to keep in touch and exchanged addresses.

Christos had come earlier to Athens and enrolled to study Physics at the university in the metropolis. By the time Petros arrived, Christos had been given a supervisory role and so the two friends started seeing much more of each other. As Petros had to find some work to support himself, he took much longer to complete his Physics degree but eventually after graduating he went into computing, a hot subject in the late 1960s. Christos, on the other hand, upon graduation proceeded to carry out a doctorate and found employment at the *Conseil Européen pour la Recherche Nucléaire* in Geneva. That broke somewhat the bond between the two although frequent business trips to Europe by Petros, who was working for an investment bank, ensured they occasionally met.

So, it was thus that the boys and girls of the Averofeio, and Alexis' pals at the Scouts, found themselves in different countries having to get used to different peoples and their customs, often trying to put down roots in places that were so alien to their own upbringing.

Those alumni of Averofeio that had settled in Athens had formed an association, with a base at the centre of the city, and those who resided in Greece visited it often and exchanged news over a leisurely lunch or dinner. A quarterly newsletter came into being which was sent to all, including those living abroad such as Alexis and Yanis in London and Christos in Geneva.

Their first reunion took place in Athens some dozen years after leaving Alexandria. The decision was taken to meet in the summer of 1973 at a beach restaurant in Lagonisi, roughly 10 km south of Athens along the coastal road. The group were thus able to escape the cosmopolitan, crowded and blissfully hot Athenian sun and enjoy the freshness of the air by the coast. Alexis, Yanis and Christos and their wives, Erica, Kate and Ingrid respectively were able to fly into Athens to attend the reunion. Also present were other school pals, including Petros and his wife Vassiliki, Michalis and his sister Myrto, Rea, Irini and Marika. Yeorgis, after his year in Tanganyika, had emigrated down under and had lost touch with his pals. Nina, who was now practicing as a doctor, was also present with her husband Tasos. As Alexis and Ismail had kept in touch, the young Palestinian was also invited and was able to attend the reunion. Irini, a graduate of a teacher training college had started to work in a secondary school near her home in Athens. Petros, Christos and Alexis were exchanging news about their respective lives while Nina and Rea talked about medicine and the latest in cancer therapy.

For dinner they started with meze including dakos, or rusks filled with olives, tomatoes and feta cheese, butter fried zucchini, saganaki, tzatziki, choriatiki, the ubiquitous Greek salad adorned with large pieces of feta cheese, shrimps with latholemono, a sauce made of lemon and oil, and grilled octopus. The main course consisted of pastichio, stuffed tomatoes and courgettes, and a large dish of paidakia, small succulent lamb chops with their characteristic flavour, having been cooked on coals. The choice of wines was unanimous: retsina, direct from the barrel, the wine with its distinct flavour which legend has it had come from sealing amphorae with Aleppo pine resin.

The conversation flowed easily as they all had so many stories to tell from leaving Alexandria to settling in their various new homes. News had filtered back from home that the situation for the majority of the expatriates living in Egypt had become desperate, accelerating the exodus to different parts of the world.

They were chatting in twos and threes and jumped from subject to subject when suddenly Ismail, who was sitting next to Nina, said to her:

"If ever your circumstances allow it, the Palestinians in Gaza would welcome you as there is a desperate need for experienced doctors to train our young graduates and assist in our hospitals. My cousin and his extended family, the Mazhiris, now live in Gaza and could help you make some contacts to enable you to work at a hospital at least for short periods. I know that with a young family and your medical practice at present this is not possible but do consider it when the children fly the nest."

Ismail, through past conversations with Nina and Alexis and indeed other members of the young Alexandrians, knew that there was a strong empathy with the plight of the Palestinians and he was ploughing his own furrow hoping that by planting a seed here and there some of his Greek friends from Alexandria may reflect more intensely about the desperate plight of the Palestinians living in Gaza, the West Bank and Israel itself. Nina listened attentively without readily responding.

"The situation in Gaza is getting worse by the month following the 1967 war," continued Ismail. "Palestine lost so much land to Israel which resulted in enormous resentment from my fellow Arabs living there. Before the 1967 war I was able to frequently visit Gaza by train directly from Cairo as there were two trains per day. There were no borders between the Gaza Strip and Egypt. Gaza was administered by Egypt and the people there were able to trade internationally by selling carpets, citrus fruit, textile products and embroidery in an economy that was by local standards very successful. They traded using the Egyptian pound as currency. There was no control of fishing in the Mediterranean waters and the inhabitants made a good living without much interference from Israel."

"And I suppose after the 1967 war everything changed?" queried Nina.

"Overnight," replied Ismail. "Israel occupied the Gaza Strip and closed the border with Egypt making it practically impossible to visit my relatives or friends. Goods had to go through Israel and alas it was the Israelis that decided what price was fair. Gaza became a caged region where freedom of movement was curtailed, and life became well-nigh unbearable. Fishing off Gaza's coast gradually became more restricted thus reducing many families, who relied on such trade, to poverty." Ismail was close to tears as he was recalling such events.

"I will bear in mind going to Gaza if circumstances ever allow it," replied Nina. Alexis and Erica approached them and Alexis introduced his wife to Nina.

"I've heard a lot about you," said Erica to Nina.

"Nice things I hope," replied Nina while glancing at Alexis.

"Of course," replied Alexis smilingly. Nina turned to Tasos, who was sitting at the other side of the table, and waving her hands signalled to him to come and join them and he and Erica were introduced.

"How are you two?" asked Alexis looking alternately at Nina and Tasos.

"Fine, although at times life here in Athens can be difficult for us expatriates," responded Tasos.

"How do you mean?" asked Alexis.

"There is resentment by the locals that we secure the better jobs. To give you an example: we all speak several languages simply because of our background so if an opening appears in, say, tourism, we have the edge and the veritable Athenians do not like it," replied Tasos. Alexis and Tasos continued to discuss the interrelation between the market, candidature for work and other issues while Nina remained silent throughout the exchange. Alexis occasionally glanced at Nina, but she appeared not to notice. He sensed that all was not well between Tasos and Nina but put it down to the pressure of the occasion when close friends meet after years of separation. The four of them switched to family issues, bringing up young children in Athens and Cambridge, where the Manis had by now settled. Although their adolescent past in Alexandria was firmly at the back of their minds, they managed to sidestep it with minimum angst and without a hint of any emotional repercussion. They were soon joined by others, thus drifting in and out of small groups gossiping, meandering and tittle-tattling happily until the late hours. After a memorable day the pupils of Averofeio departed, promising to keep in touch and to meet again at another reunion in the not-too-distant future.

Alexis and Erica stayed with Alexis' parents in Athens and spent the best part of their vacation in his parent's little holiday cottage in Nea Makri, a resort not far from Marathon. Their little ramshackle cottage was surrounded by numerous fig and olive trees which gave welcome shade from the relentless midday sun. Mary Mani was also present at the cottage, while Alexis' father would join them late afternoon after driving from his new job in Athens. He now worked for the Consolidated Construction Company (CCC), a Palestinian multinational conglomerate, a company that undertook to build many major projects, such as motorways and power stations all over the Middle East. Owing to the tense situation after the 1967 Six Day war with Israel and its Arab neighbours, the company had decided to relocate its headquarters in Athens.

After an early morning swim on the rocky beach facing the cottage Alexis, his mum and Erica breakfasted on goat's yogurt and honey and prepared the main meal for the evening. They then spent the rest of the day reading and chatting about many diverse subjects concerning their respective lives in Athens and Cambridge. Mary Mani having been cut off from mainstream news while living in primitive Benghazi, was not able to follow the aftermath of the Six-Day War. However, when they moved to Athens, she made sure to keep abreast of local and foreign news from TV, radio bulletins and newspapers. She cast her thoughts back to the long discussion at their Alexandrian apartment with some of his pals and Joshua's family about the Israeli-Palestine conflict following the 1956 war and wished to know whether Alexis had kept in touch with events in that part of the world.

"Were you able to follow the momentous events following the Six-Day war in '67?" asked Mary as they sat under a large sykia tree in the cottage, sheltering them from the midday sun. Its large well-built and twisted branches extended way beyond its trunk and bore delicious figs which they readily plucked and ate. Alexis raised his head above his current read of Quentin Bell's biography of his aunt, Virginia Woolf, and said after some reflection:

"It was at a crucial stage during my doctorate, so I missed all the details and analysis that followed but I was devastated by the speed and rapidity of Israel's victory. I meant to discuss this with you here but have not had the opportunity to do so," said Alexis as he put his vast tome down.

Mary Mani, sensing that her son and daughter-in-law were eager to discuss the war and its aftermath, continued:

"There was a lot of tension between the Arab countries surrounding Israel. This made the job of the United Nations peace keeping force in Sinai, acting as a buffer zone between Israel and Egypt, that much more difficult. A good deal of warlike statements emanated from all sides and by May 1967 it appeared that hostilities may ensue. Although the Egyptian army and air force far outnumbered those of the Israelis, the latter were far better equipped and trained for a sudden onslaught. There are reports surfacing now that the state of affairs regarding the non-readiness of the Egyptian army to confront a full-frontal assault from Israel was deliberately being kept from President Nasser."

"Look ," butted in Erica and continued, "I read an article in the *Guardian* relating to the issue regarding water sharing in the region, principally between Syria, Lebanon, Jordan and Israel. Wasn't there a problem following an agreed plan to share the water resources?"

"You are correct," replied Mary Mani. "Early in 1953 there were clashes between Jordan and Israel regarding sharing water resources around the Sea of Galilee and President Eisenhower gave the task to a special emissary, Eric Johnston was his name I believe, to formulate a plan to share the water of surrounding rivers. His plan which became known as the Jordan Valley Unified Water Plan was in principle accepted by Israel and the nations of the Arab League but…" Mary hesitated. "There was concern from the Arab League that allowing such quantities of water to be diverted from the north of Israel near the Sea of Galilee to the arid and barren south of the country which was heavily populated would allow the rapid development of the country and as a result make it even more difficult for the displaced refugees to return back to Palestine one day. Israel pressed ahead and in 1964 completed their National Water Carrier project which drew off water and transported it down south through pipelines, open canals, tunnels and reservoirs. The Arab League at a summit in Cairo openly expressed their resentment that Israel was allowed to flourish always having at the back of their mind the loss of the Palestinian homeland and issued a statement which was quite belligerent threatening to divert the Jordan River headwaters to the Yarmouk river in Jordan."

"But the *Guardian* article stated that this was economically and technically extremely difficult to implement," replied Erica.

"Quite so, it was indeed, but the Israelis took the opportunity, especially when ultimately military action against Israel was threatened, to destroy any heavy earth moving equipment used for diverting the water away from its intended destination in the south."

"Could this be a major factor in starting the 1967 war?" asked Alexis

"I do not think so, because the Arab nations abandoned this water diversion following the attacks by the Israeli military in 1965, two years before war broke out in June 1967. Let us say that for some Israeli ministers it may have been a contributing factor, always fearing that with a free West Bank the Jordanians may at any moment resurrect such a water diversion plan," replied his mother.

"Let us return to the issue of the calibre or the training of the soldiers that many commentators suggest had left a lot to be desired in the Egyptian army," continued Alexis.

"Sorry, I diverted us from the 1967 war, but that article seemed to suggest that this was an important moment in time when looking at what happened two years later," said Erica unapologetically.

"No, no, the water diversion was a major issue and had it been allowed to proceed it would have starved Israel of precious water resource, so I think you had made a very valid aside as to the origins of the 1967 war," went on Mary and continued, addressing Alexis' question. "It now appears that commissions and promotions were offered as a result of knowing influential government and army officials rather than on merit. Put simply, the whole structure of the armed forces was such that it lacked the leadership in the officers who, in the event of war breaking out, would lead the troops on the front lines but more crucially the means of communication between the various units was very primitive. All in all, Egypt was not ready to confront the highly trained and efficient IDF and it showed in the rapidity with which the Israelis gained ground once hostilities started."

"But who started the war?" butted in Erica.

"Didn't Nasser block the maritime access in the Gulf of Aqaba, thus not allowing ships in or out of the Israeli port of Eilat?" replied Alexis in response to his wife's question.

"That is true, and Israel considered it as a very hostile move and *casus belli*," continued Mary. "Further, the Egyptian President asked the United Nations to remove its buffer forces from the Sinai Peninsula so as to place his forces in defensive positions."

"You mean Nasser did not do that to attack Israel but to defend Egypt from a possible retaliatory move by the Israelis."

"That is what is emerging now from various sources," replied his mum and went on. "Israel used that as an excuse to stage a full assault on Egypt by first attacking the Egyptian airfields and destroying most of the 400 odd Mirage fighter jets which were not warned so were not airborne."

"But I believe that the Egyptians relied on a powerful radar system high up in the Jordanian mounts. Did they not warn the personnel in the airfields?" asked Alexis.

"This radar detected the Israeli planes heading towards Egypt but, alas, owing to either untrained personnel or malfunctioned equipment the warning of an imminent attack never reached the airfields. Thus, within a few hours Egypt was defenceless from the air which gave the IDF time to move and capture the Sinai Peninsula in its entirety." Mary paused as her son and daughter-in-law were listening intensely. She continued.

"The major plan, however, was not to capture Sinai but while the major powers were debating how to react to such events it gave the Israelis time to pursue their ultimate goal of occupying the West Bank, the Gaza Strip, the Golan Heights and eventually to annex East Jerusalem which until then was predominantly inhabited by Arabs. In statements that emanated from various Jewish combatants and leaders, months and years after the attack, it was clear that uniting Jerusalem and claiming it as the eternal capital of Israel was a major goal as well as capturing the West Bank which to some orthodox Zionists is part of the biblical home of the Holy Land of Judea and Samaria. The sad truth is that Israel would not sanction returning any part of the West Bank in any future peace agreement."

"So in essence what you are telling us," said Erica, "is that Nasser blocking the Gulf of Aqaba was a huge mistake and gave the pretext for the Six-Day War, the goal of which was to annex huge parts of Palestine and not to capture Sinai?"

"Quite so, but there was also another issue," replied Mary. "You see, before the war, the IDF felt very vulnerable fearing that any coordinated attack by the surrounding Arab nations would be difficult to defend the pre-1967 borders. With annexing many parts of the West Bank, they felt safer."

"But am I not correct," interrupted Alexis, "that the United Nations after considerable debate passed Resolution 242 which in effect asked Israel to return what it had gained in that war?"

"This is such an important Resolution that I scribbled it down. Bear with me, I have it somewhere on my desk." She trotted into the little cottage and fetched a book from which she extracted a little envelope onto which she had scribbled in pencil the following which she read aloud:

"First the Charter requires the withdrawal of Israeli armed forces from territories occupied in the recent conflict and secondly, termination of all claims or states of belligerency and respect for and acknowledgment of the sovereignty, territorial integrity and political independence of every state in the area and their right to live in peace within secure and recognized boundaries free from threats or acts of force. It was Lord Caradon, the British Ambassador to the UN who sponsored these statements..."

"Well," interrupted Alexis, "here we go again. Perhaps he felt guilty about his government not fully adhering to the infamous Balfour Declaration statement and tried to amend matters." Mrs Mani, grimacing at her son, continued.

"It is now five years since the UN passed Resolution 242 and still Israel occupies what it acquired in June 1967 and holds many Palestinians in prison. The issue of building large Israeli settlements in the West Bank gives Palestinians much concern. I am sure the goal is to populate the West Bank with thousands of Israelis which will make it much more difficult to claim that the West Bank is wholly a Palestinian stronghold."

"It was sad to hear of the death of Nasser. I suppose, such a humiliating defeat was difficult to live with?" Alexis responded.

"I daresay it was a contributing factor," she replied.

"You should have read the obituaries in the British press and the comments of some eminent politicians on TV after Nasser's death. All of a sudden they started elevating him to supreme heights of respectability for what he had achieved for Egypt in his brief reign whereas before his death he had been the arch villain," said Alexis.

"This is typical of the way some of the media are reacting. However, what I wanted to stress was that there was a meeting of the Arab League in September after the Six-Day War in which, after some deliberations, the leaders participating declared without equivocation: I quote, 'No peace with Israel, no recognition of Israel, no negotiations with them'," concluded Mary.

"Mm," muttered Alexis. "That plays into the hands of the victors because instead if implementing Resolution 242, after it was declared in November 1967, they continue to occupy the captured lands, build and indeed expand new settlements."

"No doubt on the pretext that the Arabs do not wish to negotiate, the Israeli government continued with its policy of acquiring more and more land which was occupied by Palestinians for decades before the British Mandate ended," added Erica.

"This is what the Israeli government has maintained time and time again. They state that the Palestinians, and its Arab neighbours, hated them and they do not waste any opportunity to declare so publicly," added Mrs Mani and continued. "The fact that after five years, since the Six-Day War, Resolution 242 has not been implemented, or to put it more succinctly, has been repeatedly blocked by the USA at the Security Council, tension has risen between the Israelis and the Palestinians with the unfortunate consequence that acts of terrorism are starting to become the norm."

"You are referring to the massacre of the Israeli athletes at the 1972 Munich XX Olympiad?" interrupted Alexis.

"That is an extreme example carried out by the Black September Group, but numerous other incidences come to mind which culminated in a terrible circle of violence with appalling results," answered Mary.

"Am I not correct in assuming that the main purpose of the attack in Munich was the demand to release over 200 Palestinians held in Israeli prisons for years without specific charges?" continued Alexis.

"Quite so, alas so far they did not release any prisoners and no doubt Mossad are hunting those responsible and given that they have succeeded in tracking down Eichmann in Brazil, I have no doubt they will succeed in locating and capturing the leaders of the Black September Group who were responsible for the Munich massacre. However, there is a more worrying aspect. Following the failure to implement Resolution 242, and assuming that no progress will be made towards resolving the Palestinian Conundrum, as you coined it," said Mary Mani while looking at her son who smiled back, acknowledging that he was the origin of this expression, "violence will be met with violence and in the years to come we will see scores of bloody incidences from both sides. Already last year, we saw this happening, from hijacking planes, shootings at airport terminals, car bombs aimed at specific individuals, letter bombs, bombs exploding in Israeli town centres and many more. If no peace settlement is forthcoming such incidences will continue."

"Where does the term Black September originate?" asked Erica.

"Has this more to do with the demise or, better, marginalization of Arafat as a prominent leader?" answered Alexis.

"That is a long story," started Mary Mani, "but you are correct. After the occupation of the West Bank the Palestinian fighters...."

"The fedayeen," butted in Alexis. Mary nodded and went on.

".....retreated from the West Bank and established strongholds in refugee villages in Jordan. From there they continued to attack the IDF and at the beginning they fought alongside the Jordanian army. Slowly but surely Arafat and his fedayeen fighters gained prominence and a point was reached whereby they challenged the Jordanian Monarchy and further attempted to assassinate King Hussein as they regarded him an obstacle in attaining their goals. After Syrian forces joined the fight against Jordan, alongside Arafat's Fatah fighters, it was the last straw and the king ordered a full-scale assault during September 1970 against the Syrian brigade and Arafat's fedayeen. They defeated them and expelled Arafat from his base in Jordan when he was forced to move to Lebanon where the Black September Organisation formed. That weakened him considerably, and more importantly he lost credibility as a prominent leader fighting for justice in Palestine."

They continued to discuss issues around the 1967 war and possible scenarios that were about to unfold. Alexis' father Mani arrived mid-afternoon, went for his customary siesta, and late into the evening they laid the trestle table under the fig tree and had dinner. The discussion lasted well into the small hours with Mr Mani recounting some of his efforts to assist European experts who were employed by CCC to meet the customs and regulations of living as expatriates in Greece. These employees were sent to various major infrastructure assignments in the Middle East.

While in Athens, Alexis and Erica met his school pals and their wives a couple more times and arranged to spend a couple of days in Monemvasia, a tiny medieval town, where some old walls and Byzantine churches still survive, linking it to the eastern coast of Peloponnese via a 200 metre causeway. After much fun and laughter, the school-pals returned to Athens and within days made their way back to their respective homes at home and abroad.

28

1973 – 1996

Mrs Mani's warning about the deteriorating relationship between Israel and its neighbours proved prophetic. A few months after the Alexandrian group dispersed, yet another war was directed against Israel, during Yom Kippur, by the combined Egyptian and Syrian forces with the principal aim of capturing the lands that both countries had lost in the 1967 war, namely Sinai in Egypt and the Golan heights in Syria. President Sadat, who had taken over after Nasser's premature death, felt a deep sense of humiliation following the 1967 war and was determined to win back militarily the Sinai Peninsula and regain some pride in the Egyptian people. The IDF was taken by complete surprise as it had not expected an attack against its forces during the holiest day in the year for Judaism, as most people, including the military, observed long periods of fasting and prayer. The attack also coincided with Ramadan, when Arabs fast for a whole month, which reinforced President's Sadat's subterfuge. Although the Egyptians made huge gains in the first few days of the Yom Kippur War, Israel, after its initial shock, gained confidence, regrouped and was able to rebuff any gains and throw the Egyptian army back towards the Canal Zone and indeed beyond it with elements of its army heading towards Cairo until the UN prompted by the major powers intervened and put a stop to such a devastating assault. A stalemate ensued while numerous negotiations began to establish a route by which Egypt could regain the Sinai Peninsula. The Israeli Government deemed it imperative to build settlements such as that in Yamit in Northern Sinai to strengthen their presence in this captured wilderness. They also discovered substantial oil reserves, such as that at Alma Oilfield off the Gulf of Suez, which they cultivated to satisfy most of the IDF's needs. Negotiations persisted, culminating in the visit of President Sadat to Israel in 1977 which helped to establish a route whereby Israel agreed to withdraw completely from Sinai in return for permanent peace with their most powerful foe in the region. Sadat's fate was sealed after his historic visit to Israel as it resulted in deep resentment within some militant factions in Egypt resulting months later in his assassination. Following talks by the major powers, Egypt was able to regain Sinai after it agreed to accept the de facto recognition of Israel, the first time that an Arab state had done so. What was more worrying however, was the gradual escalation of terror incidents following the Yom Kippur War.

Israel finally withdrew its remaining forces from Sinai and reluctantly agreed to dismantle the settlements, the last of which was that at Yamit in the northern region. The inhabitants of this settlement threatened to barricade themselves in their houses, vowed to resist arrest and commit mass suicide when the IDF forces came to complete the withdrawal. Fortunately, the IDF handled the withdrawal with sensitivity resulting in a peaceful abandonment of Yamit in 1982. Alexis rang Ismail days after the withdrawal was complete.

"Good news about the complete withdrawal of Israel from Sinai," said Alexis and went into some of the details reported on the BBC news.

"It is indeed good news," replied Ismail. "However, have you heard what Ariel Sharon mentioned on air a few days ago? I saw the interview on the Al Jazeera TV network."

Alexis admitted that he had not.

"Well, he reminded his listeners that this was the third time that Israel had had to withdraw from Sinai under pressure from the major powers. After the 1948 war, Israel, having captured the Northern part of Sinai, was forced to withdraw following intense pressure from Britain and the USA. Similarly, after the 1956 war they had to withdraw from the whole of the Sinai desert when threatened by the USA, their main supporters, with sanctions and loss of aid if they did not. And more recently they had to reluctantly withdraw following a peace treaty with Egypt. But the crucial bit in his speech was his assertion that this was the last time Israel would give up any territorial gains elsewhere in occupied Palestine..."

"And of course that includes the West Bank," interrupted Alexis.

"Sadly, yes," continued Ismail, "and he went on to

spell out that Israel would reinforce the settlements in those regions which goes smack against UN Resolution 242. In fact what he did not state, but it was implied, was that by giving up the Sinai Israel had lost their supreme vantage point high up in the mountainous region where their radar and other communications equipment could give early warnings of manoeuvres and impending attacks against them. The cost of abandoning Sinai and relocating some of their bases in the Negev desert was estimated to be millions of dollars for which, of course, the USA would compensate them."

"Events in Lebanon do not look very promising," continued Alexis, "particularly the deteriorating relationship between the Sunni Arabs and Christians in the coastal towns and the Shia Muslims in the Beqaa Valley."

"You must remember" replied Ismail, "that after the French withdrew, they left behind an administration which favoured the elite Maronite Christians and Sunni Muslims who antagonised their Shia counterparts. But what had aggravated the situation was that with the formation of the State of Israel in 1948, Arabs were thrown out or expelled from Palestine and many thousands became refugees in Lebanon. The Maronites, who were siding with the West, faced strong resistance from a pan-Arab force, including members from the Palestine Liberation Front. As we speak there is much confusion as to who supports what grouping and what the outcome will be," concluded Ismail.

"Of course, let us not forget the emergence of Hezbollah. How did this movement come about?" asked Alexis who was aware of its existence but not much else.

"This adds another dimension to the confusing events that are unfolding in the region," replied Ismail. "You see the revolution in Iran in 1979, when the Shah was ousted, had a great impact in Lebanon where the Shias who had long suffered suddenly felt a kinship with Iran's revolutionaries and thus formed the paramilitary unit which became known as Hezbollah. In fact, this unit protected the PLO and its leader against Israeli forces that invaded Lebanon with the intention to capture Arafat."

"But what about the Israeli journalist Uri Avnery," asked Alexis, "who met Arafat in Beirut in January of this year? This is really historic because subsequently in Ramallah they talked about possible peace in Palestine as Uri reported in Haaretz months later."

"Well, let us see what transpires because Uri has been called a traitor by some in Israel despite the fact that he was a member of the Irgun and fought against the British during the dying days of Mandatory Palestine and subsequently against the Palestinians in the 1948 war," concluded Ismail.

After their talk Alexis and Ismail spoke very infrequently due to family commitments and work, as Alexis travelled extensively throughout the globe.

During 1983 and 1988, tit-for-tat assassinations took place between the PLO's Force 17, a commando unit which was part of the Fatah movement, and Bayonet, a targeted killing unit of Mossad's operations Division Caesarea. Inmates upon release from IDF's Unit 504 of Camp 1391, a high-security prison in North Israel for high-risk Palestinians, gave reports of untold misery, including torture with prisoners being kept in tiny unlit cells which lacked the most basic necessities. Very few inmates survived although news about the existence of this prison filtered out years later when prisoners were exchanged.

Meanwhile the passage of time saw the families of the Averofeio School pals grow with Nestor the son of Nina, Hermioni the daughter of Alexis, Myrna the daughter of Christos and Marinos the son of Petros, all born within a few years of each other. These children grew to know one another well, following frequent visits of their families to Athens, Cambridge and Amsterdam where Christos and Ingrid had ultimately settled. In the mid-1980s, Alexis saw both his parents pass away due to protracted illnesses. The loss of his mother was a huge blow because she was also his mentor and latterly a fellow traveller in matters pertaining to politics, philosophy and the arts. In the mid-1990s Hermioni had embarked on a course in Psychology at Manchester, Nestor and Marinos both attended the university in Athens, while Myrna followed law at the University of Amsterdam. A bond had gradually formed cementing their friendships and they started communicating directly with each other despite residing in different countries often bypassing their parents.

Of the school-pals that were close, only Petros lived in Athens and made sure to attend the functions at the Alexandrian Club in the centre of Athens. He did, however, notice that Nina and Tasos rarely attended these minor reunions and rumours started going around that all was not well between them. The announcement in the mid-1970s of their separation, followed a couple of years later by divorce proceedings, did not come as a great surprise to Petros. Following her divorce, Nina immersed herself in her practice and while her son Nestor attended secondary school, she took a route to become a qualified surgeon. To achieve her goal, she carried out a few years of general training followed by core surgical training in a hospital in Athens. In the early 1990s, after Nestor got a scholarship to the USA, she embarked on specialised surgical training at a hospital in Grenoble.

Alexis too was going through trauma of his own. In the early 1980s he and Erica travelled to South Africa where Alexis was on a lecture tour. On the way back to England they stopped in Harare to visit some friends who had lived in Zimbabwe since independence. Erica, always adventurous, wished to experience some white-water rafting and their friends suggested they stayed a couple of evenings at the Victoria Falls Hotel. With reservations made, they flew in a twin-engine plane to Victoria Falls via Hwange National Park. On the morning of the second day Erica went to the White Water Office to book her adventure while Alexis stayed on the hotel's veranda editing his second technical book.

Later that morning when the police searched for him at the hotel, Alexis knew that something dreadful had happened. Erica, he was told, was thrown out of the raft and hit her head on some rocks and was pronounced dead at the scene. Alexis was devastated by the news and with the help of his friends in Harare arranged to fly Erica's body back to England.

Erica's freak accident affected him deeply, but he found solace in his work and the passage of time aided the healing process. Some short-term relationships came and went without any desire for a long-term commitment. Petros had informed Nina of Alexis' tragic loss and he also informed Alexis of Nina's divorce. After a long time and still no contact between Nina and Alexis had been made Petros, aware of Alexis' pending business trip to Athens, seized the opportunity and invited them both to his house. At that meeting Nina talked to Alexis of her separation and divorce but without any incriminations or malice towards Tasos, simply stating that after some years they realised that they were incompatible. Alexis listened attentively and expressed his regret at Nina's divorce. He then explained the tragic circumstances of Erica's freak accident. They were both lamenting the loss or parting of loved ones but without expressing opinions or judgements. They were simply stating facts with Alexis wishing to exorcise the pain he felt at the loss of his wife while Nina wanted to drive out any guilt she may have felt about the end of her marriage. The four talked candidly, with Petros and Vassiliki every now and then disappearing for a while from the scene thus allowing them precious time on their own to dwell on their platonic young love, angst, regret and remorse. They promised to keep in touch by letter. Gradually, more letters were exchanged between them relating news of their children, their work and the circumstances in which they found themselves. Was that an attempt to ignite the spark that had lain dormant all those years since the Alexandrian days? It was hard to tell.

29

Athens, Gaza Strip 1996-1999

Alexis, now in his early fifties, let Nina know that he was attending a seminar in Athens. Could they meet? Nina agreed.

Alexis was expecting Nina at any moment. He was shaving in his hotel room at the Grand Bretagne in Syntagma Square, overlooking the Acropolis and Mount Lykavittos, when he heard a knock on the door. He wiped any soap from his face, proceeded to the door and opened it. Nina stood smiling.

"Welcome," said Alexis while offering his hand to guide her into the spacious room. Nina made her way to the large window overlooking the city and looked at the Acropolis in the far distance, just discerning the columns of the ancient half-ruined Parthenon as the mid-afternoon sun glistened on this eternal, rocky elevation towering at the centre of Athens. To the Athenians the Parthenon symbolised the victory of the ancient Greeks over the Persian invaders.

Nina turned, faced Alexis as he was putting on a short-sleeved shirt. "I brought you a little present," she said, handing him a small parcel. Alexis opened it and saw a silver identification wrist bracelet complete with chain with his name inscribed and underneath in small letters was a further inscription in French, "*souvenir de nos rencontre à la plage du Glymenopoulo*". Alexis was close to tears as he clicked the chain on his left wrist, particularly when he saw Nina's lips quiver and her glittering eyes holding back tears. He somehow managed to control his emotions, as he approached Nina and extend his arms towards her. Holding each other's outstretched arms, they stood momentarily in the middle of this unassuming hotel room and finally embraced, both remaining silent, eyes closed. Alexis was first to regain his composure.

"I thank you for this," he said while clasping the little bracelet with his right hand. "That evening at the Glymenopoulo beach all those years ago has remained vivid in my mind, fleetingly surfacing and quietly fading at moments of deep reflection. It was so special to meet you on the eve of my departure from Alexandria." He paused, then said:

"Let us have a drink at the roof-bar."

They took the lift and headed towards Alexander's bar on the terrace. They ordered a couple of anise-flavoured tsipouro, the strong pomace brandy from Epirus. Apart from the short periods that they had been left alone at Petros' house, this was the first time they had met alone after their brief encounter at Glymenopoulo's beach all those years ago; no ties, no personal commitments, no preconceived ideas. Alexandria formed their bond, the essence of the city they abandoned still enveloped them as they reminisced of times past. They talked like animated youngsters not believing that they had finally come together but sure something strong was embracing them. They digressed from their Alexandrian past, discussing their subsequent lives, raising their families, adolescent kids, their education, traumas that had befallen them but tried not to dwell too much on Erica and Tasos as that would have brought too many painful memories.

Suddenly, there was quite a commotion down below as tourists gathered at the Tomb of the Unknown Soldier in front of the neoclassical Old Royal Palace watching the changing of the guards. They looked down on the symbolic ceremony while finishing their drinks. Alexis suggested they take a closer look at the tomb before dinner. They took the lift and headed for the tomb, an art-deco-shaped limestone wall. The sculpture depicts a dead soldier lying naked on the ground, wearing an ancient Greek helmet with a circular shield in his left arm, giving the impression that he is about to stand up and resume battle. With the ceremony over and tourists dispersing, Nina stepped forward to read the two inscriptions either side of the sculpture lifted from the *History of the Peloponnesian War* by Thucydides: on the left it stated *There's one empty bier made up for the unidentified ones*, while on the right *The whole earth is the sepulchre of famous men.* They returned to the hotel and the porter fetched Nina's Mercedes and at Alexis' suggestion, headed for a remote taverna at the foothills of Mount Pendeli in the north of the city, where he and his pals had dined a few times.

They arrived at around nine o'clock and made their way into the taverna's kitchen to observe what was on offer. They ordered, sat at a table on the far side sipping a carafe of regional retsina, the local resinated wine served direct from the barrel.

"By the way," said Alexis seriously, "in England bottled retsina tastes like turps."

"Turps? What do you mean?" uttered Nina.

"You know turpentine, the organic solvent derived from tree resin." They laughed as plates of a variety of mezes landed on their table. Nina started picking at this and that and looking at Alexis and said:

"Those inscriptions on the tomb make a poignant reminder of fruitless wars around the globe..." She hesitated. Alexis realising that Nina hadn't finished her sentence replied:

"Go on."

"Were you aware that I have spent six months working in a hospital in the Gaza Strip?"

"No," he replied frowning, his forehead suddenly wrinkled, "when was that?"

"About nine years ago in mid-1987, Nestor had already graduated from Athens University and in early August was on his way to the USA on a postgraduate scholarship starting that autumn. Having divorced, I thought my expertise in medicine would help the situation in the Strip. Do you remember the first reunion when Ismail was also present?" Alexis nodded. "After chatting to him he suggested if ever I wished to spend some time there helping out in a hospital he would be able to arrange it as he had relatives in Gaza and he knew some doctors and surgeons from his time at Alexandria University."

"If I remember correctly, later that year there was a major confrontation with the Israelis which lasted for many weeks," said Alexis.

"It was a major confrontation alright, which took many in Israel by surprise but also the PLO leaders. In the end they called it an Intifada?" answered Nina and went on.

"I arrived in early September and although outwardly there was calm, one could sense a kind of pervasive instability throughout the Strip. As I discovered living there for months, it doesn't take much to start an uprising but towards the beginning of December isolated incidents, like those in the city of Nablus and Jabalia refugee camp in Gaza where both Israelis and Palestinians were ambushed and killed, triggered a major confrontation. It was very tense being there at the time. There were strikes, disturbances, countless rallies, stone throwing or, more seriously, Molotov cocktails at the IDF, who responded by brutally killing and maiming many protesters, of whom many were young children, not hardened agitators. I know this for a fact because they would bring the wounded to the Dar Al Shifa hospital where I was stationed which was a few kilometres from the northern border with Israel. Alas, some did not survive their horrendous injuries. The year I was there dozens were killed and thousands were wounded, some seriously enough."

"Mm, an Intifada," murmured Alexis. "Do you think it was justified?"

"The Palestinian Intifada was a protest against the continuous occupation by Israel of the Strip as well as the West Bank. It was exactly 20 years since the 1967 War and during that time there was a huge expansion of Israeli settlements in the occupied West Bank, often dissecting areas where the Palestinians lived for decades making visiting relatives or attempting to cross checkpoints for working in Israel itself very difficult. You know some Arab friends I met in Gaza told me that Begin when he was PM would never refer to the occupied area of West Bank as such but instead for him it was Judea and Samaria. This angered many Palestinians who could see that their land was being confiscated and transformed into part of Israel often with the names changed to link them to their biblical equivalent. The indigenous Arabs were often beaten, supressed, their houses demolished and brutally treated by the IDF, so indeed something had to be done as a way of protest. Many believe that it was instigated by PLO leaders, including Arafat or Abu Jihad, but I saw the uprisings at close quarters, and it seemed spontaneous by the people rebelling against their treatment." Nina paused, reflected and went on.

"It is fair to say that Abu Jihad from his exile home in Tunis had set up youth organisations in Gaza and the West Bank which no doubt fuelled the discontent against Israel and the IDF."

"Am I not correct that special units of Mossad targeted Abu Jihad and assassinated him?" asked Alexis.

"I had already left Gaza when he was killed in April 1988 while staying in Tunis with his family. There was a huge outcry after his assassination, but one has to put this into its proper context which is that in the 1980s many retaliatory incidences took place between the PLO and the IDF. Israel so far has not admitted to the killing of Abu Jihad but Ismail's first cousin, Muhammad El Mazhiri who has many influential contacts in Gaza, told me that it was highly probable that Mossad operatives were behind the assassination. He was, after all, one of the founders of the Fatah movement in Palestine."

Alexis was by now listening very attentively to Nina as she described her six months living and working amongst the peoples in the Strip.

"How did you manage to enter Gaza as it was then controlled by the IDF?" asked Alexis.

"Muhammad arranged it. I flew to Cairo, met Ismail and some of his contacts drove us to the Rafah crossing via Sinai. As a Palestinian, Ismail had a permit to travel to visit his relatives and I was able to be smuggled in."

"No doubt by bribing some guards," butted in Alexis. Nina smiled and said, "It was the only way to be let in. We were met by Muhammad on the other side and I stayed with his family for a few days before I found an apartment near the hospital. Muhammad and his family made me very welcome, but I was viewed with suspicion by others who could not understand how and why I was there. It was the first time that I learned of the true horror of what had happened in 1948 and in 1967 after the two wars. Stories filtered out by Gazans who were imprisoned for seemingly subversive activities and their treatment in captivity was horrendous. Young women were humiliated by their guards, often stripping them naked, beating them and subjecting them to awful acts which went totally against humanitarian laws. Often the accusations against those captured were simply not informing on the activities of their brothers or sisters or for not admitting that they may retaliate in future against the death of a sibling. It was horrendous to hear of these tales from people who were released after years of confinement."

Alexis was au fait with the current situation in Gaza and the West Bank which was under the military wing of the IDF but listening to Nina who had been at the Strip with first-hand experience was very revealing. He went on to relate the discussion in their apartment in Rue Canope with his mates, his mum and the Schumann family following the 1956 war.

"I was told about your research into the Arab-Israeli conflict and how passionately you feel that something needs to be done to alleviate the suffering of so many innocent people living in the Strip under terrible conditions," said Nina.

"How did you know?" asked Alexis.

"At our first school reunion, Petros mentioned it to me having overheard my conversation with Ismail about going to Gaza. Petros remembered vividly the arguments relating to Palestine, particularly the skill with which your mum steered the discussion and the exchanges between her and Joshua Schumann. At first Ismail did not explain to me the horrors that the Gazans were going through under their occupation but while we were there, we had lots of discussions about what was happening in the Strip and the suffering of the population there. I did not realise that over 70% of the Gazans are refugees from what was Palestine following their expulsion in 1948. I went again in 1990 and left just before the restrictions intensified following the next Intifada a year later. What about yourself? Have you heard from Ismail recently?"

"I haven't heard from him recently, but I knew that he made frequent visits to Palestine in the 1980s. Surprisingly, he had not mentioned your visits there. I wonder why?"

"Perhaps I asked him not to but cannot remember," she replied.

Alexis and Nina spent a few hours in that little taverna away from metropolitan Athens discussing numerous instances in their young lives in Alexandria: so many gaps to fill, so many reminiscences, so many friends scattered around the world. As they were both passionate about the injustice that had been inflicted on the Palestinian people, they often reverted to discussing issues affecting the Gazans. After a pause in their conversation Nina said:

"The Intifada must be seen in the context of what

happened when President Carter put enormous pressure on the Israeli Government around 1977 to accept the presence of the PLO in the Geneva talks. He was the first American President to mention that peace in the Middle East required the establishment of a homeland for the Palestinians to the west of river Jordan. The Israeli Government wished to interpret that as a homeland for the Palestinians in the West Bank under Jordanian rule rather than self-rule. President Carter's adept diplomatic move was to issue a joint communiqué with his co-chair in the Geneva talks, the Soviet Union, that a precondition to attending the Geneva talks by both Israel and the PLO was that a home for the Palestinians had to be established, the legitimate rights of the refugees should be acknowledged and that Israel had to withdraw to the pre-1967 borders. So, it was all positive for the Palestinians when President Carter went so far as to explicitly state that US aid to Israel may be curtailed if his conditions were not met."

"So, what happened?" uttered Alexis eagerly.

"Alas, in the final analysis President Carter backed down under severe pressure from the domestic Jewish organisations in the US such as AIPAC and others and in fact it was Moshe Dayan....."

"One of the architects of the 1967 victory," butted in Alexis. Nina nodded and continued:

".......after visiting President Carter and after following much discourse between their advisors who was forced to issue a joint statement to the effect that Israel did not have to abide by the US-Soviet Union Geneva statement in order to participate in the talks. But it is fair to say that there was progress in Geneva in that a scheme was agreed where the Palestinians would be offered not a state but self-rule in Gaza and the West Bank with elections and with a Palestinian police force being established. Let us see what transpires."

They switched to other subjects concentrating mainly on their children and work. It was past one o'clock in the morning when Nina dropped Alexis at the Grand Bretagne.

"Would you like to come to my home tomorrow after your meetings? We could have a bite to eat on the balcony overlooking some magnificent views of Mount Parnitha?" Alexis readily agreed, they kissed and parted.

The following evening, Alexis hailed a taxi outside Grand Bretagne and made his way to Nina's place in the village of Vrilissia in north Athens. She greeted him affectionately, asked him to pour a drink and left him in the comfortable lounge overlooking the distant mountain range of Attica. It was dusk and the Athenian twilight was in full swing. Nina laid the table on the balcony where they enjoyed a delicious meal of grilled octopus with feta salad followed by chunks of squid in dark piquant source made of red chillies, spring onions, baby tomatoes, tamarind paste with mint and coriander. They continued their discussion of the previous evening probing deeper into the Palestinian Conundrum, the Intifadas, the peace talks, the schism in the Palestinian hierarchy, and remained on the balcony well past midnight. The panorama of the darkened mountains ahead, with its dense forests of Aleppo Pine and Greek Fir enveloped by a myriad of plants such as tulips and crocuses, could not be seen and gave a feeling of eeriness disturbed intermittently by the ever-present sound of the chirping crickets rubbing their forewings.

"Nina, that was delicious," uttered Alexis. "I should be on my way."

Nina looked straight at Alexis. "Would you like to stay?" she uttered continuing to look straight at Alexis; her slim figure stood out against the paler walls of a distant cottage.

After what seemed an interminable interlude, both looking at each other, he whispered, "There are many reasons why I should not."

"I would like you to stay," she pressed.

"Yes, I would like that," he replied. Nina approached Alexis as he sat in his rattan chair looking at the star-studded sky and placed her right hand on his left shoulder. Was this an acknowledgment of their emotional, soul-searching past, an understanding of minds, a statement of melancholy? Alexis could not discern. Just the mere fact that Nina had placed her hand on his shoulder that serene summer evening in the most beautiful of ancient cities was magical. They slowly entered the apartment, switched the balcony lights off and shut the connecting doors.

The following day, well into the afternoon, Alexis was scheduled to conduct a panel discussion, so he stayed and breakfasted with Nina. Catching a bulletin about the future of the Oslo accords in the Newspaper he said to Nina:

"Wasn't the news of the assassination of Yitzhak Rabin last November dreadful?"

"Awful," she replied, "and to think that he was gunned down at the end of a rally in Tel Aviv in support of the Oslo accords. Although he was not in government when I was there, many Palestinians thought that he was the one most likely to start a dialogue with the PLO and were very optimistic even though elements within the PLO, such Hamas, were not supportive of the Oslo accords."

"The assassin, an ultra-religious person, was no doubt influenced by the repeated pronouncements of Likud's leader that withdrawing from any Jewish land was unacceptable," continued Alexis. "Apparently he objected to giving back any land in the West Bank because that would deny Jews their biblical heritage which was strengthened by building more and more settlements. You know as we speak there are some 120 odd settlements there..."

"Illegal settlements according to the international community," interrupted Nina. Alexis nodded and continued. "Is it not ironic that whenever there is the likelihood of some peace initiative succeeding, the protagonists are assassinated? The same happened to the UN appointed envoy in Palestine, Count Bernadotte who was the Swedish President of the Red Cross and in 1948 when he was considering the division of the protectorate during the dying days of the British Mandate and he too was gunned down. If successive governments do not suppress the ultra-Zionists, if such a description applies, then what hope is there for the region?"

"None, I am afraid, and I think of the countless families I met in Gaza and the West Bank and indeed in Israel itself and in settlements throughout the occupied territories who long for peace."

"Surely, the overriding question is what will happen next, how can peace be resurrected?" said Nina. "Ordinary Palestinians are suffering by massive deprivation. After I left, a wall separating Gaza from Israel and the West Bank was being mooted and now it's there for all to see. It imprisons the Palestinians in Gaza Strip and makes crossing the border to work or visit other parts of the West Bank that much more difficult. It makes my visiting Gaza nowadays very much more complicated."

"I cannot even begin to imagine the suffering of ordinary Palestinians living under these conditions," said Alexis.

"When I first visited Gaza, Ismail was with me and we walked the various streets in Gaza City and he introduced me to shopkeepers and traders in all walks of life. I met a lovely lady, Ahlam who runs a haberdashery shop and next to her was a coffee shop owned by her husband Khalil."

"Ahlam, what does it mean?" asked Alexis.

"She explained to me that when she was born her parents wanted her to dream of a beautiful future and named her one who dreams a lot," replied Nina. "I would go to her shop after the hospital and buy various items that I needed such as pins, zips, sewing thread and we would talk about the situation and she would relate stories of her youth in her village in the West Bank. She was young when the 1967 war started and after that they were forcibly removed from their homes and came to the Strip. We would often go next door, chat to her husband and his guests over endless cups of lemon teas or coffees. Her shop and adjacent coffee shop were severely damaged during the 1987 Intifada but patiently they repaired the damage and continue to trade. There are countless similar stories I can relate to you which the people bore with fortitude hoping that one day peace will prevail. When their hopes are raised, following peace talks such as those that took place at Oslo, we have dramatic incidents like the assassination of Rabin."

"Given also that Hamas and the Islamic Jihad are not playing ball does not help either."

"Indeed," she replied regretfully.

After their meeting at her house in Vrilissia, Alexis and Nina started gradually seeing each other more frequently although they kept their separate abodes in Athens and Cambridge. They made frequent visits to and from the two cities and Nina became acquainted with Hermioni, Alexis' daughter. On the occasion when Nestor was at home his mum arranged for Alexis to fly to Athens and meet him. It was therefore possible on many occasions to spend time with each other and occasionally in the presence of their respective children.

Following the Oslo II Accord, the airport in the Gaza Strip opened in 1998 thus facilitating access to the region and in August 1999 Alexis accompanied Nina to the Strip. She was able to enter easily as she was deemed an essential humanitarian worker having enrolled with the United Nations Relief and Works Agency for Palestine Refugees in the Near East (UNRWA). Alexis joined its sister body of the United Nations High Commissioner for Refugees (UNHCR) having secured his pass using a UN contact.

Nina renewed her acquaintance with Muhammad and Alexis was able to meet some of Ismail's other relatives such as Ibrahim and his wife Leila and members of their extended families and their wider circle of friends. They fostered links with residents such as Ahlam and Khalil, frequently visiting their shops where other Arabs would congregate and spend time talking to them in their native language as both Nina and Alexis were fairly fluent in Arabic. Through informers Shin Bet got wind of their presence in Gaza and started following the movements of these two ex-Alexandrians but all their enquiries led them to believe that they were bona fide members of the huge humanitarian effort based in the Gaza Strip. Nevertheless, they liaised with security forces in Europe and the USA after finding out that Nina was once again in the Strip before the start of the next millennium, this time accompanied by Alexis.

While working in Gaza in 1999 they were introduced to the newest member of the El Mazhiri family, Muhammad's grandson, Ramzi, who was then only a few months old. Nina took to the infant and over the years formed a close bond following his progress at school and beyond.

One evening while talking to Ahmal at her haberdashery shop, they met a tall, softly spoken Gazan with a good command of English. His name was Mahmood Sistani, an industrialist who was in his mid-forties with receding hairline and round face. Originally from a refugee family that had settled in the Gaza Strip he was a graduate from the Faculty of Commerce from the Islamic University of Gaza. When another customer walked in Mahmood turned to Alexis and Nina who were standing next to Ismail, and said:

"Would you like to meet some friends of mine tomorrow evening? A couple of colleagues specifically asked me if both of you could join us? We will provide transport as it is quite a distance from Gaza City?" Alexis and Nina were bewildered by such an impromptu invitation, particularly as it was offered by a stranger. Perhaps, they thought, it was not so unexpected as by now they had met a good number of Gazans who were aware that these two Alexandrians cared deeply for the plight of the local people, particularly after they realised that Alexis had conducted in-depth research on the subject and could confidently put an argument for the injustice that had befallen the Palestinians. Ismail nodded in approval which was a comfort to both as they trusted him implicitly.

The following evening Ismail came to the hospital where Nina was finishing her shift. Alexis was chatting to some injured Arabs following numerous skirmishes that were occurring nightly at the border between Israel and the Strip. They followed Ismail out of the hospital who led them through a number of narrow streets finally making contact with an Arab waiting by a car and they were driven to Khan Yunis district in the south of the Strip. Although it should have taken just short of one hour via the main central highway the car chose a meandering route, often joining the coastal road, to avoid any informants who may have spotted the car and followed them. After an hour and a half the car came to a halt and they were led into a spacious house, then out into the back courtyard across numerous small alleys, finally reaching their destination. They were taken to a large basement at the back of the house where people of all ages, including Ismail's cousins, Ibrahim and Muhammad, stood chatting. Mahmood Sistani introduced Alexis to some of his associates. Most of them were well educated from universities in Gaza or the West Bank and some of them had attained prominent positions within the Strip. Alexis and Nina soon cottoned on to the fact that Mahmood himself, after completing his studies in Gaza, was able to gain a scholarship for postgraduate work in the USA. He had distant family who had settled at Bay Ridge, a neighborhood in the southwest corner of the New York City borough of Brooklyn. This area was the home of thousands of Palestinian refugees who had left their homes after the 1967 war with Israel. He ended up at Manhattan College and carried out an MBA in Business Administration specialising in entrepreneurship and globalisation. He had already started collaborating with other Palestinian entrepreneurs in Israel itself as well as the Gaza Strip and the West Bank. Prior to the assassination of Rabin, many Palestinians had high hopes of a settlement with Israel and looked beyond to the time when a new Palestinian State would require entrepreneurs and businessmen who would foster links with the outside world, including Israel, and encourage start-ups. Rabin's assassination was a setback but did not deter Mahmood and his industrial partners who continued to pursue with vigour the attainment of their goals.

Although those present had a limited knowledge of French and English, Alexis and Nina were able to communicate fairly easily with the Arabs. Mahmood continued to introduce Alexis to some of his colleagues while Nina was speaking to Muhammad and his cousin. They were immediately grateful for their presence not only that evening but making the effort against all odds to visit Gaza and offer some much-needed voluntary work. Alexis joined a group who were chatting about the rights and wrongs of the situation in Palestine when one of them pointedly looked straight at Alexis and said:

"I believe you sympathise with our cause against the treatment we have received from the Israelis since Al-Nakba day." Alexis and Nina were well accustomed to quotes of Al-Nakba or Catastrophe Day, as the Palestinians referred to the day when the State of Israel was formed, signalling to the world over the plight of the many that were displaced from their homes. Alexis acknowledged the reference to Al-Nakba by nodding his head. The Arab continued:

"Ismail and his cousins told us that over the years you have delved into our history and followed many events and news items concerning our plight and that you are not afraid to discuss these issues with your peers, colleagues and friends whenever the opportunity arises."

"It is the injustice that has been inflicted on you and your fellow Palestinians, the embodiment of which is the huge number of refugees displaced from Palestine after the British Mandate terminated and are scattered all over the region and of course further afield," replied Alexis. He then went on to describe how he saw the situation unfolding, how the 1967 war was pivotal to developments that had happened since and changed the uneasy coexistence that reigned between the Israelis and Palestinians prior to it.

"Prior to the 1967 war," said the Arab, "we tolerated each other: the Israelis would visit us in Gaza and often preferred to deal with us as our goods and services were much cheaper than what was offered in Israel. But after the war it all changed as they occupied our territories and started building many settlements."

"I know, one cannot underestimate the significance of the 1967 war and one can now understand the motivation behind forcing such a war," replied Alexis. "The Israelis continue to this very day to acquire as much land as they can to construct more illegal settlements in the occupied territories and despite the protests of countless countries in Europe as well as protests from some groups in the USA over the intervening 30-odd years, Israel's attitude towards the Palestinians had not changed one iota; on the contrary, it has hardened."

Alexis was now in full flow, describing past events but at the same time learning from people on the ground about the atrocities that were committed by the Irgun and the Stern groups and latterly by the IDF and the inhumane treatment of its inhabitants since Al-Nakba. After an hour or so with Alexis having gone from group to group, repeating old arguments and listening to horrendous stories of massacres and mistreatment, they were all ushered into an adjoining room where an assortment of local foods were laid on a couple of folding tables. Alexis took a small plate and chose some grilled fish, stuffed with cilantro and green peppers and served himself some Zibdieh, a local favourite clay pot dish of shrimps baked in a stew of olive oil, red peppers and peeled tomatoes. He took some pita bread, sat down next to an older man who had kept quiet for most of the discussion and started eating. The Arab smiled at him and said:

"We are very grateful for what you and your partner have done and indeed continue to do here. It is very important particularly to hear you talk about Palestine in such a passionate and convincing manner."

"But I haven't said anything that is not widely known and especially to you people who have lived through such horrendous and miserable times. More to the point, I am a foreigner......"

"Ah," interrupted the old man, "it is because you are neither a Jew nor an Arab but an expatriate from Alexandria, albeit from mixed parentage as I understand, that your views carry that much more weight. You do not owe any allegiance to any of the factions in our region so you can be objective. You speak for the ordinary Palestinian, not the angry militants or intellectuals. We need our voice to be projected far and wide, well beyond these shores, we want the man in the street in Europe and beyond to understand our plight and to feel the angst that we feel daily in our lives so that pressure can be put on the Israeli government and its supporters..."

"You mean the USA."

"Predominantly, but other groups too, in order to intensify the efforts for peace and get some justice for our refugees. I say that because as soon as the PLO is mentioned in any discussion many foreigners think of the group simply as a 'terrorist organisation' and dismiss it out of hand, although currently some serious efforts have been made to reach a settlement."

"It is so ironic," replied Alexis, "that Irgun and the members of the Stern group were regarded as terrorists by the British and the world at large during the dying days of the Mandate but 30 years after Menachem Begin, an Irgun member, was elected PM of Israel and was hailed as a hero? Was he a terrorist or freedom fighter during the Mandate? After all, he was the leader of the group responsible for blowing up the King David Hotel and killing over 90 people, mostly civilians. Similarly, Nelson Mandela was released from prison nine years ago under the gaze of billions of people around the globe. He too conducted subversive activities and terrorised the Afrikaners in South Africa so was he a freedom fighter or a terrorist? The same applies to the PLO and other paramilitary organisations which fight to overturn huge injustices that have perpetuated over decades."

Alexis and Nina continued to mix and talk with other members of Mahmood's group deep into the night.

"A car will drive you back to the city," said Mahmood. "I have enjoyed meeting you and hope to meet you again in the not-too-distant future when you are next here, hopefully under better conditions."

They dispersed and were driven back to Gaza City.

30

Gaza Strip, Jerusalem, June 1999

Following his escape from Alexandria, Alexis had lost touch with Joshua Schumann. During the first reunion of the Averofeio School, Ismail had informed Alexis that Joshua had settled in Israel and was a prominent figure in West Jerusalem. Following Alexis' and Nina's closer involvement in 1996 Ismail, through his contacts in Palestine and Israel, related news to them about Joshua, particularly his involvement in the building of some settlements not far from East Jerusalem in the West Bank. Alexis had already mentioned Joshua's escape to Nina and when they were presently in Gaza, they could not help wondering how close they were to Joshua but because of border controls and security issues, were unable to make contact. They were therefore pleasantly surprised to receive a message that Joshua knew that they were in Gaza and invited them to visit the family in West Jerusalem.

Joshua was now approaching 79 years of age and was the patriarchal figure at the architectural practice he had started over 30-odd years ago, the day to day running and decision making was conducted by his son Avi and his co-directors. Although he remained backstage his son would seek every now and then his advice on some issue which had its origins in the 1960s when the practice was in its embryonic stage.

After the premature passing in 1987 of his mother Hannah, Avi Schumann and his family returned to the patriarchal home in the Musrara neighbourhood, a fashionable part of West Jerusalem barely 50 metres from the Old City Walls and Temple Mount. Joshua was very grateful to his son and daughter-in-law, Golda, for this gesture as he welcomed the company of his immediate family and looked forward to spending more time with his adolescent grandson, Shimon. He thoroughly enjoyed recounting stories about his early life in cosmopolitan Alexandria where from an early age he and his family had not regarded themselves as being part of the Jewish Diaspora as they felt entirely integrated amongst the other expatriate communities.

"Were you expelled from Alexandria, grandad?" asked his 15-year-old grandson.

"Not really," he replied, "but after the Suez War the situation became very tense and many of my compatriots were expelled, not only from Egypt but many other Arab countries in the region. Our family was very well known and had very good contacts with Arabs in Alexandria and other influential people but as time marched on and the exodus of the expatriate communities of Alexandria gained momentum, it became prudent to escape..."

"Wow grandad, really?"

Joshua went on to relate the steps that led to his escape in his boat from the Yachting Club and his last encounter at his house in Rushdi with young Alexis.

"Apart from one or two close friends, the only person that knew of my escape was young Alexis Mani, who at the time was a bit older than you are now and was the son of a very close friend of our family, Mary Mani. He came to our house to invite me to spend Easter Sunday with them, as your grandma, your dad and auntie had already left Alexandria for Zürich to receive specialised treatment for grandma's illness for which urgent attention was needed. As luck would have it, it was two days before my planned escape."

"What happened then?" pressed young Shimon.

"I was in the process of smashing many loved possessions and getting rid of important documents that I did not wish to fall into the hands of the Egyptian officials when I heard a knock at the front door. I looked through the keyhole and saw Alexis standing there. I assumed that he had heard the thumping coming from the lounge. I hesitated for a moment not really knowing how to react, but soon realised that it would have been futile to ignore his presence and I let him in. I could not hide what I was doing as he could immediately see the devastation all around so I had to confess my scheme and make him promise to keep what he saw to himself for at least 48 hours until my departure. He also promised not to tell his mum until dawn the following Sunday. As it transpired, he kept it from Mary for over 24 hours."

Joshua related this episode and many other stories

which fascinated the young Shimon as he had heard similar stories from his father, Avi, when he too was an adolescent growing up in Alexandria.

Soon after Avi and his family moved to the patriarchal house in the early 1980s, Joshua was still the dominant figure behind the practice but was gradually grooming his son to eventually take over. After he had completed his schooling, young Shimon graduated with a degree in Law from Tel Aviv University and he spent a few years in an investment bank in London. He returned to Israel in the early 1990s and at the suggestion of his grandad joined the Israeli leading conglomerate, MIVI, which was headed by one of Joshua's long-term associates Yuval, head of the Arvartz family. From very humble beginnings MIVI, within a span of 30 years, had expanded to include industrial systems, communications, consumer electronics, security, defence and construction. Shimon met Yuval and his son Moshe and heir to the conglomerate, and they offered young Shimon the job of overseeing human resources within a number of MIVI companies. Within a few years Shimon was made head of a number of companies and subsidiaries of MIVI.

Joshua was now an established figure within the orthodox Jewish community in Jerusalem and had feelers in many government establishments and other quangos. He also had links to the secret service Shin Bet and was often asked for his opinion on some foreigners or deemed undesirables by the Israeli Government who wished to enter Israel and the occupied territories including Gaza.

A contact at Shin Bet visited Joshua at his practice. They exchanged the usual pleasantries, but Joshua knew that there was something more serious behind his visit.

"My sources inform me that you knew Alexis Mani when you were in Alexandria."

"Good Lord," exclaimed Joshua, "where did you come across this name? Indeed, I knew his family well."

"Would it surprise you to learn that at this very moment Alexis Mani and his partner Nina Phundas are in the Gaza Strip and have participated in some clandestine meetings, the latest of which took place in Kahn Yunis only yesterday?"

"Well, well, well," replied Joshua in genuine astonishment and called Avi in from his office to relate what he had just been told.

"Clandestine, are you sure?" queried Avi.

"Our informers in Gaza confirmed that the route they took from Gaza City to arrive at their meeting in Khan Yunis was very circuitous," replied the Shin Bet Officer.

"Be that as it may, there must be a misunderstanding. Let us invite Alexis and his partner to our home. We have so much to talk about," exclaimed Joshua without any hesitation.

The Shin Bet officer was not happy with Joshua's suggestion and looked at Avi who nodded with approval at his father's proposed invite.

"I would advise against it," pressed the officer. Joshua went on.

"Nonsense. I assure you, you have nothing to fear from Alexis Mani. Although I do not know his partner, I can certainly vouch for him." He hadn't quite finished his sentence when fleetingly the evening in Alexis' apartment all those years ago, where the issue of the Palestinian Conundrum was discussed at length, flashed through his mind and, stepping towards the large window overlooking the walled Old City of East Jerusalem, he uttered:

"On reflection I am not surprised that he is spending some time in Gaza. Do you know what he is doing there?"

"Apparently his partner, Nina, is a doctor and a qualified arterial surgeon and is ostensibly helping in a hospital while Dr Mani is carrying out some seemingly humanitarian work although we have our doubts about his true motives."

"Is he a medic too?" asked Avi

"Apparently not. His doctorate was in Engineering."

"Have they registered with any aid organisation?" pressed Joshua.

"Yes, they are both with the UN, but one wonders what supervisory role the local UN officials in Gaza provide to ascertain their bona fides?" replied the Shin Bet Officer.

"Do you have his contact details?"

The Shin Bet officer handed Avi a piece of paper with Alexis' and Nina's whereabouts and contact numbers and shortly afterwards, having once again been reassured of the authenticity of these two Alexandrians, he left.

The following day Joshua contacted Alexis and invited them to his home in Jerusalem. Alexis and Nina took a cab to the Erez crossing, crossed the border and entered Israel. Joshua's chauffeur greeted them and guided them to a Mercedes saloon for the one-hundred-odd kilometre drive to Jerusalem. The car was reinforced with steel plates and special glass windows to resist a bomb or a hail of bullets. As they approached the outskirts of the sizeable town of Ashkelon the driver pointed to a large construction site in the distance with dozens of cranes and said:

"This will be one of our desalination plants intended to produce I believe some 50 million cubic metres per annum." Alexis and Nina stared at the site. Alexis explained:

"This will be a sea water reverse osmosis plant converting sea water to drinking water." Alexis and Nina looked at each other and wondered whether this facility would allow some of the water to be diverted to the Strip. Soon after, the car veered north east towards Jerusalem. As they approached the outskirts of Jerusalem at Mevaseret Zion the driver pointed to the 1949 armistice line which divided the West Bank from Israel.

"The so-called Green Line," whispered Alexis to Nina.

"Now one can understand why the Israelis maintain that this line is really indefensible, justifying to the outside world the 1967 onslaught against their Palestinian neighbours essentially redefining the borders, and are reluctant in any peace talks to withdraw back to the Green Line," replied Nina.

"Dare I say to the consternation of the international community including the USA," replied Alexis. Nina nodded in agreement. The car sped along Jerusalem's northern suburbs and veered south towards the city centre. The car joined Shivtei Israel Street, turned left into Daniel Street and came to a stop in front of an impressive edifice. Avi opened the door and with a big smile hugged Alexis. Alexis introduced Nina.

"Welcome to Jerusalem. It has been such a long time since we last saw each other. You haven't changed much," he said to Alexis and made way for them to enter the spacious entrance hall. "Come, Joshua and my sister are waiting in the drawing room."

"Now this is a surprise and a half," uttered Joshua when he saw them and warmly hugged Alexis.

"Hi Rivka, said Alexis to Avi's sister. You have hardly changed." She smiled and hugged Alexis.

"May I introduce Nina, an old friend from our Alexandrian days," Joshua, Rivka and Avi embraced Nina in turn.

"Welcome to our home," said Joshua.

"Now let me see, how long is it since we last spoke on that fateful Friday when you came to our house at Rushdi?" Alexis, on receiving news of the invitation to Joshua's house, had recounted the incident to Nina and made a mental note of the years that had elapsed.

"40 years. As you recall, I was a mere adolescent then and now I am an old man in my fifties," replied Alexis jokingly.

"Nonsense, an old man you say?" said Joshua looking at Alexis.

"Welcome to Jerusalem," said Avi's wife Golda as she entered the room followed by Shimon and his wife Adina. "I have heard so many stories of when you knew Joshua in Alexandria all those years ago." Introductions made, they shook hands.

They sat comfortably in the drawing room, were offered drinks and started reminiscing about their respective pasts, their lives in the intervening years, their traumas with their families, Hannah's passing, their offspring, their upbringing, their respective lives in Israel, Cambridge and Athens without once mentioning the continuing troubles in this region. Rivka was still living in France and was now working for a major multinational company in Paris heading their law department. She had remained single and was visiting her family and spending a month or so seeing old friends and acquaintances she had not seen since she had left and made her home in France. Nina having spent some time in Paris chatted to Rivka quite happily about her time there and they exchanged notes about their stay and experiences in the French capital.

As dusk approached, they were led into a spacious dining room and sat at a large rectangular table laid with individual mats showing aspects of Jerusalem's holy sites, silver cutlery and crystal glasses. They had a sumptuous dinner with many offerings to satisfy the various palates. After dinner they withdrew to the adjacent drawing room.

"What brings you to Gaza?" asked Joshua.

"In one of our reunions in Athens, Ismail was present..."

"Ah yes, Ismail, I remember. How is he doing?" asked Joshua.

"He is still in Alexandria and travels quite extensively so he was able to join us at our school reunions in Athens," replied Nina, "Once he found out that I was a qualified doctor he mentioned the dearth of qualified medical staff in the Gaza Strip and alluded to the fact that if ever in the future I had more time, and I was willing, he would make some introductions and I could assist for brief periods in various hospitals over there. At the time I had my practice in Athens and was going through my divorce so things were very tricky. But in the late 1980s with my son Nestor having gone to study in the USA, I realised that I could offer my help and through Ismail's contacts that was readily arranged but still I had to go through the legal channels and register as an authorised voluntary medical doctor and surgeon." Suddenly Joshua turned to Alexis and said:

"Whatever happened to that transmitter?" All eyes turned to Alexis who in an instant commanded centre stage.

"Yeorgis, a fellow scouter, and I took it to the Boy Scouts and hid it amongst all the other camping equipment. As to its whereabouts after I left Alexandria, and more to the point, when the grounds were demolished and assigned for constructing much needed dwellings for the ever-expanding population in the city, as Ismail informed us at the reunion, I cannot say. I would have liked to have been a fly on the wall when the transmitter was discovered."

It was wise of Joshua to divert the conversation away from the troubled Gaza Strip as he deemed it not prudent to discuss this issue during their very first meeting after a 40-year gap. They continued to reminisce about the Alexandria they had left behind, relating stories that Golda and Adina were not aware of and they hinted at the magnetism of the place. Although in the late-50s the old cosmopolitan charm of the city was on the wane, it retained a mystique that held the various expatriate communities together. However, reports had come out of Alexandria that the expatriate communities had considerably dwindled during the 40 intervening years, that many new Arab neighbourhoods had mushroomed in what were once affluent European *quartiers* and that the whole essence of the city had radically changed. "I still have in my possession the picture you handed me the last day we met depicting the little boy – very Rembrandt-like, remember?"

"Indeed, I do. Where is it now?"

"It is hanging proudly in my office at St John's College in the Cambridge. I can return it if you wish?"

"No, keep it, otherwise it may remind me of the last weekend I spent in Alexandria and the trauma of those last few days."

It was past midnight and Joshua persuaded them to spend the night at the house as the curfew upon entering Gaza would raise all sorts of questions and whether their special passes as aid workers would get through some of the control zones. They readily accepted, and Golda led them to a guest room on the top floor with panoramic views of East Jerusalem's Old City. The unmistakable golden Dome of the Rock, the Arab Shrine, loomed ahead on Temple Mount, the hill that for thousands of years had been worshipped by Muslims, Christians and Jews. They stood gazing at the site for some time without saying anything. Alexis was the first to break the silence.

"This Mount has been so divisive over the years. I wonder how many can be housed in this shrine?"

"Many hundreds, even more, I have been told that its interior is vast." she replied.

"Here you are, I brought you a nightie and pyjamas as you did not come prepared for spending the night. Hope they fit you. Have a pleasant sleep," said Golda and disappeared down the stairs leading to the master bedroom of the house. Alexis and Nina stood silently for a while longer by the large window staring at the Old City in the foreground unable to quite absorb the significance of the magnificent panorama that lay before them and what it had meant to peoples of different religious beliefs over the centuries. Occasionally they would turn to one another and make a comment about a feature that caught their attention or the movement of people and of the guards near the shrine and the Al-Aqsa mosque nearby.

Meanwhile Joshua and Avi stayed downstairs.

"Hm, clandestine meeting in Kahn Yunis," started Avi. "it doesn't make sense"

"I do not know what to believe," replied Joshua. "Perhaps I can find out tomorrow."

The following morning after breakfast Rivka, Nina, Adina and Golda left, heading to the nearby Damascus Gate to enter East Jerusalem, to walk through the Old City and meander through its inimitable alleys. Avi and Shimon said their goodbyes to Alexis as they left for their respective practices while Joshua led Alexis to his large office, adorned with oak-panelled walls and multiple floor-to-ceiling bookcases filled with an impressive collection of books, pamphlets and old manuscripts. Joshua turned to Alexis offering him a comfortable reclining chair in which to sit.

He lit a large cigar and sat opposite Alexis while drawing and exhaling the smoke without saying anything but clearly deep in thought. Alexis perceived that an interrogation-style conversation was in the offing and looked straight at his senior with equanimity. He prompted:

"Is there something on your mind Joshua?" Joshua

looked at him, brought the cigar to his mouth, took a few more puffs and brought it down to hang between his fingers replying:

"What brought you to Gaza?"

"I thought you may ask me about Gaza. Nina and I....."

"Was she your sweetheart in Alexandria?" interrupted Joshua.

"Nina and I," replied Alexis hesitantly, "go back a long time to when we were very young. So, after many years of following different paths and many family developments that I will not bore you with, about three years ago we met again in Athens. It was then that she told me that she had been to Gaza to assist in their hospitals. We soon both realised that we shared common views about the situation in the occupied territories and indeed in Israel." Alexis paused to see Joshua's reaction to the words 'occupied territories' but none was forthcoming, so he went on.

"In fact, I did not realise that over 70% of the 1.5 million or so inhabitants in the Gaza Strip are UN-registered refugees expelled from their homes in 1948. The way I feel about the Palestinian-Israeli problem should not come to you as much of a surprise having been present in our apartment in Alexandria all those years ago when we discussed at length the Palestinian problem when mum and some of my close friends were present."

"Of course, the Palestinian Conundrum as you put it. I do remember and indeed the detailed discussion we had with your mum. Is she still with us?"

"Alas, no she passed away some 15 years ago."

"I am so sorry. Mary and I first met in the mid-1930s when our families lived in Cairo and your brother Pavlos was a toddler. I do miss our times in both Cairo and Alexandria; these were precious times remembered with much love and affection despite the circumstances that led us all to leave."

"I know," whispered Alexis thoughtfully. Joshua regained his composure and went on.

"Enough harping about the good old days. What do you think your brief visit to Gaza will achieve?"

"Nothing specifically, but recently I found that I had some free time and wanted to accompany Nina and used a UN contact to get me a visa. As you may be aware, for the time being the authorities have relaxed the entry requirement and I wanted to see for myself how the Gazans coped with the situation as it exists at present."

"What about your secret visit to Khan Yunis last week? Was that part of your fact-finding mission?" pressed on Joshua.

"You are well informed, Joshua."

"Living in Israel, one has to be."

"There was nothing secret about our visit to Kahn Yunis. We simply met some of Ismail's friends and colleagues..."

"Why, then, the circuitous route to get there?"

"Well, even though the meeting was taking place in the Gaza Strip there are many spies and informants that will report any gathering. Simply, the fact that you know about this meeting shows that Shin Bet were spying on us and monitoring our movements."

"How sure are you that the PLO was not behind such a meeting?"

"Do you mean the Palestinian Authority, or do you mean militant remnants of the PLO?" Joshua smiled acknowledging Alexis reference that the Palestinian Authority that was established following Oslo, and now headed by Arafat, was much more peace-orientated as opposed to factions within the PLO movement who regarded acts of terrorism as more appropriate in achieving the results they sought.

"Look," continued Alexis, "I have no evidence that PLO activists were there, nor have I ever been introduced to anyone from the PLO or subsequently from the Palestinian Authority. No doubt in that meeting there may have been PLO sympathisers or members of the Palestinian Authority, but Nina and I cannot confirm or deny their presence. Besides, at that gathering, consisting primarily of intellectuals, we discussed issues concerning the future relations between the Palestinian people and Israel."

"Alexis, you cannot imagine what it is like to live under constant threat of a missile being ejected from Gaza or the West Bank towards many cities in Israel, including Tel Aviv and Jerusalem. One does not know whether a passenger, in a bus or train, is a suicide bomber or an ordinary Palestinian living amongst us. How many times did Arab leaders in the past express the wish to, and I quote, 'throw us in the sea'? I could relate to you countless of incidents since coming to live here in Israel..."

"I know, Joshua," interrupted Alexis.

"Hear me out," responded an insistent Joshua. "The Kiryat Shmona massacre for example, where 18 people were killed, half of them children, or the coastal road attack in 1978 where over 33 civilians were killed of which 13 were children, or the murder of Danny Katz in 1983 who was only 14 years of age for Christ's sake, and this year the suicide attacks on buses at Tveria and Haifa. The list is endless and of course without mention of the appalling terrorist acts abroad such the killing of our athletes at the Munich Olympics." Joshua paused and looked at Alexis' serious countenance.

"Of course, I understand the grave situation that exists here," replied Alexis, "but the response of the IDF to any act of terrorism is to adopt what is termed 'collective punishment', meaning they destroy scores of houses and shoot at countless Palestinians. To give you an example, they killed over one thousand Palestinians, many of whom were innocent bystanders and children, following the Intifada of some ten years ago, and well over ten thousand were imprisoned, many without a trial. Joshua, can you not put yourself in the shoes of a Palestinian Arab living in the occupied territories..." – stressing the words 'occupied territories' as he wished to observe Joshua's reaction, but alas Joshua still retained his aloofness – "... and being the son or grandson of those expelled from their homes in either 1948 or 1967? No prospects, little opportunity of betterment, deprivation of life's basic necessities, even needing permits to enter Israel to seek work: so what do they do? They rebel, often violently as in the Munich Massacre, because even a peaceful prospect is all too often violently supressed by the IDF."

"Jews were killed, too, prior to 1948 and the other wars and thousands were expelled from many Arab countries in retaliation," replied Joshua.

"I am not denying this, but the scale of the ethnic cleansing of both sides was orders of magnitude different. Look at the disappearance of many villages and their inhabitants, for example during 1948 in Deir Yassin, Lydda, Safsaf, Saliha, Jaffa Gate incident, Ein al-Zeitun and Al-Husayniyah while a score of other incidents in 1967 such as at Imwas and Bayt Nuba. I am giving you a few potted examples but equally I do not deny that the Zionists suffered too, such as at the Ben Yahuda Street bombing, and the massacres on the Hadassah medical convoy and at Kfar Etzion."

"You must understand," said Joshua, "in the dying days of the British Mandate many of the Jewish people who had emigrated to Palestine brought with them appalling stories of persecution and maltreatment not only from the Nazis in Germany but from many other governments which were hostile to the Jewish people living amidst their indigenous populations and craved for a home of their own. If the Jews formed a home in Long Island or Uganda, as it was once suggested they should, it would have been fighting against the Americans or Ugandans but as it so happened it was against the Arabs in Palestine in the Holy Land as many Jews will attest. They were willing to die to establish a base; they brought with them a load of baggage, hate, scars of remembrance of appalling past events, and they were ruthless in the pursuit of their goals. They were fighting for their survival, there was nowhere else they could go to, it was a home in Palestine or death of the Jewish people and their dreams."

Alexis was taken aback by the depth of emotion displayed by Joshua's summation, expressing the helplessness of the Jewish people in the Diaspora who were driven to Palestine and were not going to accept any other option which would uproot them yet again to other parts of the globe but were determined to stay put. Joshua went on.

"The boundaries drawn after the armistice in 1949 were totally ineffective in that Israel felt vulnerable from the constant threat from their Arab neighbours which in retrospect may have been more rhetoric than substantive."

"You are quite correct that it was mostly rhetoric as the Arab leaders realised, particularly after the 1967 war. Truth be told, they were never going to be a match for the IDF in winning any future war even if all the neighbouring Arab countries combined their forces. However, regarding the borders that you have just alluded to, it suggests, does it not, that Israel will never return the occupied territories in the West Bank and Jerusalem despite what pronouncements are made to the contrary when peace talks resume. They left the conquered areas of Sinai and the Golan Heights but that was the last time any land seized was given back fulfilling the pledge made by Ariel Sharon at that time," stressed Alexis. "Joshua, look at the events here in your city. Soon after the Israelis defeated the Jordanian occupying force in Jerusalem, not very far from where we are sitting, Israel demolished the 800-year-old Mughrabi Quarter, expelled 600 of its residents, destroyed 135 homes and instead erected the Western Wall Plaza? Is that not a very provocative move?" Joshua remained silent, puffing his cigar while Alexis continued.

"Look at the expansion of Jerusalem's municipal boundaries, to include newly-occupied territory in the West Bank, an annexation, which according to my sources in the UN the international community has never accepted? Many of the houses there were built for Israeli citizens. By the way, I was astonished to have been told that the Palestinian Arabs living in Jerusalem are regarded as residents not citizens." Joshua was taken aback at the depth of knowledge Alexis was revealing about the efforts of the Israeli government to consolidate their hold on Jerusalem and to annex or occupy large chunks of Palestinian land in the West Bank. It was evident that he had done a great deal of research, cross-referencing his facts which Joshua could not refute.

Joshua took advantage of a lull in the conversation to ask Alexis if he would like more tea. Alexis nodded and Joshua proceeded towards the double door, summoned the Arab servant and ordered more tea and slices of lemon. Joshua took a long walk back to his seat via the set of wall-to-ceiling bookshelves, gazed momentarily at the sky-blue horizon as he passed by the tall panelled window, and sat opposite Alexis who pressed on.

"Further, around 1974 the Israeli government established the Ma'ale Adumim settlement in the West Bank, to the East of where we are here," with Alexis pointing in the correct direction across the room, "and which I believe is now one of the biggest government-sponsored settlements." Alexis had struck a chord. Joshua's wrinkled face became very serious and at the same time very sad. He remained taciturn and momentarily almost uncommunicative.

"If I am not mistaken, it was your practice, was it not, that bid and secured the contract for the design of dozens of dwellings and other infrastructure projects within Ma'ale Adumim?" Finally, Joshua looking down at the Persian carpet, said:

"It was at a time of great difficulty regarding our practice. Despite the gold bars that I had brought in from Egypt I had to bribe a number of officials to enable me to start a new practice and secure premises. Besides, that settlement would have been built come what may, despite the protestations of many liberals within our community. If it wasn't us it would have been my rivals."

"But there are so many more settlements that have sprung up in the West Bank, and more are being contemplated despite promises to the contrary by the Israeli government. What is more, are you aware that the international community regards these settlements as illegal under international law? As a result of the building of these settlements, some of which are not even sanctioned by the Israeli government, the land in the West Bank available for agricultural purposes for the Palestinians farmers shrinks year on year, reducing their opportunity to make ends meet and feed their families. The irony of all of this, for Christ's sake, is that to acquire more land Israel enacted the Ottoman Land Registration Act which came into force in 1858."

"Is this what you discuss in your gatherings?"

"Let us put it this way," replied Alexis, "Nina and I do not refrain from voicing our opinions on the injustice that has been done to hundreds of thousands of Palestinians for over 50 years without anybody seemingly being able to do anything about it. We do also comment at the futility of sabotaging any talks, be it from the Arab or the Israeli sides. What is more, through such meetings and spending time in Gaza in between our voluntary work we have met countless refugees who have related stories and incidents that have taken place during their lives. These are horrendous occurrences of maltreatment and abuse, hate and utter misery."

"Following Oslo, there is renewed optimism," uttered Joshua.

"I grant you there was indeed, even amongst the most vociferous Palestinians who were against conducting any negotiations with Israel, a mood change. That said in the plan the Palestinians only had control of less than 3% of the occupied territories while Israel was responsible for order and security for the largest part which incidentally was agriculturally the most fertile. There was of course some in the Knesset who did not like this peace initiative and called it a very black day for Israel, insinuating that they were selling their soul especially at the thought of Israel withdrawing to the pre-1967-war borders. The exact borders were not specified because of the very sensitive nature of this issue. But having said all that look what happened to Rabin."

"This was very regrettable as the assassin was a loner belonging to an Ultra-Orthodox Jewish sect."

"How sure can you be that there will not be any other loners waiting in the wings when other future Zionist leaders get close to striking an agreement with the Palestinian Authority?" went on Alexis.

"Views are changing within Israel," said Joshua and went on. "For example, Peace Now, the movement which was formed some ten years ago, has consistently argued that the Israeli government should undertake talks with the PLO. Also, great strides have been made during the past few years by prominent Israeli and Palestinian businessmen to cooperate and foster new forums which look beyond the present hostilities. I would like you to meet a close associate and friend, Yuval Arvartz, who has created a series of very successful enterprises in Israel and is in contact with prominent Palestinian industrialists in the West Bank and Gaza who share similar visions for the future."

"Are you still chatting?" said Golda as she entered the room followed by Nina, Adina and Rivka. Ignoring her question Joshua went on: "Have you had a good look around?", addressing the question to Nina.

"We have indeed, so much to absorb in so little time. The old walled city is really fascinating with so much history involving Christians, Jews and Arabs" she replied. Nina realised that Joshua and Alexis were having a very private tête-à-tête, guessing pretty much what the topic of the conversation might have been.

"When are you heading back home?" asked Joshua.

"We intend to stay a few more weeks before leaving Gaza," replied Alexis.

"I will contact Yuval's office to see if he is about, as he constantly travels, and then arrange for all of us to have dinner together."

"Fine, do let us know."

"Will do."

They bade one another farewell, while Golda urged Nina to keep in touch and Rivka handed Nina her address in Paris and asked her to meet when she found herself in that city. They were soon on their way back to Gaza's Erez border crossing, driven in Joshua's chauffeur driven armoured Mercedes. An unmarked Israeli internal security car followed them as they left Jerusalem, keeping its distance but always in a position to observe the course of the chauffeur-driven limousine. When they left Jerusalem and were heading towards Ashkelon, officers of Shin Bet switched cars so a different unit took on the pursuit. When they saw them heading towards the Erez crossing point, they signalled to their headquarters that all was well.

In the meantime, that evening back in Joshua's household Golda and Avi were quizzing Joshua about his chat with Alexis. Shimon and Adina were also present.

"We have nothing to fear regarding Alexis," said Joshua. "He and Nina have some very strong opinions about the injustice that was inflicted on the Palestinians during the 1948 and 1967 wars. From what he was saying I am sure he is not involved in any subversive activities but talks freely about the plight of the Palestinians to any group that cares to listen to his views and the fact that he is not Arab or Jew but an Alexandrian Greek adds credence to his arguments."

"Does he also recognize the Israeli point of view, in that we are surrounded by a number of belligerent nations that would not hesitate to destroy us given the opportunity?" butted in Shimon.

"He does to a certain extent, and he has stressed time and time again that he and Nina do not like to take sides as they recognize the arguments of both the Palestinians and the Jewish people. One can discern, however, that his views although altruistic, are more pro-Arab," replied Joshua.

"How did you find Nina?" asked Adina to Golda.

"Oh, very pleasant, but I got the impression that she was a bit restrained, let us say, rather inhibited in openly expressing her views particularly as we were walking on the Temple Mount," replied Golda.

"Do you reckon, Dad, that Shin Bet will contact you again?"

"I daresay they might."

"What will you tell them?"

"I would repeat what I have just said to you all. I do not see an immediate danger of an illicit or subversive nature in their activities. But who knows, depending on how the situation develops their meetings with various groups in Gaza may attain more sinister agendas and without realizing it Nina and Alexis could find themselves having to defend their actions. What worries me is the possibility that these meetings could quite easily have been instigated by militants rather than friends and colleagues of Ismail and his family."

"Who is Ismail?" asked Adina.

"He is the son of a Palestinian refugee whose family managed to settle in Alexandria and met Alexis when they were both very young."

"Do you trust Ismail?" asked Golda.

"People in the security service here believe that some of his associates when he was at the University of Alexandria may be linked to militant factions in Gaza or with Hezbollah in Lebanon."

"The plot thickens," added Shimon.

"On several occasions Dad and I met Ismail when he was a teenager attending the University of Alexandria," said Avi. "He was quietly spoken and at the time did not show signs of a belligerent attitude towards the Jews or the Israeli government. Evidently, he was sad that his parents had to abandon their house in Lydda but having settled in Alexandria, and being far away from the situation unfolding back in Palestine, devoted himself to his schooling and studies and assimilated with the Alexandrian expatriate communities and was even latterly accepted into Alexis' Boy Scout and school groupings."

"We must accept," went on Joshua, "that what Nina and Alexis are doing is quite commendable, particularly in the eyes of most Gazan citizens, but let us hope that they have not taken on more than they had bargained for. After all, the situation in Gaza is quite fluid with lots of factions vying for supremacy and they will not hesitate one bit to land them in some trouble if it should so suit them."

"Do you reckon altruism is still what guides them?" asked Shimon.

"From my chat with Alexis, yes I do," replied Joshua.

"Come, let us have dinner," urged Golda and the family made their way along the spacious corridor leading to the beautifully furnished dining room at the far end of the house.

Meanwhile Alexis and Nina returned to their flat not far from the Erez crossing towards the coast and within walking distance of the Dar Al Shifa hospital where Nina was based. She went straight there as they were short-staffed for the afternoon shift. Alexis reflected on his chat with Joshua. Was he fair and did he push him too far he wondered? Was he surprised that Joshua settled his family in Israel as opposed to Paris or any other place in Europe? He was wealthy enough to have homes in both places so was it Zionism that drove him to Israel? What were his motives back in Alexandria and was he mixed up in sabotage activities or was he doing favours to other Jews involved in subversive activities? Alexis switched off the lights of his apartment so that his presence was not so obvious from the outside and glanced out down the street from behind the curtains. He spotted a male dressed in a long Jellabiya in the process of buying two roasted corn on the cob pieces from a street vendor while every now and then looking up at Alexis' flat. No doubt, he reflected, Nina's movements would also be monitored. He was not unduly concerned because his conscience was clear that he had not thus far been involved in anything subversive or illegal, but he realized that from now on they were both marked people. For the remainder of their stay in Gaza, Alexis and Nina watched their steps very carefully and went about their business of carrying on their voluntary work and fulfilling their obligations without giving Shin Bet operatives or their informants in the Strip the slightest provocation or excuse to arrest and interrogate them.

The invitation from Joshua arrived within days of

their meeting back in Jerusalem. Joshua booked a table for lunch at the Eucalyptus restaurant near his home and invited Yuval Arvartz and his son Moshe to join them. Alexis and Nina were picked up by Joshua's chauffeur-driven Mercedes and arrived at the Eucalyptus at noon. Introductions were made and lunch ordered, when Yuval suddenly turned to Joshua and said:

"Yousef should join us shortly." Joshua nodded and within minutes Yousef Al-Fayeen and his nephew Ali walked in. Apparently, the Palestinians were well known to both Joshua and Yuval, and exchanged pleasantries. Joshua introduced Alexis and Nina to Yousef and Ali.

During the course of the lunch Alexis and Nina found out that the 63-year-old Yousef was head of the Al-Fayeen clan, the most prominent Palestinian family with business developments all over the Middle East. After graduating from the An-Najah University in Nablus he carried out postgraduate studies in business administration at the University of Chicago. He returned to Palestine and within a few months started buying and selling oil and gas throughout the Middle East. He then set up a communications company and branched out into manufacturing electronic goods. After a succession of other commercial and trade dealings he founded the Al Quds University with campuses in Jerusalem and nearby neighbourhoods, Abu Dis and Al-Bireh. He was a philanthropist and by the end of the millennium he had amassed a considerable fortune, purportedly being the richest person in Palestine. He controlled his businesses from a holding company in London. His nephew was also a successful businessman who founded a prominent newspaper in Nablus.

"What we are trying to achieve," said Yuval, "is co-operation between like-minded industrialists and entrepreneurs whose aim is to further the wellbeing of all inhabitants of Palestine and Israel. The hostilities do not help but progress is being made towards some peace initiative."

Alexis and Nina stared at him without responding. Yuval went on.

"I have it from the highest authority in Palestine that every effort will be made to assist us in our joint Palestinian-Israeli endeavours to bring economic prosperity to all concerned."

Putting two and two together, it became fairly obvious that the highest authority Yuval referred to was none other than Yasser Arafat himself with whom Yousef had formed a very close bond since the early days of his PLO leadership. Rumours abounded that the initial wealth creation of the Al-Fayeen clan was due to funds and contracts he was able to secure for himself and other family members given his proximity to the leader of the PLO movement.

"So, you see, Alexis, it is not all doom and gloom and some positive steps have been taken for the betterment of everybody in the region," concluded Joshua.

Following this impromptu lunch Alexis and Nina were encouraged to reflect that behind the scenes of devastation and utter misery, strong efforts were being made, post-Intifada, to foster a spirit of greater cooperation in Israel and the occupied territories.

On their way back to the Strip, Alexis, while glancing at some settlements on the outskirts of Jerusalem, said to Nina, "We must not condemn the actions of Arafat in picking Yousef to help kick-start some much-needed infrastructure and investment in the West Bank. If it was not the Al-Fayeens, it would have been another clan. He simply knew Yousef personally, trusted him and from what we were told at lunch it worked, resulting in the employment of thousands of Palestinians who otherwise would have remained impoverished without being able to provide for their families."

"It saddens me though that there is little evidence that any of these funds or projects were channeled towards the Strip," replied Nina and continued to discuss the implications of their lunch with two of the most powerful and influential businessmen in Israel and the West Bank. Before they left Gaza they spent some time with the Muhammad family and brought presents for little Ramzi who gave Nina the most heart-warming smile, radiating the genuine innocence of a newly-born, growing up in one of the most deprived of regions of the Middle East.

A few months later the incoming Israeli PM pledged to assist the settlers and reneged on the promise to freeze the building of more settlements. Without stating so publicly he was, from the start, against the Oslo peace initiative and new settlements or outposts near larger existing settlements once again sprang up in the occupied territories.

31

Gaza Strip, Ramallah, 2001-2014

In the early years of the millennium there was renewed tension in the region due to the repercussions following the alleged involvement of Al-Qaeda in the 9/11 Twin Towers attack in New York. Despite such a toxic mixture of war and insurrection there was a notable hope that an agreement might be reached in Palestine following a flurry of peace talks involving the PLO and Israeli leaders including mediators from Egypt and the USA. In early 2004 Alexis and Nina were able to travel to the Gaza Strip with relative ease, particularly as by then they both had official papers which established them as essential aid workers. They formed a large network of contacts within the Strip and the West Bank where Alexis gave talks to audiences who loved to hear the comforting views of someone who shared their plight and sympathised with their aspirations and focussed on the injustice that had been inflicted upon millions of ordinary Palestinians.

In 2005, after the Israelis agreed to forcibly remove the Jewish settlements from the Strip, genuine hope arose that here was the beginning of the end of hostilities between Israel and the Palestinians. This was reinforced by the publication of a visionary report from the prestigious think–tank in the USA the Rank Organisation which, at the instigation of the octogenarian architect and donor Guilford Glazer, commissioned a scheme dubbed The Arc. It called for the establishment of a Palestinian State to the west of East Jerusalem engulfing a number of towns in the West Bank starting from Nablus in the north, traversing to Ramallah and Bethlehem and then on to Hebron in the south before veering back southwest towards the Gaza Strip. The scheme would incorporate a high-speed railway link and an aqueduct which would resolve the acute water shortage which had bedevilled the Strip as well as parts of the West Bank for decades. As soon as the plan was introduced to the leaders of the Palestinian Authority, the deputy planning officer was said to have had tears in his eyes. At last a visionary scheme had surfaced, albeit from a think-tank in LA, which gave hope to peace. But alas it turned out to be too good to be true and the plan was shelved. Alexis and Nina tried in vain to contact Joshua, Yuval, Yousef and Mahmoud, all of whom offered diverse reasons for the failure to implement ranging from doubts on its viability to lack of funds.

With the death of Arafat, the leadership of the Palestinian Authority's Unity Government fell to an ageing and ineffective leader, who resumed the negotiations with Israel. However, given the inability of the negotiators between the Palestinian Authority, Israel and its mediators to reach an agreement during the first five years of the millennium, time after time airing feeble excuses for the failures, in 2007 the Palestinian National Unity Government collapsed, splitting into two factions. Hamas took control in the Gaza Strip following success in the elections leaving Fatah, based at Ramallah, in charge of the West Bank. The Israeli government regarded such a split as an extremely hostile development and renewed with vigour the restriction of travelling in and out of the Strip as well as openly announcing the wish to bring Gaza's fragile economy to its knees by boycotting the export of goods and restricting imports. This period proved very frustrating for Alexis and Nina who found it much more restrictive to visit Gaza City due to the Israeli military clampdown on travel between the West Bank, Egypt and especially the Strip. Because of the tense situation between Israel and Hamas the established crossing points at Rafah or Erez could not be used and smuggling them in through the newly excavated underground tunnels was no longer possible because the Egyptians had closed them.

There followed the start of a very tense period for Gazans as sporadic hostilities escalated to violent and brutal confrontations between Hamas and the IDF. The three-week violent war during December 2008 and January 2009, codenamed Operation Cast Lead by Israelis or the Gaza Massacre by the Palestinians, made it impossible for Alexis and Nina to be smuggled into the Strip despite willing conspirators such as Ismail and his extended family network. Israel blamed Hamas for firing rockets towards their border towns while the Palestinians blamed the IDF for breaking the delicate ceasefire and continuing the stranglehold on the Strip.

Although Alexis and Nina felt frustrated, they bided their time and waited for a calmer period before even considering going back to the Strip. Within a few years the situation had improved and Ismail informed Alexis and Nina that he could smuggle them into the Strip with the aid of some associates. In early 2011, Alexis and Nina flew to Cairo and met a contact of Ismail's who drove them at night along the main road in Sinai towards the Strip. At El Arish they left the main road leading to Rafah and followed the small coastal road on the North of Sinai Governorate. Upon reaching the coast they switched to another car and headed towards Al Qarya as Suwaydiya following the narrow-laned Taba-Rafah Road. About two hundred metres from the border between Sinai and the Gaza Strip they embarked on a small boat which finally brought them to the southern part of the Strip. Muhammad, who as ever took it upon himself to organise their entry into the Strip, had brought his grandson Ramzi along at the disembarkation point to the great consternation of both Nina and Alexis. However, as soon as the young 11-year old said to Nina, "Hello, Auntie," her anxiety evaporated, and tears of joy filled her eyes as she embraced little Ramzi. They were ushered into an old Citroën DS Estate and driven to the north of the Strip. At traffic lights the car slowly sank to the ground as the engine-driven hydraulic system was depressurized giving the feeling that one was hovering along.

"Tell us about school!" said Nina as they switched cars and were hurriedly bundled into a little Fiat on their way to their flat in Gaza City.

"Oh, school is OK, I do not like mathematics, but I am happy with most other subjects," replied Ramzi. Nina, pointing at Alexis, turned and replied:

"Uncle Alexis is a wizard at mathematics, and he will be able to help you." Alexis looked at Ramzi, smiled, acknowledging Nina's remark, and looked out of the window. Unfolding in front of his eyes was a deteriorating Strip. Gazans looked depressed, shops dimly lit and with abandoned rubbish in the streets. The car followed the back streets to avoid Hamas' check points and Shin Bet informers who disguised themselves as Arabs as they mingled with the indigenous population and remained invisible. Muhammad dropped Nina and Alexis at their apartment near the hospital. Nina immediately went to the office of UNRWA to inform them of her unexpected presence in the Strip and to be assigned some work. The secretary handed her a note. It was from Mahmood Sistani informing her that he wished to discuss some developments, and would she and Alexis make contact when they were next around.

The three of them met the following day at a café in the Mall in Gaza City.

"I wanted to let you know of some interesting development concerning Yousef Al-Fayeem whom I believe you had met many years back," started Mahmood.

"We do know Yousef and his nephew Ali; Joshua arranged for us to meet both of them," replied Alexis.

"Following the break of the National Unity Government in 2007, Yousef was so frustrated by the infighting between Fatah and Hamas that he formed a new political movement, the Palestinian Forum," continued Mahmood.

"Political movements mean nothing really especially, here in the Middle East," replied Nina rather dismissively.

"Hear me out," said Mahmood and went on. "He has repeatedly turned down a suggestion to be Prime Minister or assume other ministerial positions within the Palestinian Authority at Ramallah, because he believes that the infighting between the two factions is counterproductive. What is more significant is that he is attempting to bring together many prominent businessmen, both Palestinian and Jewish, with the view to exerting pressure on the ruling parties to get together and settle." They discussed the ins and outs of Yousef's initiatives for some considerable time and before parting Mahmood promised to keep in touch and update them with any new behind-the-scenes initiatives.

Not far from the Dar Al Shifa hospital lay a small park with giant slides, swings, mini rock-climbing walls and other attractions for young kids. Ahlam on her way home would often come across Nina as she left the hospital and they would make their way to the park to meet little Ramzi and his friends enjoying the activities after school. Often they met Ramzi's mum, Karima, and all three would sit on a bench looking at Ramzi climbing a tree using a rope ladder or jumping from branch to branch occasionally losing his balance, falling down and starting again. He would then scramble up rope nets and navigate obstacles in Viking ships. Ahlam and Karima would relate episodes in their childhoods to Nina who listened attentively to events, some happy, more often painful, and interspersed with a modicum of hope pinned on the Hamas leadership who had promised that now that they were in charge the situation in Gaza would improve. The youngest of the three women, Karima, would remain silent for long periods listening to the other two, trying to suss out what drove Nina and her partner to come to Gaza.

At the end of play Nina would often ask Karima if she could take the little boy for a pizza, à deux, wishing to spend some time with the young Gazan and to get to know him better. They would spend a happy hour in a pizzeria not far from Muhammad's family home and eventually return home. Nina would teach little Ramzi French and English. The young boy was fascinated by his adopted Auntie who was so different from all the relatives and the other women in his entourage. Nina would give him short exercises to carry out at his leisure and discuss at subsequent meetings. He thus excelled in languages at school but surprisingly there was no resentment from his pals. Alexis would sometimes join them and the three of them would saunter back home along the narrow winding backstreets of Gaza City.

"Tell me, Auntie, about the world outside Palestine?" little Ramzi would ask. "Is Athens a big city with fast cars, large buildings and sandy beaches like these here in Gaza?" Nina would go on to explain the history of the Parthenon, the ancient Greeks, Alexander the Great, and the great city of Alexandria he had founded.

"I met your Uncle Alexis there when I was young, well when we were a little bit older than yourself," she would say.

"Do you visit Alexandria?"

"There are trips that our old school friends organise every now and then, but we rarely go with them."

"Why?" Ramzi would ask innocently.

"We all have great memories of Alexandria and our homes are now elsewhere. Sometimes it is too painful to go back and to see all the changes that have been made over the years. At our school, although it still exists, only a handful of pupils attend the classes, so it is sad to see how things are at present."

"I am sad sometimes and I do not really know why. Perhaps it is to do with the bombs that fall near our neighbourhood every so often, it is very scary. My family does not like the Israelis. When I ask my parents, they tell me that I am too young to understand. Am I too young?" Nina was taken aback by the innocent approach of the questions from an 11-year-old. She would often distract the youngster by focussing on something that was happening around them.

Over the years Alexis, and especially Nina, had formed a strong bond with the young boy. On the occasions when they were smuggled into Gaza, they would spend quality time with the youngster whose adolescence they followed closely amidst the turmoil of Intifadas and fruitless attempts to reach a peaceful settlement.

The visits to Gaza, albeit very infrequent during the last decade, nevertheless remained clandestine as far as their children Hermioni and Nestor were concerned. When they were away from their bases in Athens or Cambridge they concealed their whereabouts and gave the impression that they were sunning themselves in fashionable resorts in Greece or Italy enjoying time together after years of separation whilst the authorities in Israel refrained from announcing to the outside world their presence in Gaza because they did not wish to admit that somehow Alexis and Nina kept slipping through their extensive network of agents, spies, informants and collaborators in the Middle East and beyond.

While in Gaza, during the early summer of 2013, Alexis and Nina received an invitation from Yousef to come to his palatial house in the outskirts of Ramallah. He had completed it towards the end of the previous millennium, and it was a replica of a large villa in Italy he was very fond of. Alexis and Nina were able to travel to his house in Yousef's chauffeur-driven Audi. They arrived early one evening and were introduced to his extended family.

"Welcome to our new home," said Yousef and greeted them affectionately. Later in the evening Yousef asked Alexis and Nina to follow him to his study.

"Do you know about my initiative, the 'Palestine Forum'?" he asked.

"Yes, Mahmood told us a few years ago when we were last in Gaza. How is it going?" replied Alexis.

"Do you remember our lunch with Yuval Arvartz and his son Moshe in Jerusalem? Joshua was present too."

Alexis and Nina nodded. Yousef went on.

"Yuval, myself and other businessmen from Israel and Palestine are launching an initiative which we will call 'Breaking the Impasse', or BTI for short. We are fed up with the inability of politicians, from both sides I hasten to add, to discuss peace terms which are acceptable to all concerned. This will be launched under the auspices of the World Economic Forum and we hence booked a venue in a hotel near the Dead Sea."

"Why now?" asked Alexis.

"The timing of our BTI is crucial," replied Yousef. "As you are aware, the US Secretary of State, John Kerry, is about to start another round of talks between the two sides to broker peace. Our Initiative gives a message that in any peace agreement the reconstruction within a new State of Palestine would require a huge industrial effort and key figures from Israel and Palestine are prepared to work together to achieve that goal. We are pleading with all the politicians and mediators to get a lasting peace based on the two-state solution." Alexis and Nina looked at each other, their facial expressions conveying uncertainty and deep concern.

"But glancing at a recent map of the West Bank published in an article in the *Figaro* earlier this year," replied Nina, "I was appalled at the extent of the Israeli settlements within the West Bank. I must ask you, what would constitute a West Bank Palestinian State? Surely, not just simply the main towns of Ramallah, Nablus, Hebron and a bit of land that has no settlements in it? The international community time and time again has stated that any two-state solution can only be seriously considered if the Israelis withdraw from their illegal settlements in Palestine and go back to the pre-1967 borders. Can you see that happening by force, using soldiers of the IDF? Because I cannot imagine the settlers withdrawing willingly."

After a grimace showing Yousef's disapproval of Nina's blunt statement, he went on. "We are only too aware of the problem the settlements in the West Bank pose but if we start putting preconditions on any talks we will not get anywhere. No doubt, the settlement issue will be discussed in the peace talks. Nobody assumes an overnight miracle but let them start a dialogue, knowing full well that the business communities are firmly committed to rebuilding a new Palestine. So, I hope you can join us at the launch."

"If we are still in Gaza we will be delighted to attend. Thank you," said Alexis. Nina nodded.

"Let us join the others," Yousef said, and led Alexis and Nina to the huge but beautifully designed sitting room where the rest of the gathering were chatting while the youngsters were engaged in mindless video games. Large wall-to-ceiling windows gave a panoramic view of the city of Ramallah in the far distance.

On their drive back to the Strip, Alexis and Nina reflected on Yousef's initiative and discussed its implications. One thing was for certain, the business community was utterly fed up with the inability of the leaders of the various factions to come to the negotiating table for a mutually acceptable solution. Alexis agreed entirely with Nina that the biggest stumbling block was the Israeli settlements strewn all over the West Bank knowing full well that they would not be abandoned, however many incentives or sweeteners the negotiators threw at them. Equally, they were aware that Hamas would not accept any solution other than complete withdrawal of Israel to the pre-1967 borders.

Alexis and Nina were still in Gaza when Yousef alerted them that BTI was about to be staged. They were able to attend the launch of the Initiative at the Dead Sea where speeches were made by key figures from both sides of the divide. Paraphrasing Yuval's statement, it read:

"We met hundreds of powerful individuals who stated that something had to be done. The message was that enough was enough. Our politicians should take this initiative seriously and act. So be it if we fail but at least we can hold our heads high and say that we have tried."

While Yousef's read:

"We are just messengers and we will leave the details to the politicians. Our goal is to break the impasse and implore the two sides to negotiate. They will have to compromise but we wish to persuade the adversaries to enter into genuine negotiations."

The Dead Sea meeting was followed by a huge media campaign in Israel and the occupied territories early in 2014, costing well over a quarter of a million dollars, pleading with the politicians of both sides and their negotiators to get serious about brokering a lasting peace agreement during the ongoing peace talks that had started a few months earlier. Alas, such a positive move by well over three hundred prominent industrialists was taking place amidst warnings from journalists on the ground, as well as the humanitarian agencies, that trouble was brewing on all fronts.

32

Athens, May 2016

Alexis and Nina left Gaza and were back at their homes in Cambridge and Athens, to-ing and fro-ing between the two abodes. Alexis had a series of meetings in Athens and Rome in early May in 2016 and was staying with Nina at Vrilissia. One evening Nina arranged a small party at her home with Petros and his wife Vassiliki as well as Irini Samara, Nina's contemporary at the Averofeio in Alexandria. Irini, now in her early seventies, had twice been married and divorced and had just become a grandma for the third time. She had recently retired as Headmistress of a private school not far from Nina's district. Vassiliki was still part-time editor of a local newspaper in Athens while Petros had long retired from a career in computing with several foreign banks based in Athens. As is usual in circumstances where pupils of the school reunite after long periods, they spent a great deal of the evening talking about their personal circumstances, such as their growing families, leisure, hobbies and part time work. Although times were difficult in Greece following bouts of austerity measures and several bailouts by the EU they were all comfortably off and tried to assist their families where they could, some of whom had emigrated to other European countries and beyond. The situation in Palestine, however, was never far from the ex-Alexandrians' thoughts that evening.

"Disappointing news from Palestine on the failure of the peace talks that John Kerry brokered two years ago and the resulting war between Israel and Hamas," started Petros, looking at Nina as they all sat in the early evening on her spacious balcony overlooking the magnificent view over mount Attica. "Have you kept in touch with the situation there?" Nina sat next to Petros as Alexis was offering another round of drinks and replied:

"Trying to untangle the situation over there and disentangle facts from rumours is an impossible task. Having spent some time in the region and talked to key figures both in Israel and Palestine as well as reading countless newspaper reports and TV bulletins, I think I have quite a clear picture of what happened two years ago. Everybody knows by now that the thorny issue is the return to the pre-1967 borders and the ever-expanding settlements in the West Bank and East Jerusalem." Petros nodded as though he understood. Nina continued.

"Would you believe that even before the negotiations started in mid-2013, Israel approved nearly 1200 settlement homes and what is more their spokesperson stated that these settlements would remain part of Israel in any future peace agreement."

"And if that was not provocative enough," butted in Alexis, who after serving drinks came and sat next to Irini, "during the height of the fight that ensued after the talks collapsed, that August Israel approved another 900 settler homes. That was not all. In October of that year Israel announced that they were going to build a further 3500 homes for settlers in the West Bank. The British Foreign Office was so aghast at such blatant disregard for international opinion that it strongly condemned these decisions as it undermined, as they put it, the trust and threatened the viability of the two-state solution."

"They were also constructing new settler units in East Jerusalem at the same time," said Vassiliki who had reported on these developments in her Newspaper column at the time.

"Over 60, to be precise," replied Alexis. "As I understand it there was a time limit to get those talks concluded particularly coupled with the fact that the Israelis agreed to release long-held Palestinian prisoners, some low level but also including some high-level military figures, as a precondition to holding the talks in the first place."

"It is fair to say that little by little they eventually released the prisoners but the mistrust between the two factions and their advisors made it impossible to continue the talks," said Nina.

"The whole issue is so depressing," said Irini. "I cannot ever see them reaching an agreement which will satisfy Jews and Arabs in Palestine. It is already 68 years since the creation of Israel and the warring parties are as far apart now as they ever were."

"What is more depressing," replied Alexis who

stood up, picked up Irini's glass for a refill, stopped at the door and continued, "is that following the collapse of the talks gave impetus for a renewed spate of violence which culminated in what some commentators refer to as the silent Intifada". Alexis disappeared towards the drinks cabinet. On reappearing he pressed on:

"Or third Intifada given that the first took place during 1987-93 which Nina experienced personally..." They all looked at Nina who nodded.

"One can assume that the second Intifada was the collective insurrections in the first few years of the millennium. However, it is only semantics to refer to first or second Intifadas; let us say there was renewed violence."

"What triggered it?" asked Petros.

"Possibly the kidnapping and murder of three Jewish boys," said Nina.

"By Hamas, no doubt," interjected Irini.

"Most commentators thought so but Hamas denied they had anything to do with it although they did not condemn it stating that there were many prisoners still in Israeli jails who, although it was promised, were never released. Of course, Israel arrested thousands of suspects including most of the military leaders in the Strip. But some investigative journalists concluded that the most likely culprits were members of the Qawasameh tribe."

"Who?" asked Vassiliki.

"This is a dissident ex-Hamas grouping in Hebron which often opposes moves by Hamas in Gaza to halt its bombings and attacks towards Israel and initiate peace talks. It is said that they initiate violence themselves which inevitably provokes retaliation by IDF and resorts to collective punishment." replied Alexis.

"You mean to say," butted in Petros, "that this clan deliberately murdered these boys to instigate renewed violence in the region?"

"That is my assessment because days later Jews abducted a young Palestinian..."

"Mohammed Abu Khdeir, I believe was his name," interrupted Nina.

"Yes, well, Israeli settlers in East Jerusalem forced him into a car the day after the burial of the three Jewish boys. They found him days later in a forest nearby and the evidence suggests that he was burnt alive. Of course, the Israeli authorities hunted the perpetrators and following their arrest tried them in a court."

"By God, what is happening over there is inhumane," said Petros.

"Look, although Nina and I have given you potted examples of incidents that sparked wide insurrection, the irrefutable fact is that frustration on the part of the ordinary Palestinian citizen rose following the death of Yasser Arafat when there was no obvious candidate of the same stature to succeed him. This coupled with the increase in settlements in the West Bank and East Jerusalem, punitive restrictions on border movement and brutal collective punishment by the IDF, doled out on them when bombings, suicides and other attacks took place, has fueled their resentment. However, that said, the few examples we have given you escalated into major insurrections in Jerusalem which spread to other parts of the West Bank and the Gaza Strip and lasted the best part of 50 days."

Alexis and Nina then took it in turn to summarise the events of the 2014 Intifada where Hamas and Fatah called for days of rage in support of the killing in Jerusalem of the Palestinian youngster. Many rockets were fired from secret locations within the Strip on a number of Israeli towns and settlements including Tel Aviv and Jerusalem, inflicting dozens of casualties. Israel retaliated fiercely by destroying close to 9000 homes and partially damaging another 5000, claiming that rockets were fired from within carefully concealed fortifications underneath some of these houses.

Over 2000 Palestinians were killed while forcing those who survived to live in rented accommodation which they could ill afford. UNWRA, with the help of international aid, promised to rebuild up to 7000 homes but the uptake two years after the war was still very slow. Israel, who measured its military casualties to be less than one hundred, continued the assault by IDF's F16 fighters and destroyed the only Power Station in Gaza thus depriving citizens of the means to run the sanitation plants, crippling the distribution of water and putting out of action sewage treatment plants while severely reducing the ability of hospitals to function properly. Amnesty International called the destruction of the power station 'a collective punishment' of its people. It further crippled the reconstruction of its ruined infrastructure by restricting the importation of bricks and mortar as, it was claimed, these could be used for building new tunnels.

Before the 2014 uprising, Alexis and Nina explained, enterprising Palestinians could make up to $15000 annually by smuggling raw materials and medical equipment as well as guns from Egypt through numerous tunnels. It was thus possible to make a considerable fortune over the years smuggling various items through these tunnels following Hamas' election in 2007. However, Alexis and Nina could not establish whether it was simply enterprising Palestinians who used that route for making a fortune or whether it was the Hamas leadership itself that controlled most of the tunnel entry and exit points thus, over the span of the past seven years, a considerable amount of money could be made by imposing tariffs on those trading goods. However, Rafah was heavily bombed by the IDF and closed the Strip's southern border with Egypt for most of the year, bar a handful of days, thus cutting the livelihood of those individuals who used it as a route to commerce.

The airport that was hailed as Gaza's gateway to the outside world, and was visited by President Clinton shortly after its inauguration, was destroyed and rendered practically useless, its impressive colonnade left in ruins. Gradually, the life of ordinary Palestinians who were not involved in schemes pertaining to the numerous tunnels was made intolerable.

"Take the fishing industry as an example," started Alexis, "which for decades leading to the 1990s employed tens of thousands of people and amounted to about $10million turnover, was reduced to a mere handful of workers with most boats lying idle in Gaza's harbour. This had to do with Israeli patrol boats restricting Gazan fishermen from venturing beyond a certain limit. After the 1994 Oslo Accord, when the limit allowed was extended to 12 nautical miles, the catch was quite good but during the past 20 years the Israelis have imposed stricter limits of six nautical miles and even on occasions only three. Within such restricted zones the sea was, to a large measure, devoid of any fish. From its maximum catch of over 4000 tonnes of fish in 1994 it dropped to as little as 1400 tonnes during the period after Hamas took control of the Gaza Strip."

"It is fair to say though that during the past five years it has steadily improved and reached over 3500 tonnes per annum as was reported by UN survey," butted in Nina and went on. "And now there is a wall in place separating the Strip from Israel itself with a buffer zone of 300 metres where anybody venturing a few metres within this zone risks being shot by IDF border guards stationed in tall towers erected on the Israeli side."

"What a dreadful state of affairs. It is a humanitarian disaster," said Irini. "Surely you are not going to Gaza, again are you?"

"Not for the time being," replied Nina. "However a

new hospital wing is being constructed and due to finish in a year or so and no doubt my services may be called on again. Besides there is a Palestinian teenager, Ramzi...."

"Ismail's grandnephew," interrupted Alexis.

"I haven't seen Ismail since our reunion many moons ago," said Irini. "Is he still in Alexandria?"

"He is," replied Nina, "and initially he was instrumental in me going to Gaza and helping out to find my feet over there. He has a network of relatives and friends in the Strip and that is how Alexis and I came across Ramzi. As I was saying, he is now about 16 years of age and about to make up his mind which university to attend. I would, at some stage, like to take him out of Gaza to continue his studies somewhere in Europe. It may not work out so I am keen to go back there soon to see what can be done."

Thus, another small gathering of ex-Alexandrians came to pass where inevitably the main topic of conversation was the Palestinian Conundrum and its implications for the region.

33

Paris, June 2016

A few days after the gathering at Nina's apartment in Vrilissia, Alexis and Nina flew to Paris on their way to England. In Paris they stayed at the Le Pavillon de la Reine, a delightful hotel, hidden behind a discreet entrance, on Place des Vosges in the arrondissement Marois. This impressive 17th-century residence, enveloped in greenery, faces a beautifully manicured garden with a pretty flower-filled courtyard. Apart from its location at the heart of the city the choice of this hotel rested on its proximity to dozens of galleries some of which Nina had earmarked and wished to visit the next time she found herself in the capital.

On arrival the hotel reception gave Alexis a handwritten note informing them that Ismail was in the city and suggested meeting them for dinner at 9pm at L'Ange 20, a quaint bistro not far from the hotel. Alexis and Nina were surprised they had received a handwritten note but knowing Ismail's obsession with anonymity the use of a mobile or by email would have alerted the security agencies of his whereabouts. They wondered, however, what was so urgent that forced Ismail to meet them in Paris.

Nina and Alexis made their way to the first gallery on her list, the Galerie *Épisodique* at Rue de Nanettes.

The theme was a series of exhibits completely disconnected from one another, episodic so to speak, where each stood alone and depicted distinct personalities. Denys Zacharopoulos, the Greek artist and his fellow creators, were exhibiting their Transitions, a movement which questioned public and private facts, history and fiction, the love of art and artists' admiration of artists. Nina found out about this movement from Myrto, who was thrilled by its uniqueness and convinced her friend to visit it if she ever stopped over in Paris on her way to England. They entered the well-lit gallery and paced slowly by the various items on display, with Nina every now and then mumbling in disapproval or exhorting the virtues of an exhibit that took her fancy. They then made for Karten Greve Galerrie, a 20-minute walk to 5 Rue Debelleyme, where a mixture of buildings, birds, and other artefacts were on display. What caught Nina's attention was a painting of a large medieval book by Felix Cytrynowicz whose interpretation of its dishevelled pages, flapping as they were held upright by a gust of wind, was stunning. Next to this medieval book stood a very impressive black and white shadowy figurine leaning on an inclined ladder by Mark Diener. It was as though the figurine was transfixed by the movement of peoples as they passed by inspecting the various exhibits. No need to interpret what the figurine intended to say, this was quite clear by the expressive stance. As they left and joined Rue Turenne on their way south to the bistro L'Ange 20, Nina thought they were being followed.

Alexis stopped at the kiosk, bought a copy of *Le Monde* and turning to face Nina pretended to browse through the Newspaper while in actual fact he examined the *va-et-vient* behind Nina.

"I do not see anything untoward," he whispered. They continued and arrived at L'Ange 20, looking forward to its traditional French cuisine. The hotel had already booked a table for 9 o'clock and as Ismail was already waiting at the bar, greetings were exchanged, Nina affectionately kissing Ismail while the men shook hands.

"What brings you here?" asked Nina while Alexis ordered a bottle of Crémant de Bourgogne, his favourite sparkling tipple, a blend of Chardonnay and Pinot Noir, with aromas of citrus fruit which give it its distinct, well-structured flavour.

"I wished to discuss something away from prying eyes," replied Ismail. Alexis and Nina glanced at each other.

"How did you get into France?" asked Alexis.

"I did not fly. There are other ways to get in," replied Ismail without any more explanation. Ismail started explaining that a group of residents in East Jerusalem had asked if Alexis could attend a meeting they were organising where he could contribute to a discussion about the bloody insurrections in East Jerusalem and the West Bank that occurred two years ago but also to comment on the findings of a World Bank Report on the future of the Palestinian economy. On the assumption of a major monetary boost in the fledgling economy, the report made certain startling conclusions.

"East Jerusalem?" asked a perplexed Nina and turning to Alexis went on. "How are you going to get there without being noticed?" she concluded as the waiter finished filling their flutes. Alexis lifted his ice-cold flute of Crémant, clinked the other two flutes and downed its content in one strong swallow.

"Wow, I needed that," replied Alexis and looking at Nina went on. "I assume with difficulty." He gave a grimace of pain knowing full well that Israel's highly sophisticated counter-terrorism measures would be difficult to evade. Alexis' movements would soon be spotted, using the latest satellite surveillance systems and unmanned drones patrolling the air space. Advanced sensors and algorithms were in place, such as the hyperspectral Ground Moving Target Indicator and Moving Target Indicator, both of which have the flexibility to operate during day and night and in all weathers. Israel's newest system, GroundEye, could provide data and high-resolution imagery capable of delivering large amounts of information to security personnel and alert any of Alexis' movements once he had crossed into Palestine or Israeli annexed territories.

"Would you at least consider their request?" implored Ismail.

"You know me," replied Alexis, "I will not shy away from the challenge of evading the authorities and speaking my mind at the gathering. If they wish to silence me, they will have to arrest me." Nina looked at Alexis rather concerned at his gung-ho approach to Ismail's request.

"You know it will be quite dangerous?" went on Ismail.

"I am well aware of the dangers involved," replied Alexis while slowly leafing through the impressive stock of wines on offer. They ordered meat dishes, so Alexis chose a bottle of Châteauneuf-du-Pape to accompany their meal. The head waiter came with the bottle, uncorked it, Alexis sampled it, nodded in approval and the head-waiter half-filled their crystal glasses.

During dinner they discussed different ways of travelling to the Middle East with the aim of being smuggled into East Jerusalem, of all places, without Shin Bet getting wind of it. Entering as a tourist using the King Hussein crossing point was deemed a non-starter as the Israeli security forces knew him well and had amassed a dossier on him. Could he fly to Antalya in Turkey and then be driven to Amman? That too was judged too difficult as he would have to cross Aleppo while the Syrian civil war was in full swing. Flying to Cyprus and crossing to Lebanon and then to Jordan via the southernmost part of Syria was another possible route but again was rejected.

"Fly direct to Amman," suggested Ismail. "I can get you a new identity so hopefully the police at the airport will not suspect you as you will be travelling on business."

"When is the meeting scheduled?" asked Alexis.

"It will be arranged as soon as they know your travel plans," replied Ismail.

"I think it would be best to fly from Athens to Amman rather than from Heathrow or Paris-CDG airports," uttered Nina.

"Agreed," replied Alexis.

"Will you tell Hermioni?" asked a hesitant Nina.

"I don't think it is wise. My daughter would try to stop me and, if not, worry unduly if she knew where I was heading," replied Alexis.

When they returned to the hotel, Nina continued to question his rationale for agreeing to participate in such a gathering when the dangers were all too clear.

"I question it because over the past 20 years you and I have gone to Gaza on numerous occasions and have drawn the attention of the Israeli security forces. Even travelling on a false identity does not guarantee the anonymity which is essential for you to get into East Jerusalem unnoticed. No doubt there are dossiers on both of us, so..."

"Stop worrying. The only crime I will be committing is entering Jerusalem under a different identity and it is for a very good cause," interrupted Alexis, as he approached Nina and embraced her. It was 20 years since they had started seeing each other regularly again and 60 years since their first encounter during the Sham el-Nessim weekend in Alexandria. The sparkle was still there as he hugged her affectionately.

Security personnel at the Direction Générale de la

Sécurité Intérieure, DGSI, in Paris were indeed monitoring the movements of Alexis and Nina. Since its formation from two separate departments, DGSI reported directly to the Minister of the Interior rather than its predecessors which came under the jurisdiction of the Head of Police. They had followed them since they landed in Paris and were alerted when they realised that Ismail had joined them that evening but concerned as they had not tracked down the Palestinian's movements prior to entering France and indeed alarmed as to how he had evaded any border scrutiny. After the Paris attacks the previous November, Israel was helping France to identify the perpetrators so there was full cooperation between Mossad and DGSI security officers. A coded signal was sent to Israel informing Mossad and Shin Bet officers of the Paris dinner at L'Ange 20. Nina was correct in suspecting they were followed as they headed to the restaurant; however, the security officers were experts in disappearing given the slightest hint of their cover being blown.

Rivka, having worked for a multinational in Paris, had joined the Israeli Embassy in Paris as head of its security section. Although she had retired from that position she was retained as a consultant on specific projects and was kept fully aware of the movements of undesirables and other suspects. The following morning Alexis was informed that a lady was waiting at the hotel's reception to meet them. They descended and met her in the foyer.

"Rivka, it is such a surprise," said Alexis. Nina and Rivka hugged. They withdrew to a quiet corner of the lounge.

"How did you know we were in Paris?" asked Alexis. Rivka took her jacket off and looked at Alexis.

"However much you desire to be incongnito during your travels, you must by now realize that after your frequent visits to the Gaza Strip, your movements are being watched."

"You mean continuously?" asked Nina in disbelief.

"More or less," replied Rivka.

"By whom?"

Rivka smiled at Alexis without replying. She then added:

"My sister-in-law Golda speaks warmly of your meeting at my father's house in Jerusalem all those years ago. And remember we had a good chat at that time and you told me about your efforts in the Strip as a humanitarian aid worker so I think I know you well enough and I sympathize with your motives."

Rivka explained her involvement with the Israeli Embassy and warned Alexis to be on his guard as his movements were being monitored.

"From what I have gathered they have nothing specific but you have both made waves with your talks when you have been to Palestine so it should not be a surprise that your movements are being carefully scrutinised," went on Rivka.

"We were about to breakfast. Would you join us?"

She accepted and proceeded to the dining room, and during breakfast continued to talk about the good old times in Alexandria, Israel, the visits to the Strip, their school reunions and other poignant memories. During their chat their reason for their frequent visits to the Strip came up time and time again. Nina at some stage said:

"The real voyage of discovery consists not in seeking new lands but observing with new eyes things that we see time and time again in the Strip."

"Very Proustian," replied Rivka. Nina smiled and went on.

"We are after all in Paris."

"Funnily enough I visited the cemetery at Père Lachaise a few months back and read some of his other quotes."

Despite Rivka's friendly warning, Alexis was not going to be put off. After all he was simply going to East Jerusalem to attend a meeting rather than massacre people at a synagogue or plant a bomb on a bus. Despite the obvious dangers he started preparing for his clandestine journey realising full well the danger in which he was putting himself.

34

Amman, West Bank, Jerusalem, June 2016

Alexis was to fly to Amman from Athens under a different identity, bearing a fake passport arranged by Ismail's contacts in Athens. A network of Palestinian operatives in Jordan would instruct him as to the best way to cross into the West Bank. Two weeks after their meeting in Paris, Alexis landed at Queen Alia International Airport and checked in at the Amman Airport Hotel.

Late in the evening there was a knock on his door. Alexis went to the door to find an envelope on the doormat. He knew that emails, texts, mobiles or social media sites were out of the question as any of these would have allowed Shin Bet's highly sophisticated surveillance systems to track him down without delay. A little apprehensively, Alexis opened the envelope and found a message stating that he was to wait opposite the hotel at precisely 8 o'clock that evening where an old Fiat would be waiting to take him to a predetermined address west of the capital. The car duly arrived, Alexis boarded and it sped northwards towards the city of Amman, veered northwest and within 20 minutes reached the town of Na'ur. The car drove towards the city centre and stopped outside the Princess Tharwat high school for girls where he was led into a room and told that a contact would call for him within an hour. At 10pm another contact collected him from the school and he was driven along Route 40 and joined Route 65 heading northwards towards King Hussein Bridge across the River Jordan. At the intersection with Route 437 the car turned left towards the border with the West Bank and started its slow decent into the Jordan Valley. As there was sufficient moonlight the driver switched off its headlights for fear of being seen by border guards. A few kilometres away the car swerved left onto a dirt track, continued its decent and after what seemed an eternity stopped some 500 metres from the border. Alexis was told to disembark and wait while the car turned back and sped off. This he did and sure enough minutes later, as if from nowhere, another Arab appeared and told him to follow. He was taken to a remote crossing point along the winding river. There were no security guards anywhere to be seen along this stretch of the river. Although the river at that point was less than ten metres wide the guide explained that because of untreated sewage, agricultural wastes and other effluents being discharged into the river for decades it was dangerously polluted despite recent concerted efforts to clean it up. It was prudent therefore not to swim across preferring to cross in a small dinghy. About halfway the guide pointed to the flickering lights of Qasr el Yahud on the Jordan side, barely 300 metres away, explaining that this was the baptismal site of Jesus Christ, at present a much-visited tourist site. The site on the

West Bank was administered by the Israeli Civil Administration and Israel's Ministry of Tourism, as most of the West Bank had been occupied by Israel after the 1967 war. Alexis nodded sagely, acknowledging the significance of what lay before him.

Soon they were in Palestine's West Bank and slowly climbed up the other side of the Jordan Valley. As they reached a stationary car on a hilltop, the car door opened and Alexis was ushered inside by another Palestinian who greeted him warmly and drove him towards the town of Jericho using small mountain tracks and unpaved lanes.

Having spent the night in a safe house off Jericho, the following evening, as dusk was setting in, Alexis was driven through a myriad of small villages and dirt roads and continued in the desert like region between the Israeli settlements of Almon and Ma'ale Adumim and headed towards midway between the Palestinian villages of Anata and al Za'im. However, the more difficult task lay ahead as he had to cross the high wall erected by the Israeli government following the previous Intifadas on the pretext that it curtailed the numerous attacks by Palestinians on East Jerusalem and hence increase the security of the Israeli citizens.

About 300 metres from the Separation Wall the car stopped and his companion introduced him to another guide who would lead him to the entrance of an underground tunnel which effectively enabled him to reach villages and settlements on the outskirts of East Jerusalem. Before he stepped into the tunnel, Alexis stopped at the entrance and gazed at this concrete monstrosity which was an affront to humanity. He carefully examined a map that his guide had given him which clearly showed that this high meandering wall was built not on Israel's land but on Palestine's occupied West Bank territory.

"Look," explained the guide, "so much fertile land has been taken away from us thus reducing our ability to grow enough agricultural produce which we badly need to support our families."

"I know," replied Alexis reflecting on his discussion with Joshua during his earlier visit to Gaza. "What is amazing is how the international communities have allowed such a gross disregard of international law to continue for such a long time."

What did Alexis feel as he looked in turn at the map and the wall? Almost certainly he was enveloped by a mixture of shame, sadness and anger. It was clear that although terrorist incidents had indeed reduced following the completion of the 708-kilometre wall, many observers pointed out that the real reason for building this snaking wall on the West Bank's land was to protect the illegal Jewish settlements from Arab incursions by erecting a physical barrier between the Arab-populated areas and these settlements. However, the barrier restricted the movement of Palestinians not only within their villages in the West Bank but also for travelling to Israel in search for work or visiting relatives in other West

Bank cities or the Gaza Strip and fuelled the animosity towards the occupying Israeli forces. But why, Alexis wondered, build Jewish settlements on the West Bank, particularly at an accelerated pace following the 1967 war, when clearly the land belonged to the Palestinians after the wars of 1948 and 1956 had ended? There could only be one answer: to annex more and more land in the West Bank so that in the future it would have to be accepted by the international community as a de facto part of Israel, with the settlements never being allowed to be dismantled. This matched exactly with the biblical aspirations of many Jewish settlers who firmly believed that the whole of the West Bank was part of the Holy Land and should be part of a wider Israel. Alexis reflected that on occasions even the Israeli Government protested against the continual expansion of settlements in the West Bank but it was only a protest to placate the international outcry and condemnation as in truth it supplied funds and manpower to aid the completion of new, and the expansion of existing, settlements.

Alexis bade goodbye to his guide, entered the tunnel and was met by another Palestinian on the other side of the wall. They headed towards Wadi Al Joz, passing Mount Scopus on their right. They walked down El Muqdasi Street reaching the Rockefeller Archaeological Museum on their right then joined Sultan Suleiman Street and reached Herod's Gate. They hesitated to make sure that they were not being followed and, taking the opportunity of some hustle and bustle caused by a group of tourists entering the Gate, mingled with them and crossed into the Old City. Proceeding south towards Temple Mount, they passed St Ann's Church on their left and reached King Faisal Street. He was then taken to a house only hundreds of metres from the Al-Aqsa Mosque. A courtyard interconnected many of the rooms of this house where he saw over a dozen people snacking on *foul* falafel with pita bread and an assortment of cheeses. They greeted him warmly, shaking his hand, and were relieved that he had made it undetected.

Shortly after Alexis arrived, some prominent Arabs gave accounts describing the awful situation that Palestinians found themselves in with lone voices from within and some from outside Palestine protesting and attempting to publicise their plight. Alexis did not have a prepared text but spoke about the concerted effort by the government of Israel to crush any attempt by the Palestinians in the West Bank and the Gaza Strip to make ends meet by expanding their indigenous industries. There was a shortage of water, daily power cuts occurred, and restricted movement of Palestinians in and out of the occupied territories was detrimental to seeking employment or visiting family and relatives. To emphasise his point, he went on to highlight the iniquity of the situation that Palestine was finding itself in, by giving an example of the Arab Potash Company on the eastern side of the River Jordan which, since its inauguration six years ago on a new site at Gawr as-Safi, was now a thriving enterprise. The company is the eighth-largest potash producing company in the world. This is a vital ingredient, he explained, in fertilisers used in plant growth and food production. One would have thought that as the West Bank's border with the Dead Sea is around 35 kilometres there would be ample opportunity for Palestinians, too, to produce and export potash and gain hugely from that natural resource.

"Alas, my friends," Alexis stressed, "this has not been possible because of restricted access and problems with obtaining permits by the occupied force on prospective investment companies and individuals." He produced facts and figures from a World Bank report claiming that the Palestinians would benefit to the tune of several hundred million dollars of exports which, quoting from their report, would be almost equivalent to the contribution of the entire manufacturing sector of Palestinian territories today. "Moreover," Alexis went on, "for the past 50 years Israel benefitted enormously by selling its goods to Palestine but Palestinian goods found fewer markets in Israel. How can it be claimed that the lack of Palestinian prosperity is the main cause of the conflict when the Palestinian economy is not given a much-needed head-start?" An earlier report from the World Bank had stated that restrictions and access to a large area in the West Bank, controlled by Israel, had hugely stunted the Palestinian economy.

"Let me quote something else from this report," continued Alexis as he opened his notepad and read. "Unleashing the potential from that 'restricted land'

and allowing Palestinians to put these resources to work, would provide whole new areas of economic activity and set the economy on the path to sustainable growth. Further, the Palestinian tourism sector could be boosted by millions, annually nearing 1% of GDP, by creating Dead Sea hotel resorts, similar to those on the Jordanian side."

Alexis went on to quote from several sources and published reports, facts and figures that showed conclusively the reasons why the Palestinian economy had for decades suffered. He did not advocate a militant response or rebellion; he was simply presenting facts upon facts that were irrefutable as they came from authoritative sources. When he had finished, he was thanked for his efforts by an appreciative audience and escorted to a room where he was to spend the night, planning the reverse trip out of East Jerusalem the following evening.

At midnight he was awoken by the owner of the house, who was distraught and informed him that plain clothes policemen were raiding the premises. Such raids were too familiar to Arabs living in East Jerusalem. As the house consisted of many rooms scattered on different floors, his host explained to Alexis that he had time to get dressed and leave. The owner pointed to the direction of the rear garden for his exit from the house. The owner assured him that somebody would be waiting on the other side of the street to guide him out of the Old City. A grateful Alexis thanked him and headed towards the 4th-century Christian Church of the Holy

Sepulchre, which also served as the Headquarters of the Greek Patriach of Jerusalem. It is said to be the place of Jesus' resurrection, hence the original Greek name of Anastasis. Alexis waited at the prescribed spot but alas no one appeared. Could he pop into the church and using his knowledge of the Greek language seek refuge from those chasing him? But as an atheist he quickly dismissed such a blasphemous course of action. After a while he realized that he was on his own in a city that he hardly knew, pursued almost certainly by members of Shin Bet. Alexis had to react quickly. He started walking towards New Gate as he knew, from studying some maps before he had set off from Athens, that Daniel Street, where Joshua's house was situated, lay in that direction and could easily be reached once he had crossed the City Wall. There were no guards to be seen so he proceeded towards the Gate and crossed it. He was in West Jerusalem – what a relief. He knew that the Schumann household was not that far away. As he continued to walk he became aware of a group of youngsters coming from the other side veering towards the heart of West Jerusalem who would soon cross his path. Alexis found a door, opened it and went through finding himself in the entrance hall of a large apartment block. He waited until the group's laughter subsided and ventured back onto the street. He was not aware that two Shin Bet officers had followed him having been alerted of his hurried departure from the house by an informant. As he crossed the street to head towards Joshua's house, they reached him and stopped him.

"Could we have your identity papers?" said one of them. Alexis froze but knew that the game was up. He produced his false passport hoping for a miracle.

"Could you come with us, Sir," said the Shin Bet Officer pointing to a car approaching from behind. Alexis had no option but to comply. The car with Alexis and the two officers sped along and within minutes arrived at the Maskobiyeh detention center in West Jerusalem. Alexis was taken to a tiny room and left for a number of hours. Through a small window at the top of one of the walls came a light indicating that it was early dawn. There were two new officers; one sat opposite Alexis while the other stood by him. Alexis was exhausted, having had no sleep at all that evening.

"What is the purpose of your trip to Jerusalem?" asked the seated officer.

"I was meeting some friends and colleagues in the Old City," replied Alexis.

"Where exactly?"

"I do not know the address as I was taken there last night."

"We know this is not your identity as you are Alexis Mani. Why are you travelling on a false passport?" Alexis had to come clean and address his subterfuge.

"Had I attempted to travel as myself I would not have been allowed to enter even though my visit was to meet old friends and acquaintances my partner and I have made over the years by carrying out voluntary work on the Strip."

"What was the purpose of the talks?"

"Exchanging ideas and discussing the future of any peace talks following the bloody insurrections of last year."

"Who is the owner of the house you went to last night?"

"I haven't the faintest idea. I was taken there."

The interrogation continued for a considerable time trying to force Alexis to reveal the names of the Arabs who had organised this meeting. He had made a point, upon receipt of the invitation, to ask no questions about who had invited him and who would be present in case he was arrested and interrogated by Shin Bet.

"I would like to contact a lawyer. I know Joshua Schumann who lives here in Jerusalem with his family and he will contact my lawyer," asked Alexis after it became obvious that they had no intention of releasing him any time soon. Alexis, blindfolded and handcuffed, left the room and was led down some steps and into a long corridor with cells either side, the heavy wooden doors of each cell fitted with large metallic bolts. He was ushered into a small unlit room where there was a pit latrine and a mattress in one corner. Inmates in other cells shouted for him to be strong and to tell them nothing. From other cells, cries of help emanated from known Palestinian militants who had confessed and were subjected to heavy punishment, allegedly without resorting to torture, but to Amnesty International their treatment amounted to torture. After the May 2012 ruling, Shin Bet had to tread very carefully on the level and methods of the agency's interrogation techniques because they could not overstep the Knesset Foreign and Security Committee who oversaw its activities. But international observers were suspecting that Shin Bet did not limit itself to aspects of security but often delved into civil matters. Radicalisation of young Palestinians was the main concern of Shin Bet who chose to imprison teachers, educators and Islamic judges. Other inmates were on hunger strike and their families were appealing to the Israeli government to release them following their arbitrary detention because of poor health. Some had been arrested, detained, interrogated and beaten for months on end following the 2015 insurrection in Gaza, and were deemed sympathizers to that unrest, although no evidence of their involvement had ever been put forward. These were predominantly young Palestinians from different neighborhoods in East Jerusalem who Shin Bet thought may pose a problem and resort to terrorism at some point in the future.

Alexis slumped onto the narrow bench and was soon asleep. After two hours he was once again woken up by the noise of the heavy bolts being slid across to open his cell door. He was taken blindfolded to another underground room for more interrogation. Deep down the authorities knew that Alexis was not involved in any insurrection or terrorist activities, but their aim was to extract fresh information about the Arabs in East Jerusalem who had arranged the meeting, so arrests and more interrogations would follow. After days of fruitless questioning, Alexis was taken up the stairs to a bright room where Avi and Golda Schumann were waiting.

"Alexis, what on earth are you doing here?" uttered Avi in disbelief seeing Alexis in such a state.

"It is a long story, but boy am I glad to see you."

Avi Schumann with his powerful connections with the Israeli government was able to release Alexis from custody. Although it was against the law to travel with false papers, Avi was able to hire a well-known lawyer who argued that the only reason that Alexis resorted to travelling under a different name was that the authorities would have stopped him entering Israel in the first place. Avi and Golda drove him back to their home in Daniel Street for a welcome rest. The following day Alexis met the ageing Joshua who was by now nearing his hundredth year.

"My dear friend," said Joshua upon meeting him at breakfast, "you are putting yourself in grave danger with such escapades. Shin Bet have you marked, and it will become more and more difficult in the future for Avi and his connections to come to the rescue. You must avoid at all costs being dragged into such situations."

"Joshua," replied Alexis as he approached the old man sitting in a comfortable reclining chair, "I am not dragged into these meetings as you put it. I willingly attend when I am asked but at the same time I am all too aware that I am putting myself in danger and one day, who knows, Shin Bet may accuse me of some illicit insurrection, however unfounded that might be. Having said that, I cannot stand by and observe the deteriorating conditions the Palestinians have to endure, particularly in the Gaza Strip, and do nothing about it."

"Do you think that Hamas' leaders care about the deteriorating conditions of the Gazans? Do they live in poverty as their people do?" butted in Avi.

"Hamas is desperate," replied Alexis, "they know they cannot defeat the IDF militarily but also know that the only course open to them is to provoke the IDF into frequent skirmishes to overreact and use excessive retaliatory force, thus inflicting on Israel the condemnation of the international community. IDF could enter Gaza at any time and destroy Hamas' forces and capture its leadership but to what end? So, they resort to methods stopping short of starving the population in order to keep the dissenting voices in the UN at bay."

"Are you also sure that Hamas is not offering shelter in Gaza to elements of the Islamic State thus denigrating their cause, however justified that may be, as the Israeli government will use this as an excuse not to have any new peace talks with Hamas? We have all seen the awful brutality of the Islamic State, the public beheadings, desecration of ancient artefacts and monuments and the appalling human right violations of recent years," replied Avi.

"I am appalled by what the Islamic State represents. However, Nina and I haven't been to Gaza for some time so lots must have happened in that period of which we are not aware," said Alexis.

"How about the leadership of Hamas?" continued Avi. "Are you aware that large sums have been raised over the years by Arab donors or through individuals who espouse the Palestinian cause, and that these funds have not been used to better the life of the ordinary Palestinians but rather to construct rockets and fund other subversive activities and, dare I say, considerable amounts must have ended up in the pockets of Palestinian leaders in Gaza and other Hamas leaders living abroad?"

"You know what is ironic in all this?" started Joshua who despite his advanced years was still very alert. "When the Hamas Movement was in its embryonic stage it was initially propped up by the IDF in order to counter the machinations of the PLO and Yasser Arafat. How history returns to haunt us!"

"Matters have changed," replied Alexis, responding to Joshua and ignoring what Avi had just revealed, "because, over the past 30 years, since President Carter put forward the notion of the establishment of a Palestinian State, the right of return for the refugees and the withdrawal of Israeli forces to the pre-1967 borders, no progress at all has been made. If anything, much more land in the West Bank has been annexed and more illegal settlements have been constructed." Joshua coughed nervously as Alexis went on. "So, I suppose Hamas has said that enough is enough and has resorted to insurrections and firing rockets towards Israeli towns and settlements." Alexis was aware of some reports, not least from a number of reputable journalists in Egypt and other Arab countries that funds collected for Hamas had corrupted many leaders who had funnelled the money into Swiss accounts, bought luxury houses and stayed in five-star hotels. Turning to Avi he continued.

"I would like to visit Gaza before I fly back to Athens. Could you arrange this for me? It will be a fact-finding tour to see for myself some of the things that you two have just told me." Avi looked at Joshua who sat in his chair, eyes shut, listening to his son's and Alexis' exchanges. The lull in the conversation between the two alerted Joshua who opened his eyes and nodded to Avi. After all it was, he who had the high-level contacts in government and the security services and had to sanction such a visit.

35

Gaza Strip, June 2016

After a day's rest Avi's chauffeur drove Avi and Alexis to the Erez border-crossing. They remained silent. The car parked near the Erez crossing point and Avi asked Alexis to wait in the car while he made his way to the customs building. He spoke to the military head for a good few minutes and emerged nodding to Alexis that permission was given and handed him some papers.

"See you in two days," he told Alexis. "Our car will be here to take you to Tel Aviv airport. Don't you do anything silly: fact finding, not a lecture tour."

"Don't worry, I will behave," said Alexis and shook Avi's hand. They exchanged understanding smiles and parted.

Alexis, entered the 2 km long, metal-grid caged passageway separating Israel from the Strip. Periodically the ominous sight of the tall watchtowers came into view complete with numerous security cameras. Beyond, in the distance, he saw the wall separating the Strip from Israel, a sight that filled him with sadness that matters had to come to this. The Gaza Strip had become an open prison housing over two million inhabitants.

Alexis, not having notified his contacts of his arrival, took a taxi to the Al Mathaf Hotel in the northern part of the Strip and booked a room for two nights fronting the shore. He descended the marble staircase leading to the poolside. He crossed the little gate and walked on to the paved promenade along the beach wishing to clear his mind of the events of the previous few nights. He walked along the coast for a good 30 minutes, every now and then resting along the iron fence and staring at the beach and the Mediterranean beyond. He had reached the Dar Al-Shifa Hospital where Nina often worked but did not feel like going inside to meet friends and colleagues. Beyond the hospital he came across a shanty town stretching a few kilometres, consisting of narrow shacks composed of scavenged man-made materials such as abandoned construction debris and the kind of flotsam and jetsam found on a desert island. He suspected that he was being followed as every now and then he saw different people, a safe distance behind him, ostensibly enjoying the mild evening and pretending not to be paying much attention to him. He returned to his room, rang Nina, changed, and made his way to the comfort of the hotel's restaurant.

The following day he started walking towards the centre of Gaza City crossing Zeitoun and headed for Khalil's coffee shop. He thought he was not followed but was not sure because as he approached the heavily populated region just outside Gaza City itself any informant or police person in civilian clothes would become invisible in the crowd. As a precaution he left his mobile at the hotel so that Shin Bet or any informants would not be able to track his movements as he meandered through the city's rundown alleys. Upon nearing the café, he recognised Khalil sitting at a table on the pavement with a couple of customers chatting, as usual gesticulating to emphasize his point. As Alexis approached Khalil from his rear, the others stopped talking, causing Khalil to turn to see what brought about their silence only to smile broadly as soon as he recognised his friend.

"Wow, long time no see, my friend," he uttered as he embraced Alexis. "What brings you here?" Alexis not wishing to divulge his escapades in East Jerusalem evaded the question and replied:

"I am spending a couple of days at the Al Mathaf Hotel and thought of visiting old friends and some of Ismail's relatives in Gaza and Jerusalem. How is the situation here in Gaza? You have had a turbulent few years since Nina and I were last here."

"Come and sit down and have your favourite brew. Tea with slices of lemon," replied Khalil as he guided Alexis inside the café and went behind the counter to prepare the refreshments. Alexis looked around. Nothing much had changed since he was last here a few years ago: the same tables and chairs, albeit some rickety to the point of collapse, some old pictures of pre-1948 Palestine fields hanging on the walls and a stack of shisha pipes on a long shelf next to a few plants in desperate need of nourishment. Four older men were playing cards while exchanging comments with bystanders witnessing their moves. Khalil came with the lemon tea and a small cup of hot coffee for himself and sat opposite Alexis.

"Matters are not good, my friend," he started. "We live in a large prison where life is unbearable, unemployment, particularly amongst the young, is sky high, people are frustrated not having any money to buy even the basic provisions to feed their families, water is not safe to drink, forcing us to boil it. Crossing the border is pretty much impossible unless there is a medical need and even then, one needs a permit. Officialdom has gone mad. It is dreadful." A friend of Khalil, who runs the bakery shop two blocks away, approached their table and was introduced to Alexis. He joined the conversation.

"We are frustrated that our politicians do not speak with the same voice as the schism between Fatah and Hamas persists," said the baker, while looking round to make sure that he was not overheard. "I have three employees who work for a few hours and when the flour and other ingredients run out they sit idle for the rest of the day. This is no way to carry on. Lots of aid goes to support our military and to buy guns and rockets instead of improving the situation for the two million people living here in the Strip."

It was the first time that somebody was openly levelling criticism towards the Hamas government ruling the Gaza Strip. During the ensuing discussion it transpired that over 80% of water was not safe to drink and because of shortage of electricity to run the sewage treatment plants raw sewage was pumped straight into the sea. There was utter condemnation by human rights organisations that Israel's blockade of the Gaza Strip by land, sea and air contravened international humanitarian laws.

"Since Hamas had won the 2007 elections, the Israelis have punished us," continued the baker. "They keep us in a stranglehold, they suppress us. This is the price we have paid for opting to choose democratically the leaders that we wish to support and who will fight for our cause."

"Do you regret electing Hamas?" prompted Alexis inquisitively.

"With the aid of hindsight possibly, but what was the alternative?" continued the baker. "The Palestinian Authority was totally ineffective in negotiating a peace agreement and was regarded by all as a puppet to Israel and its superpower ally. Arafat did what he could and after his death the PA took over and for decades the same situation has persisted with no end to the plight of our people living in refugee camps in neighbouring Arab countries, the West Bank and here in Gaza. We therefore gave Hamas the opportunity to strike a peace settlement, but the Israelis never gave them a jot of a chance to succeed. Instead, on the pretext of being a militant organisation, they tied the noose even tighter and have condemned us to a life of poverty and misery." The baker was very passionate in the condemnation of the political stalemate that had resulted following the success of

Hamas in gaining control in the elections. Alexis took advantage of a lull in the conversation and asked Khalil about Ahlam.

"She is fine, getting older like me and just managing to make ends meet. Go next door and say hello. I will join you in a minute." Alexis left the two men and entered the haberdashery shop. Ahlam was serving a customer so Alexis hung around momentarily observing the little shop. It looked meagre with little merchandise and with evidence of some damage to the back wall following the latest Intifada two years earlier. In one corner was a stool next to a small table with some special implements used to repair stockings and darn socks. As the customer left, Ahlam turned to Alexis, stepped forward and embraced him warmly.

"It is so good to see you Alexis. Is Nina at the hospital?" she enquired.

"No, Nina has not come with me this time. She is busy in Athens writing a newspaper column, so I decided to spend a few days here and visit old friends," said Alexis trying to deflect Ahlam's next question about the real purpose of his visit.

"I was chatting to Khalil and his baker friend and I gather things are not good. I am so sorry."

"The most frustrating aspect of all this is that people here are starting to feel helpless; the situation is so bad that nothing can be done to make things better. Gazans are forgotten people despite the protestations of countless international organisations. Nobody is listening, nobody cares," uttered a tearful Ahlam. "How do you explain the death of four nine-year-olds on our beach here in Gaza by the IDF? Israel stated that it was an awful mistake, collateral damage reported another Israeli spokesperson." Ahlam paused, wiped the tears off her face then continued:

"The situation here in Gaza impacts our everyday life. I waited this morning for one hour to refill my gas bottle as electricity is often cut-off, but they only filled half the bottle as there is also a shortage of gas. It is intolerable."

Shortly afterwards Khalil joined them.

"What happened at Shuja'iyya two years ago is so shameful," said Khalil, "many casualties including children."

"Yes, your friend the baker alluded to Shuja'iyya as I was leaving the café," uttered Alexis.

"Shuja'iyya is a very densely populated region in Gaza City, close to where we are, with some 100,000 inhabitants..."

"Yes, I know," interrupted Alexis, "some of Nina's colleagues at the hospital live there."

"Well, I hope they were not hurt. The Israelis stated that they dropped leaflets warning residents to abandon their homes as this area was about to be heavily bombed by their F16 fighters. They claimed that Hamas were launching hundreds of rockets towards Israel from underground bases deep inside that neighbourhood and furthermore they also claimed that Hamas used our people living there as human shields."

"Friends that live there," butted in a tearful Ahlam, "said to us that Hamas forcibly prevented some residents from leaving their homes during the bombing so that they were held as hostages in order to intensify the international condemnation of the assault following their deaths. I do not know what to believe any more." Khalil and Alexis looked at each other. Khalil summed up the situation.

"What is also true is that the shelters were overflowing as thousands had already moved in. Other residents said afterwards that they were not aware of the danger as electricity was off so without TV or radio bulletins they were unable to keep abreast of the pending assault. Hundreds died, including many children, and many more wounded. The Israelis called Shuja'iyya a terrorist fortress but does one believe that?"

"One wonders whether a CDE was carried out before the air attack," asked Alexis.

"CDE, what is that?" asked a bewildered Ahlam.

"Collateral Damage Estimate," butted in Khalil looking at Ahlam. "It is a way of assessing civilian casualties prior to an attack."

"Oh," murmured Ahlam.

"I suppose a CDE was irrelevant in those circumstances as the IDF knew they would inflict heavy casualties of innocent people as a consequence of their decision to attack Shuja'iyya," said Alexis.

"CDE is the stuff you see in films, but I am afraid, my

friend, it does not apply to our unfortunate people living in the Strip," replied Khalil.

As another customer walked in the shop wanting her stockings mended, Alexis bade goodbye to his friends and headed towards Gaza City, soon reaching the shopping mall. He walked through the lively atmosphere but as he left the mall and reached the smaller alleys surrounding the shopping centre the contrast was striking. The disorder in the streets was almost palpable; the shells of countless abandoned houses following the last war stood defiantly against the bright skyline and the sound of scantily dressed kids roaming aimlessly was heart-breaking.

Alexis reached Ibrahim's apartment.

"I heard you were in Gaza. Come and sit down," said Leila as she opened the front door. "Ibrahim went out but will return shortly."

Alexis and Leila talked and exchanged news about Nina, Ramzi and other members of the family. Almost certainly Ibrahim would be in the know about Alexis' visit to East Jerusalem although there again, Alexis reflected, in order to keep his latest trip a close-guarded secret it could be that Ismail had not informed any of his close relatives. Wishing once more not to divulge the reason for his presence in the region he broached the plight of the Palestinians living in appalling conditions in the Strip.

"I just saw Khalil and Ahlam about an hour ago," said Alexis. "I know how desperate the situation is here in Gaza. They told me about the state of the drinking water, the lack of electricity and gas."

"We cannot continue like this," replied Leila, "Matters will come to a head. Another war, Intifada, call it what you like. The Israelis have taken everything from us: our livelihood, our dignity, the future of our families – but what hurts most is that they have taken our land and that we cannot forgive. When you go back you must tell your friends and colleagues of our plight, you must continue to fight our cause. I know you and Nina have done this ever since you first set foot in our Strip but please also inform people in high places in governments, the decision-makers that can influence our leaders to follow a different course." The desperation in Leila's countenance was all too obvious. It was the second time within a few hours that Alexis had heard local people criticizing their own government.

Ibrahim entered the apartment and approached them. "Surprise, surprise to see you here without Nina," he exclaimed. Alexis did not know whether Ibrahim was pretending not to be aware of the latest saga at East Jerusalem or whether he was hiding it even from his wife.

"As I explained to Leila, Nina is busy, so I thought of popping in and visiting my friends here," replied Alexis smilingly. They continued to talk. At some stage Ibrahim turned to Alexis and said:

"Would you like to see how the other side lives?" Alexis was intrigued. Leila was smiling.

"The other side?" he uttered.

"Come, I will show you," he replied and, turning to his wife, "I will be back within a couple of hours."

Alexis was keen to see another aspect of Gaza's daily life and followed Ibrahim down the staircase of the three-storey apartment block. As they headed for the bus stop Ibrahim said to Alexis:

"I am sorry for the subterfuge. I know about your misfortune in East Jerusalem but Leila does not know. We are all very sorry about your arrest. You see, Shin Bet knew that you had entered the West Bank and had you followed wishing to identify our friends in the Old City that organised the meeting. However, the frequent switching of our operatives worked and Shin Bet lost sight of you after you entered the Old City. Unfortunately, as is often the case, an informant alerted Shin Bet of your whereabouts and as they approached the house they spotted the Arab who was to escort you out of the Old City. They arrested him and then saw you coming out of the house. The important aspect of all this is that your visit was a success. Were you badly treated at the detention centre?"

"It was unpleasant, but I was not tortured. Luckily my ex-Alexandrian contacts in West Jerusalem came to my aid."

"You mean Joshua?"

"His son also."

"Well, it helps to have friends in high places."

"Did Shin Bet arrest the owner of the house where we conducted the meeting?"

"They did and interrogated him for a few days but released him after realising that no subversive activities were discussed at the time."

They took a bus and soon arrived at a place in the northern part of the Gaza Strip where a show-jumping competition was in progress. The competitors in their jackets, riding shirts and breeches, complete with helmets and tall riding boots, were executing various dressage manoeuvres in a sport which most Europeans would regard as elitist. How could any family in the Strip afford to pay $200 per month stabling fees, let alone be able to purchase horses costing a few thousand pounds, wondered Alexis. Anxious parents and relatives sat at tables under umbrellas in an area reserved adjacent to the arena. Riders and horses were performing a series of *Piaffes*, a calm and collected elevated trot on the spot, or Passages, where the horse performs a highly elevated and extremely powerful trot, followed by extended and collected Gaits. Alexis and Ibrahim sat at a nearby table and ordered some tea. Alexis glanced across at these people and asked himself how they could afford to fund such a minority sport. Perhaps these were families of prominent Palestinians, or government employees, or families of the Palestinians who had remained in the Strip and made a success of the situation in which they found themselves. He was perplexed but not surprised that horse jumping was the chosen sport as there is a long tradition with horse breeding and horse racing throughout the ages within the Arab fraternity, using some of the best horses that money can buy. The quandary was that equestrianism was taking place in one of the most deprived and run-down regions in the whole of the Middle East. As they were watching a youngster completed his dressage successfully, Mahmoud Sistani approached their table.

"Welcome to our Club," he said shaking Alexis' hand and greeting Ibrahim in the usual way of gesturing one of his hands in a circling fashion around his chest.

"Are your children competing today?" asked Alexis.

Mahmoud smiled and replied:

"Oh no, my children are too young. I own this Club," while looking at the parents clapping another youngster dismounting his horse and clapped too. He turned back to Alexis and noticing his perplexed countenance he went on.

"Amidst the doom and gloom of daily life here in the Strip it is important to give people some light relief," he said, and turned to Ibrahim to discuss some development he was involved in. Alexis cast his thoughts to smuggling goods through the myriad of tunnels as a way of making money and wondered whether these people were the recipients of some of the tunnel revenues but could not discount the fact that some could have been genuine businessmen in the Strip's fragile textile or agriculture enterprises.

"Alexis, it was nice seeing you. Next time you are in the Strip we must have lunch here at the Club. We have a new cook who has produced some marvellous dishes.

I must dash off as I have a meeting at Abasan al-Saghira in the south." Alexis shook hands and Mahmoud disappeared into the clubhouse. Alexis glanced at Ibrahim and, with his hands pointing to the crowd on the terrace, said:

"Who are these people?" Ibrahim was vague about who these people were, perhaps he did not know himself or was he reluctant to reveal their identity? However, he had made the comment of "seeing how the other side lives", implying that this was a Palestinian elite with privileges far beyond what most Palestinians living in the Strip could enjoy. He deflected the question.

"Would you dine with me tomorrow evening?" asked Ibrahim while leaving the club. "There is a quiet place off the city centre, serving traditional Palestinian food, so let us meet there."

"I would love to," replied Alexis while Ibrahim hurriedly noted down the address. They agreed to meet at eight and parted.

The following morning Alexis took a taxi and headed for the Al Mezan Centre, the independent human rights NGO with its headquarters in the Jabalya refugee camp. Since its establishment some 17 years ago, the purpose was to represent Palestinians whose every single right had been violated and to assist in countless humanitarian issues and uphold international law as well as the rule of law in Gaza as part of the occupied territories. He and Nina had met its head, Iqbal, on numerous occasions as he had participated in some of the meetings that Alexis and Nina were invited to.

Iqbal informed Alexis that two of the hospital staff and their families that Nina knew and were living at Shuja'iyya had been killed in the recent attack by the F16s. Alexis knew that Nina would be devastated when she found out and would have to wait for an appropriate time upon his return to break the news. Iqbal went on to update Alexis about some of the factions that had mushroomed in Gaza during the last decade. Many groupings were formed, be they secular, religious, radical or military, all vying for recruiting youngsters to their ranks and with youth unemployment reaching unsustainable proportions there were many who succumbed.

"Hamas' Iz ad-Din al-Qassam Brigade is by far the largest and most prominent fighting force which claims to be over 25,000 strong. There is also the Police Special Force," continued Iqbal, "a unit which is supposed to police and patrol the Strip, but it can also, at a stroke, switch to being a combat force and defend the Strip should the need arise."

"Ever since I entered Gaza, I have had the feeling that I have been followed and was wondering whether the person is part of the Special Police or an Israeli informant?" asked Alexis.

"He could be either, but I am not surprised given the frankness and, dare I say, passion with which you usually address issues concerning Gaza and Palestine," relied Iqbal smilingly.

"From what I learned during this visit, Israel's tight

grip is strengthening," said Alexis.

"Well, the situation deteriorated enormously after the last Intifada. You see there are new assault methods that Israel is deploying, such as unmanned combat drones, some carrying aircraft ordnance such as missiles, and armoured aircraft patrolling day and night over the Palestinian skies and, interestingly, unmanned patrol boats remotely controlled from their headquarters on Israel's shores ready to pounce on any suspicious activity from seemingly innocent fishing boats."

"What about Hamas, have its leaders been questioned about the plight of the Gazans?" asked Alexis.

"Rarely," replied Iqbal, "but last year a young journalist managed to approach the leader of Hamas as he was leaving his headquarters and questioned him about the conditions here in the Strip. His reply was simply that, I quote, 'the people can withstand the siege, however hard that may be.'"

"I wonder whether he believes his own statement?" asked Alexis.

"It is not for me to say, but all I can add is that I perceived a wry smile as he looked across the many cameras that were recording the interview. Perhaps he was addressing the international community rather than his own people."

"What about the relationship between Daesh and Hamas?" asked Alexis probingly. "On my walks I thought I saw a Daesh military compound not far from a Hamas check-point. Is there an understanding between the two?"

"It is difficult to discern the truth these days but recently Daesh has accused Hamas of siding with Fatah and expounding a more tolerant approach to appease Israel and get a settlement. There are so many factions at play here, not least jihadists sympathetic to Daesh in Gaza which Hamas is attempting to crack down on to the dismay of Daesh. On the other hand we have here in the Strip the Ibn Baz Islamic Institute in Rafah whose director runs a bakery and is a more tolerant Salafist advocating discussion and debate rather than violence. It is practically impossible to assess the relation at present between the two organisations but one thing is for sure, there is enmity between the two and it goes back a long time despite attempts at reconciliation."

"How about your organisation? Are you well supported?" asked Alexis anxious to find out how humanitarian organisations were able to fund their operations in the Strip.

"Our main support comes from the Representative Office of Norway to the Palestinian Authority, the Open Society Foundations, the Sigrid Rausing Trust, ICCO and Kerkinactie, the Dutch-based inter-church alliance and Medico International in Germany. We could do with additional groups which support us but we are resilient and have survived many funding crises," went on Iqbal. "The main problem arising from the frequent border skirmishes, and indeed Intifadas, between the IDF and Hamas, is the inability to replace our humanitarian workers as access to Gaza is restricted. You see, Israel controls the airspace, our territorial waters and the crossing points. It has also rendered the airport in the south useless."

"I know what you mean, as Nina and I found it difficult to enter the Strip but we put it down to my frequent talks to Arab groupings here in Gaza which made me, and by association Nina, personae non grata. But restricting access to bona fide aid humanitarian workers borders on the scandalous."

"It is worse than simply not allowing frequent turnover of humanitarian workers into the Strip, as it also restricts documenting violations of human rights and international humanitarian law. We cannot get staff from the West Bank because Israel restricts all travel between the West Bank and the Gaza Strip which, by the way, the UN recognises as one Territorial Unit."

"But surely," responded Alexis, "you should be able to get foreign aid workers through the Rafah crossing which is controlled by Egypt and not Israel?"

"You would have thought so but alas this is not the case. Egypt has kept the Rafah crossing closed claiming that there were insurrections between an affiliate of the Islamic State that had clashed with Egyptian border forces following the coup that deposed President Mohamed Morsi. It is an absolute disgrace that Egypt, a supposedly friendly Arab country, gives excuses for closing the Rafah crossing for almost three years, stating security issues at the border, when they know full well that allowing foreign aid workers to enter would help the well-being of ordinary Palestinians by documenting atrocities and maltreatment not only by the IDF but also by elements within the Hamas Police and Jihadist patrols."

"How does Israel justify its actions?" asked Alexis.

"Well, they repeat time and time again that allowing the flow of Palestinians to and from the Strip to the West Bank, in essence, aids the transfer of terrorists between these regions so only allowing passage to exceptional humanitarian cases..."

"And I suppose the traffic of humanitarian workers in and out of Gaza does not qualify as such," interjected Alexis.

"Quite, without the fresh flow of staff and volunteers as well as professional experts in and out of the Strip all the organisations based here struggle to carry out their work and monitor instances which violate international humanitarian laws. They cannot travel abroad and attend forums and conferences where these issues are aired and familiarise themselves with instances of abuse against the law in other parts of the world," responded a desperate Iqbal.

Alexis stayed at the centre for another hour, was introduced to various employees and was briefed as to what each of them was involved in.

Early in the evening Alexis made his way to the restaurant situated in the outskirts of Gaza City. He arrived at eight and asked whether Ibrahim was there. The owner directed him to an inner room at the back, away from the other diners and most importantly from the prying eyes of police or informers who might have followed Alexis. There he joined up with Ibrahim and was introduced to a few other Palestinians, some of whom knew Alexis from his previous visits to Gaza and two colleagues of Nina's who knew her well. They all greeted Alexis affectionately and sat themselves round the table. The owner brought out a series of large silver oval serving plates filled with an assortment of delectable Levantine cuisine. These included kibbeh, a local dish made of bulgur, minced onions and finely ground lean beef; lamb and goat with cinnamon nutmeg and clove; maqluba, a lamb dish cooked with rice and fried vegetables placed in a pot; matbukha, a cooked dish of tomatoes and roast bell peppers seasoned with garlic and chilli peppers; and tabbouleh, a vegetarian salad of finely chopped parsley, tomatoes, mint, onion, bulgur wheat flavoured with olive oil, lemon juice, salt and pepper. Alexis picked up a warm pita, sliced it open, separating its two sides, and inserted some foodstuffs making an appetizing sandwich.

One of the doctors in the group told of the day when two of his colleagues and their families were tragically killed in the bombardment at Shuja'iyya. Although they were aware of the dangers of living in that neighbourhood they had family ties in the complex and the school was nearby.

"Do we know for sure whether the basements of these houses were used to fire rockets towards Israel?"

asked Alexis.

"There are rumours to that effect, but nobody can tell for sure," was the answer. There followed an uncomfortable pause, the silence of which spoke volumes. Ibrahim was first to break the awkwardness around the table.

"I was told that your stay in Jerusalem was quite eventful," he said. The others looked at Alexis quite eagerly to find out what had happened. Alexis glanced at Ibrahim, who nodded that it was fine to discuss this in front of the others present. Evidently, they were all in the know.

"You might say that," answered a smiling Alexis and went on to explain that although his travel to Jerusalem had had its dangers and the meeting went alright, it was after it had concluded that officers from Shin Bet came to the house he was staying in and from where he had to flee after being alerted by the owner. Alas, Shin Bet, who was monitoring his movements, caught up with him at New Gate as he was exiting the Old City and arrested him. As he was explaining his arrest and treatment at Maskobiyeh detention center in Jerusalem, a young waiter came to the back and informed the owner that two suspicious looking gentlemen had entered the restaurant and were quietly looking at the menu. "Could they have followed Alexis?" he asked the group.

"They could be Shin Bet," said one of them.

"No, they would not dare cross into Gaza. They would be lynched," replied the restaurant owner. "They are probably police or informants working for Shin Bet. Let me have a look." The owner disappeared to investigate only to return shortly afterwards to inform the group that all was well as the two Arabs had ordered and looked quite innocent. They continued to discuss in groups of twos or threes.

"Is there a way by which I could make contact with somebody in authority here is Gaza? There are many questions that I would like answers to but when I raise such questions in my talks I get conflicting answers or no answers at all," asked Alexis. All eyes turned to a young man who had not contributed much to the conversation thus far. He was sitting a couple of places away from Alexis. Conscious that everybody was staring at him he leaned forward and said:

"Do you wish me to arrange such a meeting?" Alexis hoped that the young man meant a member high up in Hamas' ruling party. The parting words of Avi rang clear in his mind: "Fact finding tour, not lectures." But here was an opportunity to meet a member of Hamas, the ruling party in Gaza since 2007, who, as rumour had it, in many instances had forced Gazans to adhere to strict Islamic law. He glanced at Ibrahim who although had not reacted one way or another, his expression clearly gave Alexis the indication that he should accept.

"I would appreciate this," uttered Alexis. The young man excused himself and left the room. Alexis turned to Ibrahim and said:

"Who is that young man?"

"He is the Adjutant for Hamas' leader here in Gaza."

"You mean Ali Al Hakimi's administrative assistant?"

"Indeed. You cannot get anywhere near the leader without his say so."

Alexis hoped the young man would arrange for him to meet Al Hakimi himself rather than any other member in Hamas' hierarchy. He did not feel threatened nor was he alarmed; however, it crossed his mind that he would be getting in uncharted waters, the consequences of which could not be predicted. The conversation continued for a while until Abdul returned. Alexis looked at the young man anxiously.

"Please follow me," he said, addressing Alexis who bade farewell to Ibrahim and the others and following the young man left the restaurant through a door at the back.

"My name is Abdul," said the young man as they approached a junction. "These two Arabs at the restaurant were not Shin Bet or informants."

"What were they?"

"Your bodyguards."

"My bodyguards? Surely not," replied Alexis in utter disbelief.

"With your talks over the years and expressing some controversial views you have made many enemies," replied Abdul.

They crossed the road and turned left into a disused yard, debris scattered everywhere. They crossed the yard, ascended some steps and found themselves in a quaint square with a few dimly lit shops but otherwise it was quite dark. They meandered along two alleys turning left then right with Abdul, looking in all directions to ensure that they were not followed. Even though they were in Gaza he did not wish to reveal the whereabouts of the Hamas leadership to anyone. They soon reached an unimpressive looking-house, where the only light was a low-wattage bulb on the porch giving at most a few metres visibility. He knocked twice, uttered a few words through a slit on the door-side and they were let in. Abdul turned to Alexis.

"I need to blindfold you, even a friend like yourself. Security, I am afraid."

"I quite understand," replied Alexis.

Alexis was then led through the house into the back alley where a car was waiting to drive them to the required location. After ten minutes the car stopped and they entered another house. Alexis was taken down some steps and through a couple of corridors which led to a small room. The blindfold was taken off and Alexis was confronted by a middle-aged Arab.

"My name is Al Hakimi," said the Arab shaking his hand. "Apologies for blindfolding you but we live in difficult times and it was necessary..."

"No need to apologise," replied Alexis and sat on a chair opposite the leader of Hamas in the Strip.

"We appreciate the efforts you and your partner have made to support our cause over the past two decades.

We are disappointed, however, that the international community has seen fit to do nothing to alleviate our situation and put pressure on the Israeli government and their supporters the USA to arrest the deteriorating position here in Gaza," said Al Hakimi and paused. Alexis, looking at the leader, asked:

"May I be blunt?"

"Of course, I expect no less," replied the Arab

"They regard you as an extremist organisation," started Alexis.

"Do you regard us as such?"

Alexis stared straight at him.

"I think you know the answer to that. You are as much a terrorist organisation as Mandela's group was during the Apartheid years, or the Mau Mau rebels were against the British in Kenya, or the IRA, or the Suffragettes, or indeed the Stern and Irgun were in the eyes of the British during the Mandate," replied Alexis. Ali smiled.

"Indeed," replied the Hamas leader. Alexis went on.

"But your people are suffering dreadfully. Lack of electricity, shortage of gas, very little money to buy basic provisions assuming these are available, the water needs to be boiled, raw sewage going straight into the sea, thousands living in shanty towns by the shore."

"That is why our people periodically rebel and protest."

"But to what end? They are shot at by the IDF from their tall observation towers as they approach the wall beyond the 300-metre buffer zone even though they use slings to throw stones over rather than shoot at the IDF soldiers."

"But our only recourse is to protest. It is the right of our people."

"Do you encourage them to protest, to provoke the IDF and be killed so that they become martyrs and gain international condemnation by the action of the IDF?"

"We do not have to coerce them to protest. Their parents and grandparents who live with them are a constant reminder of the suffering, torture and humiliation they endured at the end of the British Mandate and during the 1948 and 1967 wars. These youngsters know nothing but misery, overcrowding conditions, insurrections with the IDF and the majority see no way out but to rebel, some of them paying the ultimate price."

"Every time there is rocket being launched against an Israeli town and people get killed or a suicide bomber blows a bus in Jerusalem, the Israeli government and especially their spokesperson simply state that, I quote, 'Hamas hate us, they wish to throw us into the sea'. When the TV commentator asked this spokesperson whether Israel should show restraint in their military response, he invariably replies that they only protect the Jewish villages near the border."

"Surely, you mean illegal settlements by the way," replied Al Hakimi. "I despair when I hear the response of European governments that Israel should be proportionate in any response."

"Unfortunately, Europe is totally preoccupied with Brexit – after all this will decide the future of some 500 million Europeans so one can understand focussing on that issue." Abdul brought in a tray with coffee and tea. Al Hakimi turned to Alexis who opted for tea and carefully placed a couple of lemon slices in the cup and stirred it. Ali stood, paced around Alexis and ended up once again opposite him.

"What does the international community expect from us?"

"I heard the foreign minister of Saudi Arabia about a month ago stating that Hamas should come to the negotiating table," replied Alexis.

"Saudi Arabia, well there is another corrupt regime who were supposed to be our brothers. Our Palestinian leaders have been negotiating for the past four decades but without being able to secure a lasting peace. It was President Carter around 1978 who was firm with the then Israeli leaders advocating that a precondition to any future settlement was for Israel to withdraw to its pre-1967 borders. He also threatened to cut the aid the USA was giving Israel unless they accepted that and negotiate on such terms. And what was the result?"

"He caved in to pressure from the Jewish lobby fearing the repercussions in pending elections," replied Alexis.

"Indeed, my friend, as you say he caved in," continued Al Hakimi, "and we are here some 38 years after and we are no nearer to reaching a settlement." Alexis was now in a tête-à-tête conversation with Hamas' top leader. He did not hold back because he was now representing the views of the ordinary Palestinian in Gaza and not the elite few who had profited by smuggling goods or the liberal Arabs, or the intellectuals abroad.

"But after Carter caved in, it was unfortunate that a schism appeared between factions within the PLO..."

"It was not unfortunate, it was necessary that we broke away from Fatah. In the end Arafat was too weak to argue our cause and when he died we had no option but to break away so that we could argue more forcefully in any negotiations."

"But it was still mainly Fatah that took part in the negotiations and you were marginalised despite winning control here in the Strip. At the time you even refused to recognise the existence of Israel and past Hamas leaders stressed time and time again that their goal was to throw the Israelis into the sea."

"But as you know we have since recognised Israel based on the pre-1967 borders but, as we speak, they have annexed and occupied practically half of the West Bank."

"But your people here tell me that the situation in the Strip was more tolerable before 2007 when Hamas took over. Then Israelis often visited Gaza to fix their cars in garages here as it was much cheaper than in Israel or indeed buy stuff they needed much more cheaply. Following the three Intifadas against Israel, the Gaza Strip has become an open prison, with a wall surrounding it, with ugly watchtowers ready to fire at protesters given the slightest provocation, a buffer zone where your people get shot at if they step into it, unemployment has soared, there are shortages of all amenities and houses demolished by the IDF in recent wars. What have you achieved for the ordinary Palestinian in the Strip today except utter misery?" Alexis paused as he perceived that Ali had suddenly acquired a very serious facial expression when confronted with such a barrage of unrestrained statements. He collected his thoughts, looked at Alexis and started.

"Does the international community expect us to declare a total truce, put down our guns, disband our fighters and go to the negotiating table?"

"That would be a start," replied Alexis bluntly.

"I tell you what will happen. Israel may end the blockade, the monstrous separation wall may be demolished, no towers, they may withdraw the IDF, they may allow us to fish beyond the 6 kilometre limit and reach the part of the Mediterranean which has a reasonable amount of fish, unemployment will reduce and the people of Gaza will start witnessing better conditions..."

"Well?" interrupted an anxious Alexis.

"Well, my friend, we will end up with another puppet regime here in Gaza similar to that in Ramallah, with self-rule in both but without an independent Palestinian state, with Israel occupying all the land they annexed in 1967, and the principle of the Right of Return of the Palestinians living in refugee camps in neighbouring countries not adhered to. Is this what the major powers are asking from us? Is this what you are asking from us?" Alexis knew that Ali was demanding an answer to the most intractable problem in modern history, the Palestinian Conundrum as he had referred to it countless times in the past.

"No, it is not what I ask of you," he uttered in desperation, "but I sincerely ask you what is the alternative? You cannot beat Israel militarily as they have the most sophisticated military machine in the world, the international community is looking at other troublesome regions, such as Yemen and Syria, the USA is at loggerheads with Iran and with the situation in North Korea – even some of your Arab neighbours do not sympathize with your cause any more. I have heard the argument that the Palestinian population is fast increasing and at some stage in the future they will rise in an apartheid-style revolution. But the regime in South Africa was hated by almost every country in the world which openly expressed their abhorrence for apartheid followed by sanctions. Can you foresee any country applying sanctions against Israel in the future?"

"We value education, so we are making every possible effort to make sure that our youngsters are well educated so they understand what happened in the past and can carry the torch in future years."

"Are they being brainwashed in schools to hate the Jewish people and all what Israel stands for? At least talking to my Jewish contact..."

"You mean the Schumann family?"

"Yes I do, they tell me that many schools have become sites of popular terror and rioting."

"Popular terror translates to a peaceful protest. We do teach them our history and we do mention what happened in 1948 and 1967. It is inevitable that we delve into our past if the human misery suffered by their forefathers is to be conveyed to the young. However, look at the reaction of the IDF. For some socioeconomic reasons some of our pupils need to cross to neighbouring villages in the West Bank to attend the appropriate school and the IDF resort to all sorts of tactics to prevent our children reaching even the school gates by numerous roadblocks and checkpoints along the way. And as the world turns a blind eye to such incidents, the IDF will continue to deprive our children of their education. Do not take my word for this." Ali reached for the table behind him and fetched a report. Pointing to the report he continued.

"A UN report this year stated that there were 2500 pupils from 35 West Bank towns and villages that need to cross various military checkpoints to reach their schools every day. The report goes on to state that at least half of these children faced some sort of intimidation and at times violence for simply wishing to cross the checkpoint to attend school. This equates to extreme harassment does it not?" Alexis acquiesced and held his head in his hands in frustration of what he was being told. Ali went on.

"UNICEF established protective teams of volunteers to make sure that the Palestinian pupils reached their school, but the UN report goes on to state that even these people were subjected to harassment and intimidation, often imprisonment. Not only were the IDF responsible for such actions but the inhabitants in these illegal settlements often introduced their own checkpoints. Despite such extreme measures, it is heartening to read from this UN report that in the West Bank and Gaza Strip the level of those educated has reached over 95%. That is an incredible achievement despite the efforts of the IDF to prevent us educating our young people." Al Hakimi stopped, stood and waved at Alexis to follow him. Through the exchanges Alexis had wanted to ask one more delicate question but could not find the opportunity. As they started to walk towards the door, he stopped also obliging Al Hakimi to stop. He could not hold back any longer and said:

"You see, your people resent rumours that the Hamas leadership abroad is enjoying a luxurious life staying in five-star hotels or purchasing houses worth over a million dollars and establishing Swiss bank accounts. How true are those rumours?

"The leadership is always on the alert to eliminate such practices from our ranks. As far as staying in five-star hotels, we only do so when the other side stays in similar hotels prior to starting any talks. Do you expect us to stay in a student hostel while the Israelis and their mediators lord it in luxury accommodation?" The leader of Hamas pressed on.

"Come next door, I wish to show you something before we break up." Alexis followed the leader down the corridor which led to another windowless room. He went to the far wall which had six enlarged maps of the West Bank showing chronologically the build-up of Israeli settlements from 1968 to 2015. As there was only a small low-wattage bulb in the ceiling Ali switched on a powerful spotlight focussing in succession on each map.

"Look," he said pointing to the first map, "in 1968 there were five settlements with 250 settlers, while in 1977 there were 38 settlements with 1,900 settlers. Last year there were 125 with 382,000 settlers. Just before the schism with Fatah in 2005 there were 123 settlements with just less than a quarter of a million inhabitants. Interestingly, although the settlements remained about the same number between the years 1997 to 2015, the number of settlers dramatically increased pointing to the fact that the existing settlements were expanding. All that activity, I hasten to add, was carried out under the full gaze of the international community which chose to do absolutely nothing save offer vague protests during successive peace negotiations." Alexis knew of the illegal settlements but was still troubled to see the expansion so graphically stretched across these maps and the sheer scale of increase since the 1967 war. Al Hakimi resumed his narrative.

"Acceleration of these settlements was carried out in two periods, first 1968 to 1977 under Golda Meir and

Yitzhak Rabin and most notably from 1977 to 1986 under Menachem Begin and Simon Peres when the settlements increased from 38 to 117. Hamas was not prominent then and the PLO under Arafat was at that time in charge of the Palestinian peace delegations. Thereafter successive leaders of various Israeli parties have continued to encourage the expansion and financing of such settlements. In fact, Ariel Sharon, who was Prime Minister between 2001 and 2006, was in effect responsible for the vast expansion of the existing settler population in the West Bank and was his way of preventing the establishment of a Palestinian State in the West Bank." Ali paused, reached his desk, fetched another map of the West Bank, handed it to Alexis and uttered, "Have a look at these illegal outposts."

The map showed the growth of unauthorised Israeli settlements in the West Bank which entered the picture following the 1993 Oslo Accord where the Israeli Government agreed to freeze the establishment of new settlements. Ali continued.

"These illegal outposts..."

"You mean illegal in that they were built without the consent of the Israeli government..." butted in Alexis only to be interrupted again by Al Hakimi.

"The international community regards any settlements in the West Bank, including outposts, as illegal, but if truth be told because the Oslo Accord forced the Israeli government to halt any further settlement activity, future settlers took it upon themselves to build new houses and schools away from existing settlements and, what is more, with the support of official state authorities with regards to all their needs including the defence of these outposts." Alexis was taken aback by such unauthorised expansionist policy clandestinely supported by the Israeli government.

"These outposts have come into being since Netanyahu was elected leader for the second time seven years ago. What is more, the cunning operation of all this development is that as these outposts grow they come closer and closer to existing settlements and recently the Netanyahu government decreed that since they are physically so close they will be deemed neighbourhoods of the nearby settlements and thus legitimised their existence." Ali paused then continued:

"So I ask you again, my friend, what sort of two-state solution do the major nations envisage when our Palestinian land in the West Bank is infested with settlements, which most of the nations in the UN regard as illegal? Is anybody serious that some of these settlements will be abandoned or forcibly evacuated to make room for our bilateral state in the West Bank? Look," continued Al Hakimi pointing to the 2015 map, "there is no room any more." Alexis came near the wall to study closely the maps and number of settlers involved.

"Furthermore," continued Ali, "a very interesting development occurred in 2005 following the death of Arafat. We had a new leader who along with most of the Palestinian leadership favoured the so-called Arc Project. Are you aware what it entailed?" Alexis nodded that he was aware of it but added, "Why was it abandoned, I suppose finance was not available as it involved millions of dollars?"

"Finance would have been no problem," replied Ali. "At the time some fellow Arab countries were willing to offer substantial funds to start it off. But the reason it was not carried forward is more subtle. I will hazard a guess. This project was very forward-looking and we largely welcomed it, despite it having originated from an organisation within the USA. The Israeli leadership realised that, had this project gone ahead, it would have stopped in its tracks the fulfilment of the Orthodox Jewish community's aspirations for its biblical promise to render the whole of the West Bank as part of an enlarged Jewish State."

"I suppose if one projects such developments it is not too difficult to envisage that in a few years we will end up with close to a million settlers in the West Bank," went on Alexis. Ali nodded in agreement.

"Where did you get such detailed information regarding these settlements and outposts? It is quite impressive," said Alexis while looking closely at the maps and probing that perhaps there was a slight exaggeration in what Al Hakimi was presenting to him. The leader of Hamas smiled and replied:

"Well, you may be astonished to know that it came from an article in Haaretz, a Jewish newspaper and written by a Jewish correspondent."

"I see," replied Alexis and went on. "I must ask you something else." Al Hakimi stared at him in anticipation.

"Since the elections, which Hamas won, there have been a number of attempts towards reconciliation between yourselves and Fatah, the latest of which has failed. A Unity Government would have much more credence and leverage in any future negotiations with Israel."

"We are still discussing issues that separate us with Fatah," replied Ali dismissively.

Alexis and Ali had talked for at least two hours about the Palestinian Conundrum with arguments and counter-arguments being thrashed about freely. Abdul came into the room and whispered something to his leader who turned to Alexis and brought the discussion to an end.

"I am afraid I must leave. We must resume our frank exchanges if ever you find yourself once more on our patch. A car is waiting outside to take you to your hotel. Give my regards to your partner. We value her work in our hospitals." The Hamas leader then disappeared, hotly pursued by Abdul. Another operative came, blindfolded Alexis once more, led him to a waiting car and on to the hotel.

In the morning Alexis checked out of the hotel and made a phone call to Athens informing Nina of his pending arrival. He then took a taxi and made his way back to the entrance of the long tunnel taking him to the Erez border crossing. Avi was there waiting for him with the chauffeur to drive him to Tel Aviv airport. He was able to travel back to Athens under his own passport with Avi accompanying him all the way to the passport and border control to make sure that there were no awkward questions at the airport or a last-minute hitch. The two remained silent throughout the journey.

"Give our regards to Nina," uttered Avi as he shook Alexis' hand, momentarily looking at the ex-Alexandrian's weary face.

Upon landing at Athens he headed straight for Nina's apartment.

"Whatever happened in Israel? I received a call from Ismail to say that you had been arrested in Jerusalem," exclaimed an anxious Nina as she welcomed him back. They embraced and Alexis sat down, utterly exhausted. After regaining his composure, he explained the events leading to his arrest, his release and subsequent meetings with Joshua, Avi and Al Hakimi.

He decided to stay a couple of days to recover from this trip and brief Nina further on his deliberations not only with Al Hakimi but also to convey news from their dear friends Khalil and Ahlam. The dreadful news of the death in Shuja'iyya of the two families of the doctors from the hospital deeply affected her.

"Our friends in the Strip send you their love, including the Schumanns," he finally whispered.

Alexis travelled back to Cambridge and Nina followed after a few weeks. She stayed at Alexis' house off Parker's Piece in the city centre.

36

Cambridge, London, 2017

Following the schism between the Palestinian Authority and Hamas after the death of the PLO leader Yasser Arafat, the split polarised politics in the region in that the Palestinians were not speaking with one unified voice but with two very different voices: The Authority, based in Ramallah, and Hamas based in the Gaza Strip. In an effort towards reconciliation the Gaza Agreement was signed in April 2014 with a view to forming a National Unity Government which would represent all the Palestinians in both Gaza and the West Bank. The National Unity Government was formed weeks later. Rumour had it that during the silent Intifada Hamas wished to depose Fatah rule in the West Bank which the leader of the Palestinian Authority called a very grave day for all Palestinians. In September 2014 in Cairo it was agreed that the Unity Government would be in control in Gaza and the PLO would take control of border crossings. However, the National Unity Government was dissolved in June 2015 following Fatah's acknowledgment that they could not operate in Gaza. Another Reconciliation Agreement brokered by Egypt was signed in Cairo in October 2017. However, many issues remain to be resolved not least who would control the weapons held by terrorist groups in Gaza. The PA insisted that any weapons in Gaza were controlled by their security forces. In essence a de facto army was envisaged before a formal state of Palestine could come into being. Such to-ing and fro-ing between the leaders of Fatah and Hamas made any possible initiative for starting negotiations with the Israeli government very difficult as they justifiably pointed out that they could not see a united Palestinian front. This was further complicated by Israel's insistence that they would not talk to any National Unity Government that included elements of ex-Hamas leadership.

Alexis, back in Cambridge after his eventful trip to Amman and Jerusalem, was monitoring the state of affairs from afar and made a concerted effort to keep abreast of developments in Palestine and read factual documents and books that appeared in the press about many facets of this intractable problem. One such book reviewed in the *Sunday Times* was entitled 'The Ethnic Cleansing of Palestine' by Ilan Pappe, one of the New Israeli Historians. Alexis' daughter was on the phone after he had drawn her attention to this new book.

"Am I not correct in surmising," she declared, "that Ilan Pappe has been heavily criticised by other Israeli historians because he had included a few incidents of alleged massacres which, they claimed, did not actually take place?"

"Well in a book of some three-hundred pages, with countless references to support his arguments, I daresay that one or two facts may not turn out to be true, but the bulk of his allegations are undoubtedly true and corroborated from other sources," asserted Alexis.

"Anyway, read it and we can discuss it further. But do not rely solely on Pappe's book," continued Alexis, "there are other books on the subject. Ben Morris, for example, is another of the New Historians that gives an opposing view as to the facts pertaining to the expulsion of the Arabs from Palestine in 1948. You will find, however, that at a certain point Morris admits that the Arabs had to be expelled from their homes in Palestine because it was necessary for the establishment and indeed the survival of the new Jewish State. One cannot deny the well documented atrocities committed by the Israelis at Deir Yassin, Lydda–Ramle and Jaffa. So, read some of the arguments of both historians and what the critics say about them."

"Will do," replied Hermioni.

"Did you manage to have a word with the PM?" went on Alexis.

"Not really," answered Hermioni frustratingly. "She is totally preoccupied by the Brexit negotiations and cannot seriously consider any other issue. The impasse over the Irish border has totally enveloped her and successive Brexit Ministers, so I am afraid I will have to wait for an opportunity, whenever that arises, to grab her attention."

"Brexit has put all other issues on hold," replied Alexis. "Let us wait and see what transpires. Nina and I are spending a few days in London and will be dinning tomorrow evening at the Ivy at around 8 pm. Would you and Stuart be able to find a babysitter and join us?"

"I cannot promise because I have to complete a report for the day after tomorrow but if I proceed well with it this afternoon and Stuart is free we will join you," said his daughter.

The atmosphere at the Ivy in London's West Street was as always welcoming. Stuart and Hermioni were able to join them as Alexis started revealing details of last year's clandestine visit to Jerusalem via Amman.

"Dad, you are pushing your luck, don't you think?" stressed Hermioni.

"I will not be gagged by anybody, although I am glad that Avi was about to offer well-needed assistance for my release," responded Alexis.

"All I can say, Alexis, is I am glad you have powerful friends in Israel," said Stuart. Nina nodded her head in total agreement. During the meal the conversation oscillated from topic to topic discussing their busy lives, grandchildren, St John's and Nina's sporadic articles in Athenian newspapers.

"By the way," asked Alexis addressing his daughter, "do you know any of the members of the Joint Committee for Human Rights? Hermioni mentioned a couple of names."

"Well, I wonder whether its report on the 'Freedom of Speech in Universities' has been completed?"

"I cannot say I have seen it although my desk at present is overflowing with pamphlets and copies of Hansard Reports which I am gradually going through. Why do you ask?" replied Hermioni.

"Cambridge University has decided to forbid an academic from chairing an event next November on 'BDS and the globalised struggle for Palestinian Rights' which featured a panel that included some speakers known to be pro-Palestinian activists."

"BDS?" uttered Stuart glancing in turn at Alexis and Nina.

"Boycott, Divestment, Sanctions, is a global movement initiated about two years ago with the aim to force Israel to stop the oppression of Palestinian people," replied Nina.

"I doubt if Israel is worried about BDS," said Hermioni while looking at Nina. "They will ignore it as they have repeatedly paid no notice to other condemnations by the international community."

"It is gathering momentum," said Alexis and went on, "and what is more Israel detests the parallels that have been drawn between the BDS movement and the sanctions that were forced on South Africa's Apartheid regime all those years ago. However, I share Hermioni's pessimism given that there have been countless demonstrations and protests espousing BDS, yet we have seen no notable actions of countries or businesses boycotting Israeli goods or services."

"I share your reservations," replied Nina looking at Alexis, "but my feeling is that the movement will gather pace."

"So, what was the outcome of banning this guy?" asked Hermioni.

"The event was cancelled. Justifiably there were protests from the Students' Union and several political associations, some stating that there was a steady number of individuals that were being ostracised because of their views," said Alexis and continued. "The interesting aspect of all this is that the University made several written statements to the Parliamentary Committee stating that preventing speakers from attending students' events could be illegal. They add that they have created 'safe places' to support students but 'no-platforming' infringed its freedom of speech policies."

"That sounds like double-Dutch to me," exclaimed Stuart. Ignoring her husband's comment Hermioni added:

"The House of Commons is correct in trying to assess the level of free speech in UK universities. As such it could be monitored and its relation, if any, to terrorism and human rights law could be traced."

"I think in the final analysis the university was quite embarrassed at having to stop this academic from chairing the panel when advocating a policy of free speech," concluded Alexis.

"That is not the end of the matter," said Nina looking at Alexis. Hermioni and Stuart turned and looked at him too.

"The university's Palestinian Society invited me instead to present a talk about the Palestinian problem," replied Alexis.

"Will you accept?" asked Hermioni anxiously while glancing at Nina.

"I think you already know the answer to that," said Nina looking at Hermioni. Alexis grimaced at his daughter implying full agreement with Nina's statement.

"I have already done so."

"When is this talk scheduled?"

"In the autumn, well after our planned reunion in Greece."

"What on earth are you going to say in just over 50 minutes?" queried Hermioni.

"I haven't as yet formulated my ideas but I am certainly not going to describe in any detail the events of the last hundred years. I am in two minds whether to address the future and describe what my solution would be, if I was in the driving seat."

All four continued to discuss this issue putting forward arguments for a more subdued approach to Alexis' lecture thus avoiding confrontation with the Jewish fraternity at the university and especially at Alexis' College, St John's. Nina and Alexis left the Ivy at just after 11 o'clock. The night was balmy, a soft welcome breeze enveloped them as they turned right into St Martin's Lane going south, passing Noel Coward's theatre on their left and soon reaching the English National Opera. They crossed the pavement and glanced at its posters.

"*Les* Pêcheurs de Perles," uttered Nina as she translated Bizet's opera in fluent French. "I was in New York visiting Nestor in the fall of 1986 and I saw the Pearl Fishers at the City Opera and remember glancing through the reviews in the *New York Times Book Review* days after. One critic was decisively not enthusiastic about its libretto but I enjoyed the performance because of Bizet's score with its melodic suppleness and warmth."

"I am not sure about its warmth," butted in Alexis, "as the 'Friendship duet', with the harp and clarinet in the background, when I hear it the passion in me rises to a crescendo."

"Crescendo, no less," exclaimed Nina.

"Well, you know what I mean."

They laughed as they crossed Charing Cross Road passing by the National Portrait Gallery and veered towards Pall Mall reaching the combined Universities Club at numbers 71-77. They sank into a large comfortable settee in the lounge to the left of the impressive atrium and each ordered a glass of their favourite tipple, a Cointreau. They sipped the brandies, absorbed in their own thoughts. Once up in one of the Club's comfortable rooms they soon fell asleep.

37

Siros Island, the Aegean Sea, July 2017

The ex-pupils of the Averofeio had arranged another reunion at Siros, the cultural island capital of the Cyclades in the Aegean, sandwiched between Kithnos and Mykonos. Siros was chosen for its proximity to Athens, which could be reached by a fast catamaran or by flying direct to Mykonos and catching a ferry. It was the end of July and the Meltemi winds were starting to blow quite fiercely; however, being blistering hot, the winds were welcomed as they tempered the high temperatures. By the end of their sojourn the Meltemi abated and windy days gave way to balmy evenings when the ex-pupils scattered into smaller groups to walk around leisurely in search of interesting archaeological sites, old churches and hidden tavernas.

On the third evening Alexis and Nina lost track of any rendezvous and set off for Lilis, a taverna high up on a mount at Ano Siros about 500 metres beyond Miaoulis Square. Evidence of the island's long Venetian occupation was all around but most strikingly Ermoupoli, the capital port, and characteristic of its neoclassical buildings, gave an air of aesthetic simplicity symbolized by its princely mansions, grandiose villas and picturesque piazzas.

They sat at a table overlooking the waveless sea, offering panoramic views of the Aegean and the isles of Rineia and Dilos in the far distance. The sky was bluish red, the horizon mostly imperceptible, the sea and sky merging seamlessly. They ordered, small plates featuring calamaria, soupies, grilled octopus while now and then revisiting their Alexandrian adolescent years, their long separation, getting at last together in mid-life, and of course gossiping about their ex-school pals and their families. A quartet was playing traditional Greek urban songs or *rebetico* on their mandolin-like long-necked string instruments.

"What was Nestor's reaction when you first told him you had gone to Gaza?" asked Alexis. Nina turned towards him, sipped her tsipouro, the pure grape pomance-brandy, fished out the sliced lemon, bit into it to savour its unique flavour, and replied:

"I suppose the same as that of Hermioni's, *n'est-ce pas mon chéri?*" replied Nina mockingly.

"Mm, my daughter was quite put out."

"Well, I explained to my son how it had all begun with Ismail's reference to the situation in Gaza and that he had relatives living there that could help me. When Nestor realised the plight of the Palestinians, he understood my decision but always fearing the worse as time progressed. When matters got worse he did not know that we kept going there and that was the best. No doubt you experienced the same reservations from Hermioni."

"I did, and she took some persuading at first when I went to Gaza with you all those years ago. She thought it was unwise, and I think we took the right decision not to tell them of our continuing clandestine visits to the Strip the past six years or so."

"There you are!" shouted Hermioni as she finally reached the top of the mount followed by all the other members of the group. "May we join you?"

"Of course," replied Alexis and waved to the waiter to extend the table to accommodate the considerably enlarged group. There was quite a commotion as the group was now 18 strong so several tables had to be placed together in one corner along the short wall at the edge of the cliff thus separating them from the other diners.

"What a splendid view," exclaimed Christos as he sat next to Nina at the centre of the long improvised dining table. Opposite sat Ismail, Kaliopi, Yanis, Vassilliki, Stuart and Myrna. Alexis stood as the extra tables were put together and sat at one end flanked by Kate and Ingrid while Hermioni was sandwiched between Nestor and Petros at the opposite end. Amalia found herself between Christos and Michael while Marinos sat next to Nina. Retsina, stored in pine barrels, other local wines and beers were soon ordered. Similar hors-d'œuvres to those already at the table as well as feta and bean salads were ordered several times over. The job of the waiter taking their main orders was made well-nigh impossible as they all talked ten to the dozen. He had to come back from the kitchen several times to confirm his hurriedly scribbled orders. The conversation flowed quite easily, continuing where they had left off earlier during the afternoon swim, about their current lives, extended families, aspirations, politics and the amazing attitude of the Twitter-happy US President, all making rude jokes but knowing full well that in the final analysis his finger was not far from the nuclear button. Aided by copious quantities of retsina and other alcoholic drinks, the conversation was quite relaxed as they chatted in small groups switching from topic to topic.

It was inevitable that at some stage the latest bout of austerity measures forced by the EU/IMF on the Greek government which in turn imposed these on its people and its implications would have been aired. It was a topic that never escaped the attention of Alexandrian Greeks when they reunited every so often. The austerity measures were first introduced in 2010 to solve the Greek government debt crisis caused by a huge budget deficit. It had a calamitous effect on the morale and wellbeing of the people and resulted in thousands of graduates from the prestigious polytechnic and university at Athens emigrating to other European countries. These, Petros argued, were the young people that Greece needed to bolster the economy and create wealth but alas they were forced to abandon their families and flee abroad. Marinos, Petros' elder son, was the embodiment of such a person having uprooted his family and was now working in New York for the UN.

"How many austerity packages have you had since

2010?" asked Stuart.

"To tell you the truth I have lost count, they must number over a dozen," replied Petros while Vassiliki nodded in agreement, "and the austerity measures during the past few years were imposed by the new government controlled by our left-wing party, Syriza." Petros was in his element as soon as austerity was mentioned and always complained bitterly about such measures, blaming the European leaders and particularly the German Chancellor as well as some major banks that he held responsible for all the evils that befell the ordinary people living in Greece. He and Vassiliki were the only ones in that gathering who were living in Athens and were subjected to the full brunt of these austerity measures. Alexis, Yanis and Christos having made their homes elsewhere in Europe did not share Petros' woes but sympathised with the predicament he and Vassiliki were faced with. Alexis tried in vain to remind his school pal that with the Brexit negotiations in full swing the European Union had a more pressing issue to consider than worrying about Greece's economic woes.

As the evening progressed Alexis had something else on his mind. Such a gathering offered a good platform to discuss the plight of Palestinian Arabs and to share with them some facts that Nina and himself had mulled over the past few weeks. So waiting for a lull in the conversation he said:

"Has anybody seen the news this evening? There was another deadly incident in the Gaza Strip next to the

Israeli border."

"I watched the news on Al Jazeera just before leaving and apparently ten Gazans were shot at as they protested near the border with Israel," said Nestor.

"I suspect some protesters may have crossed into the buffer zone," said Christos.

"Is there ever going to be a resolution to the Palestinian problem?" butted in Myrna.

"Well, as long as the US supports Israel the stalemate will continue ad infinitum," said Marinos who, as Director of the UN Development Programme and based in New York, had his finger on the pulse of the US international policy. By now all of Alexis' pals and their children knew that Alexis and Nina had gone to Gaza several times over so with an element of hesitancy they refrained from expressing strong opinions about the conflict. Alexis and Nina followed their sentiments but without any specific focus the conversation kept drifting to other topics. A few months after he returned from his eventful trip to Jerusalem, Alexis showed Nina an article in the *Guardian* by Nathan Thrall detailing the real reasons why the endless talks and summits to resolve the Palestine-Israeli impasse had failed. They read it and reread it to absorb the intricacies of the arguments and to corroborate the facts with other sources. Alexis, as he sat amongst his pals and their children on that graceful island in the middle of the Aegean, reflected on the role his mum had played back in 1956 after the Arab-Israeli war in the Canal Zone when some of his close pals including the Schumann family had gathered in his apartment in Alexandria to celebrate his birthday. It was now the turn of Nina and himself to act as mentors and steer the discussion along its tortuous path. Alexis grimaced at Nina; she responded at once with a nod and Alexis waited for an opportune moment to switch the discussion back to the Palestinian issue. The quartet of bouzouki musicians turned to a few well-known romantic songs with a number of the diners partaking in the singing. Alexis seized the opportunity as the quartet stopped for a well-deserved break and started:

"I came across an article which outlines very succinctly the reasons why the stalemate persists and it has nothing to do with what is usually written in Presidents' memoirs or put across at think tanks, which wrongly argue that the extremists are setting the agenda. Further, the real reason does not rest on issues such as time was short or there was insufficient preparation before a summit, or that the negotiators mistrusted their opposites. The real reason is more subtle and it is to do with the fact that Israel is quite happy with the status quo."

"I thought you might say that," butted in Christos.

"Is the two-state solution I keep hearing about still viable?" asked Vassiliki, looking askance at her husband Petros who was still mulling over aspects of Greece's punitive austerity measures.

"There is a general consensus that with a little effort from both sides, not least doing something regarding the settlements in the West Bank, a two-state solution may be viable," answered Nina.

"So why has it not happened?" asked Amalia in frustration.

"Just consider what has happened since I left the hospital in Gaza over 20 years ago," started Nina staring at her daughter-in-law who posed the question, "The Oslo Accords..."

"In 1993," butted in Alexis. "Yes, quite so," replied Nina and went on. "They looked extremely promising in reaching a lasting peace after the negotiations between Rabin and Arafat. Incidentally, these two, together with Shimon Peres, were awarded the Nobel Peace Prize in 1994 for their efforts. However, an ultra-zealot Zionist took a different view and deemed it a betrayal of the Zionist dream and in 1995 gunned down Rabin after a rally in support of the Oslo Accords. Then, a few years later the 'Wye River Memorandum' also offered a promising solution but unfortunately the Israeli Labour Party did not join Netanyahu's coalition."

"What was the essence of this memorandum?" asked Michael, Myrna's other half.

"A commitment of a substantial withdrawal from the settlements in West Bank," replied Alexis. Nina nodded and went on.

"Then we had the Camp David Summit which could have resulted in a peaceful agreement if only the US had taken a more balanced approach by consulting the Arab states instead of paying too much attention to internal politics of the Israeli government." Nina paused for a moment while all eyes around the large table looked to her to end her summary of the main events. Alexis took over.

"President Clinton was certainly firmer than his predecessors when at the end of December 2000 he outlined the parameters for an agreement which could have been accepted by both parties but alas this did not happen."

"Why on earth not?" asked Christos.

"For the apparently naïve reason that the plan was presented too quickly and with a further condition that if they did not accept it within a short period the offer would lapse."

"It really does not make any sense not to allow sufficient time to consider Clinton's proposals carefully," said Hermioni.

"You would think so," continued Alexis, "but the other obstacle was that this proposal was made in the dying days of his administration and weeks later he was out of office."

"I wonder whether President Clinton felt guilty in not brokering a lasting settlement during his Presidency and tried during the last weeks of his administration to push a deal through knowing fully well that it would not succeed?" butted in Yanis.

"There we go," responded Petros who knew his school pal very well. "Yanis is in his element with his conspiracy theories." They all laughed out loud pointing fingers at Yanis who accepted nonchalantly the accusation.

"I don't know about that but let us say it is very strange to start something as delicate as these negotiations knowing that time was running out," replied Alexis.

"OK, whatever the reason for starting late in his presidency, why didn't the next president adopt this scheme and run with it?" asked Ingrid.

"We must remember that that was when the Republicans had just snatched power," butted in Nina

"I daresay in dubious circumstances as there seemed to be some irregularity when counting the votes in Florida," butted in Yanis.

"Be that as it may," continued Alexis, "we then had the Taba discussions in Egypt where both sides were close to an agreement but apparently time ran out. But I suspect the real reason was that Ehud Barak did not wish to alienate some voters in the pending Israeli election, by raising the Palestinian issue even though there was a possible solution to the conflict. Had he done so he would have faced certain defeat against Ariel Sharon."

"What a mess," uttered Petros in despair.

"Well, you call it a mess but perhaps it was meant to fail," continued Nina. "But, finally, there were two major initiatives in 2003, the Road Map to Peace initiated by the US and the Geneva Accord both of which could have led to peace."

"What scuppered those two initiatives?" asked Kate in frustration.

"Unfortunately, there was a Likud Prime Minister

who was very hawkish," replied Nina.

"But also," interrupted Alexis, "we had an Intifada which did not help matters."

"I believe there were three Intifadas if you include the incidents which started in 2014," said Christos.

"Certainly," continued Alexis, "these bloody insurrections did not achieve the effect the Palestinians had hoped for, but one could understand why Hamas resorted to such fruitless tactics. Life in Gaza is so horrible; it is like being caged in an open prison without seeing an end. It was a desperate move knowing that it would never succeed but there was hope that the outside world would realize their awful plight and put pressure on the superpowers to force both factions to the negotiating table. Many independent observers and media commentators had predicted such an uprising given the multiple failures for a peaceful agreement during the past two decades. But one must admit the Intifadas were not at all helpful and gave fuel to the Jewish propaganda..."

"As a result many Palestinians lost faith in any peace initiative and rebelled, interrupted Nina.

"From what you are telling us it would appear that somehow, somebody, or a government or the US lobby or whoever, does not wish to reach peace," said Kaliopi who had remained silent throughout the exchanges. She glanced at her husband Marinos and then looked in turn at Nina and Alexis. Alexis and Nina in turn glanced at each other and exchanged a wry smile. The crucial message was slowly and surely being crystallized in the minds of their children that peace was being blocked in preference to preserving the status quo.

"While it is very disappointing that these early peace initiatives all failed, what is more disheartening is that recent talks did not succeed either," said Nestor.

"Quite so," continued his mum. "In 2010 Mahmood Abbas and Benjamin Netanyahu were close to an agreement; if only Israel had agreed to halt the construction of further settlements in West Bank and accept $3bn aid from the US."

"But," said Ismail, "Israel will never agree to either abandon their settlements or stop building new ones. Some Zionists believe that, biblically, Palestine belongs to the Jews and building more and more settlements will eventually fulfil their dream of capturing the whole of the area occupied by my people in early 1948."

"Yes, but that is not the view of most Israelis," responded Alexis. Nina continued.

"In 2013 there were also some secrets talks between Abbas and Netanyahu with Secretary Kelly of the USA as intermediary but he unfortunately imposed an artificial deadline by holding separate talks with the two factions. Furthermore, Kelly held more talks later that year, and early the following year. One wished that he had spent equal amounts of time talking to the two factions rather than spending a disproportionate time with the Israelis and hardly any time at all with the Palestinians."

"And, what is more," interrupted Alexis, "he made inconsistent promises to the two sides regarding the settlement issue and the release of Palestinian prisoners."

"So, although many reasons were put forward for the impasse," continued Nina, "the obvious reason was never disclosed. That is, that one side preferred the status quo rather than seeking peace."

"Surely," said Ingrid, "it cannot be the Palestinian Arabs who wished to retain the status quo as their life in Gaza is miserable by all accounts."

That was the startling conclusion following Alexis' and Nina's description of the events that led every single time to failure. There were two principal players in this dispute and as the Palestinians would have gained quite a lot from an agreement it became evident that Israel wished to maintain the stalemate, as long as they were allowed to do so by the USA.

"The most important aspect of all this," continued Nina, "is that the Palestinian Arabs will only accept what by international law everybody agrees should be offered: that is, a Palestinian state on the pre-1967 borders but with minor adjustments that would allow Israel to retain some settlements. The capital would be in East Jerusalem with sovereignty of the Noble Sanctuary or al-Aqsa mosque compound and of course to have some land continuity with the rest of the West Bank."

"But the issue of Jerusalem is really the sticking point, is it not?" asked Vassiliki.

"This is a difficult issue but in the context of what we are discussing here not really," replied Alexis, "because everybody accepts that Jerusalem is a major problem but before it is considered there were other issues that could have been resolved quite easily. So leaving Jerusalem on one side, for the sake of the argument, the Israelis would withdraw their forces from the West Bank, the Palestinian refugees would be offered some compensation and the Right to Return to Palestine but obviously not to their original homes and Israel should accept responsibility for the refugee problem..."

"Partial responsibility," interrupted Nina.

"OK, partial," replied Alexis, "but not on a scale that would drastically change the land that Israel occupies today. So, over the years the Palestinian negotiators have not deviated much from that position, except with some minor modifications and they expect that one day with the help of the major powers such a homeland will become a reality. We must also bear in mind that the situation in Ramallah has been made much more bearable by pumping a lot of money to support the Fatah government and its institutions so Palestinians living there are not as desperate as those living elsewhere."

"Particularly in Gaza," said Nina who had first-hand experience of the situation there.

"Would Israel accept this pre-1967 sort of agreement?" asked Stuart.

"That is the nub of the problem," replied Alexis. "The cost of making no deal is much less than what it will cost them morally and in monetary terms otherwise. How can Israel explain to some settlers that they will have to abandon their homes and convince them that this is a sensible solution? The Israeli government will be confronted with internal rebellion even before the sensitive issue of the Table Mount is considered."

"Is this how the Jewish people call the Noble Sanctuary or the Al-Aqsa mosque compound?" asked Hermioni.

"Yes," replied Nina "and would you believe it a few months ago the Israeli government held its weekly cabinet meetings in tunnels under the Al-Aqsa mosque to commemorate the liberation of East Jerusalem following the 50 years they had annexed it." The group looked at Ismail who had remained thoughtful for the latter part of the discussion and took the opportunity to stress a point about the occupation of Jerusalem. Ismail started:

"I saw a report in Al Jazeera that confirmed what I knew from my own relatives that Israel makes life very difficult for Palestinians to access the compound for Friday prayers. Only those above a certain age are allowed in while the majority in the West Bank must apply for a hard-to-obtain permit from Israeli authorities."

"And there are over three million," added Alexis and waved to Ismail to continue.

"Quite. Of course not all will wish to pray every week but nevertheless such restrictions cause huge problems at checkpoints when thousands at any time queue to go through to East Jerusalem and on to the Sanctuary."

"The separation wall does not help either," added Alexis who had come across it a year earlier on his ill-fat-ed trip to Jerusalem. "It is a monstrosity and an affront to human dignity."

The band of musicians came back from their break and started playing some hypnotic syrtaki and bouzouki tunes which brought back happy memories of Petros' party all those years ago when Christos, and his then girlfriend Marika, led the youngsters in a classic exposition of Greek dancing.

"*Ela* Christos!" shouted a mildly inebriated Petros as he stood and waving his hands and feet haphazardly continued addressing his school pal "*Opa!*" he exclaimed, streaming with emotion. "Show us the proper way of dancing the *Sirtaki!*". All eyes turned to Christos who was reluctant to acquiesce.

"I haven't danced these tunes for ages." Ingrid took the initiative, stood, approached her husband and gently lifted him out of his seat. Offering little resistance Christos made his way to the front of the gathering, stood upright, raised both his hands above his head, keeping his feet stationary, eyes shut. Alexis knew that the show was about to begin. He glanced at Nina, memories coming flooding back as they continued to stare at each other. With a grimace showing pathos, Christos started moving his feet slowly to get accustomed to the syrtaki that echoed all around the Lilis. Other diners looked on with astonishment at the sight of such elegance coming from this slim-looking mature individual. It seemed as though his movements were totally in tune with the sounds emerging from the bouzouki instruments. He slowly moved along a few steps back and forth then with a slow-motion pirouette and a rhythmic up and down approached Ingrid and with hands on each other's shoulders they started moving to and fro. Following a few minutes of serene expression of Greekness, Christos approached in turn each of his pals and their partners, first Petros and Vassiliki followed by Yanis and Kate. The six of them continued to link shoulder to shoulder and dance the syrtaki, eyes fixed on Christos who was leading them, waving by now a red handkerchief in his free hand. However, it soon became fairly obvious that one integral couple was missing from this chain. It did not go unnoticed to all that Nina and Alexis was the only couple present in Siros who were both in Alexandria at Petros' party and both had taken part in such a meandering chain of Greek dancing. Christos looked at them and waved them to join in. Alexis looked again at Nina whose eyes had remained fixed on him, bringing unprecedented memories of their innocent adolescence. It was on the eve of their fateful beach rendezvous and yet here they were after all these years united in love and spirit, sharing a rare moment with all their loved ones. Resembling a couple of humanoid robots they stood up and with the seriousness that the occasion deserved joined the human chain of aged adults dancing to the noisy applause of their children and their partners. Hermioni could not help casting a thought on the tragic loss of her mum Erica, and stared at Nestor. He was looking askance at the black sea, his thoughts no doubt momentarily elsewhere. The four school pals and their partners, locked in an embrace, danced to many tunes including 'Zorba the Greek', until the quartet of musicians stopped. They all bowed and stooped as they withdrew smiling to the comfort of their seats, sweating, breathing heavily. Plates of watermelon were already on the table and were welcomed by all.

Alexis had a mission and knew that lots of arguments regarding Palestine had not yet been thoroughly aired. He let everybody move to other topics before resuming the narrative. Nina and Alexis were in full accord with the arguments put forward in the *Guardian* article. They were aware that compulsory repatriation of the Zionists from some of the settlements would have to be carried out by the IDF whose share of soldiers who held strong religious belief was quite substantial. Also, the IDF leaving the West Bank would put Israel in a much weaker position as far as gathering intelligence about the movement of ex-Hamas militant elements which in turn would have facilitated easy access to other parts of the West Bank and spread its insurgents over Palestine. The Israeli authorities would not be able to control the flow of Arabs to and from the occupied territories. Israel would not have access to the West Bank's natural resources, including water, and they would not benefit from the present situation where they had full control of Palestinian customs and trade. As if by a miracle, Stuart brought the discussion back to the issue in question. To Alexis and Nina that was very satisfying as it demonstrated that the younger generation was still eager to learn more about the Palestinian Conundrum.

"I suppose in all this the Jewish lobby is still very prominent in the USA and gives comfort to Israel," uttered Stuart.

"It always has been and will be so, and monetary support for Israel will always be plentiful," replied Nestor, who, living in the USA, had first-hand knowledge of the ties between the Jews in the States and those who had emigrated to Israel.

"And of course, with the president being so pro-Jewish the situation will continue as long as this administration lasts," added Amalia. Nestor following his wife's comment said:

"Remember also that with the president being so pre-occupied with his Russian connection..."

"Yes, but although one hears many reports and facts emerging weekly nothing has been proven categorically that there was collusion during the American election?" interrupted Alexis.

"Every time anybody within the CIA or the FBI comes closer to revealing important information they are fired," butted in Amalia.

"Isn't that proof that the President has something to hide?" asked Ingrid.

"The *New York Times* and other media such as CNN," continued Nestor, "have this year consistently tried to prove a link with Russian officials and the president's entourage, and probably his son, but he retaliates and comes up with the notion that it is all part of 'fake news'." Nina, sensing that the conversation was drifting away from the central theme, brought matters back to the Palestine-Israeli issue.

"So, it is quite obvious that Israel had withstood all the criticism that has been levelled at its state over the past 50 years and would prefer to retain the status quo rather than have to sustain the huge costs of moving to a pre-1967 border, with all the difficulties that that would entail. And furthermore, this is despite the fact that some of its more liberal elements wish to alienate themselves from the occupation of the West Bank and desire to have open rather than the present clandestine contacts with some of the Arab states."

"Of course, the USA is totally preoccupied with Iran and North Korea, not to mention the huge trade wars with China, so instead of pressing ahead with the peace process they opt to continue their annual support for Israel of a few billion dollars and turn a blind eye to the vociferous protests from some UN nations when a particular resolution concerning Israel is vetoed by the US administration," said Ismail.

"The USA gives more to Israel in aid every year than to all the other countries put together," said Marinos.

"So, it appears that the Israeli government would be foolish to accept reverting back to the pre-1967 border issue when the alternative is a stalemate that costs much less," said Hermioni.

"This is exactly what it boils down to," added Alexis

with Nina nodding in complete agreement. "And they will ignore any future criticisms about the building of new settlements, or the recognition of the State of Palestine by some countries."

"But there is no such Palestinian state, is there?" asked Yanis.

"Well, I meant symbolically, as there is self-rule in Ramallah so one can claim that there is a quasi-state of Palestine with its own government."

"Would Israel continue to ignore any warnings that this situation cannot continue ad infinitum?" asked Kate.

"Some commentators," replied Alexis, "do make the stark warning to Israel that if they do not offer Palestinian citizenship or sovereignty, then they run the risk of becoming a non-state, I mean a kind of an apartheid state without being a Jewish state or a democracy. At present it is only a fear but a realistic one and the perception is that if that stage becomes a reality Israel will then make concessions and will agree to a two-state solution. But in the meantime, it is cheaper and more sensible for them to do nothing and absorb all the criticism that is levelled at them given the proviso that America will always support them monetarily and morally. The ideal situation for Israel in the meantime is that if life in the occupied territories becomes unbearable enough Arabs will emigrate away from The West Bank and Gaza..."

"But the Arab population in the occupied territories is increasing at an alarming rate. Surely the Israelis are aware of that fact?" said Ismail.

"That is something that will happen in the future; in the meantime some Israelis pray that the West Bank joins Jordan and Gaza forms part of an enlarged Egypt and the problem of a future Palestinian State disappears altogether," continued Alexis.

"The point is," butted in Nina, "as long as the Oslo Accord remains in place and is not superseded by something else, the major powers will not demand that Israel grants citizenship or sovereignty. In reality, Israel runs an apartheid type regime in the areas it controls."

"You mean it has annexed," said her son.

"Well, that is a moot point, but leaving that on one side by simply stating that it controls the areas, Israel continues to suppress and dominate the Palestinians against their free will. Everybody hopes that Oslo remains a transitional stage to an independent Palestinian state sometime in the future."

"The crux of the matter," said Alexis, "is that Israel has a very attractive fallback option. Why, the argument goes, make peace which will cost quite a lot morally and in monetary terms when the alternative, that is the fallback option, is much cheaper and more to the point is allowed to be maintained by the Western powers?"

"But is it not a fact that in the areas that Israel controls there is a huge number of non-Jewish people, Arabs and Christians alike?" stated Myrna.

"Indeed, and absurdly the Western powers will not call Israel a non-democratic country," said Hermioni.

"Surely," concluded Kate, "the obvious solution is to make Israel's fallback position more difficult."

"If you look at the history of US-Israel relations since the creation of Israel, this is exactly what ex-US Presidents have done," replied Alexis. "For example, President Eisenhower put pressure on Israel and indeed their co-conspirators France and Britain to withdraw from Sinai after the Suez debacle. President Ford in 1975 held back funds promised to Israel unless they withdrew from Sinai two years after the Yom Kippur war," added Nina.

"And on it goes," continued Alexis. "In 1977 President Carter threatened to hold back assistance to Israel unless it withdrew from Lebanon." Alexis and Nina were now in full flow, citing facts that most of their contemporaries were not aware of and showing a thorough grasp of the issues that faced the Palestinian Conundrum.

"President Carter," went on Alexis, "threatened both sides that if they did not sign the agreement, aid would be curtailed. Similarly, the US Secretary of State James Baker forced Yitzhak Shamir to attend the negotiations in Madrid otherwise he was not going to honour the ten billion dollar loan guarantee promised to Israel to enable the repatriation of Soviet Jews to Israel."

"And, alas, since then," interrupted Nina, "the USA has not put any more pressure on successive Israeli governments. Since Oslo, the US government has made Israel's fallback position easier to maintain. This was accomplished by making the life of the Palestinians in the West Bank a bit more bearable and successively vetoed any UN Resolutions that went against Israel. In addition they put pressure on the PLO not to confront Israel in international institutions. At the same time they ensured that Israel was militarily more secure and stronger than all its Arab neighbours by donating huge aid sums and steadfastly defending the actions of Israel against international criticism."

"How come the world has allowed such settlements to increase against opposition not only within Palestine but from many countries in the UN?" asked Marinos.

"Cries to dismantle these arise consistently by academics, the media, even by liberal Jews of the diaspora," said Nina. "The paradox is that the USA has refused to recognize Israel's sovereignty beyond the pre-1967 lines, and yet..."

"And most of the countries of the EU," interrupted Alexis.

"Yes," replied Nina, "but sticking to the US first, although they differentiate between Israel and the occupied territories they do not do anything to force Israel to abandon their expansionist programme of building more settlements in the West Bank."

"But that is exactly their long-term goal, eventually to occupy all of the West Bank hoping one day the world will accept their occupation and offer de facto recognition of a greater Israel," said Alexis.

"In fact, Israel does not at all like this policy of differentiation as it believes that it delegitimizes the State and fears the consequences," added Nina.

"You mean imposing sanctions?" asked Kate.

"That is the ultimate weapon that the outside world has against Israel which may cripple the country economically, but the USA will no doubt veto such a move if it ever arises in the UN as they have done so far with countless other Resolutions," replied Alexis.

"As the USA apparently adheres to differentiation between the State of Israel and the occupied territories," continued Nina, "one would have thought that its administration would put pressure on Israel to halt their expansionist programme but in fact it does the opposite. It shields further actions against the Israeli government on more settlements because, the argument goes, as the USA does not recognize the settlements they should really put pressure on Israel to stop these but alas the USA turns a blind eye on further settlements pretending that they are powerless to do anything about them."

"But the USA supports Israel with aid so stopping this aid would force the Israelis to think again," said Petros.

"But they continue to support them, no doubt the Jewish lobby in the USA has a lot to do with such support," said Amalia.

"So, in a way the policy of differentiation which to any unbiased observer should bring pressure on Israel to change their settlement strategy has the perverse opposite result of helping to prolong the occupation," said

Alexis.

"The odd thing about all this," replied Nina, "is that liberal Zionists in the USA, other thinkers of the diaspora who side with left-of-centre parties in Israel, as well as the editorial board of the *New York Times*, although they all support differentiation it creates the notion which permits them to be both pro-Israeli and anti-occupation."

"How convenient," butted in Kaliopi with frustration.

"How about penalizing the financial institutions, real estate agents, government agencies and middlemen that heavily profit from operations in the occupied territories particularly when they are not based in these territories, but their headquarters are in Israel?" asked Vassiliki.

"There is a lot of talk about pressurizing these groups but unfortunately critics of the occupation prefer softer policies which are totally ineffective," said Alexis.

"How about labelling the products that come out of the occupied territories so that it is abundantly clear where these have originated?" asked Stuart.

"That is easy to do, but going beyond and imposing sanctions on the democratically elected government that created the settlements, confiscating land and legalizing the outposts, is inconceivable," answered Alexis.

"Because if that were to happen it would delegitimize the whole of the raison d'être of Israel and indeed it would require doing this by force which they constantly have shied away from," concluded Nina.

"Didn't Moshe Dayan once say, I quote, 'The USA gives us money, arms and advice. We take the money and the arms but we decline the advice'," said Hermioni jokingly.

"Well, one wonders how such blatant statements are allowed to remain unchallenged and such inconsistent policies by the USA are permitted to obscure the real arguments?" said Michael.

"Would it not be marvellous if the two factions got together and decide that one country may be the answer?" ventured Kaliopi naively.

"That is highly unlikely because the raison d'être of Zionists is a country they can call their own and they were hell-bent on establishing it after the British Mandate was over. The consequence of one country is that the majority would be of non-Jewish origin and democratically they would lose their unique identity," replied Alexis and continued.

"The stark reality from Hamas' and the Palestinians' point of view is that they are faced with a brutal and very well-trained opponent and what is more every time the Israeli spokesperson appears on TV to answer for their bloody and ruthless military response they come up with the well-rehearsed slogan that, I quote, 'the Palestinians hate us and try to make life in the settlements very insecure'. And guess what?" They all looked at Alexis in anticipation as he concluded his sentence: "The Israeli government spokesperson was so effective in rebuffing any criticism, that he was eventually promoted as Israel's ambassador in London."

"Wow, that is a massive leap for somebody that time and time again regurgitated the same tired arguments," uttered Petros.

"Be that as it may, a measured response from the IDF is never the answer, they simply have to kill a number of protesters to teach them a lesson," stressed Alexis while he glanced over towards Nina effectively asking her acquiescence to announce to the group something they had discussed earlier that day. She looked back at him and nodded to go ahead.

"By the way," continued Alexis, "Nina and I are once again going to Gaza to help in a hospital and visit the many friends that we have made over the past 20 years."

"How long are you going for?" asked Nestor who turned to Hermioni to see if she knew of their pending trip. She did not.

"We haven't decided exactly when we are leaving or for how long, but I assume it will be for a few months' stay," replied Nina. "They are constructing a new hospital wing and help is needed to run it."

"So you will be there during the Nakba period around April and May next year?" asked Hermioni who was well aware that there would be trouble during that period.

"So?" challenged her father looking straight at her.

Silence enveloped the little group of Alexandrians with Nina's and Alexis' children looking at each other and considering the myriad of grave implications following what Alexis and Nina had just revealed. Fleeting glances were exchanged by all in various directions around the large table unable to add anything beyond what Nestor and Hermioni had just voiced. Kaliopi broke the uncomfortable silence surrounding the Alexandrian group.

"What is Nakba?"

"Nakba means catastrophe in Arabic and signifies the period of some weeks of passive resistance by the Palestinians to remind the world of their expulsion from their ancestral homeland during the dark days of 1947-48," replied Nina. The group fell silent, each with their own reflections on what Palestinians meant by referring to the anniversary as 'catastrophe' and focusing on the plight of miserable Gazans who longed for peace whilst knowing it to be as unattainable as ordinary life itself. Alexis and Nina took it in turns to discuss the significance, of the annual ritual, when the Palestinians feel utter despair at losing their homeland following the creation of the State of Israel compared to the absolute rejoicing of the Zionists for what they regard as their Independence Day. How can 24 hours be so contrasting to two peoples sharing a common land and living next to one another?

It was late in the evening when shortly after this long discussion the group started descending the small mount where the restaurant was situated and followed the myriad of meandering streets downwards, finally reaching the eastward side of the *limani*. They walked in small groups each with their own thoughts, often exchanging a brief comment of the night's discussion and traversing, crisscrossing or revisiting the infinite spiral where the evening's arguments had led them.

Alexis and Nina were walking behind the group. She said, "I wondered whether we pressed them too hard."

"You mean relentlessly."

"Hm, I guess that is what I mean."

"We did, but unless these facts are shouted about as loud as one can, and as many times in as many circles, groups, and the media, the ordinary person in the street would not have a clue about the real plight or wretchedness of the Palestinians, especially Gazans, and I think, ultimately, it is only world-wide pressure from the public that may have an effect on what happens in the future. I hope that our school pals, their siblings and our sons and daughters will conduct similar discussions at their numerous gatherings so these issues are understood more vividly by the world at large. Even though there are authoritative books written on the subject, by Chomsky, Pappe, Said, Jones, Baroud, Thrall and many others..."

"Don't forget the one we spotted and bought at Waterstones just a few months ago by Ian Black, entitled *Enemies and Neighbours*, the Middle East Editor of the *Guardian*..." interrupted Nina

"Of course, I do, very authoritative and a harrowing read I must admit," replied Alexis and went on

"As well as the relentless online bombardment of

facts and bulletins by Jeremy Hammond's *Foreign Policy Journal*, these will alas reach only a tiny minority as they are daunting, harrowing, hard-hitting, full of misery and despair. In fact not the kind of book people would pick up to read on holiday," concluded Alexis.

The front of the little port at Chora, past midnight, was still buzzing with tourists and locals in cafes and restaurants with strings of rebetico, the popular urban Greek music which saw a revival, decades ago. Elsewhere, weary sojourners sipped colourful cocktails, now and then swallowing a mouthful of cashew nuts or shelled pistachio nuts from several ornate bowls. They were enjoying a peaceful warm summer's night seemingly without having a care in the world. As Nina and Alexis walked along the edge of the long waterfront, small speedboats and fishermen's trawlers were moored alongside massive yachts, no doubt belonging to nameless oligarchs, Greek ship owners or city magnates, the vessels bobbing rhythmically in the dark waters of the port, the *limani*. The tall lean sailless masts of the huge yachts swayed in the light breeze. A dragger was entering the little port having pulled a trawler into deep waters after sunset. Nina turned to Alexis.

"Are we sure about going to Gaza?"

"They need you and that's what matters most."

They walked towards their hired cottage high up on a steep road in the district of Manna overlooking the *limani*. As they arrived at the entrance to the cottage they glanced towards the *limani*: the lights of Ermoupolis flickered sporadically as though conveying messages from the little cottages of the town. They looked at each other, smiled and entered the cottage.

38

Cambridge, October 2017

The Main Lecture theatre, at the refurbished Old Divinity School at St John's Triangle site, was packed with dons and undergraduates. The atmosphere was very tense, full of anticipation for what this ex-Alexandrian, now academic, was about to reveal and what he would concentrate on during the limited time allotted. The lecture was organised by Friends of Cambridge University Palestine Society.

"*Bon chance*," whispered Nina, as she knew what this occasion meant to him. Alexis smiled. He took a handkerchief from his pocket which he had earlier laced with some Acqua di Gio, Georgio Armani's eau de cologne, and took a couple of deep breaths. This was a sign that he too felt a bit anxious when he had to deliver an important lecture, particularly on a subject that was so dear to his heart but, by contrast to all other routine lectures, he did not claim any expertise. Following a brief introduction by the society's president Alexis stood up, approached the lectern, adjusted its height, placed a few notes on it and looked at the audience. He had already checked the cutting-edge audio-visuals at his disposal to avoid last-minute glitches. After thanking the society's president for the invitation he began.

"As you are well aware the Israeli-Palestine Conundrum goes back well over a hundred years. If I were to choose a crucial date or statement I would opt for the Balfour Declaration. We are now well conversant with what Arthur Balfour had in mind: simply the creation of a state for Jewish people and this is stated quite succinctly and without ambiguity in the first paragraph of his much-quoted statement. However, many historians, particularly Jewish academics, omit to state the last part of the Balfour Declaration which goes on to state without any equivocation or uncertainty the following which I quote, 'it being clearly understood that nothing shall be done which may prejudice the civil and religious rights of existing non-Jewish communities in Palestine or the rights and political status enjoyed by the Jews in any other country'. Conveniently this is omitted and largely forgotten when the conflict in Palestine is debated. So after many insurrections, conflicts, ethnic cleansing, the Nov 29th 1947 UN Partition Scheme, three major wars with Israel's Arab neighbours, vetoed UN Resolutions, building of settlements, illegal I hasten to add according to international law, countless failed attempts for negotiating peace, three Intifadas, leader and prominent mediator assassinations, murders, suicide bombers, rockets and mortars firing on Israeli towns, IDF's brutal responses followed by criticisms of the disregard for the inevitable collateral damage, ignoring humanitarian issues including adherence of International Humanitarian Law, leaders' egos, two-state solution on the pre-1967 borders..." Alexis paused to regain his breath, looked at the audience and continued. "We are where we are: no solution to the conflict with each side blaming the other." Alexis' opening statement managed to captivate the audience's attention. They were transfixed by his every word. He went on.

"I will concentrate most of my talk on why the present administration in Israel is hell-bent on making the two-state solution an impossible dream. In the two-state solution it is proposed that the Gaza Strip and a large part of the West Bank will form the new independent Palestinian State. Would the two regions be linked? Ideally yes, but let us leave that on one side." Alexis paused, then he continued.

"The Palestinian leadership, be it Fatah or Hamas or preferably a Unity Government, always argued that such a two-state solution would be based on the pre-1967 war borders. Well, let me show you five slides on the build-up of Israeli settlements." He projected these PowerPoint slides, allowing time for the audience to absorb the details on each one, as they showed chronologically the increase in settlement growth in the West Bank from 1967, where only a few settlements existed, to around 125 in 2015. The respective increase of settlers during the same period was from an initial 250 to around 382,000.

"The current estimate of the number of settlers in the occupied territories is now nearing 400,000," added Alexis as he concentrated on the last slide.

These slides left the majority of the young audience

shell-shocked, some wincing, aghast with such blatant expansionism. The larger of these settlements, expanded to include outposts and neighbourhoods, were those at Maaleh Adumim, Modi'in Ilit, Beitar Ilit, Givat Zeev, Beit Aryeh, Alfie Menashe, Oranit, Kedumim, Ariel, Eli, Efrat, Kiryat Arba. Numerous smaller ones scattered throughout the West Bank from Jenin in the north to Hebron in the south.

"These slides are not Palestinian propaganda but are contained in an in-depth report by Yotam Berger published only a few months ago in Haaretz, the Israeli News Agency," said Alexis and went on. "And many of these settlements had large outposts located quite near which increased the overall area of the original settlement and made it more secure." Alexis reached for the small bottle of sparkling water and, opening it purposefully, took a mouthful or two.

"I should have also mentioned that some of these new sites are termed neighbourhoods because they are very near the original settlements so the settlers argue that they are not new but simply an extension of the original ones."

"The international community," continued Alexis as he turned and looked at the audience, "considers that such Israeli settlements violate the Fourth Geneva Convention's prohibition on the transfer of an occupying power's civilian population into occupied territory. But, and here is the interesting bit, the Israeli government maintains that the Fourth Geneva Convention does not apply to the Palestinian territories as there was no sovereign country called Palestine claiming, I assume, that its peoples were stateless and the land administered as a mandate by the British. This is despite the fact that Palestinians have lived in these lands for centuries. So, the Israelis annexed this land," with Alexis turning and waving his hands at the last slide displaying the settlement infested West Bank, "without caring a hoot about what the rest of the world thinks. This goes smack against the second part of Balfour's Declaration which I referred to earlier. Of course, the International Court of Justice and the International Committee for the Red Cross reject the Israeli government's interpretation." He stopped, faced the audience and continued.

"This state of affairs is highly undesirable and puts a major stumbling block on the two-state solution, that of an existing Jewish state and another for Palestinians. However, no commentator has ever advocated that the new state of Palestine would only be the Gaza Strip. It is inferred that the new state of Palestine, if ever it came into being, would consist of the Gaza Strip as well as land and towns in the West Bank. But because of these Israeli settlements there is a much-reduced area in the West Bank that may truly constitute the other part of the new Palestinian state. Further, because of the position of some of these settlements it presents a great obstacle in defining a clear border in the West Bank between these settlements and the bit that would constitute the other part of the newly created state of Palestine." Alexis approached the desk, picked up the small bottle of sparkling water he had just opened, half-filled a glass and drank a good deal of it. He returned to the lectern.

"Such Israeli settlement expansion into the occupied territories goes against Resolution 2334, which the Security Council on December the 16th last year passed by 14 votes to one abstention, that of the USA. This resolution had some strong statements regarding Israel's illegal settlements which it called a flagrant violation of international law. For example, one entry includes the following statement: 'expressing grave concern that continuing Israeli settlement activities are dangerously imperilling the viability of the two-state solution based on the 1967 lines.' This suggests that the countries on the Security Council that supported this Resolution still believed that a two-state solution was still viable." Alexis momentarily paused and continued.

"Israel's Supreme Court forced the evacuation of the settlers from the Amona outpost built illegally on Palestinian land in March of this year and as a result months later the Israeli government approved the establishment of a new settlement, named Amichai, no doubt to house the settlers that were evacuated. Earlier this year another settlement was approved, that of Shvut Rachel East with nearly a hundred dwellings to be built, but of course they do not accept that this is a new settlement. A government spokesperson insisted that it was a neighbourhood of the Shilo settlement. And guess what? The Shvut settlement was nowhere near any built-up area of

Shilo so eventually the two will be amalgamated and the Shilo settlement will become much bigger. Further, the Shvut settlement is near the Amichai settlement so the expansion goes apace without anybody being able to do anything about it. It is quite accepted by the majority of commentators that many Israeli leaders, including Ariel Sharon and the present PM, wanted to expand the settlers living in occupied territories to such significant numbers rendering the establishment of a Palestinian state pretty nigh impossible. And with the Amichai and Shvut Rachel East settlements they are achieving this. Now, what is fairly obvious is that since the 2016 presidential election, it is very clear that the US administration is in full agreement with such an expansionist policy evidenced by abstaining from endorsing Resolution 2334." Alexis, visibly animated, went on.

"How can the major countries accept such blatant disregard for human dignity and decency?" Alexis turned and focussing on the audience continued. "I tell you how Israel can continue on such a grotesque path of expansionism, simply by the support of the current President of the USA who on the one hand promises the deal of the century as far a solution to the Palestinian Conundrum is concerned and on the other agrees to endorse the massive aid to Israel, to the tune of $10 billion for the next ten years, as was promised to them when the previous president stepped down." Alexis stopped to gather his thoughts. He then went on.

"So, to summarise: looking at the 2015 slide with

the settlements and the continuing establishment of the new settlements, outposts and neighbourhoods, I have just outlined it is clear that a two-state solution is progressively becoming a non-option unless the Palestinian leaders accept that the new state of Palestine is simply that of the Gaza Strip and expansive areas in the West Bank around the cities of Ramallah, Hebron and Nablus. For the foreseeable future I cannot see that being acceptable, so the stalemate continues." Alexis stopped momentarily and glanced at his notes. Then he went on.

"Of course, I hasten to add, my premise suggests that a one-state solution, meaning one secular state for both the Jewish and Palestinian people living side by side, although highly desirable and would be the ideal solution, is at present as unattainable as man reaching Mars. Frankly, it is pie in the sky." The audience laughed out loud.

"So, having outlined the various options one would be forgiven if one raised their hands in despair and simply stated that this is an intractable problem with no solution in sight. In fact, some commentators refused point blank to discuss the Palestine-Israeli problem when it was aired publicly and were asked what could be done. Adopting such an attitude condemns millions of Gazans and pockets of Palestinians living in the West Bank to a miserable existence." Alexis, after a brief walk about in front of the audience, continued.

"However, we are where we are. Instead of regurgitating the same arguments that have been stated in many books, expounded in pamphlets, newspaper articles or published online, let us concentrate entirely on the conditions that will have to be met to at least enable to attain a measure of stability in the region and to start a meaningful dialogue between the two factions." Alexis, focussing solely on his PowerPoint presentation, stated each condition in turn with bullet points, emphasising elements and elaborating on each one separately.

"Here we go. The existence of the state of Israel is accepted and its safety guaranteed, without equivocation, by all neighbouring countries. I know this has been done already but it must be clearly repeated. No utterance such as 'we will throw them back into the sea' must ever be made again.

"Israel immediately halts any new or projected settlements in West Bank particularly on the outskirts of Jerusalem. Furthermore, the Israeli government stops funding the building of settler outposts or the so-called neighbourhoods and, in fact, declares these illegal and orders the IDF to physically remove these which by and large were built on Palestinian owned land.

"Israel ends the blockade in Gaza, dismantles the wall of separation and allows immediate access to Gazans to travel to other parts of the West Bank and to Israel to seek work. This should end the near-starvation existence of its two million inhabitants.

"A worldwide effort commences immediately to rebuild the infrastructure of the Strip, including its airport. Massive aid is needed to the tune of $50-$100 billion which must be international with wealthy countries contributing the larger part including countries in the Middle East such as Saudi Arabia and Qatar.

"Fishing limits off the Strip to be extended to areas rich in fish without interference from Israeli patrol boats or missile-loaded drones.

"These measures will alleviate the immediate suffering of the Gazans, would raise their standard of living and would render a forthcoming political solution more palatable.

"The question that remains is whether there will ever be an independent Palestinian state? To be frank, I doubt it. There may be a reference to autonomy and jurisdiction of areas and towns in the West Bank with again pumping substantial aid to improve the conditions there and in other areas of the West Bank where the Arabs predominantly reside.

"The Palestinian Unity Government, if ever it comes into being, must drop its insistence of the pre-1967 borders with Israel as a pre-condition to initiating talks. This is imperative because otherwise Israel would have to forcibly resettle about 125 settlements and rehouse nearly 400,000 settlers. This is neither realistic, nor feasible.

"So far, such a scheme would alleviate the lives of most Palestinians but their desire for an independent State remains. Many unanswered questions remain.

"The relationship between Fatah and Hamas? The status of East Jerusalem? The return of the refugees, albeit the majority are either very old or have passed away? Their children and grandchildren may be lured to Gaza and other parts of the West Bank such as Ramallah, Hebron and Nablus and accept a quasi-state possibly linked to Gaza via a corridor which may form the basis of an independent Palestinian State.

"There are also issues relating to the Jewish people. The claim that all of the West Bank forms part of the biblical heritage of the Jewish people must be dropped." Alexis, in his peripheral vision, perceived an uncomfortable movement of some of the audience's Jewish attendees as they heard the last statement. He continued.

"I am aware that to some ultra-orthodox Jewish settlers this will be unacceptable but I am proposing a compromise and as such extreme elements from both sides must be dealt with by their respective governments." Alexis turned back to his PowerPoint presentation.

"Israel reaches an amicable arrangement with the settlers of some isolated settlements in the West Bank to repatriate them either in other larger settlements within the West Bank or within Israel. This will ensure that more land is made available in the West Bank for a future independent Palestinian state if ever that comes into being. Should these settlers accept to be citizens in the West Bank then they should be allowed to stay put.

"Israel accepts the principle of Right of Return of Palestinian refugees to the West Bank, to parts of East Jerusalem or to the Gaza Strip. Israel, with the help of external funding, compensates the refugees for the loss of their homes.

"I am aware that Peace Now, the Israeli Movement that was initiated in 1978 and advocates peace through public pressure, uses the Geneva Accord's initiative proposed border as a reference point when unauthorised settlements or outposts are being discussed. Unfortunately, the border they refer to is the one that existed before the 1967 War and as I stated above this is unrealistic. Peace Now must come up with an alternative or, let us say, more realistic border.

"Lone revenge attacks from either side should be swiftly and decisively dealt with by the authorities from either side.

"The reconciliation process starts immediately.

"Once the lives of Palestinians in the Strip and the West Bank become more tolerable then the process of finding a political solution should begin. I do not propose to detail here with what that would entail but the above may prove a conduit to start the discussions.

"Would Hamas accept such a massive economic boost without considering at the same time the question of how and on what condition would a permanent Palestinian state be borne? Only time would tell. Would the rockets fired at Israel stop and would the IDF retaliatory measures abate? I cannot predict that either."

Alexis paused each time another condition was stated and expounded on the pros and cons. The conditions stunned the audience, in that although there were aspects that each side would find hard to adhere to there were elements that both would readily accept.

The chairman opened the discussion. "Yes, we have one here," he said, pointing to a middle-aged gentleman. The roving microphone was given to the questioner.

"You stated at the beginning that a one-state solution is pie in the sky. Could you please elaborate?" Alexis approached the questioner.

"I am aware of the book by Dr Karmi, entitled *Married to Another Man*," replied Alexis, "advocating a one-state solution. That book was written over ten years ago and where has it got us?" Alexis turned towards the screen, collected his thoughts and proceeded.

"Yes indeed, would it not be great if both Palestinians and Israelis could live peacefully in the area originally occupied by the British during their mandate?" replied Alexis. "But, for the life of me, I cannot see this happening any time soon. Something extraordinary must occur to trigger such an initiative. Even if the US President is defeated in the 2020 elections and a Democratic leader is elected that would not mean an immediate shift of America's thinking. The Jewish lobby in the US is still very strong and despite the fact that some liberal thinkers start to question the continual support for Israel there are no indications that this is about to change. Remember what happened when a number of presidents, from Eisenhower to Carter and beyond, tried to force successive Israeli governments to change their policies? Alas, they all finally succumbed to internal pressures and backed down. Further, Israel, having made a pact with Egypt, arguably their biggest neighbouring foe, and with Iraq and Syria in tatters, that only leaves Iran that can possibly challenge them militarily. With its awesome military strength, Israel can withstand any regional pressure. Further, to return to the one-state solution, we have to consider what happens when elections take place. The Palestinians outnumber the Israelis and unless some very clever electoral system is put in place the Jewish people would eventually lose their identity. I do, however, accept that it should not be beyond the wisdom of legislators to devise a method of apportioning votes in a way that would satisfy both Jewish and Arab aspirations."

"But look what happened in South Africa," suggested another questioner. "Nobody thought that the Afrikaners would relinquish power and now we have one state for the Afrikaners and the rest."

"The circumstances," replied Alexis "were totally different. Apartheid was disliked by practically the whole world, and sanctions were biting. Israel on the other hand is supported by more than 30 countries worldwide and I cannot see any circumstances where sanctions would be applied in the near future."

"Do you mean the BDS movement is ineffective?" continued the questioner.

"BDS was launched over ten years ago. Its essence was, and still is, that the Palestinians are entitled to the same rights as the rest of the world," replied Alexis.

"However, has it been successful? Do we see the Israeli economy collapsing? Further, BDS's principle is the end of occupation and colonisation of Arab lands. Doesn't such a statement threaten the self-determination of the Jewish people? So how does one reconcile BDS with what has happened so far in Palestine?"

"There are countries that do boycott Israel," persisted the questioner.

"Well, apart from the neighbouring Arabs countries in the Middle East, who else supports the boycott? I will tell you, Algeria, Malaysia, Oman, Saudi Arabia, Brunei, Bangladesh, Libya and Kuwait. That list does not constitute a formidable force which could hurt Israel. So the promotion of BDS is a noble aspiration but with limited..." Alexis' struggled to find the right word, finally stating, "...clout, I am afraid."

After a pause Alexis continued. "I have some trade figures here which I looked at a few months ago. The major partners are the USA, Germany and Britain. To the USA and Britain, Israel exports more goods than imports from them and with Germany there was a massive imbalance in deficit of some three million dollars. So for BDS to bite such trade has to stop. So far it has not."

The chairman spotted another youngster who tried a couple of times to raise her hand. Pointing towards that direction, the chairman allowed the question.

"The Palestinians rejected the partition plan in 1947. They have no moral ground for asking for an independent state, let alone a two-state solution anymore." Alexis slowly made his way towards the questioner, stopped a few paces away and replied:

"The partition that was rejected 70 years ago gave the Jewish people half of Palestine when at the time they occupied 8% of the land and had a population half that of the Palestinians." Alexis consulted his notes and found the figures he was looking for. "There were some 1.2 million Palestinians and just over 0.6 million Jewish inhabitants. Further, when Count Bernadotte tried to offer an amended partition plan which would have distributed the land more equitably, advocating that it would be an affront to human dignity not to allow the displaced refugees the right to return, he was duly assassinated by members of Stern." The youngster who asked the question sank quietly in her seat.

Another questioner asked: "Could you elaborate: between the pre-1967 borders and the new borders, should both sides accept your proposal?" Alexis, returned to the podium, looked at the questioner and after a short pause replied.

"As it is inconceivable for Israel to ask the IDF to dismantle the large settlements from the West Bank, a new border would have to be established which carefully meanders through these large settlements and Palestinian West Bank. The USA will always support the settlements morally and monetarily so these will stay put. A commission would have to be set up to look at ways to retain some of the large settlements in the West Bank as part of Israel and what is left in the West Bank together with the

Gaza Strip will form the new Palestinian state."

"A tall order, particularly if one considers the proliferation of the illegal outposts in West Bank which were supported by the Israeli government as well as the present US administration. I believe there is a survey currently being conducted by Peace Now which suggests that contrary to the promises to halt settlement construction new ones, as well as new outposts, are being envisaged," replied the questioner.

"This is indeed sad," replied Alexis. "If what you say bears any truth then there is little hope of any solution. If the intention of the Israeli government is to continue to build more settlements until more than a million settlers reside in the West Bank then all is lost. I must reiterate: the only hope is the complete cessation of any expansionist programme in the West Bank and, more to the point, the government of Israel must negotiate the relocation of some of the smaller settlements. After all, what I am putting forward is a compromise solution and as such some sacrifice will have to be made by both sides."

Another questioner raised her hand. Microphone in hand, she started.

"Why do you assume that Israel will go along with what you have outlined? What is in it for them?"

"Although, Hamas and Islamic Jihad inflict minimal damage on Israel and the settlements, the Israeli people would welcome a resolution which minimally affects their status quo, that is, they would only have to negotiate the removal of a few settlements and abandoning the present stranglehold on Gaza. Deep down there are those in Israel who wish for peace and the measures I put forward allow for the attainment of a lasting solution with minimal changes."

"So why then would the Palestinian Authority or Hamas accept your premises?" the questioner persisted.

"Their people in Gaza are suffering and I sincerely hope the Gazan people would accept my compromise solution because they would benefit economically; they would have acquired a state of their own and the long-term pledge of the Right of Return of the Palestinian refugees will have been fulfilled. Furthermore, Israel is militarily very strong and has sophisticated military equipment ranging from Pereh-type guided missile carriers and Wolf armoured personnel carriers to possibly long range quasi-ballistic missiles while its unmanned aerial vehicles provide up-to-the-minute surveillance against any hostile action. A compromise with Israel is the only solution I can think of in order not to prolong the agony that the citizens of the Gaza Strip face daily." Alexis paused then went on.

"Let me tell you what I foresee will happen more and more in Gaza if the status quo persists. A colleague in Gaza took me to a football pitch not far from the city centre where we witnessed a match in progress between two local teams. We made a short video of it which I would like to show." He fetched a memory stick from his briefcase and loaded it into the PC. It showed 22 males, ranging from boys to men, all hobbling on long wooden crutches supported under their armpits kicking the ball with their good legs as they lurched back and forth between the two goal posts. Their wounds were sustained as they protested at the border with Israel, with the IDF soldiers deliberately targeting their legs in order to maim rather than to kill. The footballers looked in defiance at the camera as the video was taken, their smiling faces sending a message to the outside world that they too were not afraid of Goliath and the day would come when their people would be victorious in Palestine's tortuous route to justice and freedom. Alexis stopped the video, turned facing the audience and uttered:

"Is this what we want to perpetuate? Utter misery? No, we do not, and a compromise must be reached at all costs, otherwise the Islamists will intensify their attacks on Israel, the murders and executions will continue and the losers will be the ordinary peoples of both Israel and Palestine. Brexit apart, the major European countries should face their responsibility square on and not hide behind grandiose statements that ultimately give the excuse for Israel to continue on its path of annexing more and more parts of the West Bank and behaving irresponsibly. The Palestinian Conundrum must be solved. The suffering of ordinary people is immeasurable, their dignity sunk to oblivion, their misery is incalculable and the day will come when the cry for justice will reach its apogee and then..." Alexis paused clearly very emotional and in some distress and uttered, "...the unthinkable will happen and we will be facing Armageddon."

Silence ensued as members of the audience were astonished by the video they had seen and on hearing Alexis' last closing comment. There was no point in asking more questions. This short video spoke volumes about the miseries of the ongoing stalemate. The chairman thanked Alexis and they all quietly dispersed.

At High Table that evening at St John's, Alexis was able to continue the discussion with his Jewish colleagues who thought one or two conditions would be difficult to accept but on balance they acquiesced that if a truly genuine attempt was made for a lasting solution most of his conditions had to be met. Their fears were that the Hamas leadership may be reluctant to accept such a compromised solution.

Within days, Nina returned to Athens. She wondered how many more enemies Alexis had made following some of his stern statements during the lecture. They started to make arrangements for their return to the Strip following news that the hospital wing would be completed by April 2018. Two months later came the announcement of the President of the USA and the intention to move their embassy to Jerusalem. Alexis was in Italy while Nestor contacted his mum following the president's announcement and therefore she was not able to contact him immediately. Alexis on his return home was driving to St John's College when he heard the news about the president's announcement and its worldwide repercussions on his car radio. Within a week he flew to Athens and discussed with Nina their pending trip to the Strip.

"I am informed that the hospital wing in the Strip is scheduled to be completed weeks before Al-Nakba day," said Nina.

"That coincides with the president's entourage going to Jerusalem to inaugurate the announcement of the pending embassy move. Obviously, there will not be a building ready to accommodate the embassy staff but no doubt the ceremony will take place with members of the Knesset and other dignitaries present," replied Alexis.

"How crass," stressed Nina, "for the President of the USA to choose such a day for the formal ceremony announcing the move of their embassy to Jerusalem? How cruel, the couple thought, for the most powerful person on Earth to pick this sensitive 24-hour period for setting in motion such diplomatic protocol against one of the most deprived peoples on earth."

"It beggars belief that the president can be so vindictive," replied Alexis. "Anyhow, we must contact Ismail and Mustafa in Alexandria to coordinate our entry into the Strip."

39

Alexandria, Gaza Strip, April 2018

Alexis and Nina flew from Athens to Alexandria and spent a few days with Mustafa and his family. Ismail joined them a couple of times. They visited old haunts, their school and other meeting places which, with the passage of time and the influx of many indigenous inhabitants from other parts of Egypt, had changed character and sadly had become unfamiliar. On the evening of the last day they boarded the tramway opting for the Victoria line and headed for Stanley Bay. They sat on the upper deck without saying much, watching other passengers embark and disembark at the various stations. There was Sidi Gaber where Alexis had arrived from Port Said after seeing Pavlos off on a liner to England. The other side of the station was Christos' family apartment where Alexis was first introduced to Tasos. Alas, the Armenian basketball grounds had long disappeared and had made way for much-needed high–rise apartment blocks. The aged tram trudged along its tracks and as it passed Rushdi they descended and headed for the rear open platform which formed one of the tram's entrance/exit points. As the tram pulled into Glymenopoulo station Alexis raised his hands and gripped the ledge where as a youngster he would hang to carry out a few pull ups while the tram was still in motion.

"It was crazy doing that. Was it to impress the girls?" asked Nina.

"Not really, because often I was travelling on my own," replied Alexis. "It was the fearlessness of an adolescent."

"And a silly one, if I may add." They left the tram and headed for Nina's family apartment. They stopped on the pavement opposite and looked up at the balcony on the first floor. There was no sign of life.

"I wonder who occupies the apartment now?" whispered Nina.

"Go and knock on the door."

"I daren't."

"Why?"

"I don't know. It was our lovely home and alas it is no more."

"After all those years you still feel for the place?"

"I suppose so, it is still painful."

"It is after all part of our old Alexandria," murmured Alexis nostalgically.

Moments later they were heading for the Corniche. Upon arrival they crossed the winding coastal road and descended the steps to the sandy beach. It was deserted but little had changed. They slowly walked along the water's edge listening to the lapping sound of the dying waves without uttering a word, enveloped in dreams of a bygone era. They stopped.

"Was it all those years ago that we met here for the

last time?" she asked.

"It was." They embraced, letting their emotions flow. Nina was first to break away and said:

"A few years back I came across Proust's *À la Recherche du Temps Perdu*, and reread it. Does it apply to the lost souls of two young Alexandrians?" Nina smiled.

"We lost each other but eventually, by fate or luck, we found each other again. That is what matters most, does it not?" responded Alexis as they started walking back towards the steps that had such a huge significance in their lives. Upon reaching the top they had one last look at the beach below, hailed a taxi and made their way back to Mustafa's house near Ramleh tram terminus. Gaza awaited them.

The following day Mustafa drove them towards the Rafah Crossing and following the same circuitous route as in the past, they entered the Strip at its southernmost location. As on previous occasions Alexis and Nina were met by Muhammad, Ismail's cousin. Alas there was no Ramzi to greet them which did not really surprise Nina as he was now over 18 years of age and no doubt at university. They were driven to their apartment and headed for their respective UN offices in Gaza city.

It was May 14th, the day before Nakba. The son-in-law of the President of the USA led a huge delegation made up of evangelical Christians, senators and many other diplomats for the ceremony announcing that sometime in the near future the US embassy will be relocated in West Jerusalem. A link lasting a few minutes was established between Washington and Jerusalem and the US President gave a short speech stating proudly that he had kept the promise he had made on his inauguration.

The television channels were awash with news from the borders between Gaza and Israel showing images of the chaos and carnage, where over 50 Palestinians were shot dead and over two thousand injured, allegedly for stepping into the buffer zone. The jubilation in West Jerusalem, where the ceremony was hailed as historic, was in direct contrast to the fate of civilian and militant protesters alike facing a brutal response from IDF guards up at their tall watchtowers in the Strip.

"President Truman," the President declared in his video link, "recognised the State of Israel when it was formed 70 years ago, and today I have fulfilled a pledge which is long overdue to declare that the capital of Israel is the whole of Jerusalem."

In response, at the unveiling ceremony, the PM of Israel stated:

"This is an historic day and the president has made history. The President is strong enough to accept Jerusalem as the capital of Israel. Balfour declared over one hundred years ago that the home of Jews should be established here in the hills of Judea and Samaria and today that pledged has been fulfilled."

Nestor was switching channels, from NBC to BBC World 24 and from CNN to Al Jazeera, to get a balanced view of what was happening in Jerusalem and the Gaza Strip. A phone call from Hermioni at Westminster interrupted his viewing.

"Did you hear what the Israeli PM has just stated?" asked Hermioni. "A somewhat incomplete statement of the Balfour Declaration."

"I did," replied Nestor, "but it is not the first time that the Balfour Declaration has been quoted short of the most important bit."

Hermioni continued, "I've scribbled it down following my dad's utterances at the reunion... *it being clearly understood that nothing shall be done which may prejudice the civil and religious rights of existing non-Jewish communities in Palestine or the rights and political status enjoyed by the Jews in any other country.*"

"Precisely," continued Nestor. "I was watching a programme on BBC's catch-up a few months back about the history of Jews and the presenter did precisely the same thing, omitting to mention the last few lines at the end of the Balfour Declaration, the lines you have just quoted, and what was the result post-1948?"

"Over 700,000 Arabs forcibly evicted from their homes in Palestine and today in Jerusalem neither the PM of Israel nor the President dare utter the full Balfour Declaration because it simply does not suit them," replied Hermioni.

"What is the reaction at Westminster?" asked Nestor.

"The Foreign Secretary was sad at the deaths of the protesters and suggested restraint in the use of live ammunition. A rather pathetic response in the circumstances," replied Hermioni.

"I am afraid this has been the reaction all along of many Western leaders. They condemn the brutal action of the IDF but are powerless to do anything about it," continued Nestor. "For as long as I can remember the US has blocked many UN resolutions and all we hear from the other countries are meaningless protests. Let me come back to you. I wish to hear what is being reported in the Middle East on the Al Jazeera Channel," went on Nestor. He turned the volume up and the voices of civilians and others came loud and clear into the lounge.

"We must continue with our protests and marches at the border. We cannot accept what is happening because if we capitulate it will be the end of our legitimate aspirations of a return to our homes in Palestine. More will be murdered but this is the price we have to pay in order not to betray our fathers and forefathers who were so brutally evicted from their homes," shouted a young protester.

An hour later Nestor rang Hermioni back.

"Have you heard from your dad?" he asked anxiously. "I haven't heard from mum. It is very worrying being that they are both in Gaza." Hermioni had not.

In fact Alexis and Nina were in the thick of it. They oscillated between the hospital and the border with Israel helping the wounded Palestinians who had been shot by the IDF border guards.

On the Israeli side beyond the separation wall in a tall outpost the IDF soldiers were changing the shift.

Young Aaron Schumann, Shimon's 20-year-old son, had just returned from a visit to his grandfather, Avi, in his spacious architectural office in West Jerusalem. Avi was going through some 3D graphics of the latest apartment block intended for a settlement in the outskirts of the city. Aaron was then driven in an armoured military carrier to the northern border between the Gaza Strip and Israel and entered one of the tall observational towers. He had just come to take up his post and relieve his colleague who had been on duty for the past few hours. Aaron was very nervous handling his Uzi-Pro blowback-operated, select-fire, closed-bolt submachine gun. He made sure that bullets were in place. He glanced at the Palestinian crowds gathered over the other side of the tall wall, seemingly running in all directions trying to help the wounded and every now and then crossing into the buffer zone while hurtling Molotov cocktails towards the high wall.

Karima dashed into the hospital where Nina was stationed and tried to find her. She went from corridor to corridor, and from room to room without being able to locate her whereabouts. She finally rang Alexis, who tried to calm Karima down.

"What is up?"

"Ramzi is not at the university in Nablus as we thought but a close friend said that he had made his way to Gaza and is taking part in the protests at the border," replied an emotional Karima.

"His is sensible, he will not put himself in any danger," went on Alexis trying to reassure an exceedingly agitated Karima.

"I will come to the hospital and we will find Nina. Just wait for me there."

Alexis grabbed a lift from an ambulance and within minutes reached the hospital. He found a hysterical Karima in the reception area of A&E being consoled by the staff. Alexis made his way to Nina's office and found her assistant directing a couple to the Trauma Clinic.

"Have you seen Nina?" he asked her.

"She is helping in Theatre II where a huge number of wounded protesters were diverted following the shootings on our border in the north," she replied.

Alexis headed for Theatre II. He could not get in as the surgeons, including Nina, were performing an operation which had reached a critical stage. He headed back to A&E.

"I have left a message for Nina to join us as soon as she finishes helping in the theatre," he said to a tearful Karima.

After half an hour, Nina emerged from the operating theatre and headed to an adjacent room where some injured protesters had been brought in. She started examining them and redirecting them to various other clinics depending on the seriousness of their wounds. She suddenly saw Alexis rushing towards her and asked:

"What is the problem?"

"Karima is hysterical because she has just been told by a student friend of her son's that yesterday evening

Ramzi had left the campus at Nablus, joined another group of university students who were smuggled into the Strip. She suspects that they are protesting on the northern part of the border."

"Let us go and find him. It is not good being there at this time."

They left the casualty section and headed for the entrance. They waited while an ambulance brought in some wounded protesters and hitched a lift to the Strip's northern border. The ambulance stopped about half a kilometre from the separation wall. They left the ambulance and looked in various directions between them and the wall. There were protesters everywhere, no coordinated attack, nor systematic charge in any direction. There were protesters as young as six or seven years old, not realising the dangers they were getting themselves to. Holding banners and small Palestinian flags they were waving them towards the IDF soldiers manning the towers. Nina and Alexis walked within metres of each other, trying to locate Ramzi and his fellow students. They stepped up their pace, gradually progressing towards the buffer zone. Suddenly they saw a bunch of youngsters shouting obscenities at the IDF and gesticulating wildly and pointing at their half-torn flags. Instantly bullets were hurled towards the group and some tumbled to the ground. Nina was near enough to recognise young Ramzi as he fell. She rushed towards the group and with her hands made room amongst the protesters to get closer to the centre of the group. Alexis shouted at her not to go any further as she was about to cross into the buffer zone but she proceeded without a moment's hesitation. Alexis followed her towards the group.

Suddenly Aaron saw a number of people crossing into the buffer zone and heading for the group of protesters about to hurtle improvised Molotov cocktails towards the separation wall. Other Gazan protesters knelt over what looked like a couple of young Palestinians wounded in the previous skirmish. Nina arrived first and waving her hands made room to reach the wounded when suddenly a burst of bullets from an Uzi semi-automatic assault weapon burst forth. Both Alexis and Nina and several bystanders were hit in the crossfire and fell instantly to the ground. To his horror Aaron realised what he had done and stopped as his commanding officer reached his post.

"What the hell happened there?" he inquired.

"I thought that a crowd was preparing for an assault so I opened fire."

An ambulance arrived shortly afterwards and collected the wounded amongst them Nina, Alexis and Ramzi. They were rushed to the hospital where Ramzi's wounds were found not to be life-threatening. Alexis was pronounced dead on arrival while Nina was rushed to the operating theatre. She, however, having lost a lot of blood, did not survive either.

Karima, her father Muhammad and all the colleagues and friends of Alexis and Nina were crestfallen at the loss of their dear Alexandrian friends.

Hermioni and Nestor were devastated by the deaths of their parents. Hermioni prepared a speech that she delivered to the House a few weeks after the incident. As the speaker of the House announced her name she stood up from the backbenches amidst a deathly silence while holding a piece of paper in her trembling hands.

"I stand here this afternoon," she started, "to lament the death of my father and his partner who were victims of wanton violence and a shoot-to-kill policy as they tried to help a group of youngsters in Gaza protesting about an intractable problem, the origins of which can be traced to a statement made in this very chamber exactly one hundred years ago. My father and Nina Phoundas cared deeply about the plight of the Palestinian people and the injustice that has been bestowed upon them following the Balfour Declaration and the massive Jewish emigration after the British Mandate in Palestine had ended." Hermioni hesitated and, regaining her composure, continued:

"They were helping the wounded around the protesters that hurled abuse and unrestrained utterances towards a brutal Force, the IDF..." and went on for another ten minutes enumerating the futility of such a prolonged and unnecessary conflict, without any country being able to halt it.

Nestor made a similar speech at the United Nations.

Following the election of a Unity Government, its Palestine rulers unveiled a memorial stone at the very spot were Nina and Alexis had fallen, with the following inscription:

You did not have to come, but you did and bravely paid the ultimate price. Palestine salutes you and mourns you. RIP.

40

Cambridge, July 2018

It was a beautiful July Saturday morning in Cambridge, cloudless, warm with a fine breeze sweeping away the sun's early morning heat. Shoppers were arriving from the surrounding villages, in buses or driving and using the numerous park and ride outposts. Christ's Pieces, the Victorian parkland in the centre of the city, with its tree-lined avenues adorned with seasonal flower beds, looked as though it was the garden of a stately house. It is over 180 years since the opulent Clarendon House, the home of Charles Humphrey, was demolished to construct the picturesque Victoria, Earl and Elm Streets. That morning it was full of bloom, with its bowling green in pristine condition following an early-morning mowing.

Erica and Alexis left their house in Earl Street and were heading to M&S on Market Square to have breakfast with their friend Mark, a semi-retired industrialist who had built a sizeable engineering company off to the west of the city. Alexis was very quiet that morning as he and Erica scaled the wooden fence into Christ's Pieces, walked by the flower beds, veered onto the tree-lined avenue leading to Christ's Lane and entered St Andrews Street. Alexis still had not uttered a word as they meandered through the gathering shoppers and using the escalator reached the café at the top. As they sat down with their croissant and tea cakes, Erica said to Mark while looking askance at Alexis:

"My dear husband is totally uncommunicative this morning." Alexis poured tea into his cup, dropped two slices of lemon into it, stirred it and sipped a fraction, nearly scalding his lips. Then he turned to both and said:

"You will not believe the recurring dream I have had the past few nights. Remarkable, the sequence of events is still so vivid in my imagination. When I woke up I had to think for a few seconds whether it was all true or was it a dream?"

"What was it about?" asked a bewildered Erica while her grimace produced a chuckle from Mark. Alexis started describing the extraordinary events of his dream, adolescence in Alexandria, the Scout movement, Nina, the injustice that had been inflicted on generations of Palestinian people, the myriad of settlements, Joshua and his family, school reunions with his pals, Balfour and the British Mandate. Although it was still memorable and remained vivid in his mind, the events were not related chronologically, Nina kept being mentioned together with a few other names such as Christos and Petros. It was a long dream, remarkable for its realism, naïve in its outcome but still powerful in the message that it was conveying. Alexis paused and sipped more of his by now lukewarm tea.

"Where did that all come from?" whispered Erica. Alexis shook his head and shrugged his shoulders. Mark said:

"I bet Freud would offer an answer to your question Erica. Psychoanalysis is what you need, my friend," and looked at Alexis. Then he pressed on:

"But, you know what? It seems you have enough material from those dreams for a nice little book. The question is do you remember clearly what happened and the sequence of events?"

The conversation switched to other topics which they usually discussed at their breakfast meetings: the latest University Challenge contest, books they had read, Brexit and families. Alexis remained mostly silent, only seldom interjecting a word here and there.

They parted. Alexis, as it was customary following their daily breakfasts, went straight to his office at St John's. He switched on his PC, stared outside his balcony window at the blue sky with the beaming sun's rays reflecting off the manicured lawns of Chapel Court, turned and gazed at the empty page on the screen and gingerly started tapping on his keyboard:

Chapter 1

The announcement by the President of the United States that a new embassy will be built in the West of Jerusalem...

Acknowledgements

I am indebted to my Alexandrian school pals Dinos Carayannis, Dimitri Lazarou and Sakis Stergiou for reading and commenting on the manuscript. I owe gratitude to three professorial colleagues at St John's College, Cambridge: Stefan Reif for reading and commenting on Chapter 12, John Kerrigan for many fruitful discussions and reassurance at the early stages of the preparation of this book and Geoff Horrocks who kept reminding me of my Greekness.

To the staff at Black Spring Press Group, particularly to Amira Ghanim and publisher Dr Todd Swift for their unfailing support and guidance. My thanks also go to Edwin Smet for carrying out the typesetting and design. Further, my deep appreciation is extended to my editor Alex Wylie whose diligence and meticulous editorial intervention was a source of huge encouragement for me. Finally, sincere thanks to my wife Margaret, who was kind enough to give my rudimentary English more fluency and for her unfailing support throughout this project.

The real Alexandrians standing in Alexandrian's Yacht Club in 2004 with their pseudonyms used in the book. From left to right: Yanis, Kate, Ingrid, Christos, Petros, Vassiliki, Erica and Alexis.

Lightning Source UK Ltd.
Milton Keynes UK
UKHW010247021021
391524UK00002B/63

9 781913 606459